Fab
Confessions
of Georgia
Nicolson

Vol. 5

Further Confessions of Georgia Nicolson:

Angus, thongs and full-frontal snogging

'It's OK, I'm wearing really big knickers!'

'Knocked out by my nunga-nungas.'

'Dancing in my nuddy-pants!'

'...and that's when it fell off in my hand.'

'...then he ate my boy entrancers.'

'...startled by his furry shorts!'

'Luuurve is a many trousered thing...'

'Stop in the name of pants!'

'Are these my basoomas I see before me?'

Also available on CD:

'...and that's when it fell off in my hand.'

'...then he ate my boy entrancers.'

'...startled by his furry shorts!'

'Luuurve is a many trousered thing...'

'Stop in the name of pants!'

'Are these my basoomas I see before me?'

♥♥Fab Confessions of Georgia Nicolson

Vol. 5

'Stop in the name of pants!'

and

'Are these my basoomas I see before me...'

Louise Rennison ♥

HarperCollins *Children's Books*

Find out more about Georgia at www.georgianicolson.com

'Stop in the name of pants!' was first published in Great Britain in hardback by
HarperCollins *Children's Books* in 2009
'Stop in the name of pants!' was first published in paperback in 2010
'Are these my basoomas I see before me?' was first published in Great Britain in hardback by
HarperCollins *Children's Books* in 2009
'Are these my basoomas I see before me?' was first published in paperback in 2010
Published in this two-in-one edition by HarperCollins *Children's Books* in 2011
HarperCollins *Children's Books* is a division of HarperCollins*Publishers* Ltd,
77-85 Fulham Palace Road, Hammersmith, London, W6 8JB

1

Copyright © Louise Rennison 2009, 2010

ISBN 978-0-00-741204-4

Louise Rennison asserts the moral right to be identified as the author of the work.

Printed and bound in England by Clays Ltd, St Ives plc

Mixed Sources
Product group from well-managed
forests and other controlled sources
www.fsc.org Cert no. SW-COC-1806
© 1996 Forest Stewardship Council
FSC

FSC is a non-profit international organisation established to promote the
responsible management of the world's forests. Products carrying the FSC
label are independently certified to assure consumers that they come
from forests that are managed to meet the social, economic and
ecological needs of present and future generations.

Find out more about HarperCollins and the environment at
www.harpercollins.co.uk/green

'Stop in the ♥ name of pants!'

A Note from Georgia

Dear chums, chumettes and, er... chummly wummlies,

   I write to you from my bed of pain. Once again I have exhausted myself with creativitosity writing 'Stop in the Name of Pants!' I am having to lie down with a cup of tea and a Curly Wurly. But that is how vair vair much I care about you all, my little pallies. I am a fool to myself, I know.

   I ask only one thing in return and that is this. All of you must dance the Viking disco hornpipe extravaganza in classrooms and recreation facilities throughout the world. It doesn't matter if there are only two or three of you, just stand up proudly, get your horns and paddles out (oo-er) and dance!!!

   Loads and loads of deep luuurve,

   Georgia
   xxx

   p.s. Some of you don't know what the Viking disco hornpipe extravaganza is, do you?

p.p.s. Please don't tell me you didn't know that Vikings had discos.

p.p.p.s. Or that they shouted "Hoooooorrrn!!!"

p.p.p.p.s. For those of you who haven't bothered to keep up with my diaries because you are just TOO BUSY, I have put instructions for the dance at the back near the glossary.

p.p.p.p.p.s. What have you been TOO BUSY doing?

p.p.p.p.p.p.s. I suppose you have been TOO BUSY to even know what the having-the-hump scale is as well.

p(x7).s. So I have included that at the back too. My so-called friend Jas (who has the hump pretty much all of the time) would be at number four with you by now (cold-shoulderosity work).

p(x8).s. I really luuurve you and do not mind that you are lazy minxes. That is your special charm. Pip pip. X

To my groovy and fabby and marvy family and mates (including my extended family at HarperCollins and Aitken Alexander).

'Stop in the name of pants!' – my latest work of geniosity – is dedicated especially to absent mates. Who have selfishly gone off to have fun. (Yes, you know who you are, Jeddbox and Elton.)

And also to absent mates who aren't really absent but lurking about somewhere pretending to be absent.

Deep in the forest of red-bottomosity

Saturday July 30th
Camping fiasco
11:30 p.m.
In my tent of shame.

Again.

The rest of my so-called pals are still out in the woods with the lads and I have crept back to the campsite aloney. I can hear snoring from Miss Wilson's tent and also Herr Kamyer's. I bet there will be a deputation of voles coming along shortly to complain that they can't get any sleep because of the racket.

11:32 p.m.

I'm going to forget about everything and just go to sleep in my lovely sleeping bag. On the lovely soft ground. Not. It's like sleeping on an ironing board. And I do know what that is like actually.

11:33 p.m.

I said coming on this school camping trip would be a fiasco of a sham and I was not wrong.

11:34 p.m.

I was right.

11:35 p.m.

I wonder what the others are doing?

11:36 p.m.

Anyway, the main thing is that I am now, officially, the girlfriend of a Luuurve God. And therefore I have put my red bottom behind me with a firm hand. I will never again be found wandering lonely as a clud into the cakeshop of luuurve. Or picking up some other éclair or tart or fondant fancy. Ditto Eccles cakes and Spotty dick or... shut up, brain.

11:37 p.m.
So, speaking as the official girlfriend of a Luuurve God who has put my red bottom behind me with a firm hand and who will never be wandering around looking for extra cakes, can someone tell me this...

How in the name of God's pantyhose have I ended up snogging Dave the Laugh?

Also known as Dave the Tart.

Two minutes later
Oh goddy god god. And let us face facts. It wasn't just a matey type snog. You know, not a – "It's all right, mate, I'm just a mate accidentally snogging another mate" – sort of snog.

It was, frankly and to get to the point and not beat around the whatsit, a "phwoooaar" snogging situation.

Thirty seconds later
In fact, it was deffo number four and about to be number five.

Four seconds later

Anyway, shut up, brain, I must think. Now is not the time for a rambling trip to Ramble Land. Now is the time to put my foot down with a firm hand and stop snogging my not-boyfriend Dave the Laugh.

One minute later

I mean, I am practically married to Masimo the Luuurve God.

Ten seconds later

Well, give or take him actually asking me to marry him.

Five seconds later

And the fact that he has gone off to Pizza-a-gogo land on holiday and left me here in Merrie but dangerous England to fend for myself. Being made to go on stupid school camping trips with madmen (Miss Wilson and Herr Kamyer).

He has left me here, wandering around defenceless in the wilderness near Ramsgate, miles away from the nearest TopShop.

Three seconds later

And how can I help it if Dave the Laugh burrows into my tent?

Because that is more or less what happened. That is *le* fact.

I was snuggling down under some bit of old raincoat (or sleeping bag, as Jas would say in her annoying *oooh isn't it fun outdoors* sort of way). Anyway, where was I? Oh yes, I was snuggling down earlier tonight after an action-packed day of newt drawing when there was a *tap-tap-tapping* on the side of the tent. I thought it might have been an owl attack but it was Dave the Laugh and his Barmy Army (Tom, Declan, Sven and Edward) enticing us into their tent with promises of snacks and light entertainment.

Four seconds later

I blame Dave entirely for this. He and I are just mates and I have a boyfriend and he has a girlfriend and that is that, end of story. Not. Because then he comes to the countryside looking for me and waving his Horn about.

We were frolicking around in the lads' tent, and Dave and me went off for an innocent walk in the woods. You know, like old matey-type mates do. But then I put my foot down a bloody badger hole or something and fell backwards into the river. Anyway, Dave was laughing like a loon for a bit before he reached down and put his arms around me to lift me up the riverbank and I said, "I think I may have broken my bottom."

And he was really smiling and then he said, "Oh bugger it, it has to be done."

And he snogged me.

When he stopped I pushed him backwards and looked at him. I was giving him my worst look.

He said, "What?"

I said, "You know what. Don't just say 'what' like that."

"Like what?"

I said, with enormous dignitosity, "Look, you enticed me with your shenanigans and, erm, puckering stuff."

He said, "Erm, I think you will find that you agreed to come to my tent in the middle of the night to steal me from my girlfriend."

I said, "It was you that snogged me."

He looked at me and then he sighed. "Yeah, I know. I don't feel very good about this. I'm not so... well, you're used to it."

My head nearly exploded. "I'm USED to what??"

He looked quite angry, which felt horrible. I'd seen him angry with me before and I didn't usually like what he had to say. He went on: "You started all this sounding the Horn business ages ago, using me like a decoy duck and then going out with Robbie, then messing about with me and then going out with Masimo. And then telling me that you felt mixed up."

I just looked at him. I felt a bit weepy actually. I might as well be wet at both ends.

My eyes filled with tears and I blinked them away and he just kept on looking at me. I couldn't tell what he was thinking. Maybe he had had enough of me and he really hated me.

Then he just walked away and I was left alone. Alone to face the dark woods of my shamenosity and the tutting of Baby Jesus.

Ten seconds later

And I didn't even know which way the tent was.

The trees looked scary and there was all sorts of snuffling going on. Maybe it was rogue pigs. Pigs who had had enough of the farm life, fed up with just bits of old potato peelings to eat and nowhere to poo in privacy. Maybe these ones wanted a change of menu and had made a bid for freedom by scaling the pigpen fence late at night. Or perhaps they were like the prisoners of war in that old film that Vati's always rambling on about. *The Great Escape.* When the prisoners dug a tunnel under the prison fence.

That's what these pigs must have done. Tunnelled out of the farm to freedom.

There was more snuffling.

Yes, but now they were hungry. Runaways from the farm just waiting to pounce on some food. If they found me, they would think of me like I thought of them. As some chops. Some chops in a skirt. In sopping knickers in my case. Out here in the Wild Woods the trotter was on the other foot.

I could climb up a tree.

Could they climb trees?

Could I climb trees?

Oh God, not death by pig!!!

The scuffling got nearer and then a little black thing scampered out of the undergrowth. It was a vole. How much noise can one stupid little mousey thing make? A LOT is the answer.

I should make friends with it really, because with my luck I will be kidnapped by voles and raised as one of their own. On the plus side, I would never have to face the shame of my red-bottomosity, just spend my years digging and licking my fur and being all aloney on my owney.

Like I am now.

Dave appeared out of the darkness in front of me. I ran over to him and burst into tears. He put his arm around me.

"OK, Kittykat, I'm sorry. Come on, it's all right. Stop blubbing. Your nose will get all swollen up and you'll collapse under the weight of your nungas and I can't carry all of you home."

It was nice in the forest now. I could see the moon through the trees. And my hiccups had almost gone. As we walked along he smiled at me and stroked my hair. Oooh, he was nice.

He said, "We haven't done this luuurve business before, so we are bound to be crap at it. I do feel bad about Emma, but that is not your fault. That is my fault. We can put away our Horns and be matey-type mates again. Come on. Cheer up. Be nasty to me again, it's more normal. I like you and I always have and I always will."

I sniffed a bit and gave him a brave, quivering but attractive smile. I kept my nostrils fully under control so that they didn't spread all over my face. As we walked along I could hear little squelching noises coming from the knicker department. With a bit of luck you couldn't hear it above the noise of rustling voles (also known as my nearly adopted family).

Dave said, "Is that your pants squelching, Gee? You should change them when we get back. You don't want to get pneumonia of the bum-oley on top of everything else."

We walked back through the trees in the light of the jolly old big shiny yellow thing, and no, I do not mean an illuminated banana had just appeared, although that would have been good.

Then everything went horrible again; there were some hideous noises coming from the left of us...

"Tom, Tom. over here. I think I've found an owl dropping."

Oh brilliant – Jas, Wild Woman of the Forest, was in the vicinity. Dave took his arm away from my shoulder. I looked up at him, he looked down at me and bent over and kissed me on the mouth really gently.

"Ah well, the end of the line, Kittykat. You go off with your Italian lesbian boyfriend and see how it goes and I'll try and be a good mate to you. Don't tell me too much about you and him because I won't like it – but other than that, let's keep the accidental outburst of red-bottomosity to ourselves."

I smiled at him. "Dave, I..."

"Yes?"

"I think I can feel something moving in my undercrackers."

Midnight

And that is when I scampered off back to Loony Headquarters. That is, our school campsite. To change my nick-nacks.

Ten past midnight

I said to Baby Jesus, "I know I have done wrong and I am sorry times a million, but at least you have been kind enough not to send a plague of tadpoles into my pantaloonies."

Sunday July 31st

11:00 a.m.

I must say, it was a lot easier getting our tent down than up. I pulled all the peg-type things out of the ground, Rosie and Jools kicked the pole over, and though it wouldn't go in its stupid bag thing, we made a nice bundle of it in about three minutes flat.

Jas and her woodland mates and Herr Kamyer and Miss

Wilson were folding and sorting and putting things in little pockets and so on for about a million years.

Ten minutes later

Rosie, Jools and me stashed our tent bundle in the suitcase holder thing at the side of the coach and got on board past Mr Attwood. The only reason we got on without some sort of Nazi investigation and body search was because he was slumped at the wheel with his cap pulled down over his face.

Rosie said, "That's how he drives."

And she is not wrong if the nightmare journey home was anything to go by.

Twenty minutes later

We were having a little zizz on the back seat under a pile of our coats when Jas, patron saint of the Rambling On Society, came on board. I knew that because she came to the back of the coach and shook my shoulder quite violently. I peered at her. She was tremendously red-faced.

I said, "Jas, I am trying to sleep."

"You didn't pack your tent up properly."

I said, "Oh, I'm sorry, are the tent police here?"

She said, "You have just made a big mess of yours in the boot. We had to take it out and pack it up so that we could get ours in!"

"Yes, well, Jas, as you can see, I am very, very busy."

"You are soooo selfish and lax and that is why you have a million boyfriends, none of whom will stay with you."

She stormed off to sit at the front near her besties Miss Wilson and Herr Kamyer.

God, she is annoying, but luckily no one else heard her rambling on about the million boyfriends scenario. I wonder if the boys are home yet?

Five minutes later

Herr Kamyer stood up at the front of the bus and said, "Can I haff your attention, girls." Everyone carried on talking, so he started clapping his hands together.

Mr Attwood jerked to life and said, "It's time to go."

Herr Kamyer said, "*Ja, ja, danke schön, Herr Driver*, but first I vill count zat ve are all pre—"

At which point Mr Attwood put his foot down and Herr Kamyer fell backwards into Miss Wilson's lap.

Quite, quite horrific.

We just watched the young lovers as they got redder and redder. Like red things at a red party.

Herr Kamyer tried to get off her lap, but the coach was being driven so violently by Mr Mad that he kept falling back again, saying, "*Ach*, I am *sehr* sorry I..."

And Miss Wilson was saying, "No, no, it's quite all right. I mean I..."

Eventually, when Mr Attwood was forced to stop at the lights, Herr Kamyer got into his own seat and pretended to be inspecting his moth collection. Miss Wilson got out her knitting but kept looking over at him.

I said to Rosie, "Just remember this – he was there when Nauseating P. Green did her famous falling into the shower tent fiasco and Miss Wilson was exposed to the world having a shower. He has seen Miss Wilson in the nuddy-pants."

I was just thinking about popping back to Snoozeland when Ellen dithered into life.

"Er, Georgia... you know when Jas said... well, when she said that you had... like a million boyfriends or something, I mean have you or something?"

Rosie said, "Ellen, gadzooks and lackaday, OF COURSE Georgia hasn't got a million boyfriends. She would be covered in them if she had."

Ellen said, "Well, I know but, well, I mean, she's only got Masimo, and that is like... well..."

Mabs said, "Yeah, Masimo... and the rest."

I said to Mabs, "Who rattled your cage?"

And Mabs said, "I'm just remarking on the Dave the Laugh factor."

Ellen sat up then. "What Dave the Laugh factor?"

Oh Blimey O'Reilly's nose massager! Here we go again, once more into the bakery of love. I am going to have to nip this Dave the Laugh thing in the bud.

I said, "Ellen, did you snog Declan and, if so, what number did you get up to?"

Ellen looked like she had swallowed a sock full of vole poo, which is not a good look.

"Well, I... well, you know, I, well, do you think I did or something?"

I said, "A yes or no any time this side of the grave would be fab, Ellen."

Ellen said she had to get her cardi from Jas's rucky and

tottered off to sit next to her. Hahahahaha. I am without doubtosity top girlie at red-herringnosity.

4:00 p.m.

Dropped off at the bottom of my road. By some miracle we have arrived home not maimed and crippled by our coach "driver" and school caretaker Elvis Attwood. He hates girls.

I don't think he has a driving licence. When I politely asked to see it after a near-death experience at a roundabout, he suggested I remove myself before his hand made contact with my arse. Which is unnecessary talk in a man who fought for his country in the Viking invasions. I said to him, "You are only letting yourself down by that kind of talk, Mr Attwood."

Two minutes later

Walked up the drive to Chez Bonkers. Opened the door and yelled, "Hello, everyone, you can get out the fatted hamster, I am home!!!"

Two minutes later

No one in.

Typico.

I don't know why they ramble on so much about where I'm going and what time I will be in, when they so clearly don't give two short flying mopeds.

Kitchen
I'm starving.

Nothing in the fridge of course.

Unless you like out-of-date bean sprouts.

Four minutes later
Slightly mouldy toast, mmmmm. I think I am getting scurvy from lack of vitamin C, my hair feels tired. Perhaps Italian Luuurve Gods like the patchy-hair look in a girlfriend.

I wonder if he has left a message on the phone for me?

Five minutes later
I really wish I hadn't listened to the messages – it is a terrifying insight into the "life" I lead.

First it was some giggling pal of Mum's saying that she had met a bloke at a speed-dating night and had got to number six with him. How does she know about the snogging scale? My mum is obviously part crap mother and part seeing-ear dog.

The next message was from Josh's mum, saying, "After Josh came home with a Mohican haircut I don't think it is a good idea that he comes round to play with Libby again. I am frankly puzzled as to why she had bread knives and scissors in her bedroom. Also I cannot get the blue make-up off his eyes. I suspect it is indelible ink, which means the word BUM on his forehead will take many hours to get off."

There was a bit more rambling and moaning, but the gist is that Josh is banned from playing with my little sister Libby.

Dear *Gott in Himmel*.

And that was it. No message from the Luuurve God. It's been a week now. I wonder why he hasn't called? Has he gone off me?

Maybe I did something wrong when we last saw each other.

one minute later
But it was so vair vair gorgey porgey.

one minute later
He said, "We like each other. It will be good, Miss Georgia."

One minute later

What he didn't say was, "I will call you as soon as I get there."

One minute later

Or "I will pay your airfare to Rome, you entrancing Sex Kitty."

Ten minutes later

God, I am so bored. And my bottom still hurts from my falling-in-the-river fiasco. So I can't even sit down properly.

One minute later

I wonder if Dave the Laugh will tell Emma about our accidental number four episode. Probably not. After all, it didn't mean anything and, as he said, we are mates in a matey way. And what goes on in the woods stays in the woods.

Thirty seconds later

Hmmm. He also said in the woods that he has always really liked me. Maybe he meant that in a matey-type mate way.

One minute later

Will I tell Masimo?

one minute later

If he doesn't ring me, I won't have to make the decision. Anyway, it was only an accidental number four, verging on the number five. It could happen to anyone.

one minute later

It could happen to Masimo and his ex-girlfriend. What was her name? Gina. Yes, it might happen if, for instance, she happened to be in Rome.

one minute later

Even if she is not there, I bet he and his mates will be roaring round Rome on their scooters smiling at all the girls in their red bikinis or whatever it is they wear there.

Probably nothing. They probably go to work in the nuddy-pants because they are wild and free Pizza-a-gogo types. They don't have inhibitions like us, they just thrust their nungas forward proudly and untamed. Probably.

In my bedroom looking in the mirror

The only thing that is really thrusting itself forward proudly is my nose. Even Dave mentioned it.

one minute later

Perhaps it has grown bigger and bigger in Masimo's imagination in the week he has been away. He hasn't even got a photo of me to remind him that I am more than just a nose on legs.

Five minutes later

Perhaps because he is foreign he is a bit psychic. Perhaps he has a touch of the Mystic Meg about him and he knows about the Dave the Laugh incident.

one minute later

Jas has probably sent a message via an owl to let him know. Just because she has got the hump with me. AGAIN. About the stupid tent business.

Lying on my bed of pain
8:00 p.m.

And I mean that quite literally because my cat Angus (also known as a killing machine) is pretending my foot is a rabbit. In a sock. If I even move it slightly, he leaps on it and starts biting it.

Also, ouch and double ouch. I can't get into a comfy

position to take the pressure off my bum-oley. I think I may have actually broken something in my bottom. I don't know what there is to break, but I may have broken it. I wonder if it is swollen up?

Then I heard the *phut phut* of the mighty throbbing engine that is my vati's crap car. Carefully easing my broken bottom off the bed and slapping at Angus, I went downstairs. Angus was still clinging to my sock-rabbit-foot even though his head was bonking against the stairs.

As I got to the hall I heard the front door being kicked. Oh good, it was my delightful little sister.

"Gingey, Gingey, let me in!!! Let me in, poo sister."

Then there was squealing, like a pig was being pushed through the letter box.

Thirty seconds later

It wasn't a pig being pushed through the letter box, it was Gordy, cross-eyed son of Angus. I could see his ginger ears poking through.

Oh, bloody hell.

I said, "Libby, don't put Gordy though the letter box. I'm opening the door."

She yelled, "He laaikes it."

When I got the door open, it was to find Libby in Wellington boots and a bikini. Gordy was struggling and yowling in her little fat arms and finally squirmed free and leaped off into the garden sneezing and shaking.

Libby was laughing. "Funny pussy. *Hnk hnk.*" Then she came up to me and started hugging my knees and kissing them. In between snogging, Libby was murmuring, "I lobe my Gingey."

Mutti came up the steps in a really short dress, very tight round the nungas. So very sad. She gave me a hug, which can be quite frightening seeing her enormous basoomas looming towards your head. She said, "Hello, Gee, did you have a larf camping?"

I said, "Oh yes, it was brillopads. We made instruments out of dried beans and Herr Kamyer did impressions of crap stuff with his hands that no one could get except Jas. And, as a *pièce de résistance*, I fell in a pond and was attacked by great toasted newts."

She wasn't even listening as usual, off in her own Muttiland.

"We went to see Uncle Eddie's gig at The Ambassador last night. It was like an orgy; one of the women got so carried away she stole his feather codpiece."

Is that really the sort of thing a growing, sensitive girl should have to listen to? It was like earporn.

one minute later

I watched her bustling about making our delicious supper (i.e. opening a tin of tomato soup). She was so full of herself burbling on and on.

"Honestly, you should have been there, it was a hoot."

I said, "Oooooooh yeah, it would have been great to have been there. Really great." But she didn't get it.

Libby was still kissing my knees and giggling. She had forgotten that they were my knees; they were now just her replacement friends for Josh. But then she had a lovers' tiff with her knee-friends, biffed me on the knee quite hard and went off into the garden, yelling for Gordy.

I said, "Mum, you didn't take Libby with you to the baldy-o-gram fiasco, did you?"

"Don't be silly, Georgia, I'm not a complete fool."

I said, "Well, actually, you are as it happens."

She said, "Don't be so rude."

I said, "Where's Dad? Have you managed to shake him off at last?"

And then Vati came in. In his leather trousers. Oh, I might be sick. Not content with the horrificnosity of the trousers, he kissed me on my hair. Urgh, he had touched my hair; now I would have to wash it.

He was grinning like a loon and taking his jacket off.

"Hello, no camping injuries then. No vole bites. You didn't slip into a newt pond or anything?"

I looked at him suspiciously. I hoped he wasn't turning into Mystic Meg as well in his old age. I said, "Dad, are you wearing a woman's blouse?"

He went completely ballisticisimus. "Don't be so bloody cheeky! This is an original sixties Mod shirt. I will probably wear it when I go clubbing. Any gigs coming up?"

Mum said, "Have you heard anything from the Italian Stallion?"

Dad had his head in the fridge and I could see his enormous leather-clad bum leering at me. I had an overwhelming urge to kick it, but I wasn't whelmed because I knew he would probably ban me from going out for life.

I gave Mum my worst look and nodded over at the fridge. I needn't have worried, though, because Dad had found a Popsicle in the freezer and was as thrilled as it is possible for a fat bloke in constraining leather trousers to be. He went chomping off into the front room.

Mum was adjusting her over-the-shoulder-boulder-holder and looking at me.

I said, "What?"

And she said, "So... have you heard anything?"

I don't know why I told her, but it just came tumbling out.

"Mum, why do boys do that 'see you later' thing and then just not see you later? Even though you don't even know when later is."

"He hasn't got in touch then?"

"No."

She sat down and looked thoughtful, which was a bit alarming. She said slowly, "Hmm – well, I think it's because – they're like sort of nervous gazelles in trousers, aren't they?"

I looked at her. "Mum, are you saying that Masimo is a leaping furry animal who also plays in a band and rides a scooter? And snogs?"

She said, "He snogs, does he?"

Damn, drat, damnity dratty damn. And also *merde*. I had broken my rule about never speaking about snognosity questions with old mad people.

I said quickly, "Anyway, what do you mean about the gazelle business?"

"Well, I think that boys are more nervous than you think. He wants to make sure that you like him before he makes a big deal about it. How many days is it since he went?"

"I don't know. I haven't been counting the days actually, I'm not that sad."

She looked at me. "How many hours then?"

"One hundred and forty."

We were interrupted by Gordy and Angus both trying to get through the cat flap at once. Quickly followed by Libby.

In my bedroom
8:45 p.m.

I can hear Mum and Dad arguing downstairs because he hasn't taken the rubbish out. And never does. On and on.

I will never behave like this when I am married. Mind you, I will not be marrying a loon in tight trousers who thinks Rolf Harris is a really good artist.

Who will I be marrying at this rate? I haven't been out of my room for years and the phone hasn't rung since it was invented.

Why is no one phoning me? Not even the Ace Gang. I've been home for hours and hours. Don't they care?

The trouble with today is that everyone is so obsessed with themselves. They just have no time for me.

Five minutes later

At last, a bit of peace to contemplate my broken bum. Oh no, here they go again. They are so childish. Mum shouted out, "Bob, you know that sort of wooden thing in the bedroom, in the corner? Well, it's called a set of drawers and some people, people who are grown up and no longer have their mummy wiping their botties, well those sort of people put their clothes in the drawers. So that other people don't have to spend their precious time falling over knickers and so on."

Uh-oh. Fight, fight!!

Then I could hear him shambling into their bedroom and singing, "One little sock in the drawer, two socks in the drawer and two pairs of attractive undercrackers on the head then into the drawer, yesssss!!"

How amazing. I shouted down, "Mum, is Dad on some kind of medication? Or have his trousers cut off the circulation to his head?"

That did it. Vati hit number seven on the losing it scale (complete ditherspaz). He yelled up, "Georgia... this isn't anything to do with you!"

I said, "Oh, that's nice. I thought we were supposed to be a lovely family and do stuff together."

He just said, "Anyway, where is your sister? Is she up there with you?"

Why am I Libby's so-called nanny? Haven't I got enough trouble with my own life? I am not my sister's keeper, as Baby Jesus said. Or was it Robin Hood? I don't know. Some bloke in a skirt anyway.

I said, "No. Have you tried the airing cupboard or the cat basket?"

Five minutes later

Things have got worse. While Mum went hunting for Bibbsy, Dad unfortunately decided to check the phone messages. He heard Mum's mate's message. I could hear him tutting. And then it was Josh's mum's message.

He had the nervy spaz of all nervy spazzes, shouting and carrying on. "What is it with this family??? Why did Libby have a bread knife in her bedroom? Probably because you are too busy pratting around with your so-called mates to bother looking after your children!"

That did it for Mum. She shouted back, "How dare you! They're MY children, are they? If you took some notice of them, that would be a miracle. You care more about that ridiculous bloody three-wheeled clown car."

Mum had called his car a clown car. Tee-hee.

Dad had really lost it. "That car is an antique."

I shouted, "It's not the only one."

Mum laughed, but Dad said, "Right, that's it, I'm off. Don't wait up."

Mum shouted, "Don't worry, I won't." The door slammed and there was silence.

Then there was the sound of the clown car being driven off at high speed (two miles an hour) down the driveway.

And silence again as it whirred away into the distance.

Then a little voice said, "Mummy, my bottom is stuck in the bucket."

9:30 p.m.
Dear God, what a nightmare. This has taken my mind off the oven of luuurve situation.

38

Libby has wedged herself into the outdoor metal bucket. We pulled her and wiggled her about but we can't get it off.

Mum said, "Go and get me some butter from the fridge. We can smear it on her and sort of slide her out."

Of course, we didn't have any butter; we had about a teaspoon of cottage cheese but Mum said it wasn't the same.

Twenty-five minutes later

In the end Mum made me go across the road and ask Mr Across the Road if we could borrow some butter. She said I could lie better.

Mr Across the Road was wearing a short nightshirt and I kept not looking anywhere below his chin. He was all nosey about the late-night butter scenario though.

"Doing a bit of baking, are you?"

I said, "Er... yes."

"It's a bit late to start, isn't it?"

I said, "Er, well, it's emergency baking. It has to be done by tomorrow."

He said, "Oh, what are you making?"

How the hell did I know? I was lying. And also the only kind of confectionery I knew were the cakes I had got from the bakery of love. The Robbie éclair, the Masimo cream horn and then I remembered the Dave the Tart scenario and quickly said, "Erm, we're making tarts. For the deaf. It's for charity."

He said, "Tarts for the deaf? That's a new one on me. I'll have to go down to the storeroom for some packets." And he ambled off.

And that is when Junior Blunder Boy and full-time twit came in. Oscar.

He looked at me and said, "Yo, wa'appen, bitch?"

What was he talking about and also what was he wearing? He had massive jeans on about fifty sizes too big for him. He had to sort of waddle about like a useless duck to keep them from falling down. And pull them up every five seconds. How spectacularly naff and sad he was. I just looked at him as he waddled over to the kitchen counter. He reached up to get a can of Coca-Cola from a shelf and momentarily forgot about his elephant jeans. They fell to his ankles. Leaving him standing there in his Thomas the Tank Engine undercrackers.

I said to him, "Oscar, you are wearing Thomas the Tank Engine undercrackers. I know this because, believe it or not, your trousers have fallen off."

He said, "Yes man, me mean to do that. Be cool, it is righteous." And he shuffled off, still with the trousers round his ankles.

I will never, ever tire of the sheer bonkerosity of boydom.

II:OO p.m.

It took us nearly half an hour to get Mr Bucket off Libby. We greased as much of her bottom as we could reach, like a little suckling pig. Eventually we cut through the top of her panties and managed to make a bit of leeway and free the bum-oley.

For some toddlers, being greased up and pulled by brute force out of a metal bucket might have been a traumatic experience. But then not all toddlers are insane. Libby laughed and sang through the whole episode, amusing herself by gobbling stray bits of butter and smearing other bits on my head. Oh, how I joined in the merry times. Not.

In addition, Gordy and Angus lolloped in to lick at the leftover butter on her botty. Soooo disgusting. Libby was shouting, "They is ticklin me!!! Heggy heggy ho!!!"

Back in bed

It is like the botty casualty department in here. My bottom, which I have had no time to attend to, is being supported by Libby's swimming ring and I have a buttered-up child rammed in next to me.

Also, have I got a boyfriend or not?

Midnight

And I am still thinking about the Dave the Laugh accidental snogging in the forest incident.

12:10 a.m.

Perhaps this is God's little way of saying, "She who lives by the red bottom gets to lie in a rubber ring."

Once more into the huffmobile

Monday August 1st
8:00 a.m.
Oww oww and double owww!! I think my botty has taken a turn for the worse. I wonder if it is swollen up?

Looking in the mirror
It does look a bit on the swollen side. Oh marvellous. I will have to ask Jas if I can borrow some of her enormous winter pants. She will have got them out of her winter store by now. She starts ironing her school pants about a month before we are forced back to Stalag 14. Which reminds me, we only

have about four weeks of holiday left. *Sacré bleu* and *merde*.

Libby has already scarpered off to get ready for nursery, so I can just have a little dolly daydream about snogging the Luuurve God. If I make a mental picture of us snogging, I might attract him to me through the psychic ethery stuff.

Ten minutes later

I can hear the postman coming up the drive. Ah, the postie. It's a lovely job being a postie; you see it in all ye olde films that ye olde parents watch. Mr Postie coming up the drive with a cheery whistle and a handful of exciting letters for the family. A "Good morning, ma'am" to the mistress of the house and then—

"I've got a bloody stick, you furry freak, and I'm not afraid to use it!!!"

Charming. Utterly, utterly charming.

I looked out of the window. Angus was sitting on the dustbin showing off to Naomi, his mad Burmese girlfriend and slag, by taunting the postie – hissing and doing pretend biffing, sticking his claws in and out. The postie had to get by the dustbin to get to the door and he was waving a big stick about in Angus's direction. Angus loves a stick. The larger the better. He lay down and started purring so loudly I could hear it in my bedroom. I don't know why he loves sticks so much, but he does. Almost as much as he loves cars.

He thinks cars are like giant stupid mice on wheels. That he can chase after.

He brought a stick home the other day that was so big, it took him half an hour to figure out how to get it through the cat flap. He did it, though, because he is top cat.

Two minutes later

It was the same with the ginormous dead pigeon. Angus backed his way through the cat flap dragging the feet first, and then Gordy heave-hoed the head bit through.

It was an amazing double act. Father and son were very impressed with themselves. Although slightly covered in feathers. They even arranged the pigeon so that it was looking towards the door and propped up so Mum could get the full benefit when she came in.

She did get the full benefit and went ballistic, jumping on a chair and screaming etc. Angus and Gordy and the dead pigeon all looked at her.

"Bloody murdering furry thugs!!!" she yelled.

I said, "Look, you are really hurting their feelings."

And then she threw the washing-up bowl at me. That is the kind of mothering I have to put up with.

one minute later

The postie has bravely got past Angus and disappeared from view as he posts our letters through the letter box. Angus has disappeared as well. Oh, I know what he is doing!

He is doing his vair vair amusing trick of lurking in the top of the hedge to leap down on the postie's head as he passes by. Tee-hee. Happy days. I wish I was a cat. At least I would get fed now and again.

I wouldn't be quite so keen on all the bum-oley licking. Although as mine is so swollen now, it would probably be easier to reach.

Mum yelled up, "Gee, come down and have brekkie and say goodbye to your family."

I said, "Have I still got one? I thought that Father had left us and would never be back. That is what he promised."

Dad yelled up, "You think you are so bloody funny, but you won't when I don't give you your ten-quid pocket money. Nothing to spend on your eyeliner or nit cream or whatever else it is that you plaster yourself with."

Nit cream? Has he finally snapped?

Mum said, "Stop it, you two. Oooh look, here is a foreign postcard addressed to Georgia – I wonder who it's from?"

Oh my giddy god's pyjamas!!! I leaped downstairs, putting the pain of my bottom behind me. Tee-hee. Oh brilliant, my brain has gone into hysterical clown mode.

Thirty seconds later

Dad had the postcard in his hand and was reading it!!! Noooooo!

He was saying in a really crap Pizza-a-gogo accent, "*Ciao*, Georgia, it is smee."

I tried to get the postcard from him. "Dad, that is private property addressed to me. If it doesn't say 'to some mad fat bloke', it isn't yours."

Dad just went on reading it. "I am, how you say, hair in Roma wive my family."

Finally I ripped it out of his hand and took it upstairs.

Mum said, "You are mean, Bob. You know what she is like."

Dad said, "Yes, I do. She's insane like all the other bloody women in this family. Hang on a minute... what the hell happened to my car-washing bucket?"

Mum said, "We had to hit it with a hammer in the end. Libby got her bottom stuck in it."

Dad said, "I rest my case."

In my room
Oh God, I am sooooo excited, my eyes have gone cross-eyed. What does it say?

Twenty seconds later

> Ciao, Georgia,
>   It is smee. I am, how you say, hair in Roma wive my family. I am hot. (You don't have to tell me that, mate.) I am playing fun. Are you playing fun? I miss I you me.
>   I call on the telefono on Tuesday for you.
>   Ciao, bellissima, Masimo xxx

An hour later
After about three thousand years and a half, the Swiss Family Mad all crashed off to ruin other people's lives and I could get on the old blower.

I nearly dialled Wise Woman of the Forest before I remembered that she had practically called me the Whore of Babylon. She is so full of suspicionosity. And annoyingnosity. How dare she suggest in front of everyone that I had been up to hanky-panky and rudey-dudeys with Dave the Laugh? She knows very well that I am going out with a Luuurve God. Who is a) hot and b) playing fun.

What in the name of arse does "playing fun" mean?

I must consult with my gang.

But not her.

I am *ignorez-vous*ing her with a firm hand and it serves her right. I hope she realises that I am *ignorez-vous*ing her, otherwise it's all a bit pointless.

Two minutes later

I may have to call her and let her know I am *ignorez-vous*ing her, as she can be a bit on the dense side.

Phoned Jas.

Her mum answered. "Hello, Georgia. Gosh, you had a fabulous time camping, didn't you? Jas said you sang and played games till all hours."

I said, "Er yes..."

"You had a great time, I bet."

"Er yes, it was very, erm, campey."

"Good. I'll just call Jas, dear. I think she's in her bedroom dusting and rearranging her owls and so on."

You couldn't really write it, could you? If I wrote a book and I said: "I've got a mate who dusts her collection of stuffed owls and follows greater toasted newts about," people would say: "I'm not reading that sort of stupid exaggeration. Next thing you know, someone will say they went to a party dressed as a stuffed olive. Or accidentally snogged three boyfriends at once." Hang on a minute, everything has gone a bit *déjà vu*-ish.

Jas came on the phone. "Yes."

"Jas, it is me, the Whore of Babylon, but I am preparing myself to forgive you."

"What are you forgiving me for?"

"Because you are a naughty pally saying things about me being selfish and lax and having a million boyfriends."

Jas said, "It's up to you how many boyfriends you have. I am not my brother's keeper."

"Jas, I know you aren't. You haven't got a brother."

"I mean you."

"I haven't got a brother either, thank the Lord. I do,

however, have an insane sister, who by the way is now probably going to be done for TBH."

"You mean GBH – grievous bodily harm."

"No, I mean TBH. Toddler bodily harm. Josh's mum has complained about her and she is suspended from nursery school. She is staying with Grandfarty and he is looking after her. She is the first person in our family to get a restraining order besides Grandad."

Jas was not what you would call full of sympatheticnosity.

"I don't think she will be the last person in your family to get a restraining order, Georgia. I am a bit busy actually."

"Jas, please don't have Mrs Hump with me. I need you, my dearest little pally wally. Pleasey please, be frendy wendys. Double please with knobs. And a tiny little knoblet. And—"

"All right, all right, stop going on."

She deffo had the minor hump, but it was only four on the having-the-hump scale. (cold-shoulderosity work).

"Jas, come on. Remember the laugh we had when we all snuck off to the boys' tent? And I came and told you that Tom was there, didn't I? Even though you were singing 'Ging Gang Gooly'."

"Well, yes, but—"

"I displayed magnanimosity, which isn't something everyone can say. But I did it because I luuurve you. A LOT."

"OK, don't go on."

"You are not ashamed of our luuurve, are you, Jas?"

"Look, shut up. People might hear."

"What do you mean, the people who live in the telephone?"

"NO, I mean, anyway, what's happened?"

"I've got a postcard from Masimo and we have to call an extraordinary general meeting of the Ace Gang."

"Oh no."

"Oh yes."

In the park
2:00 p.m.
Naaaice and sunny. I wore my denim miniskirt and halter neck and some groovy sandals. I will have to do something with my legs, though, because they give me the droop, they are so pale. Rosie had some eye-catching shorts on; they had pictures of Viking helmets all over them. She said, "Sven had them specially printed in my honour. Groovy, aren't they?"

I said, "That is one word for them."

Rosie said, "Sven has got his first dj-ing job next weekend and I am going to be his groupie. You all have to come."

Ten minutes later

We settled down in the shade underneath the big chestnut tree by the swings. The bees were singing and the birds a-buzzing, dogs scampering around, people eating ice creams, toddlers sticking ice creams in their eyes by mistake etc. A lovely, lovely summer afternoon, ideal to sort out the game of luuurve.

We had just passed round the chuddie and decided for Ellen where she should sit after about eight minutes of: "Well, erm, I should sit in the shade really, don't you think, because of the ultraviolet, but, erm, what about, erm, not like getting the sun and then like maybe not getting enough vitamin D because that would be, like, not great. Or something."

Finally she sat with her top part in the shade and her legs sticking in the sun because we told her no one had ever got cancer of the knees. Which might or might not be true, but sometimes (in fact, very often, in my experience) lying is the best policy. Especially if you can't be arsed talking about something boring any more.

One minute later

I don't know why I bother lying because Ellen has gone off to the loos to run her wrists under cold water so she doesn't get sunstroke of the arms.

Jas still hasn't turned up. I wonder if she has progressed to number six on the hump scale and is doing pretend deafnosity?

Thirty seconds later

The Ace Gang started talking about the camping trip and sneaking out to see the lads at night.

Mabs said, "I had a go at snogging with Edward."

Jools said, "What was it like?"

Mabs chewed and popped and said, "Quite groovy. We did four and then a spot of five."

I said, "Oh, so *you* missed out four and a half as well. I said I thought it was a WUBBISH idea that Mrs Newt Knickers came up with. Who apart from her and Tom would do hand snogging?"

Mabs said, "What do you mean 'as well'?"

I said, "What do you mean 'What do you mean as well'?"

Mabs put her face really close to mine. "Georgia, you said,

and forgive me if I'm right, 'Oh, so you missed out four and a half as well.' Which means, 'Oh, so you missed out four and a half as well AS ME.' Meaning you must have missed out four and a half with someone. The only someone around was Dave the Laugh."

Uh-oh, my red-herringnosity skills were letting me down.

Mabs was going on and on like Jas's little helper. "So what did you get up to with Dave the Laugh by the river?"

I said in a casualosity-at-all-times sort of way, "Ah well, I'm glad you asked me that. Because suspicionosity is the enemy of friendshipnosity. The simple truth is that Dave and I were playing, erm, tig. Yes, and I accidentally fell in a stream and then I went back to my tent because I was, er, wet."

Rosie said, "You and Dave were playing tig. I see. One moment. I must give this some serious thought. Luckily I have my pipe."

Oh no.

Two minutes later

Good Lord, I am being interrogated by Inspector Bonkers of the Yard.

The inspector (i.e. Rosie with her pipe and beard on)

continued, "You expect us to believe that you and Dave the Laugh gambolled around the woods playing a little game of tig?"

I said, "Yes."

Rosie said, "You are, it has to be said, my little chumlet, even dimmer than you look."

Ellen came back then, just in the knickers of time. I smiled at her and said in a lighthearted but menacing way, "You haven't told us about Declan. It is Ace Gang rules that we do sharesies about snogging."

Rosie and Mabs raised their eyebrows at me, but I *ignorez-vous*ed them.

Ellen heaved herself into her Dithermobile and said, "Well, Declan showed, well, he showed me something and—"

Inspector Bonkers of the Yard winked, sucked on her pipe and went, "Ay ay."

Ellen went even redder and more dithery.

"No, I mean, it was his Swiss Army knife."

Inspector Bonkers got out a pretend notebook. "All right. So you looked at his knife and then did you snog?"

Ellen said, "Well, when we were, like, leaving to go back to camp – he gave me a number three and then—"

"Then quickly went on to number four."

"Well, no, he..."

"He missed out number four and went straight for the nungas?"

"No, well, he – he, like, he said, he said, 'See you later.'"

Oh dear God, we were once more in the land of S'later. Will we never be free?

One minute later

But at least it stopped anyone going on about the Dave the Laugh fiasco.

One minute later

Jas turned up. She looked quite nice actually, if you like that mad fringey look. She said, "I was just talking to Tom on the phone. He's playing footie this arvie with the lads. He's got some new boots."

I said, "No!! Honestly!"

And she gave me a huffty look. I don't want to have more rambling lectures from her, so I went and gave her a hug and a piece of chuddie.

Anyway, we had just settled down and I'd got out my

postcard from Masimo to show the gang, when Jools said, "Oh God, Blunder Boys alert!"

They were shuffling about by the bushes at the far end of the swing park. Mark Big Gob was absent, probably carrying his tiny girlfriend around somewhere. Junior Blunder Boy was with them though. I noticed he had a belt round his elephant jeans. So now he didn't look like a twit any more. He looked like a twit with a belt on.

Mabs said, "Don't look at them and they'll get bored."

I said, "Can we get back to the matter I hold in my hand?"

Rosie went, "Oo-er."

I gave her my worst look and went on, "What do you think 'I am playing fun' means?"

Ellen said, "Well, erm, I don't know but you know, well – well, you know when a boy says 'See you later', well, like when Declan said 'See you later' and that was, like, three days ago now. So, er, this is, like, later, isn't it? Or something. And he hasn't, like, seen me."

Even though we were actually officially having the official Ace Gang meeting officially for me (as I had officially called it), I did feel quite sorry for Ellen. And also it has to be said it would be a bloody relief if she did get off with Declan.

Then she would leave Dave the Laugh alone.

Not that it is any of my business whether she leaves Dave the Laugh alone or not.

I mean, he has a girlfriend anyway.

Probably.

Unless he has told her about the accidental snogging and she is even now taking kickboxing lessons for when she next sees me.

Anyway, shut up, brain. He has got a girlfriend, which is good because so have I.

Well, not a girlfriend exactly, but an Italian person.

Who incidentally does not have a handbag.

Or a sports bra.

Whatever Dave the so-called Laugh might say. Why is Dave the Laugh sneaking about in my brain???

Jools said to Ellen, "Maybe he's a bit shy."

Ellen said, "Yes, but he, I mean, he showed me his Swiss Army knife."

I looked at her. What is the right response to that? I said, "Well, maybe he is a bit backward then?"

Ellen looked like she was going to cry. Oh Blimey O'Reilly's Y-fronts, if she starts blubbing, I'll never get round to talking about the Italian Stallion.

I said quickly, "I know... Jas can ask Tom to get Declan and the lads to come along to Sven's gig, and hopefully that will be a good excuse for him to get his knife out again (oo-er) and everything will be tickety-boo and so on."

Ellen looked a bit cheered up.

I said, "Now, shall we get back to the official meeting? What do you think 'I am playing fun' means?" And that is when an elastic band hit me on the cheek.

"Owww, bloody owww!!!"

Amazingly, not content with being complete losers, tossers and spoons, the Blunder Boys were flicking rubber bands at us from behind our tree. And then hiding behind it as if we wouldn't know where they were. Like the Invisible Twits. Not.

I got up and went behind the tree where they were all larding about, puffing smoke from fags and hitching their trousers up. Dear God. I said to one of the speccy genks, "What is it you want?"

And he said, "Show us your nungas."

They all started snorting and saying, "Yeah, get them out for the lads."

Rosie came up behind me and loomed over them. She is not small. She said, "OK, that's a good plan. We'll show you our nungas, but first of all we need to see your trouser snakes, to check that all is in order."

Ellen and Jools and Mabs and even Woodland Jas came and ganged up in front of them.

I said, "Come on, lads, drop the old trouser-snake holders."

They started backing off, holding on to their trousers.

Jools said, "Are you a bit shy? Shall we help you?"

They started walking really quickly backwards as we kept walking. Then they just took off and got over the fence at the back of the park.

Twelve minutes later

The Ace Gang wisdomosity is that "I am playing fun" and "Are you playing fun?" roughly translated into Billy Shakespeare language is "I am having a nice time but am missing you. Are you having a nice time but missing me?"

Which is nice.

So all should be smoothy friendly friendly, except that there is always a Jas in the manger.

After about two hours of talking about it, we were all going home and I just innocently said, "So what do you think I should wear when he phones up?"

And Jas immediately climbed into the huffmobile for no apparent reason. She was all red and flicking her fringe around like it was a fringe-ometer.

"Why is it always like this with you, Georgia? Why don't you just say and do normal stuff? For instance, if Tom wanted me to go to the nature reserve with him he would say, 'Jas, do you want to go to the nature reserve with me? There is a conservation day and we could clear some of the canalside of weeds.'

"And I would say, 'Yes, that would be fab, Tom.' Simple pimple, not stupidity and guessing what 'playing fun' means and what to wear on the phone."

What was she rambling on about now?

I said, "Jas are the painters in, because I think you are being just a tad more mentally unstable than normal."

She really had lost her cheese now, because she shouted at me, "Look, I haven't got any sun protector on and I am almost bound to get peely peely now thanks to you going on. And the short and short of it is that HE IS CALLING YOU TOMORROW AND YOU CAN ASK HIM WHAT HE MEANS!!!" And she stormed off.

Blimey. We all looked at one another.

I said, "I think it's owl trouble."

In bed
What am I going to wear for the phone call though? I wish I wasn't so pale; I think people can tell if you are a bit tanned. Even down the phone. I bet I can tell immediately if he has a nice tan.

Two minutes later
Actually, if he is tanned I think I might faint. I can't stand him being much more gorgey than he already is.

Five minutes later
Should I prepare a speech? Or at least a normal conversation. With some handy topics in case I mislay my brain or it decides to go on an expedition to Outer Loonolia.

One minute later
So let's see, what have I done lately?
  Loads of stuff.

Five minutes later
I don't think I will mention Miss Wilson exposing herself to Herr Kamyer.

Two minutes later

Or breaking my bum-oley in the river.

Four minutes later

In fact, perhaps it's better to leave the whole camping fiasco to one side. I will only have Dave the Laugh popping into my brain. I will stick to lighthearted banter.

Should I tell him about the tarts for the deaf episode?

Three minutes later

Or Junior Blunder Boy's Thomas the Tank Engine undercrackers?

Two minutes later

None of it sounds that normal, to be frank. I will stick to world affairs and art.

Two minutes later

I could ask him what he thinks about the foreign exchange rate. Well, I could if I knew what it meant.

one minute later

Where is Rome anyway? Is it in the boot bit of Italy? Or is Spain the booty bit?

I'm really worried about tomorrow now. I will never sleep and then I will have big dark rings under my eyes and...

zzzzzzzzzzzzzzz.

Tuesday August 2nd
9:30 a.m.

I was just having a dream about being in Rome with the Luuurve God. I had a cloak on and Masimo said, "So, *cara*, what have you come to the fancy-dress party as?" And I dropped the cloak and said, "A fried egg."

The phone rang and I practically broke my neck tripping over Angus and Gordy, who just emerged from the shadows.

I couldn't say anything because I was so nervous.

Then I heard Grandad say, "Hello, hello, speak up."

I said, "Grandad, I haven't said anything yet."

He was in full-Grandad mode. "You'll like this: what do pigs use if they hurt themselves? Ay ay??? Oinkment. Do you get it, do you see??? Oinkment!!! Oh, I make myself laugh. Are you courting yet? You should be – there's nothing like a bit of snogging to perk you up."

Oh dear God, my grandvati was talking about snogging.

Now I have finally experienced every kind of porn. This is mouldyporn.

Two minutes later

I managed to get him off the phone by saying good morning to Libby (she purred back), and promising to visit and have a game of hide-and-seek with him and the other residents. I don't mind that so much, as when it is my turn to hide I just go to the shops and then come back half an hour later and get in a cupboard. It keeps them happy for hours.

I do love my grandad though. He is one of the most cheerful people I know and now he is going to have Maisie as his new knitted wife. Aaaahhh.

Mum was wandering around in the kitchen like Madame Zozo of, erm, Zozoland. In a semi-see-through nightie. It's her day off and she looked like she might settle in for hours. I must get rid of her.

I said in an interested and lighthearted fashion, "What

time are you going out? In a minute or two? To make the best of the day?"

She sat down, actually resting her basoomas on the tabletop, presumably because she was already tired of lugging them about. Please save me from the enormous-jug gene.

She said, "I thought you and I could go out and do something groovy together."

Groovy?

I said, "Mum, are you mad because I tell you this for free a) I am not going out with you and b) the same with knobs on."

Mum said, "Hahaha, that worried you. Are you having a bit of a nervy spazmarama attack about Masimo ringing you?"

I was truly shocked. "Mum, it is not a nervy spazmarama, it is a spaz attack, which is number six on the losing it scale – hang on a minute. How do you know about a spaz attack anyway? Have you been snooping through my private drawers?"

She didn't bother to reply because she was too busy eating jam with a spoon out of the jar. She will get so fat that she will get trapped in Dad's clown car and have to drive endlessly up and down our driveway begging for snacks from passers-by. Good.

When she stopped chomping, she said, "Me and my mates

have loads of sayings and stuff. We have a real laugh. It's not just you and your mates, you know. I have a life."

I tried not to laugh.

"In aquaerobics the other day Fiona laughed so much at the instructor's choice of music that she weed herself in the pool. When she told me I nearly drowned. We had to all leave the class and I don't think we can go back."

She was hiccuping and giggling like a twerp. Is it any wonder that I find myself in trouble with boys when I have this sort of thing as my example?

I left the kitchen with a dignitosity-at-all-times sort of walk. I have a call from the cakeshop of luuurve to think about.

Back in my bedroom
Ten minutes later

What shall I wear, what shall I wear? I tell you this, I'm not going to wear anything yellow after the fried egg dream.

I could wear my bikini. My red one with the dots on it. They tend to wear red bikinis all the time the Italian girls, probably even if they work in banks and cafes and so on. Maybe not for nursing though; it might not be hygienic. My mum said that when she had an Italian boyfriend she was on the beach and this bloke rode up on a motorbike. And this girl who just had on the bottoms of a bikini and some really high heels came jogging up. She got on the back of the bike, lit a fag and they roared off with her nunga-nungas flying.

Back in the kitchen
9:45 a.m.
Why won't Mum go out? I have my bikini on underneath my ordinary clothes ready to rip off when the phone rings.

Five minutes later
She is just rambling on and on about herself. I already know more than I want to know about her.

9:55 a.m.
Oh nooooooo. Now she is talking about "feelings" and "relationships" and what is worse is, it's not even my feelings or relationships, it's hers!!! How horrific.

She says she feels that she doesn't share many interests with Dad.

I said, "Well, who does?"

69

She didn't even hear me, she just went on and on. "I think when I met him I was a different person and now I've changed."

10:10 a.m.
The Luuurve God is going to phone any minute and she will still be here.

Mum said, "I don't blame him, but people do change and want different things."

I said quickly, "Yeah, yeah, you're so right. I think you need a change – a change of, er, scenery. You need to go out into the sunshine and meet your mates and ask them what they feel. Maybe go for a slap-up meal. You've only had a pound or two of jam today, you'll be peckish. Go for a pizza and maybe have some *vino tinto* because you know what they say about *vino* in Latin. *In vino hairy arse.* Just give yourself space."

"Do you think so? Just enjoy myself and don't feel guilty?"

I nodded like billio.

Fifteen minutes later
Thank the Lord, Baby Jesus and all his cohorts. She's gone. All tarted up. It is so typically selfish of her to have a midlife crisis when I am expecting a phone call.

Half an hour later

Oh, I am so full of tensionosity. I haven't been able to eat anything apart from oven chips. With mayo and tommy sauce. And a choc ice.

Perhaps some popcorn would be good for me. It's practically health food really. In fact, don't hamsters eat it? And they are as healthy as anything. Running round and round in those little wheels for no reason, dashing up and down ladders. Ringing bells etc.

Shut up, brain! I am giving you a final warning.

Twenty minutes later

I tell you this, never cook popcorn. I don't know what happened, but I did what it said on the packet, chucked it into some hot oil in a pan and it just sort of exploded everywhere. How do you get popcorn out of light fittings?

And your hair?

And nose?

And bikini bottoms?

Angus has just done that cat thing. You know, the high-speed slink across the room with the belly nearly touching the ground. Why do they do that? Why?

Two minutes later

Now he is doing fridge staring.

Ring ring.

Ohmygiddygod. The phone. I bet all my lip gloss has disappeared. But if I go and reapply, he might ring off. Oh good, I was at number nine on the ditherspaz scale already.

I smiled as I said in my deepest voice, "Hello?"

"Georgia, have you come over all transsexual? Has he phoned yet?"

"No, he hasn't, Jas. Not that you really care."

"Yes, I do, otherwise why would I phone up to ask you whether he'd phoned you yet?"

"I don't know."

"Well, there you are then."

"You might have called just to be glad he hasn't called, knowing you."

"Well, I didn't."

"Oh, OK, thanks. Goodbye now."

"Don't you want to talk to me?"

"Er, well, not just now, Jas."

"Oh."

"I'm putting the phone down now."

72

There was a sort of a sobbing noise. Then a trembly little voice said, "Tom and I had our first row last night."

Oh for heaven's bloody sake.

I said, "What happened? Did he diss one of your owls?"

She was gulping and her voice was all trembly. "No, but he said, he said, what did I think about him going to uni in Hamburger-a-gogo land. And I said I didn't really want to go to Hamburger-a-gogo land, I would rather go to York. And he said that might be a good idea."

What is this, *EastEnders*?

Thirty minutes later

Good Lord. I think I know everything that is in Jas's head now and I tell you this for free, I wish I didn't.

Tom thinks they should go to separate unis or something so that they can be sure that they are made for each other. I did say to Jas, "Well, you can safely let him go. What other fool is he going to find to go vole hunting with him?"

But it didn't seem to cheer her up as such.

In the end I've said I'll go round to hers later after the Luuurve God has called.

God help us one and all.

one hour later

I am now officially going mad.

Phone rang

I said, "Yes! What is it?"

And then I heard his voice. "*Ciao*, er, is please Georgia there?"

It was him!!! Praise God and his enormous beard!!

I took a big breath and said, "Hello, yes, Georgia Nicolson speaking."

Blimey, why am I suddenly speaking like the queen?

Masimo laughed. "*Ciao ciao*, Georgia!! *Bellissima!!!* It is you! *Un momento per favore.*"

Then I head him speaking off the telephone and laughing, and there were other voices and then loud smacking noises like kissing.

Maybe it was kissing.

Was he actually snogging someone else while he was talking to me? That seemed very lax, even for the Pizza-a-gogo types.

Then suddenly he was back talking to me again. "Oh, *cara*, *mi scusi*, my brothers, my family, they are all going to the beach – later, when it is night we are having how you say in English – a bum-fire?"

74

A bum-fire? That seemed a bit mean. Setting people's bums on fire. But perhaps that is the old Roman ways emerging again.

Then he was laughing. "You are not saying anything. I have this wrong, no?"

I said, "*Sì*." And we both laughed. It was marvy speaking in different languages.

He said, "Have you missed me?"

And I said, "Oh, *muchos* and a half."

He laughed again. We were laughing and laughing.

"Me too. How was your camping?"

Uh-oh. The forbidden topic. I must remember my rule about not saying anything and get things back to world politics and so on as soon as possible. I said, "Oh, it was pretty crappio."

He said, "Tell me something from it."

"Well, you know, not much happened. Erm, Nauseating P. Green fell into the so-called toilets and it fell down and Miss Wilson was in the nuddy-pants having a shower with her soap on a rope. And then later Herr Kamyer sat on her knee and that was all that happened."

He said, "I have, how you would say, the mad girlfriend."

Oooooh, he had called me his mad girlfriend. How cool was that?

We talked for ages. Well, I said stuff and he asked me what it meant mostly. I wish I could speak more Pizza-a-gogo-ese; it's more difficult speaking to someone on the phone anyway because you can't see their face. And then he asked me when I am coming over to see him.

Good point, well made.

I haven't even asked my parents about the 500 squids I will need. If they would stop banging on about themselves, I might get a chance to ask. I didn't like to say that I didn't have any money, so I just said, "I think, probably in two, *due* weeks."

He said, "Ah, that is long. I wish you were here and then we could again, what do you say – snog. And I could touch you and feel your mouth on mine. And look into your lovely face. I was thinking about your beautiful eyes and I think they are so lovely, it makes my heart melt."

Crikey, he had turned into Billy Shakespeare. Or Billio Shakespeario, who wrote the famous Italian plays *MacUselessio* and *King Leario.*

Shut up, brain. Now this minutio. Stoppio, nowio. It still wouldn't stop it (io).

I was quite literally tripping around on a cloud of luuurve. Sadly, the four pints of Coke I had to keep me going before he phoned now wanted to come out and join me.

I tried pressing my bottom against the stool but sooner or later something was going to give. I needed to go to the tarts' wardrobe vair vair badly. But because my vati was too mean to get a modern phone that you could walk about with I was stuck. I didn't want to say, "Oh, 'scuse me, I have to go to the piddly-diddly department" because that would start another one of those international incidents. So I said, "Oh no, someone is at the door. Can you just hang on for a mo?"

He said, "*Sì, cara*, I wait."

And then weirdly the doorbell did ring. How freaky-deaky is that? I wonder who it was. Well, whoever it was, they weren't coming in. I nipped into the tarts' wardrobe. Then the shouting began.

"Georgia, come on, open the door! We know you are in there."

It was Grandad. And he wasn't alone. I could hear Libby and Maisie. Dear God.

I couldn't keep them out for long because they would probably start knitting a rope ladder and get through my bedroom window. Perhaps I could persuade them to go away.

There was a bit of a silence and then Grandad said, "We've

got snacks," and he posted a sandwich through the letter box. I think it was spam.

I went back to the telephone. "Masimo, I have to go now. My grandad is posting sandwiches through the letter box."

He laughed. But he laughed alone. Then he said, "Phone me when you can. The *telefono* is Roma 75556666121." He did kissing stuff down the phone and then he was gone.

I didn't even remember to say when shall we speak again or anything because I was so flustered by the elderly loons. And I wanted to write the number down before I forgot it.

Five minutes later
People will not believe this, I know, but Maisie has knitted Libby a miniskirt and matching beret for her bridesmaid's outfit.

An hour later
They have gone, thank the Lord.

Four minutes later
Hearing Masimo's voice has made everything simple for me *vis-à-vis* the General Horn, ad-hoc red-bottomosity etc.

I am putting the accidental snogging scenario with Dave

the Laugh into a snogging cupboard at the back of my brainbox. A snogging cupboard that I will never be going into again. I have locked the door and thrown away the key.

Well, I didn't throw it away actually, but I have put it somewhere that I will never be able to find again.

One minute later
The snogging cupboard is in fact next to another cupboard that has got other discarded boy stuff in it. Like the Mark Big Gob stuff. The resting his hand on my nunga-nunga episode, for instance. Which I have also completely forgotten about and will never remember.

One minute later
That cupboard has also got the snogging Whelk Boy fiasco in it. Erlack a pongoes.

One minute later
And that cupboard is next to the set of drawers that has pictures of Robbie the original Sex God in it. Funny I haven't heard anything from him since I sort of dumped him. I hope

he is not on the rack of love. Although that would be a first. Usually it is me that is on the rack of love.

Thirty seconds later
I'll just close the drawer now.

Ten seconds later
I wonder if Robbie has got the megahump with me? I daren't ask Tom. Especially as he might be Mr Ex-Hunky.

One minute later
I hope Robbie is not too sad without me. I don't like making boys cry. Although to be frank I would rather they were crying than me.

Life can be cruel.

Especially if you are vair vair sensitive like I am.

Two minutes later
I don't know what to do with myself now. I am full of excitementosity. And tensionosity. And just a hint of confusiosity.

one minute later

Maybe I should fill in time by learning some Pizza-a-gogo-ese. For when I go over. Only being able to say *cappuccino* is going to wear a bit thin after a few days.

Masimo said he was off to some party tonight in Rome.

Five minutes later

Should he be out having fun while I am hanging about like a monk in a monkhouse? That is the drawback to being the girlfriend of a rock legend, you have to hang around a lot.

I may be driven to going round to listen to Wild Woman of the Forest ramble on about Hunky.

On the way round to Jas's

If I am nice to her, she may smash open her secret piggy bank and give me spondulies to go to my beloved.

Or else I could just steal the piggy.

Round at Jas's

Both her little eyes were swollen up. I put my arm around her and said, "Jas, I have found that when you are troubled, it is often better to think of others rather than yourself. I think you would feel much better if you got me some milky coffee and Jammy Dodgers and I told you all about me."

I had only just started when we were interrupted by Jas's mum saying there was a phone call from Rosie for Jas. Did she want to take it on her phone in the bedroom?

Jas and I each listened on an extension. I was nestled up among the Owl Folk and Jas was in her mum and dad's bedroom on the other extension.

Every time I ask for an extension and so on, Dad has a complete nervy spaz saying rubbish stuff like, "Why don't you just have a phone glued to your head?" And so on.

I am not surprised that Mum says she doesn't share many interests with him. What I am surprised about is that she shares any.

Ro Ro said, "*Bonjour*, groovers. I have had *la bonne* idea. Don't you think it would be groovy and a laugh for us to work out some backing dances for Sven's gig?

I said, "*Mais oui*, that would be *beau regarde* and also *magnifique* and possibly groovy."

Jas said, "Well, as long as they are not silly."

Rosie and I laughed, then I said, "We could have a Nordic

theme. We have many Viking dances in our repertoire: the Viking disco inferno, the bison dance. We could make up another one."

Rosie said, "Yeah, grooveyard, we could have furry miniskirts and ear muffs."

Home again
9:00 p.m.
I have cheered Jas up and told her we will think of a plan *vis-à-vis* Tom.

I didn't mention the piggy bank, but I think it is on the shelf near her bed. Behind her mollusc collection.

9:19 p.m.
I don't know why I didn't realise I was born for the stage before. It is blindingly obvious even to a blind man on blind tablets that I am a backing dancer. That will be my career. I will travel with the band giving the world the benefit of my Viking disco inferno dance and so on. And it is very convenient romance-wise because with Masimo as the lead singer of the Stiff Dylans and me as backing dancer, we can travel the globe of luuurve.

The turbulent washing machine of luuurve

Friday August 5th
Early Evening

Masimo hasn't called again. Officially it's my turn to call him on the number he gave me. That is what I would do if he was a girl, which he clearly isn't, even if Dave says he is.

Shut up about Dave.

I feel a bit shy about calling Masimo. In one of my mum's mags it said, "Be a teaser, not a pleaser." And it said you should never ring a boy; they should always ring you. So essentially, I am once more thrashing about in the washing machine of luuurve.

Oooh, what shall I do? Maybe I should send him a postcard.

Five minutes later

But if I go out and buy a postcard, he might ring while I'm out. I wonder if Mum has one lurking about in her drawers. Oo-er.

In Mum's bedroom

Honestly, this house is like living in a tart's handbag. I've found a card but it is of a girl walking by with huge nunga-nungas and a bloke on a veg stand holding two melons in front of his chest. The caption is "Phwoar, what a lovely pair of melons!" What is the matter with my parents?

Two minutes later

But even if I did manage to send a card, when would I say I was coming? I still haven't managed to steer the conversation around to Mutti and Vati giving me the spondulies for my trip.

One minute later

However, I have more than romance on my mind. Masimo will have to understand that my career comes first sometimes. There is a rehearsal round at Rosie's tonight for our planned disco inferno extravaganza, so I'd better get my dance tights out.

Sunday August 7th

Waited for the postie at the gate yesterday, but he didn't have any letters for me. I asked him if he was hiding my mail, but he didn't even bother to reply.

More damned rehearsals for Sven's dj-ing night today. I am so vair vair tired. I am a slave to my art.

9:45 p.m.

I am quite tuckered out with dancing. Even though it is still practically the afternoon, I may as well go to bed.

In bed

Sven turned up at Rosie's while we were there and snogged the pants off her (oo-er).

We all felt like a basket of goosegogs.

In fact, when we were walking home, Jas said, "I felt a bit jealous."

I tutted. But actually I felt a bit jealous as well.

9:50 p.m.

The door slammed and I heard Vati come in. Accompanied by Uncle Eddie, a.k.a. the baldy-o-gram since he took up taking his clothes off for women. They pay him to do it, that is the weird thing.

Dad yelled, "The vati and the baldy-o-gram are home, sensation seekers!"

Ten minutes later

I can hear the sound of sizzling from the kitchen and the cats are going bananas. That will be the twenty-five sausages each that Dad and his not very slim bald mate will be having.

Now I can hear the spluttering of cans of lager being opened.

Neither of them will be able to get through the kitchen door at this rate.

Five minutes later

They must have chucked a couple of sausages out into the garden for Angus and the Pussycat Gang because there is a lot of yowling and spitting going on.

And barking.

And yelling.

Oh, here we go. Mr Next Door is on the warpath.

I looked carefully through my bedroom curtains as I didn't want the finger of shame pointing my way.

Yes, there was Mr Next Door in his combat gear (slippers and towelling robe) shouting, "Clear off!!!"

He's a fool really. Angus will think he wants to play the sausage game with the Prat Poodles.

One minute later

Ah, yes. Angus has bounded over the garden wall and he is having a sausage tug-of-war with Whitey. Mr Next Door has gone for his broom.

I'm not going to look any more as I may accidentally glimpse Mr Next Door's exposed bottom in the furore.

10:15 p.m.

Dad and the baldy-o-gram are arsing about, laughing and giggling like ninnies in the front room. Dad yelled upstairs, "Georgia, my dove, your pater and his friend are engaged in a very serious business matter. Would you get another couple of cans from the wine cellar. You may know it as the 'fridge'. Thank you so much."

I just shouted down, "Not in a million years, O Portly One."

He shouted back, "I will give you a fiver."

Huh, as if bribery is going to make me his slavey girl.

Two minutes later

When I went into the front room with the cans of lager, Dad was lying on the sofa like a great bearded whale.

Uncle Eddie winked at me as I came in.

Dad said, "So, Eddie, what is your life like, now that you are a sex symbol?" Uncle Eddie belched (charming) and said, "Well, Bob, Georgia, it has its ups and downs like most celebrity lives. For instance, last night I got mobbed by women in the chippie after the gig. Which is nice. And I got free chips and a pickled egg. But, on the other hand, when I got home I found they had bloody stolen another of my feather codpieces. Which I have to have handmade."

Oh, how vair vair disgusting. Now I have been exposed to every sort of porn in this house: mouldyporn, kittyporn, earporn and now baldyporn!!!

Speaking of kittyporn, where are Angus and Naomi? And cross-eyed Gordy?

Back in my room

It's all gone suspiciously quiet. I looked out of the window over Next Door's garden. I can't see the pussycat gang, but I can see Gordy.

Four minutes later

I am concerned that Gordy is hanging around with the wrong crowd. He is actually playing with the Prat Poodles and, I can hardly believe my eyes, he is chewing on their rubber bonio. It's not right. It's probably just an adolescent phase he is going through.

11:29 p.m.

I went down to get a drink of water and a Jammy Dodger to ward off late-night starvation. Mum came in a bit red-faced from too much *vino tinto*, or just sheer embarrassment at being her. She went into the front room where Dad and Uncle Eddie were practising some sort of dance for Uncle Eddie's act. I couldn't bear to go in and have a look, but I will just say this, the music they were using was "I'm Jake the Peg, diddle diddle diddle dum, with my extra leg" by Rolf Harris.

Mum slammed off to bed without saying goodnight.

Dad came out of the front room and said to me, "Uh-oh, women's trouble!"

Midnight

I must get away from here. I must get to see the Luuurve God. Dad owes me a fiver for being his slavey girl. So that means I have only £495 to go.

I wonder if he will believe me if I say he promised to give me £50 to get his lager?

Monday August 8th
8:30 a.m.

I am still not used to having the bed to myself. I wouldn't say I am exactly missing Libby, but I feel a space in my bed where her freezing bottom used to be. Even Angus didn't come in last night. He's probably too bloated with sausage to haul himself up the stairs.

In the kitchen

Oh brilliant, Mutti and Vati are not speaking AGAIN. They are so childish.

Dad yelled from the bedroom, "Connie, have you seen

my undercrackers?" And Mum went on buttering her toast.

There was a long silence and then Dad said, "Er, hello... is there anybody there?"

I looked at Mum and she was chomping away on her toastie.

I said, "Mum, I would like to discuss dates with you, about my Italian holiday. Do you remember that we agreed I would go next week? Well, do you think I should travel to Rome on the Friday or the Saturday? It would be better on the Saturday because then Vati could drive me to the airport. It would be best all round, don't you think, that he hired a proper car. For safety and embarrassment reasons."

Dad yelled again from the bedroom, "Connie, stop playing the giddy goat. I'm going to be late. I cannot find any of my undercrackers."

Mum said to me, "You don't need to worry about the lift and so on."

I said, "Thanks, Mum."

She said, "You don't need to worry about a lift because you are not going anywhere."

What???

Then Dad came into the kitchen, with a towel wrapped around what he laughingly refers to as his waist. He said to

Mum, "Where are all my undercrackers?" Mum pointed to the kitchen bin.

Dad went ballisticisimus. And a half.

It didn't really seem the right moment to ask him about a lift to the airport. Or the £500 I would need for proper spendies, so I skipped back up to the safety of my room.

Fifteen minutes later

Well, it's good that the whole street knows about my dad's undercrackers and my mum's insanity. It makes for a tighter community spirit.

I do think that Dad should learn that, as our revered headmistress Slim says, "Obscene language is the language of those of a limited imagination."

Tuesday August 9th
10:00 p.m.

Jas has driven me insane today with all her Tom talk. I think she is hoping he will just forget about the going to different universities and having their own space fandango.

Well, let sleeping dogs lie is what I say.

Although it is not what Gordy says. He is worrying me.

I was calling him and tapping his food tin with a spoon earlier when Mr Next Door popped his head over the fence. He said that Gordon was sleeping in the Prat brothers' kennel.

I said, "Yeah, you'll never get him out, I'm afraid. They will have to sleep in the house."

And Mr Next Door said the weirdest thing.

"Oh, they are in there with him."

Blimey.

Wednesday August 10th

Ok, it's over a week now since I heard from Masimo, so I'm going to send a cool postcard. I've got one of a kitten covered in spaghetti being fished out of a pan with a ladle, and you can't get much cooler than that in my humble opinion. So here goes:

> Ciao, Masimo,
>
> It is me here. It was vair fabby and marvy to hear your voice.

Hang on, he might not know what vair means, or fabby or marvy. Blimey, it's going to take me the rest of my life to write this postcard. I'll do it tomorrow.

Thursday August 11th

I keep looking at the number I have got for Masimo. What would I say if I called him? And anyway, if he likes my eyes so much, why hasn't he got on the phone again?

Lunchtime

Even though I am plunged once more into the turbulent washing machine of luuurve, I am quite looking forward to going to Sven's dj-ing gig on Saturday.

We are having final rehearsals round at Rosie's for our backing dance routines. Honor and Sophie, the trainee Ace Gang members, are getting their big break because they are allowed to join in the rehearsal sessions. Although they won't be doing the real thing as there is not enough room on the stage and not enough ear muffs to go around. But that is showbiz for you.

We are going to do our world-renowned (well, lots of people have seen it at Stalag 14) Viking bison disco inferno dance. Also as a world premiere in honour of Sven's gig, we have come up with a dance called the Viking disco hornpipe.

It is a new departure for us as it involves costume and props. Of course, we have used props before – the horns in the Viking and bison extravaganza. And also bubble gum up the nose for the snot dance. (Incidentally, we have left out the snot dance from our programme for the night as Jools said she thought that prospective snoggees might find it a bit offputting.) So, as I say, we have used props before but we have never toyed with both costume and props.

In the Viking disco hornpipe extravaganza we will be wearing ear muffs and mittens, for the vair vair chilly Viking winter nights. And we will also be using small paddles.

At Rosie's
Evening

Jas is being annoyingly droopy.

Especially as Rosie had traipsed all the way to the fairy dressing-up shop for kiddies in town, to get the muffs. And they had special tinsel and everything. Jas wouldn't wear the ear muffs because she said it was "silly".

I said, "Jas, if we didn't do stuff just because it was silly, where would we be?"

She was still on her hufty stool and said, "What are you talking about now?"

It is vair tiring explaining things to the vair dim, but it

seems to be more or less my job in life.

"Jas, do you think that German is a silly language?"

She started fiddling with her fringe. (Incidentally, another example of 'silliness', but I didn't say.) She was obviously thinking the German thing over.

I said, "Quickly, quickly, Jas."

"Well, it's a foreign language spoken by foreign people and that can't be silly."

"Jas, they say *SPANGLEFERKEL*. The word for snogging in German-type language is *KNUTSCHEN*. WAKE UP, SMELL THE COFFEE!!!"

In the end she got her muffs and mittens on.

one hour later

The official Viking disco hornpipe dance is perfected!!!

(Just a note, costume-wise: the ear muffs are worn over the bison horns. It is imperative that the horns are not removed, otherwise it makes a laughing stock of the whole thing.) So:

The music starts with a Viking salute. Both paddles are pointed at the horns.

Then a cry of "Thor!!!" and a jump turn to the right.

Paddle, paddle, paddle, paddle to the right,

Paddle, paddle, paddle, paddle to the left.

Cry of Thor! Jump turn to the left.

Paddle, paddle, paddle, paddle to the left,

Paddle, paddle, paddle, paddle to the right.

Jump to face the front (grim Viking expression).

Quick paddle right, quick paddle left x 4.

Turn to partner.

Cross paddles with partner x 2.

Face front and high hornpipe skipping x 8 (gay Viking smiling).

Then (and this is the complicated bit) interweaving paddling! Paddle in and out of each other up and down the line, meanwhile gazing out to the left and to the right (concerned expression – this is the looking-for-land bit).

Paddle back to original position.

On-the-spot paddling till all are in line and then close eyes (for night-time rowing effect).

Right and left paddling x2 and then open eyes wide.

Shout "Land AHOYYYYY!"

Fall to knees and throw paddles in the air (behind, not in front, in case of crowd injury).

Friday August 12th
In my bedroom

Dear Masimo,
   Ciao. Last night we were practising our new Viking hornpipe dance. At first we had trouble with our paddles and Rosie nearly lost an eye, but by the high hornpipe skipping we had an...

Hang on a minute. Maybe he doesn't know what a Viking hornpipe is. Or paddles. Or skipping. Good grief, international romance is vair tiring.

Saturday August 13th
OK, if I haven't heard from the Luuurve God by the fifteenth, I will take it as a sign from Baby Jesus that I should get on the blower.

Mind you, I don't know what I would say about when I am coming over. I found £1.50 down the back of the sofa. And that would make £6.50 towards my fare except that I accidentally bought some new lip gloss (raspberry and vanilla flavour) at Boots.

♥

Monday August 15th

10:30 a.m.

Another postcard from the Luuurve God!!! Yes, yes and three times yes! Yesittyyesyes!!!

Oh, I am so happy. He posted it ages ago, so the post in Pizza-a-gogo land must be as bad as it is here.

Two minutes later

I bet our postie has taken postie revenge for having to lug huge sacks of letters round. I bet that is what he does. I bet he doesn't deliver people's mail, he just pretends to, and he has a hut in his back garden bursting with letters and postcards.

Anyway.

The postcard has a picture of a bowl of pasta on the front and it says:

> Ciao, cara Georgia,
>
> Plees come for to see me. I am having the hunger for you.
>
> Masimo xxxxxxxxxxxx

Wow wowzee wow!

That is it!! As soon as I can persuade Mum and Dad to give me spondies, I am off to see my Italian boyfriend.

Hmmm, it sounds quite groovy to say that. Not "My boyfriend that goes to Foxwood School and will probably work in a bank" but "My Italian boyfriend, who will be a world-famous pop star!"

Yessssss!

Tuesday August 16th

I tried special pleading with Mum today *vis-à-vis* money. She said, "Don't be stupid. I haven't got £500 and even if I did have, you would not be getting it to go and see some Italian bloke in Rome. Gorgey or not. You can have a tenner. Make it last."

I hate her.

Wednesday August 17th

I have gone through nearly the whole having-the-hump scale. From number one (*ignorez-vous*ing) to number six (pretendy deafnosity) and Mum hasn't even noticed.

Thursday August 18th

2:30 p.m.

Blimey, life is quite literally a boy-free zone. No sign of Dave the Laugh, no sign of Robbie. I haven't even seen the Blunder Boys around. Which is good. But weird. Even Tom has gone off to stay with some mates at uni for a few days.

Sooooo boring.

And hot.

I would do light tanning in the garden but every time I get comfy Angus comes and starts digging near me. (Not with a spade, with his paws. If he did have a spade, it wouldn't be quite so boring and annoying.)

Viking hornpipes a-gogo!!!

Saturday August 20th
Sven's Viking extravaganza gig night
6:30 p.m.
In my bedroom. I am meeting the rest of the gang at the clock tower. Jas is coming round here and we are walking up together so that she "doesn't miss Hunky". Good Lord.

   We have got our ear muffs and mittens and horns in little matching vanity cases that Rosie also got from the fairy shop. She says that Sven gets a lot of his stuff from there. Blimey.

6:45 p.m.

At the back of my mind. I'm a bit worried that Robbie might turn up tonight. I know he hasn't gone off to Kiwi-a-gogo because I feel sure I would have heard it on the Radio Jas news round-up. Even if I didn't ask.

6:50 p.m.

Jas turned up at mine with her vanity case.

The vanity cases are, it has to be said, a bit on the naff side. Very pink and glittery. Jas said, "They look just like ones that fairies would use."

I gave her my "Are you mad?" look, but she didn't notice. She is too busy being a piggy-bank hogger.

However, I feel free to carry silly fairy vanity cases and to wear my horns ad hoc and willy-nilly because there is not going to be anyone at the gig that I need to impress, now that Masimo is my one and only one.

7:00 p.m.

Yippee and thrice times yippee!! I am allowed to stay at Jas's. And I don't mean my parents have allowed me to stay. Lately they don't even notice if I am in or out, they are so busy with

104

their own 'lives'. I just said, "I am staying at Jas's tonight," and they went, "OK."

It was Jas I had to persuade to let me stay. She has been in and out of her huffmobile for the last week, but I have promised not to mess about with her owls or steal her piggy bank, so she says I can stay.

Anyway, there is no point in going home. Dad is out all the time with Uncle Eddie and his other sad portly mates, going to "gigs" or pratting around with their loonmobiles. Mum is out all the time as well because Libby is still round at Grandvati's. So, apart from the kittykats (who are also out all the time), I am practically an orphan anyway.

Buddha Lounge
8:00 p.m.

Quite cool vibe in the Buddha Lounge and rammed already. A few people I know and loads of peeps from Notre Dame School.

Jas is busy pretending that she doesn't care whether Hunky turns up or not. She thinks he might be back from his mates' tonight, but she says she has too much pridenosity to try and find out. I am not going to mention his name either, or ask about Robbie, because it will just be an excuse for her to drone on and on about the "vole years" and what larks she and Tom had by the riverside shrimping and so on. Or whatever they do. Hand snog probably, but I won't think about that now.

In the tarts' wardrobe

Ellen was in a complete ditherama and tiz wondering whether Declan would turn up. She was shaking and dithering so much that she accidentally got lipstick in her eye. That is how much she was dithering. Mabs was almost as bad about Edward.

I was tarting myself up in the mirror and said, "Oh, I am so vair vair glad that I am free to enjoy myself, unlike you lot – I shall dance, I shall let my nungas run free and wild, my nostrils can flare and obliterate my face to their heart's content. Because there is no one here tonight that I am bothered by. I am simply the girlfriend of a Luuurve God."

Mabs said, "Has he phoned since he last phoned?"

I said, "In the language of luuurve that would be called 'over-egging the pudding'."

She said, "He hasn't phoned then."

I smoothed down my internal feathers because she was slightly annoying me. Calm calm, think luuurve, think warm Italian nights and soft lips meeting in the shadow of the leaning tower of Pisa... or whatever it is they have in Rome. I said, "Actually, I am going to take the pasta by the horns and I am going to phone him and tell him that I am coming over."

Jas came out of her Tom coma. "Have your parents actually agreed that you can go? To Italy? By yourself to stay with a boy? Who is older than you?"

I tossed my hair in a tossing way like someone who has tossed their hair all over the world might do.

"Sì."

All of the Ace Gang looked at me.

Jas said, "That is a big fat lie, isn't it?"

"Sì."

Back on the dance floor

All right, I haven't actually got the parents to agree a date for me to go. Or give me the money or anything. But they will be too busy with the custody battle – about who doesn't get the children or the cats when they split up – to bother about me popping over to Italy for a few days.

That is what I feel.

I will get on the old blower tomorrow to let Masimo know I am coming, and then I will start my buttering-up-the-elderly-insane plan.

8:30 p.m.

Sven walked on to take over the decks to that song "Burn, baby, burn, disco inferno." He was wearing a fur cloak and bison horns and, joy of joys, the old lighting-up flares!! And he had his own vanity case!!! Yesssss!

The lights went crazy and he stood over his decks as we all clapped and went mental.

I said to Rosie, "You should be very, very proud. You, without the shadow of a doubt, have the maddest boyfriend in town."

She said, "I know. I can't wait to get off with him again."

8:35 p.m.

It is really alarming watching Rosie and Sven. She is dancing in front of him, sticking her bottom out at him and so on, and he is winking at her and licking his lips. I can't watch this, it's Nordyporn!!!

9:00 p.m.

Funny, there not being many people we know here. No sign of Tom or Declan or Edward or Rollo or, erm, who else – erm... oh, I know, Dave the Laugh. And his girlfriend.

I, of course, don't really mind for myself but the rest of the Ace Gang are driving me mad with all their: "Oh, I wonder why Rollo isn't here yet?"

"Oooh, I wonder where Edward is. Do you think he's with Tom and the rest and they have gone somewhere else?"

And Ellen going on and on. "Erm, it's, like, I wonder if, like, do you think that, er, Declan is, like, with Tom and the rest and they have gone somewhere else?"

I am beginning to feel a bit full of tensionosity, so I have decided to take diversionary action before I start babbling wubbish like Ellen. I said, "Let's do our dance routines now, get this party started."

I went and told Rosie, and Sven said over the microphone, "In one minute we haf the dancing girls in their horns!!!"

Rosie disentangled herself from him (which took about a million years of licking – honestly) and we dashed off to the tarts' wardrobe and got dressed in our horns. I felt so vair vair free. It must be what being a Blunder Boy feels like. No

♡ 109

matter what you do or how you are dressed, you are just not aware of being a prat.

I said, "Right, let us bond now. Group hug!!!"

We did the group hug and one quick burst of "Hoooorn!!!" And we were ready for our big moment.

Out in the club

We are gathered at the side of the little stage that Sven is on. I like to think we look attractively Nordic. With just a hint of pillaging and extreme violence about us.

For our grand finale (the Viking disco hornpipe extravaganza) we have put our paddles, ear muffs and mittens in a little pile by a speaker. All the crowd were looking at us.

Sven put on a traditional Viking song "Jingle Bells", we adjusted our horns and off we jolly well went:

Stamp, stamp to the left,

Left leg kick, kick,

Arm up,

Stab, stab to the left (that is the pillaging bit),

Stamp, stamp to the right,

Right leg kick, kick,

Arm up,
Stab, stab to the right,
Quick twirl around with both hands raised to Thor
(whatever),
Raise your (pretend) drinking horn to the left,
Drinking horn to the right,
Horn to the sky,
All over body shake,
Huddly duddly,
And fall to knees with a triumphant shout of
HORRRRNNNNN!!!!

It was a triumph, darling, a triumph. Even Ellen managed not to stab anyone in the eye. The crowd went berserkerama!!! Leaping and yelling, "More, more!!!"

Sven said over the mike, "OK, you groovster peeps, this time is your turn!! Let's go do the Viking bison disco inferno dance," and he put "Jingle Bells" back on and we started again.

Everyone joined in with us. The whole room did stab stab to the right, and even the huddly duddly and fall to the knees bit. It was marvy seeing everyone down on their knees yelling, "HORRRRNNN!" And people say that teenagers today do nothing for people.

I'm a star, I'm a star!!! I shouted to Jas above the noise, "I want Smarties in our dressing room. I want a limo for my mittens – I want EVERYTHING!!!"

And then it was time for the *pièce de* whatsit: the Viking disco hornpipe extravaganza. We put on our ear muffs and mittens, and picked up our paddles. Then we got into position with our backs to the crowd and when they had quietened down, we waited for our musical cue. As the dub version of *EastEnders* sounded out from the decks, we raised our paddles proudly. The music was going: "Na na na na naa naa naaaa, na na na-na naa na na na na naa naa, duff duff duff, na na na naa naa naaaa..."

We turned round to face our audience and as we did so, the doors flew open and Mark Big Gob and the Blunder Boys walked in. Oh, brilliant.

Still, what did we care? We would get our bodyguards to toss them aside like paper towels from the paper-towel dispenser in the loos. They could go down the piddly-diddly hole of life!!!

We did the dance with gusto and also vim, and everyone applauded and went crazeeee again at the end. They were yelling, "More horn, more horn. We want more horn!!!"

God, I was hot. I said to Rosie, "I can't do it again without some drink. Send one of our runners for drinks."

Rosie said, "Righty ho."

She came back a second later and said, "Who are our runners?"

And Jas said, "We haven't got any, she has just gone temporarily insane."

But she said it in a smiley way.

one minute later
We did the dance again and everyone went mad AGAIN!!! This was the life. Even though Ellen caught me a glancing blow with her paddle.

Then the Blunder Boys started shouting wubbish in their dim way.

We just ignored them and were coming down from the stage when Mark Big Gob yelled out, "Oy, you, the big tart in the middle, give us a flash of your nungas." He was shouting at Rosie.

Sven took off the record he was playing and stood up.

There was silence.

He took off his fur cape and adjusted his horns.

Oh dear God.

Sven slowly stepped down. His flares lit up and he walked towards the group of Blunder Boys. Everyone else was backing off. People were saying, "Calm down, calm down, leave it out, lads."

Well, apart from Rosie. She was behind Sven, saying, "Go on, big boy, tear their little heads off."

Two minutes later

Now Sven is big, but there were about eight of the Blunderers facing up to him. I was a bit frightened actually.

But then it was just like a Western because the doors opened again and in came Tom and Declan and Edward and Dom and Rollo and a load of their mates and, last but not least, Dave the Laugh.

Dave the Laugh looked at what was going on and then said to Mark Big Gob, "Mark, go and get your coats and handbags. You and your sisters are leaving."

Three minutes later

There was a bit of argie-bargie from the Blunder Boys.

One of them said to Dave, "Who's gonna make me leave?"

And Dave went and stood over him and said, "I am."

And the Blunder Boys said, "Oh, OK, well, I was just asking, mate."

And there was some shoving past people and spitting from the Blunder Boys as they went off to the door. Declan and Tom and Dave did a gentle bit of frogmarching Mark through the door. And there was a lot of shouting and kicking of cars once the Blunderers were safely out in the street.

Unfortunately the venue owners had called the police, and we heard the police sirens outside.

Sven said, "Now that is how to have the good Viking night."

Dave the Laugh found me. He was holding his hand as if he had hurt it. He smiled at me and said, "Are you OK, Miss Kittykat?"

I said, "Oh, Dave, thank goodness you came. What has happened to your hand?"

He said, "One of the hard lads bit me – I may never play the tambourine again."

It was luuurvely to see him. And I felt really odd that he was hurt. I wanted to stroke his hand; in fact, maybe I should. I may have healing hands.

I was just thinking about doing it when I heard a voice say, "Dave, Dave, are you all right??? Oh God, your hand!! You poor thing, let me help you."

It was Emma, dashing about like Florrie whatsit – Nightingale.

Dave looked at me and gave a sort of rueful smile. He said, "Too many trousers spoil the broth," and got up and did pretendy limping off with Emma.

His girlfriend.

Twenty minutes later

We were all turfed out. The police gave Sven a warning and asked us if we wanted to dob anyone in. I wouldn't have minded seeing the Blunder Boys behind bars, preferably in a zoo. However, as Sven had in a way started the proceedings, we just mumbled a bit about things getting out of hand. "Sorry, Officers" etc. And tried to shuffle off home.

I saw Jas and Tom talking together in the dark over by a bench. Oh Good Lord, I would be doing goosegog all the way home now if they made up.

I tried to think of something to say that would make Jas get in her huffmobile with Tom. Or perhaps I should just go and stand between them in a friendly way and not go away. Take my goosegog duties seriously.

Thirty seconds later

A policeman came by me and said, "Stop hanging about here. Clear off home now and don't cause any more trouble."

That's nice, isn't it? No words of comfort. No "Now don't you worry, young lady, the nasty boys won't be bothering you any more. Here's £5 for a cab home to see you safely on your way."

In fact, as he looked at me I sort of recognised him. Uh-oh, he was the one who had brought Angus home in a bag one night after he had eaten Next Door's hamster. Unfortunately, Angus didn't like the bag and had attacked the policeman's trousers.

Then he recognised me. "Oh, it's you. I might have known. How's your 'pet'? Hopefully gone to that big cat basket in the sky."

I said, with dignitosity at all times, "Thank you for your kind inquiry, Officer. I must go home now. Mind how you go and remember, it's a jungle out there. Be safe."

Do you see? Do you see what I did? I pretended I was a policeman to a policeman!!!

But I was walking quickly away from him as I said it and calling to Jas, "Jas, we have to go now. The nice officer of the law said so."

Jas came over smartish. She is terrified of policemen and is the bum-oley licking expert around them. She said, "Thank you so much, Officer. You do a wonderful job." Oh, pleeeeease.

Then she waved back at Tom. He blew her a kiss and she sighed. Good grief. Can't they stay split up for more than half a day? It's pathetico.

We walked on home. I said to Jas, "Did you see Dave the Laugh getting stuck in to save us?"

Jas said, "Yeah, Tom was keeping me behind him so that I wouldn't get hurt. And when one of the Blunder Boys said to him, 'Do you want some, mate?' he said, 'Oooh, fear factor ten,' and did a judo hold that we learned when we went on our survival course and just marched him to the door. It was fab."

Oh, shut up about Hunky.

I said, "When I said to Dave, 'Are you OK? Have you hurt your hand?' he said, 'I may never play the tambourine again'! He is quite literally Dave the Laugh."

Jas said, "Oh no, you've got your big red bottom AGAIN!!"

Have I?

In bed with the owl (and her mates)
1:00 a.m.

Jas has built a small barrier of owls between us, but has said that if I don't wriggle about I am allowed to sleep in her bed because it has been such a traumatic night of violence. Blimey, she should live round at my house if she thinks this has been a traumatic night of violence. My bedroom is littered with dismembered toys, and if I move in bed, I am attacked viciously by either Angus, Gordy or Libby. Or all three of them.

Jas said, "Tom still thinks we should go to different unis or see the world or something. He said we might never know if we have done the right thing otherwise. But it doesn't mean he doesn't love me."

I said, "Well, what do you think?"

She mused (that is, flicked her fringe and cuddled Snowy Owl). "Well, I like fun as much as the next person."

I said, "Can I just stop you there, Jas. You have to be realistic if we are going to get anywhere. You do not like fun as much as the next person. Your idea of fun and the next person's idea of fun are vair vair different."

"Well, all right, what I mean is, maybe Tom is right that we are too young to decide everything now. Maybe I could do things by myself and that would be good."

I sat up. "That is the ticket, pally. I mean, there are many advantages to not having a boyfriend, you know. You wouldn't have to pretend to be interested in wombat droppings and varieties of frogspawn."

She looked puzzled. "I'm not pretending."

"Er, right, well..."

God, it was hopeless. Everything I thought of, Jas had an answer for. She doesn't want to let her red bottom run free and wild. She doesn't mind the vole-dropping stuff and looking interested. She IS interested. She doesn't want to flop around in her jimmyjams if she wants to because she already can, because Tom, Hunky the Wonderdog, likes her just the way she is, whatever she looks like.

In a nutshell, Tom is her one and only one and that is the end of the matter. I wish I were her.

Well, of course I don't wish I were her. That would be ridiculous. I'd have to chop my own head off for a start, because I'd be annoying myself so much.

Sunday August 21st
Home
11:00 a.m

I have got post-gig comedown, I think. Everything was tickety-boo when we were doing the dancing and it was a laugh. And even the fight was sort of exciting. But then seeing Dave the Laugh go off with Emma, and Jas talking about being with Hunky, it's sort of made me a bit full of glumnosity.

And I haven't spoken to the Luuurve God for ages; anything could be happening.

Boo and also poo.

It's all gloomy in the house: even though it is sunny outside it is raining inside. Well, not really, but you know what I mean. Mum has gone off with Libby, I think trying to placate Josh's mum. I'd like to think it's because she cares, but really I think it's because Grandvati has gone off for a camping trip with Maisie. She has probably knitted the tent. Who knows where Vati is; he is never in these days.

I didn't think the day would ever come when I said this, but I wish they would get back to 'normal'. I would even try not to be sick if they touched each other.

What if they split up? They would make me do that choosing thing. The judge would say that I could decide who I lived with.

It is so clearly not going to be Dad. I may warn him that he is dicing with never seeing me again by his brutal lack of care for me. He will not give me the least thing. I tried to ask him for a couple of hundred squids towards my trip to Rome yesterday, and he laughed.

Two minutes later

I wonder if he will laugh quite so much when all he has to remember me by are the press cuttings of me on world tours etc. Doing backing dancing for the Stiff Dylans in exotic locations. And when I do interviews in showbiz mags, and they ask me about my father, I will say, "I would have liked to have been close, but once the family split up and my work took me all over the world, I sort of outgrew him."

I won't add "like he outgrew his trousers" because that would put me in a bad light pop culture-wise.

Five minutes later

Hey, maybe I could say that if he will give me £500 to go to

Pizza-a-gogo, I will consider seeing him three or four times a year for an afternoon.

Excellent plan!!!

Ten minutes later

Phone rang. At last. I bet this will be my Pizza-a-gogo Luuurve God-type boyfriend on the blower from Roma *bella*. I have got an Italian book for idiots, so I must look through it. Mind you, if it is anything like our French or German textbooks it will be rubbish. They are always to do with losing your bike. They are not based on real life; there is nothing about how to snog in different languages. Absoluto stupido and uselessio.

And also too late-io.

I picked up the phone and said, "*Ciao!*"

"Oh, erm, *ciao* or something – er – I, well, it's me or something. I don't know if—"

"Hello, Ellen."

"Georgia... Could I – I mean, are you in?"

"No, I'm sorry, I'm not."

"Oh, well, will you be in later or something?"

"ELLEN, I am answering the phone. How can I not be in???"

Half an hour of ditherosity later

Miracle of miracles, Declan has actually asked her on a date. They're meeting by the clock tower tomorrow evening, so she has come to the Luuurve Goddess (*moi*) for advice.

It passes the time helping others.

I said, "Ellen, here in a nutshell are my main top tips. Don't drink or eat anything, not even a cappuccino, unless you know for sure your date is an admirer of the foam moustache. If he is – dump him. Secondly and vair vair importantly, do not say what is in your brain. And, above all, remember to dance and be jolly. Although be careful about where you do spontaneous dancing. If you do it in a supermarket, he will just think you are weird."

4:00 p.m.

Right, this is it. I can't stand waiting any more. I am going to quite literally take the Luuurve God by the horns and ring him up.

I've been going through my Italian book for the very very dim. (It's not actually called that, but it should be. It has got the crappest drawings known to humanity. I think it must be the same person who did the illustrations for our German textbook about the Koch family. Under the section "Fun and Games" it has got a drawing of some madman with sticky-up hair and big googly eyes juggling balls. That cannot be right in anyone's language.)

Anyway, I have worked out what to say from the section called "Talking on the Phone".

4:30 p.m.
I think I have got the code right and everything.

Rang the number. Ring ring. Funny ring they have in Pizza-a-gogo land.

The phone was picked up and I said, "*Ciao.*"

A man's voice said, a bit hesitantly, "*Ciao.*"

I wondered if it was Masimo's dad. What is the word for "dad" in Italian? I hadn't looked it up. It couldn't be "daddio", could it?

I thought I would try. "Er, *buon giorno,* daddio, *je suis –* erm, *non non – sono* Georgia."

"Georgia."

"*Sì.*"

Masimo's dad said, "Ah, *sì.*" Then there was a bit of a silence.

♥ 125

Oh, buggeration. How do I say I want to speak to Masimo? I said, "Io wantio – *un momento, per favore.*"

I scrabbled through the book. Oh here we are, a lovely big ear drawing to show me that it is the on-the-phone section. "I want to speak to..." I read it out slowly and loudly: "*POSSO PAHR-LAH-REH A MASIMO?*"

There was a silence and then a Yorkshire voice said, "Po what, love? You've lost me."

It turned out that I was actually speaking to a Yorkshire bloke on holiday in Rome.

I said, "Oh, I'm sorry, but you said *ciao* and I thought you were Italian."

The Yorkshire dad said, "No, I'm from Leeds, but I do like spaghetti."

Two minutes later

Anyway, he was having a lovely time, although you couldn't get a decent pickled egg in Roma apparently, but he wasn't letting that spoil his fun.

Blimey, it was like a Yorkshire version of Uncle Eddie. He was rambling on for ages like I knew him.

Ten minutes later

In the end I got off the phone. I must have got the number wrong. Or misdialled it. I could try again. No, I couldn't take the risk of getting hold of "Just call me Fat Bob" again.

Big furry paw of fate

Tuesday August 23rd
In the kitchen
5:30 p.m.

My darling sis is back at Chaos Headquarters (that is our house). Mum said, "I've managed to get Libby off with a warning. She can go back to nursery later this week, but I have to promise that she won't be allowed to play with sharp implements. So don't let her have any of your knives and so on."

"Mum, I haven't got any knives. It was you that let her have the scissors to cut Pantalitzer doll's hair. Has Josh got the word BUM off his forehead yet?"

Mum said, "Blimey, that was a fuss and a half, wasn't it? It was only indelible ink, not poison."

I said, "Mum, some parents actually, like, DO parenting. They act like grown-ups; they protect their young."

Mum was too busy flicking through *Teen Vogue* to listen.

6:00 p.m.

Libby is preparing a cat picnic on the lawn. Some crushed-up biscuits on a plate and three dishes of milk. I can see Angus, Naomi and Gordy skulking off to hide. They have been made to go to her cat picnics before. And once you have had your head shoved violently into a saucer of milk and a spoonful of Jammy Dodger rammed down your throat, you don't accept another invitation easily.

Time to start buttering up the mutti.

I said, "Mum, if I stayed with you and not Dad, well he would pay like maintenance and child support and so on. And I could use a bit of it, say like £500, because it would be mine really, wouldn't it? It's like me that is being supported, isn't it?"

Mum went, "Hmmm, but I would need a lot of help round the house."

I said, "Yep, yep, I could do that. It would be like sort of earning my own money and I could pay my own way to Pizza-a-gogo land and then it would be all right, wouldn't it? Because actually it wouldn't really be costing you anything because I would be being paid out of my own money really. And you want me to be happy and have a boyfriend and so on; even Ellen has got a boyfriend now. And when you leave Dad you might get one. You never know. Never say never."

Mum said, "Georgia, are you saying that you would be prepared to do the ironing and help around the house and be pleasant?"

I said, "Oh, *mais oui*, yes!!"

"OK, well, start on that big pile of Libby's stuff in the washing basket."

Lalalalalala. It's the ironing life for me. Quickly followed by a snogtastic adventure in Luuurve God Heaven.

Half an hour later

How boring is housework? I tell you this for free, I will not be doing any more of it when this is over. I said to Mum, "I think I have got ironer's elbow. It won't go from side to side any more, it will only go up and down. I hope it hasn't ruined my backing dancing career."

7:15 p.m.
I am a domestic husk.

I said to Mum, "I think I will go on Saturday as I suggested."

She said, "Yeah, good idea."

I said, "I will ask Dad if he can drop me off at the airport."

"He's away that weekend, he and Uncle Eddie are going away fishing or prancing around in the clownmobile. He says it will give him time to sort his mind out."

I said, "So can you take me then?"

"Take you where?"

"To the airport."

"Why are you so interested in watching planes all of a sudden?"

"I'm not interested in watching them. I am only interested in getting on one to go to Pizza-a-gogo."

"Well, that is not going to happen, is it."

And that was that.

She never intended to let me go, she just wanted me to do

the ironing. That is the sort of criminal behaviour I have to put up with. I know you read all sorts of miserable stories about kids being holed up in cellars by their mean parents and called "Snot Boy" all the time, but I think my story is just as cruel.

As I slammed out I said to Mum, "Mum, I quite literally hate you."

At Rosie's in her bedroom
8:00 p.m.

Rosie's parents are out again. It's bliss at her house. I think she only sees them about twice a year. I told her what happened. She said, "That is crapola, little matey. When you are all stressed out and having a nervy spaz you have to look after your health – have a Jammy Dodger and some cheesy wotsits."

As we crunched through a couple of packets I said, "I am just going to sneak off anyway, creep out at night with the money I will get from my guilty dad and hitchhike to the airport. Or maybe get one of the lads to take me. Do you think Dom might do it?"

Rosie was really into it now. "Brilliant plan. Just say, devil take the hindmost and *ciao*, Roma!!!"

9:00 p.m.

I was going to call Dom about taking me to the airport, but I sort of chickened out. If I could, I would ask Dave the Laugh because he would understand. Or maybe not. Maybe asking my matey-type matey person to take me to catch a plane to see a Luuurve God is not megacool.

Anyway, he would only go on about my lesbian affair with Masimo.

Still at Rosie's
9:20 p.m.

Making a list of what to take with me clothes and make-up-wise. It will be hot, so I will have to take most of my summerwear, bikinis and flip-flops.

I said, "Do you think I should take a book to read on the beach for those quiet moments?"

Rosie looked at me. "What quiet moments?"

10:00 p.m.

Oh, I feel quite pepped up now. In fact, I think I will start packing when I get in.

As I was leaving Rosie's I said, "Thank you, tip-top pally."

She said, "*De rigueur.* Hey, and don't forget your passport, chum."

I laughed.

on the way home
Fifteen minutes later

Hmmm, where is my passport?

An hour later

I'll tell you where my passport is. At Dad's bloody office, that's where.

Why? What sort of person takes official documents to work with them?

My dad, that is what sort of person.

I said to him, "Why would anyone do that?"

He said, "They're all there. I know you, you would lose yours or put make-up on it or Angus would eat it. This way I know where it is."

I said, "Well, now I know where it is as well, so why don't you go and get me MY passport. Which is issued to me in MY name. By her Maj the Queen. Because it is MY passport. Do you see? Not yours. And while you are in the safe, you may as well get me the £500 child support you promised me."

He said no.

I said to Dad as I stormed off to bed, "Dad, I quite literally hate you."

Ten minutes later

So this is my life:

I am best friends with some Yorkshire bloke called Fat Bob.

I will have to explain to my marvy and groovy new pop idol Luuurve God boyfriend that I am not allowed my own passport.

And I have got £1.50 to get to Pizza-a-gogo land.

What could be worse?

Midnight

Libby put an egg under my pillow to "get a baby chicken".

It has gone all over my pyjamas.

Wednesday August 24th

8:00 a.m.

I am the prisoner of my utterly useless and mean parents. Just because they have a crap life they are determined to make mine crap as well. I would have said that to them if I were speaking to them. Or they were speaking to each other.

In my bedroom
Dad came knocking on my door.

I said, "The door is locked."

Dad pushed open the door and said, "You haven't got a lock on your door."

I said, "You might not see the lock but the lock is there, otherwise I wouldn't be."

But he's not interested in me. He said, "Look, I am going away for a few days and—"

I said, "What is it like to be able to walk around on the planet wherever you like?"

He said, "You're not still going on about visiting this Italian Stallion lad, are you? He'll be back in a week or two anyway."

"Dad, I might not be alive in a week or two – things happen. If I were a mayfly, I would be dead in about half an hour and that would have been my whole life."

He just looked all grumpy, like a big leatherette grumpy fool. What was he wearing? A leather jacket.

I said, "You're not thinking of going out in that jacket, are you?"

He said, "Look, don't start. I've just come to say goodbye and to say that, well... you know that Mum and I have been, you know, not hitting it off."

"She threw your undercrackers away."

"I know she bloody did. Most of them were covered in cat litter when I fished them out."

Oh really, do I have to listen to this sort of thing? I will quite literally spend most of my superstar money on psychiatric fees. He still hadn't finished though.

"Don't worry too much, we'll sort it out, and if, well, if things don't get any better, sometimes people have to..."

Oh no, I think he might be going to get emotional. If he starts crying, I may well be sick. But then he did something much, much worse; he came over and kissed the top of my head.

How annoying. And odd.

one hour later

As Mum went off to "work" she said, "You look a bit peaky."

I said, "It's probably a symptom of my crap life. Which is your fault."

She just ignored me.

I know what she is up to though. She isn't bothered about

♥ 137

me having rickets or something, she just fancies a trip to Dr Clooney's. That will be the next thing. She'll start peering at me and saying stuff about my knees being a bit knobbly or that I don't blink enough or something and then suggest a quick visit to the surgery. She will have to drag me there.

10:40 a.m.
The post arrived. I may as well check if there is anything for me.

One minute later
Oh joy unbounded, there is a postcard from the Luuurve God!! It has a picture of a donkey drinking a bottle of wine on the front. Is that what goes on in Rome? You never know with not-English people.

Shut up, brain, and read the postcard from the beluuurved.

> *Ciao, bella.*
> *I am mis you like crazy. I am not for long to wait to see you. Todaya we go to the mountains. I have song in my heart for you.*
> *Masimo xxxxxxx*

138

Aaaaaahhhh. He has a song in his heart for me. I hope it is not "Shut uppa you face, whatsa matta you". Or, as it is in the beautiful language of Pizza-a-gogo land, "Shut uppa you face, whatsa matta you".

Oh, I sooo want to see him.

I wonder if I had a whip-round of the Ace Gang I could get the money. I bet Jas has got hundreds stashed in her piggy bank. But then what about my passport? Maybe I could make a forgery?

I HATE my parents.

Evening

To celebrate our last days of freedom before we get sent back to Stalag 14, we have decided to have a spontaneous girls' night in. We are all staying round at Jools's place because she has her own sort of upstairs area with her own TV and bathroom.

Now that is what I call proper parenting. Getting a house big enough so that you don't actually have to have anything to do with your parents. No growing girl should ever run the risk of seeing either her mutti or vati in undercrackers.

11:00 p.m.

I've perked up a bit.

Rosie, Jools, Mabs and me are in one huge bed and Jas, Ellen, Honor and Sophie are in the other one.

Jas amazed me by saying, "Actually, it's quite nice being single for a bit, isn't it? You can really let yourself go mad and wild. I mean, this is the first time I've worn my Snoopy T-shirt for ages."

I said, "Blimey, Jas, calm down."

Rosie said, "What we all have to remember is that yes, boys and snogging are good, but luuurve with a boy may be temporary and Miss Selfridge and Boots are yours for life."

Vair vair wise words. Then we got down to serious business.

Mabs said, "Well, I dunno really, what do you think of this? I saw Edward in the street, across the road with his mates, and he did that phone thing... you know when you pretend you have got a phone in your hand and you do a dial thing. Meaning, you know, bell me."

We all looked at her.

I said, "So have you?"

She said, "No, because I didn't know if he meant, like, I'm going to bell you or you should bell me. I'm sort of all..."

I said, "Belled up?"

140

And she nodded.

Blimey.

This was worse than s'laters.

Ten minutes later

We've decided that Mabs can't take the risk of an ad-hoc bell-you fandango and therefore the only thing to do is to accidentally bump into him and see what happens.

Jools said, "I know that they play five-a-side in the park on Thursday arvies, so we could accidentally on purpose be there. The last time I saw Rollo he said the same to me. He said, 'Give us a bell.' But then I did and he seemed sort of busy. He was on his way out to practice and he said, 'Give us a bell later.' But I didn't because that was like a double fandango: give us a bell and also s'later. Nightmare scenario."

Hmmmmm.

Then Ellen told us about going out with Declan.

I said, "Please don't tell me you went to a penknife shop for the evening."

Ellen said, "No, we, well – erm... he and I—"

I said, "I know you feel sort of sensitive about this and, you know, shy and a bit self-conscious, but you are among your own kind now; you are with the Ace Gang – your best pallies, your bestiest most kindiest maties. So let me put it this way – WHAT NUMBER DID YOU GET UP TO ON THE SNOGGING SCALE AND ARE YOU GOING TO SEE HIM AGAIN???"

Forty years later

So, just to save precious hours, I will sum up Ellen's evening with Declan. After a lot of chatting and Coke drinking (good choice drink-wise *vis-à-vis* foam moustache etc.), Declan had said goodnight and they had done one, two, three and a bit of four. Hurrah, thank the Lord!!!

On the down side, as she went into her house Declan had said, "We must do this again sometime." And gone off.

We decided that "sometime" is in fact s'laters in disguise.

I told them my mum's theory about boys being gazelles in trousers that must be enticed out of the woods (i.e. away from their stupid mates). We decided that the best thing was to be alert for sightings of the gazelles (playing footie etc.) and to be attractively semi-available.

Jas then got all misty-eyed about first meeting Tom. She said to me, "Do you remember when I first saw Tom and he was so hunky, working in the shop? And we had a plan to make him notice me. And I went into the shop to buy some onions and then you came in and made out like I was the most popular girl in the school sort of thing. And the rest is history."

She looked a bit sad and said, "Quite literally, the rest might be history."

To cheer her up, and also to stop her moaning on about the vole years, I suggested we get down to talking about serious world matters. Like the beret question for winter term. Could we improve on last year's lunchpack theme?

Sophie said, "My very favouritist was 'glove animal'. Couldn't he come back for a reprise this term?"

Midnight

We were comparing notes snogging-scale-wise and also saying what number we thought people had got to.

Jools said, "Do you think Miss Wilson has ever snogged anyone? If so, what number do you think she has got up to?" Erlack.

I said, "No man alive could get through all that corduroy."

Rosie said, "Oh, I don't know, she has a certain charm. I think I may be on the turn actually, because I thought she

♥ 143

looked quite fit when I saw her in the nuddy-pants with her soap on a rope."

We all looked at her. Sometimes even I am surprised by how mad and weird she is.

I said, "Jools, swap places with me. I am not sleeping next to Lezzie Mees." And then Rosie started puckering up at me. I stood up in bed and started kicking her off and she grabbed my ankles and pulled me over.

Mabs yelled, "Girl fight, girl fight!" and we started a massive pillow fight. At which point the door opened and Jools's mum came in. Oh dear.

She looked very serious. Here we go with the "We give you girls a bit of freedom and you just take advantage, when I was a girl we didn't even have pillows, we slept in a drawer and—"

But she just said, "Georgia, your mum is on the phone for you. You can take it on the extension up here if you like, dear."

I wondered why she was looking at me so funny? Maybe Mum was drunk on *vino tinto* and having an Abba evening with her friends and had decided to start a new life with a fireman that she met at aquaerobics. Well, I tell you this for free, I am not going to live with her and Des or whatever he is called.

Mum was actually crying when I picked up the phone. Oh

brilliant, she had already been dumped by Des and I would have to listen to her rambling on about it for the rest of my life.

She said, "Oh, darling, I am so, so sorry." Then she started crying again.

I said, "Er, Mum, I will not be moving in with you and Des."

She didn't even bother to reply; she was just gulping and crying. Actually, I was a bit worried about her because she did sound very upset. Oh blimey.

She went on, "Mr Across the Road came over – and oh, it was so – when I opened the door, I thought, I thought he was carrying a baby – all wrapped up in a blanket... and then, oh love, and... and, oh, one of his paws fell out of the, out of the blanket and it just... hung there... all limp."

And she started weeping and weeping. I couldn't understand what she meant.

I said, "What do you mean? Whose paw?"

And she said, "Oh, darling, it's Angus."

I couldn't speak and my brain wouldn't work. I could hear Mum sobbing and talking but she sounded like a little toyperson on the end of the phone.

"Mr Across the Road found him at the bottom... of our street... by the side of the road – you know how much he liked cars... he, he thought they were big mice on wheels, didn't he – and he must have been – and he was just lying there."

Then tears started coming out of my eyes, all by themselves, just pouring out of my eyes and plopping on my pyjamas. My mouth was dry, and I felt like I was choking on something.

Mum was still talking. "Georgia, love, please talk to me. Please say something, please."

I don't know how long I stood there with the tears falling, but then I felt a big pain in my heart like someone had kicked it and then stuck a knife in it. And I think a noise came out of me – you know, like when people are in pain and they make like a deep groan. It didn't feel like my voice, just like someone in pain very far away.

I think it must have been real because the next thing I knew Jas had her hand on my shoulder. She said, "What's happened, Gee? What's the matter?"

I couldn't say. I could only cry and shake. Jas took the phone out of my hand.

"Hello? It's Jas. What has happened? Oh no. Oh no."

As she was speaking Jas had her arm around me. "Yes, yes, I'm here. I'll look after her. I'll come with her in a taxi. Yes, yes, I'll look after her. We are all here; we'll take care of her."

146

By now the Ace Gang had come out into the hall and when they saw me, they all came and hugged me. I just wanted to be unconscious, I think. I wanted to tear my head off so it wouldn't have anything in it.

I can't really remember what happened, but I know I was shaking so much that Jools's mum wrapped me in a big blanket, and then the taxi arrived. I cried and cried into Jas's shoulder and she made those noises that people do – not really words, just like "there, there – sshhhh" – like you do when little children have nightmares. She was rocking me.

When we got to our house all the lights were on in the front room. I could see Mum looking out of the window as we pulled into the driveway.

When I tried to get out of the cab I couldn't make my legs work and the cab driver got out of his seat and came and picked me up. He said, "Don't worry, love, I've got you."

He carried me into the house and when he put me down, Mum and Jas got hold of an arm each to make me safe. As he went the cab driver said, "Look after her, there's no charge. God bless."

My voice was all croaky when I tried to speak. I said, "Where... is he?"

And Mum said, "I put him on the sofa."

It was really weird going into the front room. It was like a gale-force wind was blowing; I was sure it was real. I could hear it whooshing against the door, trying to keep me out. I felt like I was walking into the wind trying to get to Angus.

He was on the sofa wrapped up in the blanket. His eyes were all closed and his mouth half open. There was a big deep red gash on his head. I went over to him and looked down and my tears splashed on to his face. How could I live without my furry pal? He wasn't supposed to leave me. In that moment I would rather it was me lying there.

I sat down beside him and put my finger on his nose and stroked it. It was the first time I had ever been able to do that. He would have attacked my hand when he – when he – and I started wailing again, just saying, "Oh, Angus, Angus, I love you, I love you more than anything."

And then a little noise came out of him. Like a little growl.

I yelled, "Mum, Mum, he's alive!!! He's moving!!! He's alive!!!"

Mum came over and put her arms around me. "I know he's still breathing, love, but when I phoned the vet I told him what had happened and what he looked like. The vet said he would have internal injuries and that really the best, the kindest thing, would be to put him to sleep. He's coming over now and going to take him to the surgery and—"

I leaped up. "He is NOT going to be put to sleep. If anyone tries to do that, I will KILL them. I mean it, Mum. It is NOT going to happen. No, you can't let him. I won't let him."

The doorbell rang.

Thirty seconds later

I must have looked like I was going to kill the vet. He looked at me and then said, "Let me have a look at the poor fellow."

He gently felt all over Angus and lifted up his legs. They just flopped back. Angus didn't make any more noises.

The vet sighed. He said, "I'm afraid there will be a lot of internal injury. I think the kindest thing all round would be—"

I just said, "No."

The vet looked at me. He shook his head.

I said, "Please try. I love him." And the tears started plopping out of my eyes again.

I stroked Angus's face and he did a bit of a growl again.

I said to the vet, "You see?"

After a minute or two the vet said, "All right, I'll try,

but I'm being honest with you, cats don't often survive this sort of thing."

He packed Angus in blankets and said he would give him X-rays and drips and anything he could at the surgery.

I said, "Thank you."

I didn't mean to but I gave him a hug.

And he's got a beard.

Vet's surgery

Angus has bandages everywhere, even on his tail. He has not made any noise since the little one when I stroked his face. He is on a drip and his tongue is lolling out.

But I am not annoyed about his tongue lolling out. I can't imagine ever being annoyed with him again about anything. If he lives, he can have anything he wants.

I said to Jas, who was still with me, "When I get home I am going to pray for Angus to Baby Jesus, and if he will let Angus live I will try to be a really good person." And I included Jas's fringe flicking in that. And my dad's leather trousers. That is how serious it all was.

Angus was going to stay in the surgery overnight and the vet said I could come the next day as soon as they opened.

He looked tired and a bit sad. And now I noticed it he also looked very beardy. No, no, I don't want the tired and sad beardy vet. I want the handsome, thrusting ER vet who says, "I've done it, he's going to pull through. Have a nice day."

Dr Beardy said, "I want you to know that I love animals very much, and I know what he means to you, but it doesn't look good. If I keep him alive, he will probably die in a few hours from something I can't fix."

I just said, "He is not going to die. That is a fact."

Jas said she'd come and stay with me at my house but I said no. I wanted to do some heavy praying. She gave me a little kiss on the cheek when she left. I know it was dark and a lezzie-free zone, but it was still nice of her.

Thursday August 25th
Dawn
I don't think I slept. I just nodded off now and again and then woke up, and for a few moments life felt normal and then I remembered. Even Gordy, not world-renowned for his caring, sympathetic nature, cuddled up next to me and didn't attack me once even when I moved my foot.

Five minutes later

Gordy came and sat on my chest and looked at me with his yellow eyes. Well, one of his yellow eyes; the other one was glancing out of the window. He was looking at me unblinking. Then he let out one of those strange croaky noises that makes him sound like he is a hundred-a-day smoking cat. And he leaped down from my bed.

I think he knows something. I think he knows about Angus and he is on my side.

Even if he is a homosexualist half-cat half-dog, it doesn't matter. Love is all you need.

Ten minutes later

Looking out of the window, Gordy is playing chase the bonio with the Prat brothers.

That is not right in anyone's book.

To think of his father lying in a vet's surgery while his son scampers around with ridiculous poodles. He has no pridenosity.

Five minutes later

I remembered my vow to Baby Jesus – about being a jolly good egg about everything. Even very annoying things.

Deep breath and – look, look at Gordy playing happily with other creatures made by God.

All right, curly, annoying yappy creatures, but God's creatures nevertheless.

I mean, not many people like maggots, do they? But that is not the point. Mr and Mrs Maggot love them. Probably. And that is what counts.

Oh shut up, brain. Just love everything and get on with it.

7:30 a.m.
Please let him be alive. Please.

I started to get myself some Coco Pops, but I couldn't eat them. Mum got up and her eyes were all swollen. I went into the bathroom and looked in the mirror. Blimey, I had no eyes. They had disappeared in the night. I was now just a nose with two eyebrows. And the places where my eyes had been ached and ached. In fact, everything ached.

Mum said, "I think I am going to ask Grandad now he's back if Bibbs can stay there for a couple of days just until this is all over – I mean, you know..."

I said, "Just until Angus comes home for convalescence you mean?"

Mum looked at me. "Georgia... you know what the vet said."

I shouted, "What does he know? His beard is so bushy, he probably can't even see what animal he's treating unless it says 'Who's a pretty boy then?' Or starts barking or neighing."

Mum said, "Calm down. He's doing his best."

I said, "He'd better be."

one minute later

Hello, God and Baby Jesus, erm, I might have given the wrong impression about Dr Beardy the vet in that I implied he was a beardy fool. But I meant it in a lighthearted and gay way.

one minute later

When I say "gay" I don't mean gay as in an "OOOOhhhh, do you like my big beard?" sort of way. I mean that I was merely being cheerful.

one minute later

Dear G and BJ, I am signing off communication-wise as

I have to go to the piddly-diddly department.

Surgery
9:00 a.m.

I had awful collywobbles tum trouble as we waited. The nurse took us down to the cat cages bit. It was so sad in there. Doped-up kittykats with drips and bandages and charts. We went over to Angus's cage and he was just lying there. He didn't look like he had moved since last night. But the little machine was going *click click*, so he was breathing.

Dr Beardy came in and said, "No change, I'm afraid. I think you had better try and prepare yourselves for him to go. All his internal organs are so swollen up from the impact, I can't tell what damage has been done, but there is sure to be some bleeding, and then—"

At home
11:00 a.m.

Mum has gone to work. She said she would call in sick and stay with me, but I know she will get into trouble. And anyway, she will get bored and start telling me stuff about her

♡ 155

and Dad and her inner dolphin. Or how she wants to fulfil her creativity by becoming a belly dancer at firemen's balls.

So, all in all, it's better to be by myself.

Five minutes later
I am so restless, I don't know what to do.

Ten minutes later
Jas rang. The Ace Gang are going for a ramble. Just a casual ramble to the park. But actually I know it is because they hope that the lads will be playing footie and that they can accidentally bump into them to solve the s'later and "sometime" fandango.

Jas was being very nice actually, although she was chewing. I didn't say anything because of my vow of nicenosity. She said, "Come with us. It will take your mind off things. You can get a nice tan while you are miserable. That would be good for when Masimo comes back."

She is being sweet to me, and she was a big pally cuddling me and looking after me when I heard about Angus. And I know she is miz about Tom, so I said I would go.

In the park

Phew, it's bloody boiling. We are all lolling under a tree. We are doing leg tanning again by having our legs in the sun and the rest of us underneath the shade of the tree. Well, apart from Rosie, who has her own method of tanning. She makes Sven stand over her head with his jacket held out to make a nice cool shadow. He is burbling on in a Sven way.

It's quite soothing listening to him talk. As Jools said, "It takes your mind off things because it sounds like it should make sense, but it doesn't."

He was saying, "*Ja* and when I take you my bride, Rosie, to my people, they will laugh and sing and kill the herring and make the hats with the herrings."

This can't possibly be true.

I said to Rosie, "Is Sven saying that his mum and dad will make you a herring hat?"

She said, "Yes, exciting, isn't it?"

Then we heard Rollo yelling from across the park. "Oy, Sven, fancy a game of footie, mate?" And Sven went off.

I sat up and I could see Rollo, Tom, Declan, Edward and Dom having a kick about.

Ellen, Jas, Jools and Mabs immediately lost their marbles.

They were trying to hide behind the tree trunk to put more make-up on.

Jools was saying, "Oh my God, do you think Rollo saw my legs? They are so pale. They didn't look so bad in the house but now I'm practically blinded by them."

Mabs said, "Do you think this is a lurking lurker on my chin or a dimple?"

Even Jas had gone into mad fringe-flicking mode. And Ellen practically dithered her own head off.

I just looked at them. How very superficial it all seemed. I don't think I could ever really care what I looked like again. I might even stop shaving my legs.

In fact, that is what I could say to Baby Jesus if he lets Angus be all right. As a mark of solidarity with my injured furry friend, I will let my own body hair run free and wild. It can shoot happily out of the back of my knees or grow so long in my underarms that I can make it into small plaits.

I won't care.

Thirty seconds later

I don't think even a wrathful god would demand that I went as far as the one mono eyebrow though.

Jools was looking over at the lads kicking a ball about. "Do you think they will come over?"

Mabs said, "Do you think we should amble over there to be a bit nearer, or is that like breaking the rubber-band rule?"

Ellen said, "Er what, I mean, what is like, the rubber band rule, or something?"

Mabs said, "You know, what Georgia told us from that *How to Make Any Twit Fall in Love with You* book, where you have to display glaciosity and let them come pinging back like a rubber band."

We were saved from thinking about a plan by what happened next.

Robbie arrived on his scooter and on the back was Wet Lindsay.

Bloody Nora. Everyone looked at me.

What was she doing on the back of his scooter? He hadn't even had a scooter the last time I saw him. Perhaps he was trying to be like the Luuurve God. How weird.

Not as weird as having Wet Lindsay clinging round your waist though.

Then, as they took their helmets off, Dave the Laugh arrived through the trees holding hands with Emma.

The Ace Gang looked at me again.

Rosie said, "Crikey."

Five minutes later

Everyone else wants to go over and watch the lads play and find out what's going on.

If I don't go, it will look like I really care about what Robbie and Ms Slimy-no-forehead-knobbly-arse are doing together. Or it might seem that I am avoiding seeing Dave the Laugh and Emma. I am quite literally surrounded by *ordure* and poo.

After a squillion years of tarting up (not me, the others. I just put on some lippy... well, and a bit of mascara and eyeliner... and face bronzer... but I only did it to be brave, not for vanitosity like the rest), we all walked over to the lads. I was right at the back. I must remember I am the girlfriend of a Luuurve God. As we got to the sidelines the lads went on playing but they were whistling and calling out stuff to us.

Rollo said, "Back off, girls, this is a man's game."

And Declan said, "Look at this for ball skills... whey hey!!!" and he headed the ball right into the goal (two coats and a can of Fanta). Then he bent down, pretended to sniff the grass and banged his bottom with his hands. And all the other boys did the same. I will say it again, because I never tire of saying it, boys are truly, truly weird.

Dave and Robbie were getting their footie boots on. Wet Lindsay looked daggers at me when she saw me. She was sitting on the back of the scooter wearing some ridiculous short skirt. How very naff to wear that on the back of a scooter. I would never do that. Well, I had done it, but I would never do it like her.

I looked away from her. I must say something loudly about Masimo in a minute. I was saved the trouble by Dom yelling out as he passed by dribbling the ball. "I got a bell from Mas and he said you were off to Pizza-a-gogo land – *hasta la vista*, baby."

And then he was viciously tackled from behind by Sven and there was a bit of an argie-bargie.

Everyone's attention was on the rumpus and I sort of sensed someone behind me. It was Robbie. I looked round at him. He looked at me very seriously. He was about to say something when Wet Lindsay called out, "Robbie, hon, could you fetch me a Coke before you go on?"

He hesitated and then turned round and said, "Sure, babe," and went off to the sweet stall. How amazingly naff and weird.

Lindsay got off the scooter and came over to me. The rest of the gang were crowded round the arguing lads and so she got me on my own. She stood right next to me and said, "If you mess this up for me, Nicolson, your life will not be worth living at school. I am head girl this year and believe me, if there is any way I can make your life difficult, I will. He's mine this time; he's sick of losers. Ta taa." And she slimed off.

Oh marvellous! How I am looking forward to Stalag 14. Not.

Then I remembered Angus and I thought, if he doesn't live, I'm not even going to go back to school. I'll get a job, or do voluntary service in a kittykat home abroad or something. I wonder how he is?

All by himself in the vet's. Maybe he's all lonely and frightened. Or in pain. Or...

I had to see him so I decided I would go to the surgery and find out what was happening. I wouldn't bother telling the others; they would understand, and besides, they were too busy tarting around in front of the lads.

I started walking off towards the gates. I had to pass quite near Dave and Emma. Dave was just about to join in the game. I must try for a naturalosity-at-all-times sort of attitude.

As I went by I said cheerily, "Hi, Emma, Dave, you young

groovers. I would hang around, but I've seen more fights than I can eat this holiday. S'laters."

Dave stopped tying his boots. "Er, Georgia, are you all right? Normally, you like a bit of fisticuffs."

I smiled in a sophisticosity-at-all-times sort of way and was about to walk on when Emma said, "I was just talking to Dave about you. I thought your Viking hornpipe dance sounded really groovy. Will you be doing it again at a Stiff Dylans gig? Are you really going to Italy to see Masimo? How very cool. Isn't that cool, Dave? It must be luuurve. When are you off?"

And she was all smiley and nice. Why? Why was she so smiley and nice? Why was her hand on Dave's hair all the time? Did she think it would fall off if she didn't hold it on?

Dave was looking at me. What was I supposed to say?

I was going to say something smart and funny or maybe even sing "O Sole Mio" if my brain entirely dropped out, but I couldn't. There is something about Dave's eyes that makes me tell the truth, so I said, "Well, actually, my cat – well, he's not very well. He was run over and – and I think, I think I will have to cancel my trip and look after him."

Oh, nooooo. I could feel the tears welling up again, I must go. And I walked off really quickly.

At the vet's
5:00 p.m.
Angus is still just lying there. The vet says there is no change and that he thought he would have "gone on" by now. He said it nicely, but I wanted to hit him.

He said, "I'll speak to your mum in the morning and see what she says. You see the thing is, Georgia, it costs an awful lot of money for him to be here and your mum and dad, well – maybe they—"

Walking home
Oh, I am so miserable. I don't know what to do. I can't give up on him, I can't. I wish I had someone to help me.

Lying in my bed
6:30 p.m.
Mum came into my room. Libby is coming home tonight. I said to Mum, "What are we going to tell her? Shall we say, oh, Libby, you know Angus that is your pussycat that you lobe, well, Mummy and Daddy can't be bothered to look after him because he is sick?"

Mum burst into tears. "Oh, Georgia, that is so mean."

164

She's right actually. I put my arms around her.

"I'm sorry, Mum, I don't mean it."

Bloody hell this is quite literally Heartbreak Hotel. And I am in the sobbing suite again.

9:00 p.m.

Libby is in bed with me. I have read her *Sindyfellow* and *Heidi* twice. Which has turned my brain to soup.

She snuggled down with me and Mr Potato Head (literally a potato with one of her hats on). Gordy came in and leaped on her and started tussling her knees under the covers. She was howling with laughter and hitting Gordy with the potato.

"Huggyhugghoghoghog. Funny pussycat. Get off now." And she just got hold of Gordy around his neck and flung him off the bed. He shook himself and sneezed and growled and she laughed.

"Heggo he laaaikes flying. Snuggle now, Ginger." And she got me in a headlock and started sucking my ear going, "Mmmmmmmmmmmmmm."

After a little while the sucking stopped and she started snoring quietly. I looked at her face in the moonlight; she is such a dear little thing really (when she is unconscious). I didn't want her to ever be sad or upset. I kissed her soft little head. Poo, it smelt of cheese. What does she smear herself with? She stirred in her sleep and put her pudgy arms up in the air. Then she sat up.

"Georgie, where is big pussycat?"

Oh blimey.

I said, "Erm, well, he's in the – kittykat hospital. He's hurt his – paws."

She got out of bed. "Come on, Ginger, let's get him." And she started putting her welligogs on over her pyjamas. She was still half asleep.

I started to say something and she flung Mr Potato at me and started waggling her finger. "Don't you bloody start, you baaaad boy. Get up."

In the end I told her that he would be snoozing and that we would go and get him in the morning and she eventually went to sleep.

Friday August 26th

Libby only went to nursery on condition that I went and got Angus.

I looked at Mum. Mum looked at me. But looking at each other wasn't going to help, was it?

9:00 a.m.
Phone rang. Oh God. What if it's the vet?

If I don't answer it, he can't tell me anything I don't want to know. But...

I answered the phone. It was Dave the Laugh.

"Georgia, what's going on?"

"Oh, Dave, it's Angus, and the vet says, and he's all in his tubes and tongue lolling and even his tail is broken, and Libby said go and get him and she had her welligogs over her jimjams, and I can't bear it."

And I started to cry. Again.

He said, "I'll come round. Cover your nungas up."

At the vet's
10:30 a.m.
Standing in front of the cage looking at Angus with Dave the Laugh.

Dave said, "Blimey. He's a bit bent."

I couldn't stand Angus being in a cage any more. In a

strange place. I said to Dr Beardy, "I have to take him home."

The vet tried to persuade me not to.

I was beginning to feel hysterical. I had to take him. I had to. If he was going to die, I wanted him with me, in his own little basket.

Dave the Laugh was ace. He even called the vet "sir" like he was at Eton.

He said to Dr Beardy, "We understand you have done your very best, sir, but now Georgia wants to take care of him, so we'll just take him home."

The vet said to me in a serious voice, "I'm just warning you that he might wake up violent and demented."

Dave said, "I'm usually in quite a good mood when I wake up, sir." Which very nearly, even in such poonosity, made me laugh.

Dr Beardy said, "I mean Angus."

And Dave said, "Actually, I think you would have needed to know him before, sir."

The vet laughed for once and said, "I did look through my predecessor's notes *vis-à-vis* the, erm, castration operation and there was some suggestion of quite wild behaviour. In fact, the notes did say never to let this cat in the surgery again."

Two hours later

When we had got Angus in the house and tucked up, things went a bit awkward. Dave was on the other side of Angus's basket looking at him. And then he looked up. And our heads were very close to each other. He said to me, "Don't cry any more, you'll make your eyes hurt." And he stroked my face.

I looked at him and he looked at me. Uh-oh.

Then he just suddenly stood up and said, "I'd better go, Kittyk – er, Georgia. I'm, well, I'm meeting Emma at six."

I stood up quickly and I smiled, although my mouth felt a bit stiff. I said, "Oh yes, yes, of course, yeah you would. Dave, can I just say – thanks so much, I don't know... I..."

For a second he looked like he was going to give me a bit of a kiss but he stopped and just chucked me under the chin and said, "Remember, I am not God in trousers but merely Dave the biscuit..." And he went.

11:00 p.m.

Angus is in the laundry room in his basket under a big blanket. He hasn't moved or anything for hours. On the way home in the cab he did a little *miaow*. It was just a little *miaow*, but it was something.

He didn't open his eyes or anything. But I think a *miaow* is a good sign.

Saturday August 27th

His eyes open now and again but they are all unfocused like he has really overdosed on catnip. Libby and me are giving him water in a little dropper thing because the vet told us to keep him hydrated.

11:00 p.m.

I have tucked in my charges and am off to beddy byes at last. I truly am a great human being. I hope Baby Jesus is noticing. I may get myself a nurse's uniform tomorrow. Libby is already wearing hers.

What if Angus really is brain-dead or can't walk any more or something? Will I have done the right thing? What if I have to push him around in a cat wheelchair for the rest of his life? I can't see any boyfriend putting up with that.

11:20 p.m.

But I would do it. If he can just come round and know who I am, that will be enough for me.

Sunday August 28th

I went downstairs to look in at Angus and he opened his eyes!!! And let out a really creaky *miaow*.

Hurrah, gadzooks and larks a mercy!!! As Billy Shakespeare and his pals would have said. Thank you, thank you, Baby Jesus!!!

I bent down to the basket and said, "Hello, big furry pally, it's me!" And I put my hand on his face and stroked it. He even purred!!! I started to cry again. Oh well, devil take the hindmost – if you can't have a blubbing fest when your cat has nearly gone to that big cat basket in the sky, when can you have a blubbing fest???

I rushed into the kitchen and opened the fridge. I had got kittykat treats just in case he wanted anything. Cream and everything.

Hey, they should make special-flavoured ice cream for cats called mice cream. Do you get it??? Do you see??? Oh good, I have gone hysterical. Hurrah!!!

I got a little dish of cream and carried it into the laundry room. He was lying there with his bandage over his head and stitches everywhere and his tail strapped up, but his eyes were open. I put my finger in the cream and put it to his mouth. At first he didn't respond, but then his tongue came out and licked off the cream. God, I had forgotten how disgusting his tongue was, it was like being licked by someone with sandpaper on their tongue. Possibly. I'll ask Rosie what it is like snogging someone with sandpaper for a tongue. She probably knows!!!

Hahahahaha. I must be cheered up, my brain is chatting rubbish to itself like normal.

I knew when Angus had had enough cream because he bit my finger quite hard. No damage in the jaw department then!

Phoned the Ace Gang to tell them the news. They are all going round to Jas's house for an all-girl barbecue.

Jas said, "Are you coming to the all-girl barbecue to celebrate?"

I said, "Which of you is going to do the barbecue?"

And Jas said, "Dad is."

"It's not exactly all-girl then, is it, Jas?" But then I thought of Jas's dad and I thought actually...

I can't go though. I'd like to because I haven't seen another human being for days. But I can't bear to leave Angus when he is so poorly.

(I said that to Mum earlier on. "Oh, I wish I had some

human company while I nurse Angus." She said, "I've been here all the time as well." I said, "As I said, I wish I had some human company." And she stropped off to have a bath. That was about two hours ago and she is still in there. I don't know what she does in there for so long; it's vair selfish.)

Jas said, "We're going to give one another manicures and try different make-up. Don't you want to have a go?"

I was tempted but I said, "No, I can't, he's still too poorly, but will you phone and let me know all the goss?"

And Jas said, "Will do, Florrie Nightingale. In fact I'll come round tomorrow in the arvie. I went for a walk with Tom yesterday, it was soooo fab. I'll tell you all about it. We actually saw a red admiral, and they are very rare. I thought it was a sign of hope and—"

I said, "Jas, I think my mum might be coming out of the bathroom and I might be able to get in there for the first time in about a year, so hold that thought about the mothy type thing and—"

"A red admiral is a butterfly actually; moths are—"

"Byeeeeeeeeeeee."

Good grief, I had nearly stumbled into Voleland by mistake.

Monday August 29th

Woke up and went to check on Angus. Found Gordy sleeping in the cat basket with him. Soooo sweet. Gordy was all curled up beside his dad.

His dad might not be so keen if he knew about Gordy's homosexualist tendencies.

Jas came round and kept me company for the afternoon. We mostly tried different sorts of sexy walking. I practised my beach walk.

Jas said, "Your feet are turning in like a duck."

"Jas, I am doing that on purpose; that is how supermodels walk."

"Is it? Why?"

"Jas, I don't know why, they just do. That is *le* rule. Why do they put their tongue behind their bottom teeth when they smile? I don't know, it is a simple rule. Let us just get on with it."

But Jas had gone off into Jasland. "Anyway, why are you practising your beach walk? You aren't going to go to Pizza-a-gogo land now. Which reminds me, Tom was talking to Dom and Dom said that Masimo had phoned him up and was really glad that you were coming. He wouldn't be if he could see you poncing around like a duck. And also if he knew that you aren't coming anyway."

I stopped for a moment to hit Jas over the head with a pillow.

She did have a point though.

I said, "Jas, will you try that number I have got? I tried it again last night and it was the same Yorkshire bloke. I slammed the phone down, but I bet he knew it was me."

She said, "No."

Which is nice.

9:00 p.m.

I wonder why I haven't heard from Masimo. He must be back from the hills by now. Do they have hills in Rome or do they have hillios?

He is expecting me to arrive any day, so how will he know when to meet me if he doesn't get in touch? Perhaps he has got the humpio because I haven't phoned him.

Phoned Jas. "Please help me find out if I've got the right number for Masimo. Pleasey, please, please."

"I've got a face pack on."

"Well, when you take it off then."

"Then I am doing my cuticles."

I slammed the phone down, she is sooo annoying. Oooooh, what shall I do??? Who might know the number?

Angus started yowling. He's getting a bit bored in his basket of pain now and I have to go and dangle stuff in front of him that he can biff with his nose.

Thirty minutes later

I had a quick mini-break from cat care.

Phoned Rosie. "Rosie, will you get Sven to pop down the snooker hall and see if any of the lads are there and if they have got Masimo's number?"

"Okey-dokey. I'll call you back, *amigo*."

Forty minutes later

None of the Dylans are in town. Now what shall I do?

Looked in at Angus before I went to bed. Gordy is in the basket, and Naomi and Libby.

She said, "Night night, me sleepin' with big Uggy."

Tuesday August 30th
10:00 a.m.

The Portly One has landed. He leaped out of his robin mobile like he had been to Antarctica instead of pretending to go fishing with Uncle Eddie. I notice he had no fish.

He kissed Mum on the cheek and she seemed a bit shy and not saying much. But at least she said hello and didn't hit him.

Dad went and looked at Angus and was quite shocked, I think. He bent down to the basket and stroked his head and I heard him say, "Poor little chap, you've been in the wars, haven't you?" Quite touching really.

I went into the kitchen and said to Mum, "Hmm, well it seems like—"

At which point we heard from the laundry room, "Bloody hell, you big furry bastard, you nearly had my bloody finger off!!!"

I went on, "It seems like dear Pater is back."

In bed

All quiet on the parent front. They are talking really quietly so that I can't hear them. But Mum did laugh once and I thought I heard some kind of slurping noise. Er, yuck. I hope they were eating jelly.

Midnight

I am eschewing Jas with a firm hand because she is obsessed with her stupid cuticles and wouldn't even help me phone Masimo.

He must phone soon, surely?

Wednesday August 31st

The phone rang. I leaped to get it. It was Dave the Laugh.

"Hi, Gee, how is the Furry One?"

I should have been disappointed that it wasn't Masimo, but to be honest, I had a really warm feeling when I heard Dave's voice.

I said, "He pretended to be asleep and ill, but when Dad put his hand on his nose, I mean Angus's nose not his own nose, because that would be a bit odd even for my dad. Well, when he did, Angus bit it."

Dave laughed, "Brilliant. So you are a bit cheered up?"

I gabbled on. "Yeah, actually it was funny, you would have laughed, but I tried to phone Masimo and I got some bloke called Fat Bob from Yorkshire and he said he couldn't get any decent pickled eggs in Rome!"

Dave said, "Right, so you're off to Rome then?"

I said, "Er, well, I don't want to leave Angus and, well, I—"

Dave said, "Actually, Georgia, I have to run, so I'll see you around. Bye."

Wow, that was a bit brutal. I wonder why he had to run? Maybe Emma had turned up or something. You would think that she could wait for just a minute, wouldn't you? Why did he ring if he didn't really want to speak to me?

How weird.

Why can't everyone just speak English?

Thursday September 1st

8:00 a.m.

Joy unbounded. Angus tried to stand up today!!! And he ate some kittykat food. Libby fed it to him with a "poon" and most of it went in his ear, but hurrah hurrah!!!

To perk him up I put on his favourite tune, "Who let the dogs out?" and did an impromptu disco inferno dance. I did the Viking bison dance and, as a special tribute to his kittykatness, I substituted paw movements for the bison horn bit. I think I am a genius dance-wise!!! And even though Angus just let his tongue loll out and closed his eyes, I can tell that deep down he is secretly thrilled at my tribute dance.

That is what I think.

I have quite literally single-handedly nursed Angus out of danger.

Well, I have had a bit of help.

It was nice of Dave the Laugh to go and get Angus with me.

Vair nice.

Two minutes later

So how come he is Mr Big Pal one minute and the next minute he is too busy to speak to me on the phone?

I hope he doesn't turn into a puppydog boyfriend that just does everything his so-called girlfriend says.

Perhaps he really, really likes Emma. Because maybe she is a top snogger.

Actually, I don't think she is. Her lips are quite thin and I bet that means that there is a bit of toothy exposure during number five on the snogging scale.

Urghh no, I don't want Dave snogging Emma in my brain. I'll hum something to block the picture out.

10:30 a.m.

Phone rang. I said, "Casualty department, Nurse Nicolson speaking."

And a voice said, "*Mi dispiace*, I lookin for Georgia, she for not here?"

Masimo!

I said, "Masimo, it's me, it's me. Georgia. I tried to phone... er phonio you-io and couldn't – I spoke to some people from Yorkshire. I don't know who they were but they were on holiday in Italy and having a lovely time, but – I – oh, it is soooo nice to hear from you."

Masimo was laughing. "Ah, Miss Georgia, you are funny. I am back from ze hills, and I am thinking when you are for to come a Roma. *Mi dispiace*... I am sorry for my English. Now I am with my *famiglia*, it is like I *stupido*... how you say, even more crappio."

I said, "Masimo, well, the thing is, about me coming to Rome, well, my pussycat – you know my..."

Damn, what was the word for cat? Surely it couldn't be cattio?

I said, "My cattio is not well."

He sounded puzzled. "You are not well? Why, what is wrong with you?"

Oh merd-io.

"Not me, my cat. You know, Angus is..."

And I started doing pathetic *miaowing* down the phone. Oh good, I was talking to my Italian Stallion sophisticated boyfriend and pretending to be a cat. Excellent.

In the end I managed to get Masimo to understand. He said, "So you are not for to come for me?"

I felt quite upset, he sounded really sad. And I wanted to see Rome, although I would probably starve to death there, and never get to the lavatory or anything. It had taken me almost all of my life to tell Masimo that Angus was ill. Why can't everyone speak English? Are they just too lazy? I didn't say that though.

Twenty minutes later

We talked and talked. Well, we tried to talk, but people kept coming in to where Masimo was talking to me on the phone and he would shout at them in Pizza-a-gogo-ese. It was all sorts of people – boys, girls, his mum, his dad, aunties, uncles, dogs, and I can't be sure but I think a parrot came in as well.

They certainly seem vair sociable, the Italianos. And quite good-natured. If my family had been in the house when I was talking to Masimo, it would have been mostly shouting and swearing – and that would have just been Libby.

Then his brother came into the room and Masimo said, "*Cara*, Roberto and I will sing for you a song from the heart."

I started to say, "Well, it's all right, I – you needn't..." But they had already started.

When they finished Masimo said, "It is an old song called 'Volare' and it mean that my love has given me the wings."

Blimey. A bit odd, but that is the romantic Latins for you.

When we said *arrivederci*, Masimo kissed me down the phone. He asked me to do the same. I must say I felt a bit of a prat kissing the phone. But that is transcontinental romance for you.

Five minutes later

I've never had anyone say they love me before. Libby lobes me, that is true, but there is something a bit menacing about the way she says it.

One minute later

And Dave the Laugh kind of said he did. What was it he said when he fished me out of the water in the woods? Oh, yeah. "And that is why I love you."

But he doesn't seem to love me now. In fact, to be frank, he seems to be doing a Jas. Also known as having the humpty with me.

Anyway, shut up, brain. Concentrate on the Luurve God in the hand, not the Dave the Laugh in the bushes.

Ten minutes later
Masimo is going to fly back to Billy Shakespeare land on the 14th. Which is ages away.

Unlike the 12th, the day we go back for more torture and ordure at Stalag 14.

I've said this once and I will say it again. What is the point of school? It is really only to keep the elderly insane off the streets, in my opinion, and to provide shelter for girl-haters.

Ten minutes later
I am quite literally on Cloud 9, luuurve-wise.

One minute later
Tip top of the Love-ometer. I couldn't be happier even if I was a hamster on happy pills scampering up my ladder.

One minute later

The only thing is, though, that I get the hurdy-gurdy knee trembling and wubbish brain whenever I speak to Masimo. He makes me feel shy. And I don't really know what he's like. I mean, when you look at the nub and the gist of the situation, I have in effect only snogged him three times.

Three minutes later

I wonder who I have snogged the most times?

I may have to compose my snogging history until one of my so-called friends can be bothered to phone me up. I am always doing the calling up, so let them make an effort for a change.

Two minutes later

Tragically, my first sexual experience involved incest. My cousin touched me on the leg when we were sharing a room. And then he suggested we play "tickly bears".

I am probably scarred for life mentally, but I don't complain. At least I don't get made to hang out with him now because he has joined the navy. So with a bit of luck he will turn gay.

186

One minute later

Then there was Peter Dyer, also known as Whelk Boy. Dave the Laugh still can't believe that all us girls actually went round to Whelk Boy's house to learn how to snog. We used to queue up politely outside his door. And he had a timer.

One minute later

In fact Dave the Laugh said, "Now that is a top job. Teaching girls to snog. It is quite literally the Horn come true."

Back to my list.

Next came Mark Big Gob.

One minute later

To tell you the truth, my list is not perking me up much so far. In fact, it is depressing the arse off me. What was I thinking of, snogging Mark Big Gob?

I can't even bear to look at him now. How could I snog him??? I think he must have sort of hypnotised me into doing it. I think I was so mesmerised by the sheer size of his mouth that I was paralysed.

Anyway, it is giving me the droop to think about it, so I will move swiftly on.

187

Then was it the Sex God? Or did I accidentally snog Dave the Laugh first?

No, I think it was the Sex God because then he said I was too young for him and I used Dave the Laugh as a red herring to make him jealous.

And it was a bit of a surprise because Dave was quite good at snogging.

In fact, very good. He did the lip-nibbling thing, which was quite groovy. But, anyway...

Then it was the Sex God deffo.

Aaah, Robbie. My first love. Funny that you can care so much about someone and then they are just another bloke. Not that I don't care about him. I do. It's just that – oh, I don't know. I hope he is not still so upset. He looked like he was going to say something to me at the footie, until Miss Octopussy Head started asking him to get her a Coke and so on. And then threatening me with torture at Stalag 14.

I can't think about it. I'll get on with my list.

Blimey, then I'm afraid it was the Hornmeister again, encouraging me towards the General Horn. Bad, bad Dave the Laugh...

Then the Sex God again.

Then Dave the Laugh.

Then the Luuurve God.

Then Dave the Laugh again.

I am beginning to see a pattern emerging here. Hmmmm.

One minute later

Of course, I have not included animal snogging, like when Angus accidentally stuck his tongue in my mouth.

Or weird toddler behaviour. Libby snogging my ear. Ditto knees.

Five minutes later

Jas phoned at last. And I was full of coolnosity with her. But she didn't notice because she only wanted to talk about making Tom so fascinated by her that he will forget about going away to college.

I said grumpily, "Well, you can start doing glaciosity right now. You must start eschewing Tom with a firm hand forthwith and lackaday."

She said, "Rightio."

Hmm. Good, that will serve her right. See how she likes not having a boyfriend around.

Ten minutes later

I am on cat patrol because Angus is trying to escape from his basket. I have tucked the blankets around him really tightly so that he can't leap about and spoil all his stitches and so on. In the end I had to clip his lead on and fasten it to the basket.

He's livid.

But he is still a bit weak and after he had yowled a bit he went off to Snoozeland.

When I went to Boboland, tired from my day of constant caring, I said to Mum, "You should try caring, Mum. It's vair vair tiring."

Friday September 2nd
Up at the crack of 10:30 a.m.

Angus is getting stronger and more mad every day. He hates being in his basket. And he has chewed through his lead. I'm going to have to get him a metal one. He is the Arnold Schwarzenegger of cat land.

Twenty minutes later

I can't stand the sound of moaning and miaowing and yowling any more. Maybe if I take him outdoors, he will calm down a bit. Besides which, he has eaten so much of his basket, it is practically just a pile of old sticks.

ll:OO a.m.
Jas came round to report on her boy entrancing skills *vis-à-vis* Hunky.

I am preparing myself to forgive her, just to pass the time actually.

I said, "Right, what did you say when you last saw him?"

She did a bit of fringe fiddling and then said, "Hmmm, I said, see you later."

I said, "Right, that's good, very good, nice and vague, give him time to wonder what you have been up to and so on. When did you last see him?"

She did more fringe-fiddling and thinking then she said, "Erm, let me see – erm, it was about half an hour ago."

"Half an hour ago! Jas, you are not as such getting this, are you? You are officially giving him space so he can come pinging back like an elastic band. Seeing him half an hour ago is not having space; that is seeing him all the time."

"I like to see him."

"That is as maybe, but it is not the key to entrancement."

"What is then?"

"You must be more mysterious and unavailable. You must gird your loins and display glaciosity and so on. You must make him jealous."

"Why?"

"Because jealous is good *vis-à-vis* entrancementosity."

"How do I make him jealous? Shall I say I found some unusual molluscs and not show them to him?"

"No. I am not talking about nature, I am talking about the game of luuurve. You have to flirt with other blokey fandangos."

"How do you mean?"

"I mean, you flirt with other blokey fandangos."

"That is all very well for you, Georgia. You are inclined to thrust your red bottom about, but it is against my nature."

Oh, she is soooo annoying.

In the end I got her to agree that she will practise flirting with other boys. And she will play Tom at his own gamey and win. She said, "Right, I'm going to start now. I am practising glaciosity. This is me being unavailable." And she tilted her nose up and flicked her fringe.

"No, Jas, that is just you looking stupid in my house

where Tom can't even see you. You have to do something that he will notice."

She had a bit of a think and then said, "Right, I'm going to phone him and say that I think he's right that we should have more space and that I need more space actually, because he has been my only one and only. And that I will see him when I have a spare moment."

"Good, that is good, Jas."

She went off to phone him and I started rooting around in the garage for a cat transporter. I hope I don't get attacked by bluebottles. Usually when dad has been fishing he leaves his maggots in their little maggot home thing, forgets about them and they turn into huge bluebottles. I peered in. No menacing humming going on – so – now then, what can I put Angus in as a sort of cat wheelchair? Aha!!! Libby's old pushchair!!! Perfect.

Four minutes later

Jas came back looking a bit flushed. I was trying to work the straps out on the pushchair and she was flicking her fringe around like a madwoman.

She said, "Well, that's done. I've told him. I said I was

having a bit of space and that he should have a bit of space. And he said OK. Which is a bit weird. What do you think he meant by OK?"

I said, "I think he meant OK. Now, where is the bit that clicks into the buckle?"

"Anyway, whatever he means, I'm quite looking forward to a bit of freedom. You know, trying out my entrancing skills and so on. What is the special entrancing walk thingy?"

I showed her the hip hip wiggle wiggle hip hip thing. And also did a bit of flicky hair.

Two minutes later

She managed the hip hip wiggle wiggle thing, but when she tried to incorporate flicky hair at the same time, she banged into a wall.

Ten minutes later

We carried Angus out to the driveway in the washing-up bowl. We tried to lift the cat basket up, but the bottom just fell out and Angus was yowling like a cat who has just crashed to the floor out of its basket.

Both of us were wearing gardening gloves. I'd like to say

194

that Angus was really looking forward to his little outing and in his catty way appreciated what we were doing for him, but the spitting and pooing would suggest otherwise.

I said to Jas as we shoved him down the drive in the pushchair, "You have to be cruel to be kind. Some things in life are not pleasant, but they have to be done. For instance, German and maths. And, well, school. I can't believe the holidays have gone so quickly and we are being forced back into the torture chamber of life."

Jas said, "I'm quite looking forward to it now. We're doing *Romeo and Juliet* in English. I wonder if I will get a part like I did in last year's production. You know, I really felt that I got into the Lady M part. It took quite a lot out of me."

I said, "It took quite a lot out of me."

But she had gone off into Jasland. Is it likely that she will be cast as Juliet? Because that is what she is thinking. Whoever heard of a Juliet with a stupid flicky fringe and an obsession with owls? Billy Shakespeare didn't write, "Hark what owl through yonder window breaks?"

Five minutes later
Angus is nicely strapped into the pushchair. I have put a

♡ 195

little blankin over him and tucked a couple of sausages under his armpit so he can reach them for a nibble.

As we wheeled Angus out of our gate Mr and Mrs Next Door were coming back from walkies with the Prat brothers. They were looking unusually unusual today in matching pink collars. And the poodles looked ridiculous too!!! Hahahaha, did you see what I did there? Oh, nevermind.

Mr Next Door looked at us wheeling Angus along and said, "He's not dead then?" And he didn't say it in a pleased way.

Naomi followed us for a while doing that mad high-pitched thing that nutcase Burmese cats do. But then, when she reached the end of the road, the big black manky cat was lurking around by the dustbins and she caught his eye. Angus went ballisticisimus when he saw Manky and tried to bite through his straps. I started pushing the pushchair really quickly. Naomi is an appalling tart; she just lay down in the road and started squiggling around on her back, letting her womanly parts run wild and free.

How disgusting. I said to Jas, "Put your hand over Angus's eyes."

Jas said, "Er, no, because I'm not mad and I don't want it bitten off."

It's awful really. Poor crippled Angus seeing his woman offering herself to other (manky) men.

I started jogging along with the pushchair, but I hadn't got my specially reinforced sports nunga-nunga holder on, so I had to stop as there was a bit of a danger of uncontrollable bounce basooma-wise.

Four minutes later

We ambled along towards the park. It was quite a nice day. I put a sun bonnet on Angus because there are some baldy patches on his head where the stitches are and he might have got sunburn. I thought he looked quite cute but he didn't agree and was trying to biff me with his big paw.

When he was under his blankin and with his hat over his face, you couldn't really tell he was a cat. I said to Jas, "It would be quite funny if people actually thought he was a baby. Then they might bend down to say 'Aaaahhh' and see his mad furry face staring out at them. And that would be a hoot and a half."

Jas said, "Yeah, groovy." But she didn't mean it because I could tell she was concentrating on practising doing wiggle wiggle, hip hip, flicky hair, flicky hair, fall off pavement etc.

In the end, Angus made such a racket and the bonnet fell down over his eyes, so I took it off. I told Jas she could wear it to keep her fringe in check but she didn't want to. She is quite literally a fun-free zone.

I said to Jas, "I bet you that the teachers are actually looking forward to going back to Stalag 14 because they have no lives. I bet Slim already has her knickers laid out ready to go. Hawkeye will be practising shouting."

Jas said, "Oh, I meant to tell you something. Tom told me goss about Robbie and Wet Lindsay."

"Jas, I told you not to do any earwigging *vis-à-vis* Droopy Knickers."

"I didn't do earwigging. Tom just brought it up. Apparently Wet Lindsay goes round to Tom's mum and dad's all the time. Even when neither of the boys are there. She just goes and hangs out with the parents. How sad is that? And they get on really well. So Tom asked Robbie what was going on, was she like the official girlfriend etc. and Robbie said, and I quote, 'Well, it's nice to have someone who is sort of ordinary around and who really likes me.' Oh, and he also said that she bakes him cakes."

I just looked at Jas. "What sort of person bakes cakes for boys?"

Jas said, "Well, I made a lemon drizzle cake for Tom when we went camping and—"

"OK, let me put this another way, what sort of twit besides your good self makes cakes for boys? It is tremendously sad and odd. It doesn't say one word about cake baking in my *How to Make Any Twit Fall in Love with You* book and it says some pretty bloody strange things, I can tell you."

Of course, for no apparent reason, Jas hit number seven on the having-the-hump scale. (Number seven is, of course, walking on ahead, one of Jas's specialities).

I said, "Jazzy, don't be silly. I bet Tom luuurved your drizzly cake. It's just odd for Wet Lindsay to do it, isn't it? She's not exactly a domestic, is she? It's not like her to do anything for anyone else, is it? Is it, little pally? I bet even Tommy wommy said that it was a bit odd, didn't he?"

Jas didn't want to say, but she couldn't help it. She said, "Well, actually, he did say he thought that she was, like, a bit insincere and that she was trapping Robbie by being nice."

Hmmm. That has made me feel a bit guilty about Robbie. If he was on the rebound because I had eschewed him with a firm hand, I had sort of made him go back out with the octopussy prat of the century. It was bad enough having him cry in front of me, but for him to then be driven into her no-forehead world was awful. I didn't want him to be with Lindsay because of me. Maybe I would have to save him from her somehow.

Twelve minutes later

We were wheeling Angus along in the park singing "Always Look on the Bright Side of Life" quite loudly to cheer him up (he was yowling along to the chorus, I like to think) when round the corner of the loos came Dave the Laugh and Emma, and Tom and a friend of Emma's called Nancy. They were laughing together.

Dave saw us first and he came over and bent down to look at Angus. "Wow, you dancer! Attaboy. You're de man!!!"

He said it in a sort of admiring way and I felt really proud of Angus. He had come back from the edge of the heavenly cat basket in the sky like supercat. And it was nice to see Dave. He looked very cool in a class shirt and he looked up and winked at me – then spoiled the moment by saying, "Emma, come and have a look at Angus; he is the kiddie."

Emma came trolling across all girlie. "Ooooh, isn't he cute?"

I should have warned her not to put her face too near Angus but, well, that is the law of nature. It's only cat spit, after all. You would have thought that it was viper juice, the way she carried on. She went scampering off into the ladies' loos and Nancy went with her.

Jas had not said a word since she saw Tom. She had gone very, very red, even for her, that is how red she was.

Tom said, "I just bumped into Dave and the girls at the snooker hall..."

Jas said, "Tom, what you do is really your business. Come on, Gee, we don't want to keep the gang waiting." And she actually said to Tom, "S'laters. Maybe bell you sometime." Has she finally snapped?

I followed after her with the pushchair, leaving Tom and Dave looking at us.

When we got round the corner, Jas burst into tears.

"How can he just go and get off with some other girl, just like that? It's only half an hour since I said he could be free."

I said, "Well, it says in my *How to Make Any Twit Fall in Love with You* book that boys don't like feeling bad, so they get another girl really quickly."

Jas said, "That's awful. What's the point of seeing anyone then or caring about boys at all?"

I said, "Well, there is some good news."

"What?"

"Well, it says that they get another girl really quickly and it is usually a disaster. And they remain frozen emotionally for the rest of their lives, so that's good, isn't it?"

But she didn't cheer up as such.

Saturday September 3rd
9:00 a.m.

Jas phoned. She said, "Tom came round and said that there was nothing going on with Nancy. He just bumped into them and they had a bit of a kick around with the other lads in the park and the girls watched. And, anyway, Nancy has got a boyfriend. She is just, like, Emma's best mate."

I said, "What did you say?"

"Well, I remembered, you know, about the glaciosity and so on. And I said, 'I suppose that when you are having space you can't always ask what someone is doing and so on but we can be friendly to each other.'"

I was amazed. I said, "Jas, my little matey, that is almost quite good tactics. You are not only displaying glaciosity, you are also incidentally displaying maturiosity as well. *Muchos buenos,* as our Pizza-a-gogo friends might say."

Then she spoiled it. "I miss him though."

I said, "Go cuddle your owls and be brave."

She said, "Am I allowed to snog him if he comes round?"

I said, "No, he has to go off and then ping back. You can't do the pinging first. It is not in the book."

Tuesday September 6th

Six days to Stalag 14. God help us one and all. But on the bright side the Luuurve God comes back in eight days!!! I am keeping up my grooming and plucking so that I do not have to do it all in one go. I am ruthless with any stray hairs. Also I am a lurker-free zone. I just wish I could find some tan stuff that makes my legs not so paley, but not orange like last time. Anyway, it doesn't really matter because we will be back in tights for school.

4:00 p.m.

Angus went for his first walk today. I put him on top of the dividing wall so that he could see the Prat Poodles. They usually give him *joie de vivre* and so on. His tail is still all bandaged up but his stitches come out next week and he is eating A LOT.

♡ 203

I popped him up there but he still seemed a bit wobbly on his old cat pins. He wobbled up and down once or twice and then crashed off over the wall into Mr and Mrs Next Door's garden. I clambered up and looked down, and he was lying in the cabbage patch. He did that silent *miaowing* thing and then got to his paws again. He started walking and then careered off into a bush. Then he got up again, walked for a few paces and crashed into the lawnmower. Oh noooo, perhaps he really did have brain damage.

I leaped down into Next Door's garden to rescue my little pally. The Next Doors were out, so the coast was clear apart from the heavily permed guardey dogs, Snowy and Whitey. They were chained to their kennel, probably to stop them larking about and getting their stupid fur all muddy. And they were yapping like billio.

I said in a Liverpool accent, "Calm down, calm down," and picked up Angus. He didn't like being picked up and struggled around. As a treat I took him quite near the Prat brothers and he gave them both a big swipe with his paw around the snout.

I took him out through the gate because I didn't think I could manage the wall and Angus the mad cat.

Ooooooh, please don't let him be a backward cat. I didn't

want to have to push him around in his pussycat wheelchair for the rest of my life.

I told Mum what had happened and she said why didn't I ring the vet, Dr Beardy.

What if he said that Angus was like a turnip cat? Would I look after him even if he was dim and didn't know how to fight any more? And started liking the Prat brothers?

Five minutes later

Yes, I would. I love him and I will look after him no matter what happens. He is my furry soul pal.

Wednesday September 7th

Amazingly, Dad was quite sympathetic *vis-à-vis* Angus being an idiot cat and said he would drive me to the vet's when he got back from work.

At the vet's
5:30 p.m.

The vet looked all beardy and serious when I told him about Angus crashing about and maybe being backward. He looked in Angus's ears and eyes and so on. Then he put him up on his table and let him walk about. Angus took two steps and then immediately fell off the table. He tried to leap up on to it again and missed and crash-landed into my lap. Which he then fell off.

It was so sad. He had been the king of leaping and balancing. His days of riding the Prat brothers around like little horsies were over. I could feel my eyes filling up.

Dr Beardy said, "It's his tail. He can't balance properly while it's all bandaged up. He'll be OK when the bandage comes off."

Oh, Allah be praised!!!

(Er, sorry about that, Baby Jesus. I don't know why I came over a bit Muslim then, but we are all in the same cosmic gang after all. Clearly I have my favourite, which is Baby Jesus, but generally I am a fan of the whole caboodle. In case any of them are also omnipotent like Big G.)

Back home

Angus has just crashed into the cat flap which he was trying to get through. Oh, I am so happy. I told Jas on the phone.

She went, "Ahuhu-ahuh." But not in a caring and listening way.

Then she said, "I don't know how you manage without a boyfriend. Who do you tell stuff to?"

I said, "Jas, I tell stuff to my little pallies, like you. Anyway, can I stop you before you go off on a Moaning for Britain campaign? I am going to ring the Ace Gang and we can have a joint celebration day for the recovery of Angus and also the reinvention of – glove animal!!!"

"Oh no."

"Oh yes."

"Oh no."

"Oh yes."

"Oh no."

"Jas, this is lots of fun chatting with you and so on – but we are meeting at mine in half an hour, so you had better dash. Pip pip."

Round at mine

I have made all of the gang coffee and Jammy Dodgers as we need nourishment to prepare us for the beginning of another term at Stalag 14.

Two hours later

My ribs are hurting from laughing. I had forgotten how much fun you can get out of a beret and a pair of gloves. It was Rosie's impression of Inspector Glove Animal of the Yard that made me laugh the most. She put on the beret and pinned the gloves underneath it as ears, and then popped her beard on and started puffing on her pipe.

It was vair vair *amusant*. I said, "I think Hawkeye will appreciate the creativitinosity that we have brought to what is in fact a boring old beret."

Jas said, "She won't appreciate it; she will just give us immediate detention."

I looked at her with my eyebrows raised. "Jas, I hope you are not being the bucket-of-cold-water girl."

Jas was going on in rambling mode. "Well, it's so silly."

Rosie went over to her and took out her pipe. "Jas, are you suggesting that I look silly?"

Oh, I laughed.

To release our girlish high spirits we danced around to loud music in my bedroom and then we lay down panting on the bed.

Ellen is going on a proper second date with Declan, and Rollo bought Jools her very own rattle for supporting him at his footie matches. She is secretly thrilled, I think, although she said she would rather have had chocolates and lip gloss.

Sunday September 11th
In bed
11:30 p.m.

My bedroom is a Libby-free zone. I've got Stalag 14 tomorrow and I want to be in tip-top condition to face the Hitler Youth (prefects). And General Fascists (staff). And the Lesbians (Miss Stamp). And other assorted loons (Herr Kamyer, Elvis, Miss Wilson, Slim our beloved huge headmistress and – well, everyone else there really).

Hark! What owl through yonder window breaks?

Monday September 12th
7:00 a.m.
Oh, I can't believe the hols are over and it is back to long dark hours of boredom and – er... that's it. Still, it's now only two days until Masimo gets back. Yarooooo!!!!

In the bathroom
7:25 a.m.
I was just about to wash my face with the special face-washing soap when I realised it wasn't there. How am I

supposed to cleanse and tone etc. if people keep moving my soap? I went into the kitchen and said to Mum, "Have you been using my special soap, which is specially mine especially for me?"

She didn't even look round. "No."

I looked in at Angus. He and Gordy were in the same basket and they were both frothing at the mouth.

7:40 a.m.
Why would a cat eat soap? Why?

8:30 a.m.
Walking really, really slowly up the hill towards Hell.

Jas hasn't phoned Tom and he has phoned her twice and she has pretended that she isn't in.

I said, just to check, "Er, Jas, you know how you pretended that you weren't in? Well, you didn't answer the phone and say 'I'm not in', did you?"

She hit me over the head with her rucky, which was a bit violent, I think. It is as well I luuurve her.

We are not doing glove animal today, we are keeping the element of surprise. Hawkeye and the Hitler Youth will be on high alert at the moment. All full of energy after the summer break. All pepped up for mass brutality and girl hating so we are going to lull them into a false sense of security by being good this week. And then going all out headgear-wise next week.

8:38 a.m.
The fascist regime has already started. As we came through the school gates Hawkeye was there like a guard dog and she had a tape measure!! Honestly! She was making sure that our skirts were an inch below the knee. Anyone who had turned over their skirt at the waist was given an immediate reprimand for their trouble. I may write to my MP or the European King or whatever.

Fortunately, I knew Hawkeye would be picking on me (as she has a specially developed hating muscle all for me), so I had pulled my skirt down over my knees once we were in sight of Stalag 14's perimeter fence.

Melanie Griffiths, world renowned for her enormous out of control nungas, was just ahead of me and Hawkeye pounced. Fair enough because Melanie's skirt was practically up her bum-oley.

Hawkeye had a nervy spaz attack: "Melanie, I would have expected better from you and, frankly, with your shape, you would do well to go for the longer look anyway."

I said to Jas, "Actually, I don't think that Melanie has rolled her skirt up. I think that her arse has grown and that has lifted the hemline."

As we shuffled off to hang our coats up I grumbled to the rest of the gang, "I bet they don't have people measuring bloody skirts in schools in Pizza-a-gogo land. I bet they don't even wear skirts at schools there, they are so liberal. I bet they wear fur thongs or leatherette hotpants."

Actually, I hope they don't. Masimo might quite like that. Oooohhhh, I can't wait for him to come back.

Assembly

Oh, hello to the wonderful world of mass boredom and *merde*. Wet Lindsay and her sidefool, Astonishingly Dull Monica, were lurking around on prefect duty. They love frightening the first formers, telling them their shoes are wrongly laced up and so on.

Wet Lindsay looked at me and said something to ADM and they both laughed. I didn't care though; I have an

Italian Luuurve God as a boyfriend. And, more importantly, I have got a forehead.

We were just queuing up to go through the doors into the main hall and listen to Slim, our revered headmistress, bore for England when the two Little Titches came bounding up. I haven't seen the Titches, also known as Dave the Laugh's fan club, since the last Stiff Dylans gig. They were all flushed and excited and the (slightly) less titchy one said to me, "Hello... hello, miss. We've got new trainers. We'll show you them later. And we saw Dave the Laugh yesterday at the shopping centre. He went into Boots and we followed him and he was getting some moisturiser and then we asked him for his autograph and he signed my maths book. He put three kisses and a drawing of a monkey."

Wet Lindsay shouted out, "You two lower-school girls get back in line and stop talking. Georgia Nicolson, take a reprimand for encouraging the younger girls to break school rules."

What, what? I had got a reprimand for standing in line while some tiny nutcases told me about their new shoes. Where was the justice in that?

God, I hate her. In fact, she has made me deffo decide to split her and Robbie up somehow. It is my civic duty. Also, if I can accidentally on purpose bend her stupid bendy stick-insecty legs round her neck, I will most certainly take the opportunity.

As we shuffled to our places I whispered to Jas out of the corner of my mouth, "I hate her. She is definitely as dead as a dead thing on dead tablets. Also, forgive me if I am right, but Dave the Laugh seems to have acquired his own personal stalkers."

Fifteen minutes later

Ro Ro really made me laugh during prayers because she dug me in the ribs and when I looked at her she had on those comedy glasses that have no lenses but do have a false nose with big black eyebrows on. I couldn't stop laughing and then she did it to the rest of the gang, so we had group shoulder heaving. I managed to pull myself together for the final amen.

I could see Wet Lindsay looking over our way, but she could only see Rosie from the side so she didn't get the full bushy eyebrow effect, otherwise it would have been detention all round. What larks!

Also the hymn was a top opportunity for "pants" work. The words were, "I long for you Lord as the deer PANTS for the rain."

The volume went up about a million when we sang "pants".

Four minutes later

Oh, go on a bit, why don't you, Slim. "Blah blah blah, visitors saying girls looked like prostitutes wearing short skirts, make-up etc etc... all girls going to be hung, drawn and quartered if they don't keep to school dress codes, blah blah. A lady does not show her knickers underneath her skirt."

Oh, I am so bored. Slim had worked herself up into such a state that I thought her chins were going to drop off. Also, *vis-à-vis* fashion etc. I am not sure that I would wear an orange dress if I were eighty-four stone. She must get them specially made. By a sadist.

Then she said, "Well girls, now let us pass on to more pleasant matters. As you know, before the summer holidays Year Eleven were lucky enough to be taken on a camping trip by Herr Kamyer and Miss Wilson. I gather that they had a marvellous time. Is that true, Year Eleven?"

Me and Rosie and the gang were murmuring, "Yes, oh yes. Are you mad? Yes, yes, cheese and onion," and rubbish, but so that you couldn't really hear it. Only Jas and her sad mates were shouting stuff like, "It was great."

Bloody swotty voley knicker types.

Then Slim asked Herr Kamyer and Miss Wilson to come up to the stage. Miss Wilson looked like she was wearing her pre-Christmas cardigan. I swear, it had reindeers on it. And Herr Kamyer had on a tweed suit and an unusual tie (knitted) and his trousers hovered proudly at ankle level, revealing attractive matching socks.

Good grief. I whispered to Jools, "It's lovely young love, isn't it?" She just looked at me.

Herr Kamyer went first. He said, "Vell, ve had ze very gut time viz the fun and larfs. Didn't ve, girls?"

We all went, "Whatever, mumble mumble."

Miss Wilson took over the dithering baton then. "It was most enjoyable. During the day we drew interesting sketches of the varied wildlife and explored our environs."

Rosie went, "Oo-er," which nearly made me wet myself but no one else heard.

Miss Wilson was back in the exciting world of tents and voles, rambling on. "But the evenings were in many ways the best times, we made our own entertainment."

Slim interrupted, "Always the most enjoyable."

Miss Wilson said, "Indeed."

God, it was like a hideous teacher love-in.

Then Herr Kamyer got the giddygoat and started being enthusiastic. "Yah, ve played some of the games I haf played when I was camping in ze Black Forest. We did the shadow animals game and Miss Vilson sang mit der girls and made ze vair *gut spangleferkel*."

Oh dear God, I knew it wouldn't be long before we were back on the sausage trail.

Actually, I didn't mind idling time away with sausages and mad Germans because we had French first lesson, and I wanted to avoid Madame Slack for as long as I could because she hates me.

As Herr Kamyer and Miss Wilson both dithered and fell down the stairs from the stage, Slim said something scary.

"Well, I am sure there will be many more expeditions and excitements in the coming terms. Also I think it would be very nice for the whole school to share in the memories of the trip, and so I have suggested that Miss Wilson run an art project with Year Eleven. It will be lovely for them to bring their paintings and sculptures and so on of their feelings and experiences of the camping trip and put them on display here in the main hall."

Rosie whispered to me, "Will you be bringing the sculpture of your snogging session with Dave the Laugh into the main hall?"

I looked at her cross-eyed and said, "I wonder if Miss Wilson will be re-enacting, through the magic of dance, her marvellous standing in a field in the nuddy-pants scenario?"

French

I have *dit* this many times and I will *dite* it again, *qu'est ce que c'est le point de français*?

I've been to *le* gay Paree, I have experienced *le* mime, I have danced *sur le pont* d'Avignon and even (as Jools reminded me) done my world-famous impression of the Hunchback of Notre Dame outside Notre Dame. But I will not be going again.

This is *moi* point. I go out with an Italian Luuurve God and there is no point in going to France except for cheese. And I do not *aime* cheese, so there you are.

Madame Slack was just waiting to give me a good verbal thrashing, and when I innocently said in our conversation section that *"Je préfère l'Italie pour mes vacances and pour l'amour. Je n'aime pas le fromage. Merci. Au revoir."* Madame Slack said, "Ah well, *je préfère les étudiants qui ne sommes pas des idiots – mais c'est la vie. Prenez vous le reprimand."*

Bloody hell, two reprimands and I haven't even had my break-time cheesy wotsits.

Lunchtime

I wonder why Dave the Laugh was buying moisturiser from Boots? Perhaps he is on the turn. I may say that to him when I see him. I may say, "Dave, your skin is sooo soft and smooth. Are you on the turn?"

Not that I will be seeing him.

Probably.

German

Rosie has been looking in her new slang book, *German for Fools.* She said to Herr Kamyer, "In my new dictionary it says that a kiss lasting over three minutes is *abscheidskuss.*"

Herr Kamyer quite literally went red all over. And I could clearly see his ankles, so I am sure about this.

He started, "Well, yes, but this language is for slang, and of course one would not say... erm—"

Rosie said helpfully, "*Abscheidskuss?*"

German is quite literally comedy magic.

Five minutes later

Wee is *pipi*.

One minute later

And to poo is *krappe*. Hahahaha.

Still incarcerated in Stalag 14
Afternoon break

Going to school is like going through life backwards in time.

I said to the Ace Gang, "Did you see Miss Wilson choking on her fizzy orange when Herr Kamyer walked past her and asked her if she was wearing a new blouse? She luuurves him. She wants him baaaad. He is quite literally a babe magnet."

Rosie looked up "babe magnet" in the *German for Fools* book. She said, "Oh *ja*, he is a *Traum*boy."

Jools said, "When does Masimo get back?"

I said, "He said the fourteenth."

Ellen said, "What time, I mean, did he say s'later or 'give you a bell' or will he like give you a bell or will you give him a bell?"

We looked at her.

It is true though. He didn't say when exactly he would be back. I don't know what time he will be arriving, morning, afternoon or night. Which means essentially I will be on high alert and heavily made up for twenty-four hours a day. And even then he might not call me until the next day. He might have jet lag.

One minute later

I will have to go to bed fully made up and dressed in case he pops round unexpectedly.

One minute later

I have just had a spontaneous pucker up.

Bell went

As we were scampering back for English (double bubble), I had one of my many ideas of geniosity. I said, "I know what we can do to stop Herr Kamyer from making us do stuff. Let us get him to correct our German translation of the snogging scale. That I will be doing during blodge."

English

Miss Wilson announced that we are indeedy going to be doing a school production of *Rom and Jule* this term. And that because of the massive success of *MacUseless*, we are going to join forces with the boys' school again. They are going to be our "technical support". Which in Dave the Laugh's case means he switches all the lights off and people fall off the stage. Yarroooo!!!

We started yelling out, "Oh joy unbounded!" "Three cheers for Merrie England and all who sail in her!" "Poop poop!" "For she's a jolly good fellow!" until I thought Miss Wilson's bob would explode.

She was slightly losing her rag and said, "Now, girls, settle down. I know that it is very thrilling but – Rosie, get off your desk and please put your beard away."

Rosie looked surprised. "But I am getting in character, Miss Wilson. This is an Elizabethan beard, specially knitted by some old bloke in tights many moons ago."

Eventually Miss Wilson was able to say that auditions were to take place on Wednesday in the main hall and that we were to read the text and think about what parts we might like to play.

Nauseating P. Green asked if there was a dog in it. She has never quite got over playing the dog in *Peter Pan*. Miss Wilson said, "No, there is no dog in *Romeo and Juliet*. It is a tragedy."

I said, "You can say that again, Miss Wilson, because Pamela is top at fetching sticks and begging."

We laughed and started muttering "Prithee, prithee, prithee!" and doing pretendy beard stroking every time Miss Wilson started describing the plot of *Rom and Jule*.

After about ten minutes the classroom door banged open. Slim came jelloiding in, shouting and wobbling at the same time, telling us that we were making too much noise and being silly. If we didn't all want to stay behind for detention on our first day back, we should shut up. Ramble ramble, wobble wobble etc.

Charming.

I said to the Ace Gang quietly, "You show a bit of enthusiasm for the Bird of Avon, our greatest old bloke in tights, and this is what you get for your trouble."

And they wonder why the youth of today doesn't learn nuffink.

4:00 p.m.

Ambling out of the science block after the last bell. God, how many years have I been in blodge learning how to bamboozle my epiglottis?

As we rounded the corner towards the main building I saw Wet Lindsay dashing across to the sixth-form common room. She wasn't wearing her uniform; she had on a short dress that showed off her knobbly knees to perfection. She glared at me as she went past, and she was undoing her stupid hair from its stupid ponytail.

I said, "That's a nice dress, Lindsay. Who went to the fitting for it?"

She just gave me two fingers.

I said to Rosie, "She's a lovely example to us all, isn't she?"

4:15 p.m.

Walking across the playground I noticed Robbie sitting on his new (quite cool) scooter on the road by the gates. Most of the girls were getting all girlish and swishing their hair about as they passed him by. He saw me. (Damn, I wish I had put some make-up on!!! I must suck my nose in and smile in an ad hoc and cool way.) He has got really nice eyes and I could still picture him the day that I told him about me and Masimo and he had let a little tear out of his eye. Actually, considering that he and I only saw each other for a short time, we had packed in an awful lot of blubbing one way and another. We had quite literally spent most of our possible snogging time at Heartbreak Hotel.

Ah, well.

He smiled sort of sadly at me as I got near him. I smiled back. He is very good looking.

He said, "All right, Georgia?"

I said, "Yeah, fine, alrighty as two alrighty things. And you?"

He said, "Yeah, cool, things are you know, er, cool. I'm guesting at the next Stiff Dylans gig... Are... will you be coming? You know with your... er... your—"

At that moment I got a sharp prod in my bum. Owwwww buggery oww. I had been stabbed in my bum-oley. I looked round into the smiling face of Wet Lindsay. Wet Lindsay and her umbrella.

Wet Lindsay said, "Hi, Robbie, ready to go, hon?"

She got on the back of his scooter and while he couldn't see her she was mouthing at me, "You are so dead meat."

Robbie fired up his scooter and said, "See you around,

Georgia." And they roared off.

I watched them and Lindsay turned round and put her finger across her throat, meaning that I was indeed dead meat.

I rubbed my bum. I would probably have a bruise there and I had only just recovered from my last bum-oley injury.

I grumbled to the others, "She is such a bitch. I can't believe he is falling for it AGAIN. It makes me think he is a bit half-witted."

Jas said, "Remember what you told me about boys getting someone else really quickly when they are upset? Well, maybe you have driven him into the arms of the Stick Insect Octopussy girl. S'laters."

Yep, it looks like I am going to have to make him dump her somehow. I wonder if she still wears those false nunga-nunga increasers?

Five minutes later

Jas has gone a different way home in case Tom is around. Then he will wonder where she is and she will have become entrancing to him.

As I have already been caught without make-up by an ex, I am taking no chances. We nipped into the tarts' wardrobe in the park and we applied mascara, lippy and so on. And I did a bit of hair-bounceability work. (I put my head upside down under the hot-air hand-dryer.) Rolled my skirt over and took off my tie, and *voilà*!!! Georgia the callous sophisticate rides again with her Ace Gang (minus Wise Woman of the Forest)!!

Funnily enough, it was just as well we had done preparation because as we started walking down the hill, Dave the Laugh caught us up. He was with Declan, Edward and Rollo. Ellen, Mabs and Jools went into giggling-gertie mode and sort of lagged back with their "boyfriends", so it was just me and Dave and Rosie.

He linked up with us and said, "Be gentle with me, girls."

Awwww.

I told Dave about the *Rom and Jule* fiasco and he said, "Excellent, excellent. Many comedy opportunities in the tights department there then." He also said he had some kittykat treats for Angus.

Awwww.

As we got to the edge of the park we heard a lot of shouting. The Blunder Boys. Yippee. They saw Dave and gave him the finger. Then Oscar came looming along with his tragic jeans and no belt and one of the spoons yelled, "Wedgie!!!" And two of them got hold of Oscar and pulled down his jeans so that his Thomas the Tank Engine kecks were exposed to the world. Mark Big Gob grabbed the top of Oscar's underpants and lifted him off his feet. He was just dangling there, literally held up by his undercrackers.

Quite, quite mind-bogglingly weird.

Dave was nodding and said, "Excellent work."

We walked on and I said, "Erm, Dave, as you are world expert on the weirdness that is boydom, can you just explain what that was about?"

Dave said, "A wedgie is when the underpants are pulled sharply upward from behind, so that they go tightly up the victim's bum-oley."

We just looked at him.

He went on. "The ultimate is, of course, the atomic wedgie, when you attempt to get the victim's pants over their head."

I said goodbye to Rosie and Dave the Laugh at my turn-off and he and Rosie went off together. Dave looked back at me while he walked backwards. He said, "S'later, you cheeky minx!"

I watched them as they went off. They were laughing and

then did a bit of spontaneous "Let's go down the disco" dancing.

I sort of wished we could have hung round together some more. I really laugh when I am with Dave.

Ah, well.

In my bedroom

If my brain keeps adding up the minutes till Masimo might be back, I'll go mad. I am going to keep my mind (well, what there is left of it) occupied by doing (and I never thought the day would come when I would say this) my homework.

Two minutes later

Now, here we go – *Rom and Jule*.

Two hours later

Bloody hell, Billy Shakespeare can be depressing. *Rom and Jule* is not what you would call a megalarf. Mostly it is just fighting, a bit of underage snogging, more fighting, and then some mad bint who calls herself a nurse and makes useless jokes about sex.

For the hilarious side-splitting finale, Rom and Jule pretend to commit suicide and then they actually do commit suicide.

Two minutes later
I know how they feel – it's double physics tomorrow.

Midnight
If Masimo gets back at nine p.m. that makes it 7020 minutes to wait. Or maybe if he comes back at two p.m. that makes it 6600 minutes. Is there a time difference between here and Italy? Ooooooh I can't sleep. What can I do? It's too early to start my make-up routine. Angus might lick it off in the night.

Two minutes later
I know, I will use the *German for Fools* book that I have borrowed from Ro Ro and finish translating the snogging scale for Herr Kamyer and Miss Wilson. I do it only to help them with their luuurve.

I amaze myself with my caringnosity.

Twenty-five minutes later
Ach, so here is the full-frontal *knutschen* scale.

1. *Händchen halten*
2. *Arm umlegen*

3. *Abscheidskuss* (hahahahahah, once again the lederhosen types come up trumps on the mirth-ometer)

4. *Kuss, der über drei minuten*

5. *Kuss mit geöffneten Lippen* (I don't know how Geoff got in here, but that is boys for you)

6. *Zungenkuss*

7. *Oberkörperknutschen – im Freien* (outside)

8. *Oberkörperknutschen – drinnen* (inside)

9. *Rummachen unterhalb der Taille* (*ja, oh ja!!!*)

10. *AUF GANZE GEHEN!!!*

Wednesday September 14th

Up at the crack of 7:00 a.m.

This is my plan. I set off to Stalag 14 with my uniform "customised". (My skirt turned over at the waist to shorten it, no tie and no beret.) I do my make-up and hair for max glamorosity. Do the walky walky hip hip flicky hair thing all the way to school until just by the loos in the park. By this time I am only about one hundred yards from the school gate. Then I nip into the park loos while my very besty pally Jas stands guardey dog outside. In the loos I take my make-up off, undo customised uniform, put on stupid beret etc.

Resume looking like a complete prat, then quickly walk in the middle of the Ace Gang and pass through the Gates of Hell into Stalag 14.

8:15 a.m.

Jas was sitting on her wall, chewing her fringe. If she isn't careful, she will develop furballs like cats do. Gordy was doing that choking and coughing thing last night and then he sicked up a fur ball. Disgusting really. Especially as it wasn't even the colour of his fur. I am hoping against hope it has nothing to do with licking the Prat brothers, but facts have to be faced, and he does spend an awful lot of time in their kennel with them.

They are entering a dog show soon and if I see Gordy coming to heel to Mr Next Door and wearing a little pink collar, my worst suspicions will be fulfilled. So far, Angus has not been fit enough to ride the Prat brothers around like little horsies like he did before. But when he does start again, imagine what he will do if he drops down on to Gordy's back.

When she saw me, Jas said, "Erm, you are a dead person. Hawkeye will keep you in detention for ever and you will have to write a zillion times, 'Although I look like a prozzie I

233

am merely a tart.'" And she started honking with laughter.

She calmed down a bit when I got her in a headlock. From upside down she said, "Nurk, I am just saying that—"

I let her go because I couldn't make out what she was babbling on about and her face had gone very red. She straightened her skirt.

"I am just saying, Georgia, that when Hawkeye sees you all dolled up like a tart she will not take it kindly."

"She won't see me all dolled up. I am only all dolled up in case Masimo is anywhere in the vicinity. Before we get to the school gates I am going to make myself look like the rest of you – boring and sad."

Jas said, "Well, Tom says he likes me looking natural."

I just looked at her. "Jas, you don't look natural."

She was going to get on to the having-the-hump scale, so I quickly said, "You look bloody gorgey, that's what you look, you bloody gorgey – thing. Anyway, this is my plan. I look all glam till we get to the loos near school, then if I see Masimo all is tickety-boo luuurve-wise. However, if I don't see him, I scoot into the loos and take my make-up off and turn my skirt down etc. Ditto at home time. I nip into the loos, reapply glamorosity, turning up skirt etc., etc. You and Ace Gang huddly duddly me out of the school gates just in case there are any Hitler Youth on girl-baiting duty. Then if Masimo is there waiting for me, I am a vision of whatsit. Do you see?"

She is, of course, being all grumpy about it but she will do it.

Ten minutes later

She was saying, "I read *Rom and Jule* last night – it's so beautiful, isn't it?"

I said, "No, it's weird. It's even weirder than *MacUseless*, and that was staggeringly weird."

Jas was off in Jasland though. "It was so romantic, and you know, when everyone, the nurse and all the Capulets were saying bad things about Rom, well, Jules just stuck with him. And I think there is a lesson there for us all."

I said, "Oh yes, what is it? Don't get married at thirteen to some twit in tights?"

Jas was looking all misty-eyed. "No, it means stick to what you feel, no matter what anyone else says. And that is why I have decided not to play the elastic-band game with Tom. I just love him and he can do whatever he wants. I will just love him."

Good grief. Should I start singing and banging a tambourine? Jas has turned into Baby Jesus in a beret.

Which reminds me, I have decided to audition for Mercutio. I have many literary reasons for this: mainly, he ponces around in tights for only two scenes and then is stabbed to death. Which, as a result, leaves many, many happy hours of lolling around backstage having a hoot and a laugh with my mates. And the lads.

Rom and Jule read-through and audition in the main hall 2:00 p.m.

Miss Wilson is already hysterical.

I said to Rosie, "Certain people are not cut out to be teachers of the young."

Rosie said, "Do you mean people with out-of-control bobs?"

And I said, "Yes."

She has brought it on herself. You would have thought that after the fiasco of the orange-juggling in *MacUseless* she would have learned not to be innovative. But you just can't tell some people.

This time she has suggested we might try puppetry and mime in our production. That immediately caused an outbreak of us all pretending to be Thunderbirds puppets. Oh, we laughed.

Then, when we had almost stopped and got ourselves under control, she said that in Ye Olde Days the audience was not very quiet and would shout rude jokes and stuff out at the actors.

Rosie said, "Like Romeo, Romeo, wherefore art thy PANTS, Romeo?"

And that once more introduced the old pants theme into everything that we did. Miss Wilson only has herself to blame.

Ten minutes later

Jas was being annoyingly Jasish. She has learned all Juliet's lines for the first two acts. How incomprehensibly botty-kissing is that? She has done it because she genuinely thinks that she is Juliet.

And that Tom is Romeo.

As I said to her, "We'd better say ta taa then, Jas, because you die at thirteen. Which was two years ago."

She just stropped off to be with the others who are taking the whole thing seriously.

Ten minutes later

I was being the prologue person and I was giving it my all at the front (oo-er). I said:

"Two households both alike in dignity,
In fair Verona, where we lay our scene,
From ancient grudge break to (and I couldn't resist the comedy opportunity) new nudity,
Where civil PANTS makes civil PANTS unclean."

Oh, we laughed. I thought that Rosie was going to have a spaz attack.

Miss Wilson was yelling, "Girls, girls stop this silliness. Saying pants all the time is not funny."

It is, though.

Twenty-five minutes later

Anyway, the horrific outcome is that Miss Bum-oley Kisser Jas is in fact Juliet. This is going to be unbearable for the next few weeks. She is soooo full of herself. Discussing stuff with Miss Wilson. I actually overheard her say, "Yes, perhaps a puppet dog would add to the whole Elizabethan feel of the production. It is very likely that Juliet would have had a little dog as a companion."

Perhaps a swift rotten tomato in the gob might add to the whole Elizabethan feel.

Rosie has been cast as the nurse, which I think is an act of theatrical suicide. Ellen is Tybalt and I am Mercutio – hooray!!!

Miss Wilson had to spoil things by saying, "I am casting you, Georgia, because although you have been silly this afternoon, I know you are not going to let me or the team down."

Jas went, "Humph."

She is at number three on the having-the-hump scale (head-tossing and fringe-fiddling) and we haven't even done the first read-through yet.

Although I don't know why we are bothering rehearsing the final scenes, because with Ellen dithering around with a sword as Tybalt, it is quite likely that none of us will survive longer than Act Two.

In the loos
4:00 p.m.

I've sent Jools on a little scouting mission to see if there are any signs of an Italian Luuurve God anywhere outside the school gates. My hands are trembling a LOT and I've nearly blinded myself twice with my mascara brush. Fortunately, we haven't had to prance around like ninnies doing sport today, so my hair has retained its bounceability factor.

Ten minutes later

Jools came into the loos.

"Oh my giddygod, Gee, he's here. He's on his scooter at the gates. And he's sort of brown, and well, I mean, I like Rollo but I mean, phwoooaaar is all I can say!!! Times ten."

My bottom nearly fell out of my panties. I sat on the edge of the sink. Blimey. My heart was racing.

Thank God the prefects were having a late meeting about discipline, because I know Wet Lindsay is just waiting to get me for something. She has a plan for me and I will not be liking it. But at least she is out of the way for now.

All of the Ace Gang came into the loos. I said to them, "Right, I am ready. I want you all to metaphorically hold my hand across the playground so that I do not fall over."

Jools said, "I haven't done metaphorical hand-holding. How does that go?"

I said, "You all walk across the playground and we chat and laugh like it is normal to be meeting a Luuurve God, but while you are chatting and so on, you are also mentally holding my pandie so that I do not fall over."

Jas, who has not come down to earth since she became Jule, was still going on like Mrs Owl the Dim. "When you

240

say mentally holding your hand, do you mean we hold your hand and go mental?"

"Jas, Jas, please do not make me mess up my hair by beating you to a pulp. You know very well what I mean. Just do it."

We laughed and chatted all the way, step by step. I have absolutely no idea what anyone said, least of all me. I had never felt so nervous in my life. I took a quick look up from my casual laughing and saw him sitting on the seat of his scooter, with his long legs crossed. My heart skipped a beat; he was quite literally gorgey porgey. How could he like me? It was like being in a film.

When he saw me he got up and took off his gloves. He was wearing a pale blue leather coat and his hair had grown. And he looked so – so – Pizza-a-gogoish!

Then he did a wave and shouted, "Ay, Georgia, *ciao, cara, ciao!*" and started walking towards me and the gang.

He said to them, "*Ciao, signorinas*, and here is the, how you say, the very lovely, *molto bellissima* Miss Georgia."

And he came right up close to me and lifted me off my feet and kissed me properly and quite hard on the mouth. No warmsy upsies. Just a proper snog. And he didn't even make it a short one. I was still off my feet and I hadn't closed my eyes because I was so surprised, so I had gone slightly cross-eyed. His mouth felt lovely but not very familiar to me. Then he put me down and he kissed me quickly and said, "Oh, I have waited long for this. Come on, miss." And he took my hand and led me off to the scooter.

I turned back to the Ace Gang and they all went, "Oooohhhhhhhhhhhh get you!" in a high-pitched camp tone.

One hour later

We drove off through the streets on his scooter. It felt soooo full of glamorosity. He accelerated up the High Street quite fast. We stopped at the lights and he put down the bike stand and got off his seat, leaving the engine running. We were surrounded by cars and there were people passing by. I wondered what he was doing. Should I get off? Were we parking at the lights and going for a cup of coffee? Or did he think I should have a go at driving? Even though I can't even ride a bicycle properly.

Then he took off his helmet and he said, "I must snog you more." Blimey. And he did. He bent down and pushed up my goggles and then kissed me on the mouth. How erm... interesting. It was nice but I couldn't really concentrate because everyone was looking at us. I could see some kid in the back of a car picking his nose. People were honking their horns and some lads were going, "Get in there, my son!!!"

Masimo didn't seem to notice. He even put the tip of his tongue in my mouth, which made me go a bit jelloid. Then he said loudly, "Ah, that is better. Now I can continue. Thank you," and he bowed to the people in cars and to passers-by.

He leaped back into his seat, shoved his helmet on (without fastening the strap... I could imagine what Jas would have said about that), kicked away the bike support and revved off.

We went to the woods and it was a lovely soft warm just beginning to be autumn evening. As we went into the trees we found a little babbling brook. It was quite literally making a babbling noise as it went over pebbles and rocks. If I had to talk to Masimo any time soon that is what I would be doing – babbling.

I felt incredibly nervous. And I couldn't think of anything to say.

That was because we snogged. It was groovy gravy and I felt all melty like I didn't know the difference between his mouth and mine.

Fifteen minutes later

I am still feeling incredibly nervous and I can't think of anything to say. But that is all right because we are in snog heaven. Having a snogtastic time.

Rosie was right – foreign boys do that varying pressure. Soft and then hard and then soft again.

I wonder what would happen if we both did the same thing at once? For instance, if we both did hard together and I didn't do yielding, well, would we end up with really stiff necks? Or if I yielded when he yielded, would we both fall over? Or if he went to the right and I went to the right as well and we clashed teeth, would we – oh shut up, brain.

Funny, when I snogged normally, my brain went on a mini-break to Loonland. It didn't usually enter the debating society competition on snogging techniques.

Then Masimo stopped mid-snog and just looked me straight in the eyes. He didn't say anything, just looked me in the eyes. I didn't like to blink because it seemed a bit rude, but in the end I had to look down because my eyes were beginning to water. When I looked up he was still looking me in the eyes. He is, it has to be said, gorgey porgey times twelve.

He has really long eyelashes and a proper nose. I couldn't

even see up his nostrils. And a lovely mouth, with just the suggestion of hairiness around the chinny chin area, like a sort of designer stubble. Not like a little vole lurking around like Dad has on the end of his face. And it wasn't bum fluff like Oscar has. And it wasn't prickly like when Grandad gave me "chin pie" but it was deffo hairy stuff.

And also, I think, although I didn't like to stare like a staring thing on stare tablets, there was also a bit of chest-type hair coming out of the top of his shirt.

Blimey.

It must be brilliant to be a boy and not have to worry about suppressing the orang-utan gene. To be able to just let it grow wild and free. Of course, you can take anything too far, and some of the lads who play footie in the park are quite literally chimpanzee from the shorts downwards. I don't know about the top bit, and I don't want to know about the top bit.

Thirty seconds later

Dave the Laugh is a bit hairy as well. Anyway, shut up about Dave the Laugh; he is not in this scenario.

Ten seconds later

And Dave the Laugh is not right about Masimo being a lezzie and that is *le* fact.

Then Masimo said, "*Cara*, it is how you say nippy nungas."

I looked down at my nungas. Please God I hadn't had a sudden outbreak of sticky-out nip nips. No sign of them – phew, I was OK. I looked up again and he said, "Brrrr." And put his coat round my shoulders.

I said, "Oh, you mean nippy noodles!" And I laughed, but not in a good way, in a sort of heggy heggy hog hog way. Oh good, I am starting to laugh like my mad little sister.

One minute later

As we walked back towards his scooter, the Luuurve God said, "My – erm – other girlfriend, in Italy, I would like for you to meet her."

What what?! Am I in a *ménage à trois* (or *uno menagio d trois* –io)?

Two minutes later

It turns out that Masimo is talking about his ex-girlfriend, the one I saw at the Stiff Dylans gig and the one he went out with before me. Gina. Anyway, she has met an English boy and they are going to get married! And he would like me to meet her when she comes over in a couple of weeks.

Blimey.

I hadn't done ex-girlfriend work before.

And she was getting married.

Wow.

And not like Rosie. Not a Viking marriage in twenty-five years time. But a real one. One without horns and probably not wearing a hat made out of herring.

My *How to Make Any Twit Fall in Love with You* book had better have a section on conversational hints with ex-girlfriends. You know, how to avoid past snogging chat.

I must never say, "So, what number on the snogging scale did you get up to, Gina? With my present boyfriend?" Get out of my head, past snogging scale!!!

We walked along a bit in silence holding hands. I couldn't think of anything normal to say. Then the Luuurve God said, "I am going to the Stiff Dylans' rehearsal tonight. Do you want for to come?"

Inwardly I was thinking, *Er, nothing would make me go and sit through two hours of nodding along and then going home in the equipment van and sitting on Dom's drum and falling through it.* Like I did the last time I went to a Stiff Dylans' rehearsal. Dom still stands in front of his drum kit any time I go near.

There are, it has to be said, about a million reasons why nothing will make me go to a Stiff Dylans' rehearsal. In fact, I would rather be covered in frogspawn. And slightly roasted.

But I didn't say that. I said, "Erm, no, I've got homework to do."

Masimo smiled and chucked me under the chin and said, "Aaaaah, the little girl has her homework to do."

He said it in a nice way. But I still felt a bit stupid. So no change there.

I was saved from being more of *la grande idiote* because we got on his scooter and raced through town.

It is vair vair groovy being with him; all the girls look as we go by. I did a casualosity-at-all-times just lightly holding on to one of his shoulders thing. Until we went round a corner a bit fast and I had to grab hold of his helmet.

When we got to my place Masimo got off and started giving me a big snog goodbye. I could see Mum hiding behind the curtains in the front room. How vair vair embarrassing. I went a bit red and said to Masimo, "Oh God, my mum is watching us."

He looked up and smiled towards the window and then he blew a kiss and said, "Perhaps she wants to join in."

Ohmygiddygod, how horrific is that as an idea? Now I am involved in Europorn!!!

When I went into the house I heard Mum scampering into the kitchen and as I closed the door she called out, "Georgia, is that you?"

I said, "Mum, I saw your head bobbing around like a budgie."

She came out of the kitchen and said, "He is quite categorically gorgey."

I didn't say anything. I just went up to my bedroom in a dignitosity-at-all-times way.

Midnight

Ah well, Angus is on the road to recovery – he is sleeping comfortably on my head. And as a precaution against him tumbling off and waking himself up, he has his claws lightly stuck into my scalp.

Thursday September 15th

It is vair vair hard work being the girlfriend of a Luuurve God. Constant grooming is required; the public expects it. However, as I do not wish to be flogged to within an inch of my life by the fascists (Hawkeye etc.), I have not applied any make-up. Just put on a touch of foundation, lip gloss and mascara. And a teeny white eyeliner line round the inside of my eyes to make them look gorgey and marvy and uuumph.

Stalag 14

When I got to the school gates this morning Masimo was there waiting for me with a present! Honestly! How romantico is that? *Molto molto* romantico. It was a bottle of perfume from Italy called Sorrento.

I've never been bought perfume before. Libby made me some perfume from rose petals and milk but that is not the same. Especially as Gordy drank it.

All the girls were going mental, flicking their hair and doing mad pouting around him. It felt quite groovy. I was doing my shy smiling and looking up and looking down business, with just a touch of flicky hair, nothing like the other fools around me. I thought maybe he would kiss my hand and zoom off but then he snogged me! Full-frontal snogging in front of everyone. And by everyone I mean Hawkeye.

As Masimo took off she appeared like the Bride of Dracula shouting, "Georgia Nicolson!! You are an absolute disgrace and a shame to your uniform. What kind of an example are you to the younger girls, behaving like a prostitute in front of them. What on earth will they think?"

Actually, I could have told her what they thought because as I slunk off to see Slim for part two of the ranting and raving, the Little Titches passed by and went, "Coooorrrr, miss," and winked.

As Wet Lindsay escorted me to Slim's office she said, "You appalling tart. Personally I think Masimo should get some charity award for even touching you."

Oh, I hate her. I hate her so much you could bottle it.

Slim rambled and jelloided on for three million and a half centuries. "Blah blah, terrible example... blah blah... shouldn't be canoodling with boys... plenty of time for that... in my day... no canoodling until we were eighty-five etc., etc..."

RE
9:45 a.m.

When I finally escaped with double detention I went and sat down next to Rosie and she sent me a jelly baby and a note: Did the nasty jelly lady scare you with her chins?

I wrote back: No, but she did say "canoodle".

I feel a bit sick.

Art room

OK, on the dark side I have double detention, but on the bright side I am a bit perked up because I am wearing my new Italian perfume given to me by my groovy gravy boyfriend. And I am among my besties, the Ace Gang, doing an art project on the camping fiasco. Instead of proper lessons. What larks!!!

Miss Wilson is beside herself with excitement again. This has been a big week for her creativitosity-wise. First her puppet version of *Rom and Jule* and now the camping-fiasco project. Her bob is practically dancing the tango.

Jas is also vair vair excited. And she is walking funny. Sort of floating along and shaking her hair about. Why?

Thirty seconds later

Oh, I know what she is doing, she is walking in what she fondly imagines is an Elizabethan way. But actually looks like someone with the terminal droop.

She has brought in her collection of newt drawings and some jamjars of frogspawn.

I said to her, "Jas, that is not frogspawn, it is clearly a bit of snot in a jamjar." She didn't even bother to reply.

I am making a hat out of leaves.

Rosie said, "What is that?"

I said, "It is a hat made of leaves and so on. It is a triumphant celebration of the great outdoors."

Rosie said, "No, it is not. It is some old leaves and it is WUBBISH."

Yes, well, that is as maybe, but it is better than her "natural orchestra" which is essentially a bit of rice in some tins and a couple of spoons.

Herr Kamyer popped by and Miss Wilson went into a spectacular ditherama at the sight of her "*traum*boy."

I must tell her about the snogging scale in German so that she is ready, should Herr Kamyer leap on her for a spot of number three – *abscheidskuss.*

Five minutes later

Jas was actually humming "The hills are alive with the sound of pants" as she arranged her jamjars.

I said to her, "Jas, do you know what 'snot' is in German? It is '*schnodder*'. Comedy gold, isn't it, the German language?"

She said, "Shhh."

I said, "Do you know what shhhh is in lederhosen talk?"

But she started humming even louder.

Two minutes later

In a spontaneous outburst of madnosity Rosie has joined in with Jas's humming and started singing, "The hills are alive with the sound of pants", accompanying herself on rice tin and spoons. She was singing, "The hills are alive with the sound of pants, with pants I have worn for a thousand years!!!"

It was very infectious. I started improvising a woodland wonderland dance which involved a lot of high kicking and leaf work.

We were yelling, "I go to the PANTS when my heart is lonely—" when Herr Kamyer put his foot down with a firm hand.

He shouted, "Girls, girls, ve will not continue ze project if this kafuffle goes on!! Vat is the big funniness *mit* pants?"

We stopped eventually but I said under my breath, "*Kackmist.*" Which means buggeration. Oh, what a hoot and a half.

4:20 p.m.

Oh goddygodgod, how boring is detention. Miss Stamp was my guard. I am sure she was grooming her moustache as I wrote out, "A predilection for superficiality leads remorselessly towards an altercation with authority."

A million times (ish).

But I have my German book on my knee. Tee hee.

Canoodling is *rummachen*. Absolute top comedy magic.

5:30 p.m.

Freedom, freedom!!!

I skipped out of the school gates, and carried on doing a bit of ad hoc skipping down the hill past the park.

Which is when Dave the Laugh emerged from the park loos!! *Caramba!* I stopped skipping but it was too late. He said, "Excellent independent nunga-nunga work, Georgia."

He had just been playing footie and was a bit sweaty. His hair was all damp. I quite liked it. He's got a nice smell.

He walked along with me and said, "What have you been up to?"

I didn't mention exactly why I had been kept behind. Well, actually, I lied. I said that I had been given detention because I had done an improvised dance to "The hills are alive with the sound of pants".

He said, "Top work."

I felt a bit bad about lying, but on the other hand I didn't want to say that I had been punished for snogging Masimo at the school gates.

Four minutes later

Dave does make me laugh. I told him about the German snogging scale and he was nodding and going, "*Oh ja, oh ja!!! Ich liebe der* full-frontal *knutschen. Ich bin der vati!*"

Then he said, "You don't fancy a spot of *rummachen unterhalb der taille*, do you? Just for old times' sake?"

I said, "Dave, how dare you speak to me like that."

And he said, "You know you love it, you cheeky *fräulein*."

I just walked quickly off. I have my pridenosity.

He caught me up and said, "Stop trying to get off with me."

I was amazed. "Er, Dave, I think you will find that it was you who asked to *rummachen*."

"No, it wasn't."

"Er, yes, it was, Dave."

"No, you thrust yourself at me. Because you cannot resist me. It is sad."

I stopped and looked at him. "Dave, I can resist you. I have an Italian Luuurve God as a boyfriend."

Dave said, "Oh, he is so clearly gay."

"Dave, he is not gay."

"He has a light blue leather coat."

"That does not make him gay; it makes him Italian."

Dave said, "I rest my case."

I looked at him. And then he just bent down and looked at me. He has lovely lips and I sort of forgot where I was for a minute. I felt my lips puckering up and... then he pushed me away from him so that I nearly fell over.

He said, "Look, Georgia, stop it, try and control yourself, you are making a fool of yourself."

I was speechless. What, what??? I didn't know what to do I was so amazed, so I shoved him quite hard. He looked at me. And then he shoved me quite hard back, and I fell over. I got up and went and shoved him again.

He said, "Look, leave me alone. Your girlfriend will be really cross and get his matching leather handbag out."

He is sooo annoying. I was just marching over to shove him again when Masimo whizzed up on his scooter.

Dave waved at him and as he went off he said, "Oooh, she doesn't look very pleased."

And in fact he was right. Masimo did look a bit cross. He smiled when I came over though and said, "*Ciao...* you are fighting with Dave?"

I said, "Erm... no, it was just that, er, he was showing me how he, er, scored a goal. And he was saying that he and his girlfriend, Emma, are coming to the Stiff Dylans gig."

Masimo looked a bit confused but then he said, "Come, I will take you for a coffee."

Coffee bar

I feel like a prat and a fool. I have just dashed to the loos to put make-up on. Funny I didn't remember I hadn't got any on when I was with Dave. So I've done the lippy mascara thing, but there is not much I can do about my uniform. I hope I don't see anyone I know.

one hour later
I tried to explain the German snogging-scale thing to Masimo and he laughed, but I don't think he really gets it.

At home in bed
Oh God, it was like twenty questions when I got home. Where have you been? Blah blah blah, school finishes at four p.m., it's now eight p.m. That's four hours gap.

I made the mistake of saying to Dad, "Dad, I am not a child.'

Then he rambled on saying stuff like, "No, you can say that again, you are not a child, you are a spawn of the Devil." etc., etc.

In my bedroom
10:30 p.m.
I tell you this: I'm not the only spawn of the Devil in my family. Some complete fool (my dad) has bought my sister (also known as the littlest spawn of the devil) a "hilarious" fishing souvenir.

It is a stuffed fish on a stand and when you press a button it starts squiggling around doing a trout dance and singing, "Maybe it's beCOD I'm a Londoner" over and over again.

10:50 p.m.
Libby lobes it. It is her new besty. And new besties always sleep in my bed.

10:52 p.m.
Bibbs is fast asleep but I'm not because I have fins sticking up my nostrils.

11:00 p.m.
Also, why has she still got her wellies on?

11:05 p.m.
Oh god, now Angus has come into my room and is trying to get on to the bed.

11:12 p.m.
I'm going to have to get out of bed and haul him in. He's already crashed into the dressing table twice and is now in the

wastepaper basket. I'll be glad when his tail is back to normal.

11:20 p.m.

So, here we all are then, tucked up together: Libby, Mr Fish, Angus, a jar of potted fish (Libby's snacks for Mr Fish) and me, hanging on to half an inch of bed.

11:28 p.m.

But I'm happy. I have a Luuurve God as a boyfriend!!! Yes, yes and thrice yes! Or *sì*, *sì* and thrice-io *sì*, as I must learn to say.

11:30 p.m.

Wait till I tell the Luuurve God about the Mr Fish episode tomorrow when he picks me up at Stalag 14. I bet he will laugh like the proverbial drain-io.

11:35 p.m.

Perhaps I will save the Mr Fish story because he didn't exactly fall about when I told him about the German snogging scale.

11:40 p.m.

Dave the Laugh did though. He thought it was a hoot and a half.

11:45 p.m.

How dare he insinuate I am a cheeky *fräulein*? If anyone's a cheeky *fräulein*, he is. And he said that I was thrusting myself after him, but it was him who asked to *rummachen*. Anyway, shut up, brain. I'm not thinking about Dave the so-called Laugh.

Midnight

I think Masimo is a bit jealous of Dave. Tee hee. I'm a boy-entrancing vixen.

12:30 a.m.

Oh, dear God, I've accidentally set Mr Fish off. How disgusting to have it writhing around in bed and singing. I will never sleep at this rate. It's like Piccadilly Cir...
zzzzzzzzzzzzz.

Friday September 16th

I woke up laughing about Dave the Laugh asking if he could *rummachen unterhalb* my *taille*. Tee hee.

Not that I want him to.

The puckering up thing was just a knee-jerk reaction. Like if you think of lemons, your mouth waters. So if someone looks like they are going to kiss you, you pucker up.

It is just biological.

Nothing to worry about.

4:10 p.m.

I cannot believe this!

Wet Lindsay came up to me as I was coming out of the loos. The Ace Gang had gone on ahead because I am meeting Masimo at the school gates. She said, "Go and get your hockey kit; you have volunteered for extra practice. Miss Stamp's thrilled with you."

I said, "I think you will find that actually I haven't volunteered and that I am going off to meet my boyfriend. Do you know him? He is a Luuurve God."

She stood in front of me. "If you know what's good for you, you will get changed and get out there on that pitch."

Merde. I would just do a runner but she would only report me and then I would have to go to the elephant house (Slim's office) and be beaten to death by chins again.

I slumped off behind her.

She hasn't even got a bottom.

We passed Miss Stamp in the corridor and she said, "I am really very impressed with you, Georgia, and it is very kind of you, Lindsay, to encourage the younger girls. I will be mentioning it to the headmistress. It is a nice change to see you out of the detention room, Georgia. Keep it up."

Buggeration.

She went off into her office.

Lindsay looked at me and gave me a very scary "smile". How can Robbie snog her? It must be like snogging a cross between an octopus and a praying mantis. Erlack.

Ten minutes later

Lindsay is making me run round the hockey pitch.

She said, "Let this just be a little lesson to you, Nicolson, about how bad life can be if you cross me. Run round the pitch four times and then you can go. I'll be watching you."

I said, "Masimo will be waiting for me."

She said, "Well, you had better run like the wind, hadn't you?" And she went off into the changing rooms. I could see her looking at me through the window.

Twenty minutes later

Dear *gott in Himmel* I am shattered. I haven't got my special sports nunga-nunga holder and it is very tiring having them bouncing about. I finished the four laps and then I limped across to the changing rooms. I was so hot. I'd have a very quick shower, apply lippy etc. and then dash out to my boyfriend.

Thirty seconds later

The door was locked!

Five minutes later

I can't believe this. It's Mr Attwood's night off and no one else has a key.

I bet it's not his night off. I bet he is doing this on purpose. He is probably lurking around somewhere laughing.

Also, where is Wet Lindsay?

In the end I had to give up on getting my clothes. I will have to go home in my trackies with a massive red head. I wonder what Masimo is thinking. I wonder if he is still there? In a way I hope he isn't because I know what he will be thinking if he sees my head. He'll be thinking: *If I wanted a tomato for a girlfriend, I would have asked for one.*

As I came out of the school building I saw Wet Lindsay getting on the back of Masimo's scooter and taking off!!

What a spectacular cow and a half she is. She'd done this on purpose. She said she would get me and she has.

There is only one reasonable solution to this.

I will have to kill her and eat the evidence.

Walking home redly

My knickers are sticking to my botty. This is quite literally a PANTS situation.

Two minutes later

As soon as I get in I am going to plunge my head into a bucket of cold water.

One minute later

Although with my luck I will get my head stuck in the bucket at which point Masimo will turn up on his scooter and dump me.

Home

When I walked into the kitchen Dave the Laugh was there, balancing something on Libby's nose. What? What fresh hell?

He looked up as I came in and said, "Blimey, you're red."

I tried to walk across the kitchen doing that hip hip flicky flick thing to distract attention from my head, but unfortunately my botty hurt so much from running I couldn't keep it up.

I turned my back to him and got a drink of water. I said, "What are you doing here?"

He said, "I just brought round the kitty treats for Angus, but Libby has eaten most of them. Still, it's the thought that counts."

I turned back to him and he looked at me. "You are quite sensationally red."

I went off into the bathroom.

He was not wrong. I looked like my head had turned into a lurking lurker.

Five minutes later

I quickly plunged my head into icy water and towel dried my hair into what I hoped was a tousled yet somehow strangely attractive style (that is what I hoped). Quick bit of lippy and mascara. I didn't want to be in the tarts' wardrobe too long in case Dave the Laugh decided to go. I expected he had come round to apologise for his awful behaviour *vis à vis* the *rummachen* incident.

Back in the kitchen
Two minutes later
I said to Dave, who was now having his hair plaited by Libby, "I suppose you have come to apologise for the *rummachen* fiasco."

And he said, "*Nein.*" Which made me laugh. He started to say, "Look, Georgia, I wanted to say that—"

At which point Mum came mumming in, talking rubbish.

She was adjusting her basoomas and flicking her hair. Surely she didn't think that Dave fancies the "more mature" lady??

She said, "Dave do you want to stay for tea? It's cool if you want to hang out for a bit."

It's cool if you want to hang out for a bit? What is she talking like a complete fool for? Oh, hang on, I think I know the answer to that one.

Dave said, "No, I'm afraid I'm away laughing on a fast camel. People to see, old people to rob, that sort of thing." And he got up to go.

Libby clung to his neck as he got up, like a toddler limpet –

just hanging round his neck. He started walking off as if he hadn't noticed he had a toddler necklace and Libby was laughing and laughing. She said, "I lobe my Daveeeeeeeeeeeeeeeeee."

Blimey, she's joined the Dave the Laugh fan club as well.

I walked Dave to the gate, trying to get Libby to let go.

As I was pulling her off Masimo turned up on his scooter. He took his helmet off and sat on the seat, looking at us. Maybe he was mesmerised by my head. It still felt vair hot. I tried to do a bit of flicky hair but it was mostly sticking to my scalp.

Dave said, "*Ciao*, Masimo."

And Masimo said, "*Ciao*, mate."

But I am not entirely sure he meant the "mate" bit.

Dave scarpered off quite quickly and Libby started burrowing through Mr Next Door's hedge. She likes to go and sit in the kennel with the Prat Poodles and Gordy. But I can't worry about that sort of thing now.

Masimo looked a bit upset and he said, "Why did you not for me wait?"

I babbled on, "Well, Wet Lindsay said I had to do extra hockey, so I had to run like a loon on loon tablets round and round, like a hamster with trackie bums on, and then I was locked out, and I saw you driving off with her on the back."

♡ 269

Masimo said, "Aaaah. She said you had gone home and could I give her a lift."

Unbelievable!!! What a prize tart she is!!

Masimo was smiling a bit now. He really was gorgey porgey. He said, "And Dave, he came here, for you to have another fight?"

I laughed. "No, he came to bring some kitty treats for Angus but Libby ate them."

Masimo held out his arms. "Come here, miss."

I went over to him and he said, "You are very, erm, slippery."

Actually, he was right. If he squeezed me too hard I might shoot out of his hands like a wet bar of soap.

Then he kissed me. Which was fab and marvy and also number four, with a touch of virtual number five.

And that is when Dad came roaring up in his loonmobile.

I stopped kissing Masimo and leaped away from him like he had the Black Death. I said to the Luurve God; "Quickly, save yourself, my father is here. You must go now while you can, otherwise he may show you his leather trousers."

But it was too late. Vati had got out of his "car" and was bearding towards us. Oh how embarrassing. He was going to say something. I knew he was. Even though I have told him he must never address me in front of people.

He said, "Evening all. It's Masimo, isn't it? Are you coming in?"

Oh nooooooo.

I said, "No, Masimo has to go. He is rehearsing."

Masimo looked at me and I opened my eyes really wide and said, "Aren't you?"

He got it and said, "Ah, yes, *ciao*, Mr Nicolson. *Grazie*, but I must now to go. The Stiff Dylans are playing this weekend."

Dad said, "Oh well, maybe I will pop by to hear some tunes, come along and show you a few of my moves on the dance floor."

Has he snapped?

Masimo revved up his scooter. He leaned over and kissed me and said, "I will see you Saturday. I am, how you say, missing you already."

I tried to walk off in a dignity-at-all-times sort of way, but as we got to the house Dad yelled to Mum, "Georgia has been snogging an Italian stallion."

How disgusting!

I feel dirty and besmirched.

And also *kackmist*.

In bed

I wonder what Dave the Laugh was going to say to me? He does make me laugh. It was vair amusing, him sitting there having his hair plaited by Libby.

Anyway, I will ask him what he was going to say when I see him at the gig.

One minute later

If I get the chance. I expect he will be with his girlfriend.

Which is good.

And fine.

Two minutes later

I know that Emma is nice and everything but she did have a ludicrous spaz attack when Angus accidentally spat at her. Which is a bit weedy.

Anyway, I have vair many other important things to worry about. If Dave the Laugh wants to go out with a weed, that is his right. But the burning question is this: what in the name of Richard the Lionheart's codpiece am I going to wear for the gig?

Five minutes later

All the girls will be looking at me because a) I am officially going out with a Luuurve God and b) I am a multi-talented backing dancer and jolly good egg.

Fisticuffs at dawn

Saturday September 17th
8:30 a.m.

Preparations begin to become the girlfriend of a Luuurve God.

And possibly backing dancer.

So first on my list is cleanse and tone.

Done.

Face mask.

Done.

Cucumber eye patches.

Done.

Plucking.

Yessiree Bob.

Puckering exercises.

Done.

Lunch

Two jam sandwiches for max energy and nutrition.

Ellen was eating fruit gums in maths on Friday and Hawkeye asked her why, and Ellen said, "It is my breakfast." Hawkeye nearly had a complete ditherspaz and f.t. combined.

She said, "Where is the nutrition in that?"

And Ellen said, "Well, because of the, you know, erm... fruit or something."

3:00 p.m.

Charming conversation practice.

Done.

(Note to loon brain headquarters: do not mention hilarious pants jokes, full-frontal *knutschen*, glove animal or horns.)

6:00 p.m.

I think I look quite fab and groovy. That is what I think. Hair bouncing around, nungas more or less under control. And

I've got new special lash enhancing mascara on so my lashes are about two foot long. Of course I will never ever be able to get it off again but in the meantime I have max boy entranceability.

6:30 p.m.
If I can't get the mascara off by Monday it will give Wet Lindsay an excuse to attack me with a blow torch or put me on gardening duty with Elvis for the rest of my life.

She's bound to be there tonight. Poncing around like a ninny.

If I get a chance to warn Robbie about her I will. I must be cunning and full of subtlenosity.

Clearly, I would rather just rip her stupid octopussy head off to save time. But there is bound to be some busybody goodie-goodie who would complain to the RSPCA about it.

Leaving Home
7:15p.m.
Dad and Uncle Eddie were tinkering with the Robinmobile as I went off. They are both wearing T-shirts with a picture of Uncle Eddie in his baldy-o-gram costume on the front of them. And underneath the picture it says, "He dares to

276

baldly go where no other man has baldly gone before."

Good grief.

At the Honey Club
8:30 p.m.

Quick check in the tarts' wardrobe.

Looking in the mirror. Hmmmm. Helloooooo, Sex Kitty. Grrrrrr.

A quick splosh of my perfume from Italy that my Italian boyfriend brought me from Italy, which is to the right on the map from Merrie Olde England. Possibly. And then my public is ready for me.

Out in the club by the bar

Sven and Rosie have excelled themselves. Their theme tonight is fur, fur with just a hint of fur. Did you know you could get matching fake-fur jumpsuits? In purple? Well, you do now.

I am a bit nervy actually. This is like my first official outing as the official girlfriend of a Luuurve God. Still, I have my Ace Gang to keep me company.

Ten minutes later

Blimey, I am goosegog girl because all the rest of the gang are with their "boyfriends". Even Ellen. Although she might be the last to know – or something.

Rom and Jule (otherwise known as Jas'n'Tom) are all over each other like a rash. It is quite sweet really. If you like that sort of thing.

No sign of Dave the Laugh and his girlfriend. Which is cool. They have probably gone out somewhere different. How should I know?

They might be round at Emma's.

You know. Messing about and so on.

I seem to want to go to the piddly-diddly department again.

In the tarts' wardrobe

Oh marvellous, Wet Lindsay and Astonishingly Dim Monica are in front of the mirrors. I don't know why they are bothering. Lindsay would need a head transplant to make her look less like Octopussy Girl.

One thing for sure, I am not going into a cubicle and doing a piddly diddly while they are looking at me.

Back in the club

I said to Rosie, when she was on a snog break, "I wonder where Masimo is?"

She said, "Why don't you go backstage in your capacity as girlfriend and say to him, 'I just came to say break a leg,' or whatever you say to rock stars? Maybe it's 'break a string' or 'break your trousers'. I don't know, but just go say it."

And then I saw the Stiff Dylans come in with their guitars. They must be due on soon. As soon as they appeared they were surrounded by girls. Or "tarts" as some people might call them.

Two minutes later

The Stiff Dylans are signing autographs. Honestly! Actually signing autographs. I can see the Luuurve God. He is there signing as well. And smiling and chatting to the girls. I wonder if I should go out and get my coat and then come back in again like I have just arrived? I could sneak out and— Then he looked up and saw me. He waved and started coming over. Hurrah!

Blimey. He has an amazingly cool suit on. I bet it is from Pizza-a-gogo land. When he reached me he put his arms around me and kissed me. Everyone was looking. I felt a bit red actually. I haven't done much public snogging. He didn't even seem to notice the crowd around us. He was just looking in my eyes and he said, *"Ciao, cara,* I will see you at the break, and then after the gig we go maybe to somewhere we can be together?"

Blimey O'Reilly's trousers, it's a bit early to get swoony knickers but I have got them on.

one hour later

The whole place is rocking. The Stiff Dylans have played a cracking set and Robbie has just gone on stage to join them. He is doing sharesies vocals with Masimo on "Don't wake me up before you go. Just go." I wonder if Robbie wrote that for Octopussy Girl?

I would.

She is standing looking at him right at the front of the stage. I said to Jas, "How uncool is that?"

She was too busy smooching with Hunky to bother to reply.

Lindsay has given me the evils since I got here but I am not at school now, and also I am with my mates. And also I am the girlfriend of a Luuurve God.

Which is a bit weird actually. Loads of girls that I don't even know have been coming up to me and saying, "Oooh, isn't he gorgey, what is it like going out with him? What kind of music does he like? What is his birth sign?" etc.

What am I? His press secretary?

I didn't mention to them that I am in fact a backing dancer.

Half an hour later

This is more like it. The Ace Gang rides again!! We are doing a shortened version of the Viking disco hornpipe to "Ultraviolet" by the Dylans. We haven't got any props so we are having to improvise the paddles and so on. It is a hoot and a half.

I waved my (pretend) paddle at Masimo, but he didn't wave back. I suppose it's a bit difficult when you are playing a guitar. He looked at me though. I like to think in an admiring way.

Two minutes later

Another fast one by the Dylans. Everyone is going mental.

And Dave the Laugh is here!!! I only saw him when he came up to me and said, "Let's twist!!" And he started doing this mad fast twisting thing, going down to the floor and then up again. Quite sensationally insane, but funny. He was yelling at me, "Come on, Kittykat. Get down!!!"

I said, "Not in a million years. Get your girlfriend to make *le idiot* of herself."

He shouted, "She's not here. You can be substitute idiot!! Come on, you know you want to!!!"

Sven and Rosie and the whole gang joined in. So in the end so did I. It was the best fun!

Ten minutes later

I am hotter than a hot person on hot tablets. And that is hot, believe me. The Dylans are just going off for a break and Dave the Laugh has gone to get us some drinks.

Two minutes later

I was so full of exhaustiosity that I sat on Ro Ro's knee. She was sitting on Sven's knee so it was like a knee sandwich.

I said to her, "You have a vair comfy knee, little matey."

And she said, "Are you on the turn?"

I was just about to hit her when Masimo came up to me and said, "Georgia, come outside with me."

Rosie said, "Oo-er."

And just at that moment Dave came back with the drinks. He handed me a glass and went, "Yeah, groove on! Nice set, mate."

Masimo smiled, but not a lot, and then he said. "You are enjoying dancing with my girlfriend... mate?"

Dave said, "Oh blimey, this is not fisticuffs at dawn, is it?"

Masimo looked a bit puzzled. He said, "What is this fisticuffs?"

Dave put his drink down on the table and started prancing around doing his impression of Mohammed Ali crossed with a fool. He was yelling, "I am sooo pretty, I float like a butterfly. Duff duff. Put em up, put em up."

He is, it has to be said, bonkers.

I was laughing. We were all laughing. Except Masimo. He said to Dave, "Oh, I see. OK. We can do it this way. I will see you outside. Mate."

Dave said, "I'm afraid I am not a homosexualist."

But Masimo handed his jacket to me and started walking towards the door.

Surely he was joking.

Dave looked at me and shrugged. And then he went outside as well. Blimey.

Jas said to me, "I told you that your big red bottom would get you in trouble and now... you see."

What what???

I'd just been doing the twist, Masimo didn't even know about the accidental nearly number five in the woods scenario. I followed them both as they went out of the doors.

In fact most of the people in the club followed us outside.

Outside

Masimo said to Dave, "OK, now we sort this out, man to man."

Were they actually going to fight over me?

I should have liked it. But...

Rosie said to me, "This is just like Rom and Jule, isn't it? If they were wearing tights. Should we lend them some?"

I said, "Look, look, lads, this is silly. Why don't you just..."

Masimo was still looking at Dave and he put up both hands like they do in movies and started circling Dave, saying, "Come on."

Jas said, "Georgia, say something! Do something normal and sensible for once."

Yes, yes, that is what I must do – display maturiosity.

I stepped into the middle of them both and yelled, "STOP!!! STOP... IN THE NAME... OF PANTS!!!"

Masimo just looked at me. But Dave the Laugh started falling about laughing. And Rosie started singing, "The hills are alive with the sound of PANTS! With PANTS I have worn for a thousand years!" And then the Ace Gang joined in.

Two minutes later

Everyone was drifting off now that there was no chance of a fisticuffs extravaganza.

Dave was still laughing. He turned to Masimo and held out his hand and said, "It's just a little joke, mate, nothing to get your handbag out for." Then he said, "Night night, Gee," and went off.

I smiled at Masimo, but he didn't smile back. He looked at me and he looked really sad.

Donner *und* Blitzen.

And also *pipi*.

And *krappe*.

I started to go over to him and he turned away from me and walked off into the night.

Two minutes later

My Luuurve God has got the hump.

In fact he has just quite literally had the full Humpty Dumpty.

But maybe it will just be an overnight hump and in the morning all will be well again.

I wouldn't mind, but I've only been the girlfriend of a Luuurve God for about a month.

And I haven't seen him for most of that time.

Has he really dumped me?

One minute later

Just because I did the twist with Dave the Laugh.

And had a German fight with him.

And accidentally snogged him in the Forest of Redbottomosity.

Which the Luuurve God doesn't know about anyway.

Two minutes later

Oh marvellous, I am once more on the rack of love with no cakes.

All aloney on my owney.

Again.

PANTS.

Georgia's Backing Dancer Portfolio

In case you haven't noticed, me and the Ace Gang (and when I say me and the Ace Gang, I really mean me) have created some of the grooviest dance moves ever invented. I have always found that a quick burst of disco inferno dancing is a fab way to get rid of tensionosity and frustrated snoggosity. So, because I love you all so much – and also because, like me, you may be considering a career as a backing dancer – I have made a portfolio of my favourite moves. Starting with dances from the early days.

The Simple Years
"Let's go down the disco"

This was really an ad hoc dance fandango. The main thrust and nub was that when a so-called teacher turned their back to illustrate something on the board, we all leaped up and did a brief burst of disco dancing, then sat down before we got multiple detention.

The Middle Years

1. The Viking bison disco inferno

We're still practising this for Rosie's forthcoming (i.e. in eighteen years time) Viking wedding. It is danced to the tune of *Jingle Bells* because even Rosie, world authority on Sven land doesn't know any Viking songs. Apart from *Rudolph the Red-nosed Reindeer*. Which isn't one.

For this dance you need some bison horns. If you can't find any bison shops nearby, make your own horns from an old hairband and a couple of twigs or something. Oh, I don't know, stop hassling me, I'm tired. It goes...

Stamp, stamp to the left,
Left leg kick, kick,
Arm up,
Stab, stab to the left (that's the pillaging bit),
Stamp, stamp to the right,
Right leg kick, kick,
Arm up,
Stab, stab to the right,
Quick twirl round with both hands raised to Thor (whatever),

Raise your (pretend) drinking horn to the left,
Drinking horn to the right,
Horn to the sky,
All over body shake,
Huddly duddly,
And fall to knees with a triumphant shout of
"HORRRRNNNNN!!!!"

p.s. In a rare moment of comic genius, Jas, who is clearly in touch with her inner bison, added this bit too. It's a sort of sniffing-the-air type move. Like a Viking bison might do. If it was trying to find its prey. And if there was such a thing as a Viking bison.

Stab, stab to the left,
And then sniff sniff.

Hahahahahaha!

2. The snot disco inferno

For this dance you will need a big blob of bubble gum hanging off your nose like a huge bogey. It needs to dangle about so you can swing it round and round in time to the music. Dance this to your favourite TV show theme tune. It goes...

Swing your snot to the left,
Swing to the right,
Full turn,
Shoulder shrug,
Nod to the front,
Dangle dangle,
Hands on shoulders,
Kick, kick to the right,
Dangle dangle,
Kick, kick to the left,
Dangle dangle,
Full snot around,
And shimmy to the ground.

Yes, yes and thrice yes!

The Maturiosity Years
The Viking disco hornpipe
And finally, the piece of resistance and cream of the cream –

the Viking disco hornpipe extravaganza!!! For this you need bison horns, mittens, ear muffs and paddles. Do remember muffs are worn *over* horns, not horns over muffs. You will feel like a fool and a twerp if you muff it up. Danced to the tune of *EastEnders*, it goes...

The music starts with a Viking salute. Both paddles are pointed at the horns.
Then a cry of "Thor!!!" and a jump turn to the right.
Paddle, paddle, paddle, paddle to the right,
Paddle, paddle, paddle, paddle to the left.
Cry of "Thor!!!" Jump turn to the left.
Paddle, paddle, paddle, paddle to the left,
Paddle, paddle, paddle, paddle to the right.
Jump to face the front (grim Viking expression).
Quick paddle right, quick paddle left x 4.
Turn to partner.
Cross paddles with partner x 2.
Face front and high hornpipe skipping x 8 (gay Viking smiling).
Then (and this is the complicated bit) interweaving paddling!
Paddle in and out of each other up and down the line, meanwhile gazing out to the left and to the right

(concerned expression - this is the looking-for-land bit).
Paddle back to original position.
On-the-spot paddling till all are in line and then close eyes (for night-time rowing effect).
Right and left paddling x2 and then open eyes wide.
Shout "Land Ahoyyyyy!"
Fall to knees and throw paddles in the air (behind, not in front, in case of crowd injury).

Excellent in every way!

For more marvy extra stuff from moi, visit

www.georgianicolson.com

- ♧ join the Ace Gang
- ♡ download gorgey stuff
- ♧ win fabbity-fab prizes
- ♡ sign up for monthly G-mails from Georgia
- ♧ post photos of your bestest pallies on the gallery
- ♡ chat to chums on message boards
- ♧ and much, much more!

The Having-the-Hump Scale

1. ignorez-vousing

2. sniffing *(in an I-told-you-so way)*

3. head-tossing and fringe-fiddling

4. cold-shoulderosity work

5. Midget Gems all round, but not for you

6. pretendy deafnosity

7. walking on ahead

8. the quarter humpty *(evils)*

9. the half humpty *(evils and withdrawal of all snacks)*

10. the full Humpty Dumpty *(walking away, leaving behind that slight feeling that you have been dumped)*

The New and Improved Snogging Scale

1/2. sticky eyes (*Be careful using this. I've still got some complete twit following me around like a seeing-eye dog.*)

1. holding hands

2. arm around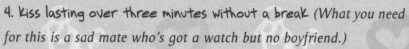

3. goodnight kiss

4. kiss lasting over three minutes without a break (*What you need for this is a sad mate who's got a watch but no boyfriend.*)

4 1/2. hand snogging (*I really don't want to go into this. Ask Jas.*)

5. open mouth kissing

6. tongues

6 1/2. ear snogging

6 3/4. neck nuzzling

7. upper body fondling - outdoors

8. upper body fondling - indoors

Virtual number 8. (*When your upper body is not actually being fondled in reality, but you know that it is in your snoggees head.*)

9. below waist activity (*or bwa. Apparently this can include flashing your pants. Don't blame me. Ask Jools.*)

10. the full monty (*Jas and I were in the room when Dad was watching the news and the newscaster said, "Tonight the Prime Minister has reached Number 10." And Jas and I had a laughing spaz to end all laughing spazzes.*)

Georgia's Glossary

arvie · Afternoon. From the Latin "arvo". Possibly. As in the famous Latin invitation: "Lettus meetus this arvo."

billio · From the Australian outback. A billycan was something Aborigines boiled their goolies up in, or whatever it is they eat. Anyway, billio means boiling things up. Therefore, "my cheeks ached like billio" means – er – very achy. I don't know why we say it. It's a mystery, like many things. But that's the beauty of life.

Black Death · Ah well... this is historiosity at its best. In Merrie England, everyone was having a fab time, dancing about with bells on (also known as Maurice dancing), then some ships arrived in London, full of new stuff – tobacco, sugar, chocolate, etc., yum yum. However, as in all tales in history, it ended badly, because also lurking about on the ships were rats from Europe – not human ones. And they had fleas on them that carried the plague. The fleas bit the people of Merrie England, and they got covered in pustulating boils and died. A LOT. As I have said many many times, history is crap.

Blimey O'Reilly · (as in "Blimey O'Reilly's trousers") This is an Irish expression of disbelief and shock. Maybe Blimey O'Reilly was a famous Irish bloke who had extravagantly big trousers. We may never know the truth. The fact is, whoever he is, what you need to know is that a) it's Irish and b) it is Irish. I rest my case.

blodge · Biology. Like geoggers – geography, or Froggie – French.

Boboland · As I have explained many, many times English is a lovely and exciting language full of sophisticosity. To go to sleep is "to go to bobos", so if you go to bed you are going to Boboland. It is an Elizabethan expression... Oh, OK then, Libby made it up and she can be unreasonably violent if you don't join in with her.

brillopads · A brillopad is a sort of wire pad that you clean pans and stuff with (If you do housework, which I sincerely suggest you don't. I got ironer's elbow from being made to iron my vati's huge undercrackers.) Where was I? Oh yes. When you say "It was brillopads" you don't mean "It was a sort of wire pad that you clean with", you mean "It was fab and groovy." Do you see? Goodnight.

bum-oley · Quite literally "bottom hole". I'm sorry but you did ask. Say it proudly (with a cheery smile and a Spanish accent).

chuddie · Chewing gum. This is an "i" word thing. We have a lot of them in English due to our very busy lives, explaining stuff to other people not so fortunate as ourselves.

clown car · Officially called a Reliant Robin three-wheeler, but clearly a car built for clowns by some absolute loser called Robin. The Reliant bit comes from being able to rely on Robin being a prat. I wouldn't be surprised if Robin also invented nostril-hair cutters.

clud · This is short for cloud. Lots of really long boring poems and so on can be made much snappier by abbreviating words. So Wordworth's poem called "Daffodils" (or "Daffs") has the immortal line "I wandered lonely as a clud". Ditto *Rom and Jule*. Or *Ham*. Or *Merc of Ven*.

double cool with knobs · "Double" and "with knobs" are instead of saying very or very, very, very, very. You'd feel silly saying, "He was very, very, very, very, very cool." Also everyone would have fallen asleep before you had finished your sentence. So "double cool with knobs" is altogether snappier.

Eccles cake · A culinary delight from the north of England. Essentially they look like little packets of dead flies, yum yum. Lots of yummy things come from the north of England: cow heel and tripe (a cow's stomach lining with vinegar). And most delicious of all, cow's nip nip (yes I am serious). What you have to remember is that the northern folk are descended from Vikings and, frankly, when you have been rowing a boat for about three months, you will eat anything.

fandango · A fandango is a complicated Spanish dance. So a fandango is a complicated thing. Yes, I know there is no dancing involved. Or Spanish.

full-frontal snogging · Kissing with all the trimmings – lip to lip, open mouth, tongues... everything (apart from dribble, which is never acceptable).

f.t. · I refer you to the famous "losing it" scale:
1. minor tizz

2. complete tizz and to-do
3. strop
4. a visit to Stop Central
5. f.t. (funny turn)
6. spaz attack
7. complete ditherspaz
8. nervy b. (nervous breakdown)
9. complete nervy b.
10. ballisiticisimus

gadzooks · An expression of surprise. Like for instance, "Cor, love a duck!" Which doesn't mean you love ducks or want to marry one. For the swotty knickers among you, "gad" probably meant "God" in olde English and "zooks" of course means... Oh, look, just leave me alone, OK? I'm so vair tired.

goosegog · Gooseberry. I know you are looking all quizzical now. OK. If there are two people and they want to snog and you keep hanging about saying, "Do you fancy some chewing gum?" or "Have you seen my interesting new socks?" you are a gooseberry. Or for short, a goosegog, i.e. someone who nobody wants around.

gorgey · Gorgeous. Like fabby (fabulous) and marvy (marvellous).

Hoooorn · When you "have the Horn" it's the same as "having the big red bottom".

in vino hairy arse · This is a Latin joke and therefore vair vair funny. The Latin term is "*in vino veritas*" which means "truth in wine". That is, when you are drunk you tell the truth. So do you see what I've done??? Do you? Instead of "veritas" I say "hairy arse". Sometimes I exhaust myself with my amusingnosity.

Jammy Dodger · Biscuit with jam in it. Very nutritious(ish).

jimjams · Pyjamas. Also pygmies or jammies.

Midget Gem · Little sweets made out of hard jelly stuff in different flavours. Jas loves them A LOT. She secretes them about her person, I suspect, often in her panties, so I never like to accept one from her on hygiene and lesbian grounds.

Mystic Meg · A mad woman in a headscarf and massive earrings who can predict the future. And probably lives in a treehouse. A bit like Jas really. Except that Jas hasn't got a headscarf or earrings. And can't tell the future. Apart from that (and the fact that Mystic Meg is a hundred) they are quite literally like identical twins.

nippy noodles · Instead of saying "Good heavens, it's quite cold this morning," you say "Cor, nippy noodles!!" English is an exciting and growing language. It is. Believe me. Just leave it at that. Accept it.

nuddy-pants · Quite literally nude-coloured pants, and you know what nude-coloured pants are? They are no pants. So if you are in your nuddy-pants you are in your no pants, i.e. you are naked.

nunga-nungas · Basoomas. Girls breasty business. Ellen's brother calls them nunga-nungas because he says that if you get hold a girl's breast and pull it out and then let it go, it goes nunga-nunga-nunga. As I have said many, many times with great wisdomosity, there is something really wrong with boys.

Pantalitzer doll · A terrifying Czech-made doll that sadistic parents (my vati) buy for their children, presumably to teach them early on about the horror of life.

Pizza-a-gogo land · Masimoland. Land of wine, sun, olives and vair vair groovy Luuurve Gods. Italy. The only bad point about Pizza-a-gogo land is their football players are so vain that if it rains, they all run off the pitch so that their hair doesn't get ruined.

red-bottomosity · Having the big red bottom. This is vair vair interesting *via-à-vis* nature. When a lady baboon is "in the mood" for luuurve, she displays her big red bottom to the male baboon. (Apparently he wouldn't have a clue otherwise, but that is boys for you!!) Anyway, if you hear the call of the Horn, you are said to be displaying red-bottomosity.

Rolf Harris · An Australian "entertainer" (not). Rolf has a huge beard and glasses. He plays a didgeridoo, which says everything in my book. He sadly has had a number of hit records, which means he is never off TV and will not go back to Australia. (His "records" are called "Tie Me Kangaroo Down, Sport," etc.)

spangleferkel · A kind of German sausage. I know. You couldn't make it up, could you? The German language is full of this kind thing, like *lederhosen and* so on. And *goosegot*.

spoon · A spoon is a person who is so dim and sad that they cannot be allowed to use anything sharp. That means they can only use a spoon. The Blunder Boys are without exception all spoons.

Spotty Dick · This is an olde English pudding named after an Elizabethan bloke called Dick. Which is nice. However, Dick was not blessed in the complexion department and was covered in boils and spots. Anyway, in honour of Dick's spots a pudding was made up that had currants all over it to represent the spots. Think how pleased Dick must have been with ye olde Elizabethan folke leaning out of their windows as he passed and shouting, "Oy, Spotty Dick, we've just eaten your head... with some custard."

squid · Squid is the plural of quid and I do know why that is. A bloke owed another bloke six pounds or six quid, and he goes up to him with an octopus with one of its tentacles bandaged up, and he says, "Hello mate, here is the sick squid I owe you." Do you see? Do you see?? Sick squid, six quid??? The marvellous juxtaposition of... look, we just call pounds squids. Leave it at that. Try and get on with it, people.

tuckered out · As anyone who has bothered to read historiosity will know, this comes from Friar Tuck, Robin Hood's big fat baldy mate. He was so fat and baldy that if he moved or danced and so on, he would have to lie down for a little zizz. Hence the expression "tuckered out".

vino tinto · Now this is your actual Pizza-a-gogo talk. It quite literally means "tinted wine". In this case the wine is tinted red.

welligogs · Wellington boots. Because it more or less rains all the time in England, we have special rubber boots that we wear to keep us above the mud. This is true.

'Are these my basoomas I see before me?'

A Note from Georgia

Dear little chumettes,

As our lederhosen friends say, "Now ist zer time to say guten tag." I don't know why they say it, but they do. And frankly, I love them for it. All right, Germany may not be Billy Shakespeare land but any country that says spangelferkel instead of sausage is top with me, comedywise... although not holidaywise.

Where was I? Oh yes, saying goodbye. As you know, I have been working like a bee (two bees) to once more give you my all (oo-er) creativitositywise. And here it is, my final oeuvre. (Now you are being silly, you know I don't mean "here is my final egg", so stop messing about.) And you will be pleased to know, I think I have pulled it off. (Oo-er.) Stop it.

So this is my final (boo hoo) diary. It is, of course, packed with the usual combination of sophisticosity and snot dancing. But be warned, there are some exciting additions - Melanie's nunga-nungas make a big and unexpected appearance, as well as other twits in tights etc.

Some of you will laugh, some of you will cry, some of you may have a little accident in the piddly-diddly department. I don't know.

But I care.
A LOT.
I do.
And even though I am away laughing on a fast camel, you will always feel my luuurve.
Are you feeling it yet?
I am.

Georgia
xxxxx

p.s. I mean it about luuurving you all, little chums.

p.p.s. I am giving you telepathic hugs.

p.p.p.s. But not in a telepathically lezzie way.

p.p.p.p.s. And remember my advice to see you through the Georgia-less days ahead...
Snog on, snog on,
With hope in your heart,
And you'll never snog alone,
You'll never snog... alone.

In memory of the original Luuurve God with the big fat red Yorkshire legs:
*Big Fat Bobbin*s.

This is dedicated to you all.
I quite literally love you all.

p.s. I hope I love you as much as you love me.
But I can't worry about that now because that is life, isn't it?

p.p.s. Perhaps I love you more than you love me, which is a bit mean as I am bothering to dedicate this book to you.

You know you luuurve it, you cheeky Fräulein!

Sunday September 18th

9:00 a.m.

Why. Oh why oh why?

9:02 a.m.

Why me?

9:03 a.m.

And I'll just say this. Why?

9:04 a.m.

One minute, I am the girlfriend of a Luuurve God, skipping around like a Sex Kitty on kittykat tablets and the next minute I am at Poo College, in Pooford. Doing a degree in Poonosity and *Merde*.

9:10 a.m.

Masimo, my Pizza-a-gogo Luuurve God, stropped off with the megahump last night. Not even stopping to say goodbye-io, or whatever they say in Pizza-a-gogo land. I may never know now.

9:12 a.m.

Why? Why oh why oh why?

9:13 a.m.

Just because I did a bit of harmless twisting with Dave the Laugh at the Stiff Dylans gig.

That's all.

9:15 a.m.

Is doing the twist such a crime?

Why would you get the Humpty Dumpty about that?

9:16 a.m.
I wouldn't mind, but he doesn't even know about the accidental snogging Dave the Laugh in the forest of red-bottomosity incident. Which I will never be mentioning this side of the grave.

9:17 a.m.
If he gets the numpty about a bit of twisting, what number on the Having the Hump Scale would he get to for accidental snogging?

9:18 a.m.
Perhaps Masimo has only got the overnight hump with me and he will be calling me soon.

9:30 a.m.
Oh joy unbounded. My vati has come barging into MY room. Which to be frank isn't big enough for him and his bottom.

    I am pretending to be asleep.

Thirty seconds later

The gros vater said, "Quickly, quickly rise and shine."

I said, "Erm... Vati... it is Vati, isn't it? Can you go away and I will pretend I haven't noticed you breaking into my room without permission. Which incidentally you will never get. Goodbye."

He came over and ruffled my hair, which is technically assault. I could get on the blower to ChildLine.

Dad was still going on and on in his dadtastic way. As he ripped back my curtains, nearly blinding me, he was rubbing his hands together and saying, "Come on, let's have some family fun. Put your wellies on – we're off to the bird sanctuary."

That woke me up. He is deffo getting madder by the minute. And also he is wearing tight jeans. Surely there is some sort of law about that.

I said, "Dad, I am far too busy to go and look at budgies. Besides, I have seen one."

He didn't take any notice and went off. "I'll be revving up the funmobile. See you in five."

He was whistling "Sex bomb, sex bomb, I'm a sex bomb". Pornographic whistling. I will probably be scarred for life.

Five minutes later

Oh, the embarrassmentosity of having a dad. He is revving up his clown "car". It sounds like a fat bloke revving up a sewing machine. Which it is really. He has painted a racing stripe down the side of his three-wheeled Reliant Robin. Even Grandad overtook the clown car the other day, and he wasn't even on his bike. He was just walking quite briskly. That is how pathetico the Robinmobile is.

One minute later

Anyway, how can I be expected to go look at budgies when I may once more be a dumpee on the rack of luuurve.

Four minutes later

Mum came mumming in.

I said, "Before you start, I'm not coming to look at budgies and that is *le* fact."

She said, "Hang on a minute, what are you doing here?"

I said, "Er, I live here."

She said, "You were supposed to be staying at Jas's though."

"Well... she was a bit... tired."

"You fell out then?"

"Maybe."

"What did you do to upset her?"

Oh, that's nice, isn't it? Nice and supportive.

"It was Saint Jas's fault actually, if you must know. She was the one who told me to do something when Masimo and Dave the Laugh nearly had fisticuffs at dawn. And then when I did do something she got the mega hump and a half with me and stropped off."

Mum came and sat on the edge of the bed. Oh Lord, now she had got interested. Drat.

She said, "Dave and Masimo were fighting?"

"Sort of."

"Why?"

"I don't know. Because I did a bit of ad-hoc twisting with Dave, and Masimo got the hump."

"So what did you do to stop them?"

"Well. I stepped in the middle of them and told them not to be silly."

Mum looked at me. "What did you actually say?"

"Stop in the name of pants."

Mum just looked at me again. She is like a seeing-eye dog.

I bumbled on. "But then Rosie started singing that crap song from *The Sound of Music* – 'The hills are alive with the sound of PANTS, with PANTS I have worn for a thousand years.' And the Ace Gang joined in and..."

"And?"

"Then Masimo just looked at me and he walked off. And not in a good way. In a having the full Humpty Dumpty way."

10:30 a.m.

The budgie lovers' "advice" is: "Don't be such a childish arse in future."

Thank you for that.

10:40 a.m.

At least I have the house to myself for a mope-a-thon. The Swiss Family Mad have roared off down the drive at three miles an hour. They'll be at the end of our street by tomorrow if they're lucky and have a following wind.

10:45 a.m.

I'm not phoning Jas because she was so grumpy with me last night for no reason.

Five minutes later

I think I may hate her actually.

Two minutes later

So in a nutshell. My so-called bestie hates me and thinks I am the Whore of Babylon and my boyfriend may hate me, even though he doesn't know the reason why he should hate me.

Six minutes later

It is sooooo boring moping.

11:10 a.m.

Masimo still hasn't phoned me. I can't stand this silence a moment longer. I am going to call an emergency Ace Gang meeting.

11:30 a.m.

Rang Jools, Ellen, Rosie, Mabs and Honor.

11:45 a.m.

I have arranged to meet the Ace Gang, with the exception of

316

you know who, at 2:00 p.m. in the park. I wanted to meet at mine, but the rest of them want to watch the footie match. They are obsessed with boys.

11:50 a.m.
I am just going to tell them all the whole truth and see what they say. Just come clean about the whole situation. Make a fresh start with my bestie mates. Truth is, after all, the cornerstone of friendship.

11:52 a.m.
Well, when I say the whole truth, I will obviously not be mentioning the thing that I am not mentioning this side of the grave. And which I have forgotten about, to tell you the truth.

1:30 p.m.
I seem to be working my way through the famous "losing it" scale. I have gone from merely having a spaz attack to being now on the edge of a complete nervy b. What if Masimo is actually at the footie match and ignores me?

What can I do?

I ask myself the question, "What would Baby Jesus do in these circumstances?"

One minute later
Of course! I must make myself irresistible to the Luuurve God by applying as much mascara as is humanly possible.

1:32 p.m.
When I went into the bathroom, Angus was sitting on the loo seat. He just looked at me when I came in and then half shut his eyes, like a halfwit cat.

I said, "Oy, what are you doing in here?"

He yawned and then he put his paw on the loo handle. Like he was flushing it.

What fresh hell?

Surely he isn't pooing in the loo?

He jumped down and skittered off out at about a million miles an hour.

How weird.

I wonder if being run over has affected his brain.

Mind you, I read about the Moscow State Circus and

they've got some cats who can pull a carriage and play chess at the same time.

Maybe I could get Angus a job in the Russian circus displaying his pulling-the-loo-handle skills.

The Russian *volk* might quite like that.

You never know.

1:40 p.m.
Oh, bloody hell, he's been in my make-up bag again.

Why would a cat eat lip gloss?

1:45 p.m.
OK, I am ready to get entrancing and alluring. I am wearing jeans and a skinny jummie, and because I am off to watch a footie match, I've put my hair into a little ponytail. *Très sportif*. It gives me a casual, sporty air.

I may wear my shades to add to my mysterious "uuumph" quality.

1:46 p.m.
Just a hint of "uuumph" but not ummphy in the "oy, you slaaaag" sort of way.

2:10 p.m.

When I arrived at our usual meeting place underneath the big chestnut tree, Sven and Rosie were there. Practically eating each other. Do they ever stop snogging?

Rosie knew I was there because she waved her hand at me.

Eventually, I went: "Hellllooooooo" for a bit until they came up for air.

Rosie took out her chuddie and said, "*Bonsoir*, sensation-seeker."

Sven leaped to his feet and picked me up (thank God I had my jeans on) and started carrying me around singing, "Oh *ja*, oh *ja*! The hills are alive wiv zer pants, hahaha, oh *ja* pants!!!"

I said to Rosie, who was reapplying her lippy, "Rosie, make him put me down..."

Rosie said, "Down, boy."

He put me down and licked Rosie's face before he ambled off like Lug the Larger to the footie field.

I said to her, "How does this happen? One minute I've got more boyfriends than I can shake a stick at and the next minute I am the Leper of Rheims."

Rosie looked at me and put her armey round me. "Would you like to sit on my knee for a bit? You like that."

I just looked at her.

Five minutes later

Jools, Mabs, Hons and Ellen arrived.

The meeting began with the official passing around of the Midget Gems. Then we discussed how to make Masimo stop having the hump and start having the Horn.

Twenty minutes later

This is our cunning plan.

I have to be nice.

That is it.

I have to be nicey girl on legs for as long as it takes to make Masimo luuurve me again.

The Ace Gang is going to help by only saying really, really nice things about me.

There was a bit of a verging on the "mentioning the thing that I will not be mentioning this side of the grave" when Ellen said, "Masimo, I mean, he like... well, he got the hump when... er... the twisting, or maybe Dave the Laugh or something... erm."

Jools said, "Ah yes, he didn't like you dancing like a fool with Dave the Laugh, did he?"

Mabs said, "It's his hot Pizza-a-gogo blood. They get vair jealous."

Rosie said, "You might have to eschew Dave the Laugh with a firm hand for a bit."

OK, well, I can knock it on the head laaarfwise with the Hornmeister.

It's a shame.

But ho hum pig's bum.

Two minutes later

But what if I don't even get the chance to be nicey-nice girl?

What if Masimo doesn't get in touch with me again?

I fear the tensionosity will drive me to not only having a complete nervy b. but I might also go ballisticisimus.

2:45 p.m.

The lads are arriving, getting their boots on and shouting WUBBISH. They don't seem to be able to just say "Hello" to each other. It's all "Aaaaaaah, you're shit!" and "On my head." "Hello, you complete tosser." Quite, quite weird. No sign of Dave the Laugh – perhaps he's not playing today. Just as well really.

2:50 p.m.
Sven has put two footballs down the front of his shirt and is swaying around like a girl. A girl nearly two metres tall, with massive hairy legs and the beginnings of a goatee.

Rosie said, "I think I'm on the turn. Svenetta is bringing out my inner lesbian."

Oh good, everyone has gone bonkers. Excellent.

I said, "Rosie, will you promise not to mention your inner lezzie if Masimo turns up?"

Rosie winked at me. "I'll try, but don't you start waggling your nungas about, you little minx."

Do you see what I mean? This is exactly what I am trying to avoid.

Five minutes later
Dom, Edward, Rollo, Declan, Sven and two others of the Stiff Dylans are all running around "limbering up".

Meanwhile, it's Cosmetic Headquarters behind our tree. In principal, I think you should be loved for yourself, and your soul shines through even if you haven't got mascara on. I know this is what Baby Jesus says and he is renowned for never having worn mascara. So, in principal, I think you should just be yourself, but in practice, I am applying just a tad more mascara.

Speaking of which, Ellen is in such a ditherama about seeing Declan that she has actually got some mascara on her teeth. How?

Two minutes later

Jas'n'Tom have turned up.

Oh yes. Here comes Miss Prissy Knickers herself. And her boyfriend, Hunky. She caught sight of us and shouted over, "Hi, Rosie, hi, Ellen, Mabs, Jools, Hons..."

She deliberately didn't say hello to me. How childish.

Two could play at that game.

I shouted out, "Hi, Hunky!" Tom waved at me and went off.

Then I noticed that Jas was not alone. She had brought two of her stuffed owls with her. And they had got little football hats and scarves on.

How pathetico.

I shouted, "Hello, owls!"

Hahahaha. I had said hello to her owls and she couldn't stop me.

Yessssss! One-nil to me!!!!!!

Nearly kick-off

The other team were from St Pat's and quite fit boys as it happens. If you like quite fit boys.

I was just having a Midget Gem to calm me down and my back was to the road when I heard a scooter approaching. It might be the Luuurve God. I got immediate knee tremblers and jelloid knickers. But I must not expose my jelloid knickers – I must exude sophisticosity. How do you do sophisticosity without turning round?

Perhaps if I tightened my bum-oley muscles that might make for a better profile rear-wise?

No, that might look like I needed a poo.

I'll just not turn round and leave it at that.

I heard the scooter come to a halt and I said to Rosie, "What's going on?"

And she said, "It's Robbie and he's got something

hideous clinging to his back."

I looked round and Wet Lindsay was on the back of his scooter.

They got off and Robbie looked across and smiled at me. I smiled back to him. Lindsay had her head down, looking in her bag. I said to Rosie, "That bag over her head quite suits her."

What was she doing?

We watched as Robbie got his footie boots on. He is certainly in tip-top condition. It is such a waste for him to be with the Bride of Dracula. Lindsay brought out a towel and a water bottle from her bag and handed it to Robbie.

Ten seconds later

She was massaging his neck. Blimey! Has she turned into some sort of Octopussy handmaiden?

I said to the gang, "I bet she comes scampering on with the half-time oranges tucked down her bra. There is enough room... She's probably got a packed lunch in there."

Which is a fact. Surely Robbie must know about her false basooma fiasco?

Erlack! I have accidentally got parts of Wet Lindsay in my brain.

I feel dirty. It was nearly kick-off time. I was behind the tree looking over at the lads and noticed that Dave the Laugh was still missing.

"I wonder where Dave the Laugh is?"

And a voice behind me said, "Why? Are you longing for the Hornmeister, you naughty Kittykat?"

I looked round and there he was, lurking like a lurker and looking very cool in his black training stuff. He was twinkly round the eyes and said to the gang, "The vati has arrived. Now we can groove."

Ellen's head practically dropped off with redness. She still luuurves him even though she is going out with Declan.

Dave said, "Well, I'd love to stay swapping make-up hints with you girls, but there are arses to kick."

As he was going by me, I said, "Erm... Dave, would you give me a call? I want to ask you something."

He looked at me. "If you are hoping to entice me into *rummachen unterhalb der Taille*, I have told you before, you are embarrassing yourself."

Oooohhhhh, he is sooo annoying.

The lads were yelling at him, "Oy, Dave, get a wriggle on, mate!!"

Dave started humming the theme from *Match of the Day* and jogging off backwards, waving at us. Then he turned towards the team and started doing run run leap like a mad gazelle. When he was a few metres from them, he did slow-motion running with his arms outstretched and his team started doing the same towards him. When they reached each other, they had a minor ruck.

Boys never cease to amaze me, never.

I wonder if he will phone me though? Masimo hasn't turned up. Perhaps he already has a new girlfriend.

Half time

Dave's team are winning one-nil. I'd like to say it is down to superior skill, but largely it's because Sven fell on to the St Pat's goalkeeper and the ball went over the line. St Pat's protested, but it's pointless arguing with Sven. He took the player who was arguing with him and lifted him off his feet and kissed him on the mouth.

The bloke was nearly sick, but he shut up and the goal counted.

Wet Lindsay did have half-time oranges.

Sadly not down her bra.

But even so, half-time oranges. How crap is that? Vair vair crap.

Three minutes later

I went and stood really near to Jas. She *ignorez-vous*ed me. So I gave a pretendy piece of half-time chocolate to one of her owls. She snatched her owly away.

Tom was there and he said, "Oh, come on, you two. Put your handbags down. Come on, Jas, speak to Georgia."

She said, "Who?"

And went off flicking her fringe to speak to Emma, who turned up to hang around Dave. Jas has only known Emma for about a minute and a half. I do hate her. It's official.

She should be on my side in my time of neednosity.

After all I have done for her.

I said that to the Ace Gang as the second half started.

I said, "She is *ignorez-vous*ing me after all I have done for her."

Ellen dithered into life (unfortunately) and said, "Er... what, erm, what have you, erm, done like, for her?"

Where to begin?

♥ 329

I said, "For a start, I have put up with her stupid fringe-flicking for about a million years."

But it was pointless trying to get anyone's attention because they were all acting like divs in front of their boyfriends.

5:15 p.m.

I thought I might have to do the Heimlich manoeuvre on Ellen when Declan asked her to the cinema at the end of the match. Well, actually, I say "asked", but what happened is that he nodded his head at her and she trotted over to him like puppy dog girl. It was like a horrible love fest at the end.

I would have more pridenosity with my boyfriend. If I had a boyfriend.

6:00 p.m.

All alone at home.

Phone rang. I nervously picked it up, but it was only Mum telling me that they are at Grandvati's for tea and did I want to go over. Is she mad?

6:02 p.m.

The rest of the gang have gone to the cinema. With their

boyfriends. Not even a thought for my tragicosity. Well, to be fair, they did ask me to go, but I would have just been goosegog girl among the snoggers.

6:15 p.m.
Angus seems to understand what I am going through. He has leaped up on to my lap.

Nice.

Aaaah. He's purring.

Really loudly actually.

Nice though.

All comfy and warmy.

One minute later
Now he's snuggling into me.

Nice.

He's all cosy on my knee and I can read my *Vogue*.

One minute later
He's snuggling into my chest now, which is nice, but a bit difficult for me to move my arms.

But he's all comfy and...

Now he's on my shoulders, like a fur cape.

He's settled down now – that's nice. He's doing his snuggling and purring.

One minute later

Now he's back on my lap... he's actually on my magazine now.

One minute later

Now he's back on my chest.

I CAN'T STAND ANY MORE OF THIS!!!!!!

Five minutes later

It's no use him just staring at me through the window. I'm not letting him in.

Three minutes later

Staring and staring.

I'm going into the kitchen to see if there is anything to stave off scurvy.

Two minutes later

Now he's staring in through the kitchen window.

6:30 p.m.

He can't stare at me in the bathroom because there is frosted glass. Hahahahaha.

He'd better not burrow in through the sewage system and pop up out of the loo.

No calls from anyone.

Not Masimo, not Dave the Laugh.

Too busy with his girlfriend I suppose.

Really, I'm too upset and tired to do my beauty routine, but as someone once said, possibly on *Big Brother*, "When the going gets tough, the tough get moisturising and plucking."

If I am once again going to be spinster of the parish, I will at least be smoothy smooth.

In the bathroom

What does Dad do with his razors? They are so blunt! I've torn my legs to ribbons. I look like I've been playing hockey with the Piranha family. Ouchy ouch ouch!!!

And ouch.

I must staunch the flow. I've probably lost an armful of blood already.

♡ 333

Phone rang

Oh my giddy god's pyjamas. I hobbled over with my legs covered in bits of loo paper and picked up the receiver. I tried for a casual, nonchalant sort of voice, one that didn't sound like I was bleeding to death.

"Hello."

"Hello, you cheeky Fräulein. You know you love it."

It was Dave. Oh, I felt so happy I wanted to cry.

He said, "So what's up, Kittykat?"

And I started.

"After you went on Saturday night, the Luuurve God got on his huffmobile."

Dave said, "And he didn't say anything?"

"No, he just looked at me all sort of sad."

"Was he crying?"

"Er no."

"Probably worried his mascara would run."

"Dave."

"I'm just being jovial Dave the Biscuit to lighten the mood."

"Well, don't be. I'm too upset."

"Look, Georgia, this is a bit tricky for me. There's Emma and well…"

"Well what? I'm only asking you to be like the Hornmeister and tell me what to do."

There was a pause and then he said, "OK, here's what we'll do. I'll casually bump into him..."

"And not mention pants or anything."

"No, I will leave pants out of it. I'll just say that there is nothing going on to have a girlie tizz about and..."

"You won't actually say the girlie tizz thing, will you?"

"Right, er well, I'll say... well, I don't know exactly what I will say, just that we were having a laugh because... that's what mates do."

"And that's true, isn't it?"

There was another little pause and then Dave said, "Yeah, well, listen, I have to go now."

And he was gone.

Had that gone well?

If so, why did I feel so funny?

10:30 p.m.

No call from Masimo.

10:32 p.m.

Still, on the bright side, we've got a budgie.

10:40 p.m.

Not for long I suspect. Angus and Gordy have been staring at it since Vati brought it home from the birdy sanctuary.

Midnight

If anyone can fix it, it's the Hornmeister. I must get the Luuurve God back. It means everything to me.

I hadn't even been able to properly show off that I was his girlfriend before I was maybe dumped.

Elepoon in your nick-nacks

Monday September 19th

Woke up from a dream where Dave had come up to me and said, "I didn't even mention pants and he went ballisticisimus."

And Dave had a pair of pants on his head.

And they weren't small.

8:15 a.m.

A bit earlier than usual. I want to make sure Jas doesn't get to Stalag 14 without me.

I want to know how Jazzy Spazzy is going to carry on her campaign of *ignorez-vous*ing me when I refuse to be *ignorez-vous*ed.

337

8:25 a.m.

Thar she blows! She senses I am here and she is putting a bit of speed on.

8:29 a.m.

Aaaah, I have got her in my sights. Her bottom is waggling away only just in front of me. I am going to do my world-renowned speedwalking.

8:32 a.m.

My nose is practically on the back of her beret.

She is still pretending I am invisible girlie, but she must be able to hear me panting.

I pulled out a Jammy Dodger and held it in front of her face. She loves a Jammy Dodger.

8:35 a.m.

Even when I ate the Jammy Dodger walking backwards in front of her she didn't slow down.

OK, I am going in.

I leaped on her unexpectedly and pulled her beret right down over her eyes. But even then she kept marching on like nothing had happened. It was only when she crashed into the postman, who was bending over filling his sack, that she had to stop and take her beret off.

The postman went bonkers and shouted at her to "stop playing silly beggars!!!!".

I have said this before and I will say it again, how come anyone who puts a badge on goes immediately insane?

And anyway, why do they need a badge?

A badge that says "postman" or "caretaker".

Don't they know who they are?

I took advantage of the brouhaha and stepped in front of Jas. Eyeball to eyeball.

I said, "Jazzy, it's me, your old pally."

She was all red and her fringe looked like a tumble-dried ferret.

She said, "I know it's you. I know it's you because every time anything bad happens or someone is shouting, you'll be around."

I said, "That's not fair. What about the time I helped you get off with Hunky by pretending that you were normal and popular?"

She shrugged and said, "Yeah, well..."

"And remember the puffball skirt incident?"

That got her.

She said, "It looked nice."

"Wrong, Jas. You looked like you had a little elepoon in your nick-nacks, didn't you?"

She shrugged, but she knew I was right really because Astonishingly Dim Monica had worn a puffball skirt to the school play and Rosie started singing, "Nellie the elephant packed her PANTS and said goodbye to the circus"!!

I had her on the ropes now and said, "Come on, little pally, think of all the larfs we've had. Come on, I need you... I need you because you are so vair vair wise. You are tip-top to the toppimost full of wisdomosity... and I am a fool."

Jas was flicking her stupid fringe, but I didn't strike her. She said, "You bring it on yourself."

I put my arm round her and held her arm down so she would stop the fringe-fiddling business. I said, "I know, Jazzy, but that is because I am full of *je ne sais quoi*."

Stalag 14

At least Jas and me are besties again. Hurrah!

Well, until she begins to annoy me again. In about a minute.

340

What is it with Miss Wilson? She's obsessed with rudey-dudeyness. Since the camping trip when she, I think deliberately, exposed herself to Herr Kamyer in the shower, she's gone sex mad.

I said to Rosie, "Is she wearing lippy? Or has she just eaten a strawberry Mivvy?"

Rosie was making a little beard for her pencil case so she was a bit "busy", but she took the trouble to look up and said, "Most people wear lippy on their lips, not on their nostrils and chin. But at least she is giving it a go."

I wish she wasn't "giving it a go".

We were having to discuss the Song of Songs from the Bible. It's about some old anciety bloke who was a king and a ye olde handmaiden-type person. I think it's mostly about snogging, but not as we know it. I said to Jools, "What does 'he put his hand on my lock' mean when it's at home?"

Jools said, "Ask her."

I had nothing else to do, and Miss Wilson would go boring on if I didn't interrupt her. And I had done all I could to pass the time, even my toenails, sooo...

I put my hand up. Well, actually, I put them both up as a sort of novelty. Like an orang-utan.

I said, "Miss Wilson, if we translated ye olde Bible into modern language – you know, that made sense – well, what number on the Snogging Scale would 'he put his hand on my lock' be?"

Miss Wilson went sensationally red, nearly as red as her nostrils and chin.

"Well, Georgia, erm, yes, that is interesting… yes, making a connection between biblical love and rituals and so forth, and, erm, modern vocabulary, erm…"

Rosie put aside her beard because we sensed a comedy opportunity. We all stared at Miss Wilson's bob.

We were not disappointed. The bob was in full bob.

German

It's not often that we get two comedy opportunities for the price of one, but happy days here we are.

Herr Kamyer had hardly had time to adjust his knitted tie before Rosie started.

She said, "Herr Kamyer, we have just had a *sehr* interesting talk with Miss Wilson."

Herr Kamyer was blinking through his glasses in a kindly and interested way. It's tragic really. He said, "Oh *ja*?"

Rosie said, "*Ja*, it is *sehr sehr* interesting. It was from the Bible. In der German Bible *vas ist*..."

Herr Kamyer said, "Der word *für* Bible in German is..."

Rosie said, "Vat ever. In der German Bible *vas ist der* translation *für* 'he put his handchen on my lock'?"

Herr Kamyer looked like a goldfish in a knitted tie. He said, "I'm afraid I do not know dis expression."

I said, "It is int der Bible, Herr Kamyer, int der Song of Songen. It ist about der *Knutschen*!"

Rosie was in her own German snogging world by now.

She said, "Would it be *Abscheidskuss*?"

I said, "Or perhaps *AUF GANZE GEHEN*!!!!!!!"

4:30 p.m.
Walking home with the gang.

Funnily enough, I sort of forgot about the Luuurve God for a while. But after the others had gone I felt really miz.

I let myself in to my "home".

No one in.

Do you know, Jas even knows what she is going to have for supper most nights.

More to the point, she GETS some supper.

Still, as long as my mum can waggle her enormous basoomas around in the swimming pool with her mates.

That's what counts.

Two minutes later

Had a bowl of Shreddies. The milk was past its sell-by date so with my luck I'll get milkytosis. Which will make my nostrils flare up to twice their size, and I will start eating grass.

In the front room

Libby, my charming but insane little sister, has christened the budgie Bum-ty.

Bum-ty doesn't look very chirpy.

Who would with two cats staring at you.

Have they been there all day?

5:30 p.m.

Ooooh, I am so vair bored. And depressed at the same time.

6:00 p.m.

The Family Mad have come in.

And Uncle Eddie is here. Hurray!!!

They caught me by surprise so I couldn't barricade myself in my room.

Uncle Eddie larged in first.

He said, "I've got one for you. Two nuns driving along at night on a lonely forest road and a vampire leaps out and on to the bonnet. The nun who's driving says to the other nun, 'Quick, show him your cross!' and the second nun shouts, 'Get off the bloody bonnet!'!!!!!"

And he went wheezing and cackling off into the kitchen.

Grown women pay money to see him taking his clothes off to music.

I don't know what to say.

Yes I do.

I would pay him not to take his clothes off.

In fact, I might go along one night to one of his baldyman gigs and shout, "Get 'em on!!!"

No. I won't do that.

I may as well go and get my jimjams on. When you are visiting the cakeshop of agony, they don't mind what you wear in there. Most of their customers are in their jimjams. With big swollen eyes. And covered in dribble.

God, I am really depressed now.

In the lounge in my jimjams

Vati came in with a pork pie. Taking his health seriously then.

He said, "What's the matter with you?"

Not that he cares.

I said, "I'm depressed actually."

He said, "Depressed, at your age? You'll be saying you're bored next."

"That is what I was going to say next."

Vati looked at me and sat down. He patted my knee with his pork-pie-free hand.

Oh dear God, he had touched my jimjams.

He said, "Do you know what my mum used to say when I was bored?"

Oh, this would be good. It was bound to be something to do with making hats out of eggboxes.

I was about to say, "I'm bored enough as it is without you telling me about prehistoric hats."

But he was rambling on.

"She used to say, 'I'll tell you what... bang your head against a wall and that will take your mind off it.'"

Charming.

In bed

7:00 p.m.

I can hear Libby trying to teach Bum-ty the words to "Dancing Bean".

I think Bum-ty might not be long for this world. He's got two cats staring at him night and day and now a mad toddler is shoving a sausage through the cage and singing.

Three pairs of mad eyes looking at you.

7:30 p.m.

Was that a scooter coming near?

7:32 p.m.

No.

Oh, good. Now I'm having hallucinations.

Of the earhole.

Ear-lucinations.

7:35 p.m.

No.

Oh yes.

Oh my God.

It IS a scooter coming up the road.

I looked through the window.

It was Masimo!!!!

Oh *merde*.

I hadn't got time to do anything.

I was in my jimjams.

I had plaited all my hair because I was so bored and depressed.

I ran down to the front room and said, "Mum, quick, I need you."

For once, Mum did what I asked her.

I told her to tell Masimo that I was out.

As the scooter came to a halt outside, I was scarpering up the stairs and I whispered to her, "Don't start a conversation with him, will you? Don't tell him about yourself."

She said, "Don't make me change my mind."

And at the top of the stairs I said, "Don't let him see Dad in his leisure trousers. Please."

Then the doorbell rang.

I bobbed down and looked through the banisters. I could only see the bottom bit of the open door.

I heard Masimo's voice. He said, "*Ciao.*"

I had thought I might never hear "*ciao*" again. Oh, what was he here for???

Mum said, "Masimo, what a lovely surprise. You look, er... lovely."

Oh nooooo, she was talking to him like he was a boy and she was a girl! Did she have her cardigan buttoned up? I couldn't remember...

Masimo said, "Er, I have come, *scusi* for my English, I have come for to give Georgia..."

Mum interrupted. "I'm afraid she had to stay late for, erm, hockey."

Masimo said, "Ah yes, she is good for hockey, I think... but I come for to give her... a letter. *Grazie mille.*"

And he was gone.

I crouched down by my window and looked out. Masimo accelerated away down the street. He was wearing a leather coat. My heart skipped a beat to see him.

In a way, I didn't want to go down and get the letter.

What if it said, *"Ciao, bella*... you are... how you say in English... dumped."

Mum came rushing up to my room.

She handed me the letter and said, "What does it say?"

I said, "It says, 'What fine weather we are having for this time of year...' Mum, I DON'T KNOW what it says because I haven't opened it yet. I am waiting to open it privately. Do you see?"

She slammed out of the room saying, "Sorry for being interested in your life."

I daren't read it.

Five minutes later
I've tried to psychically feel what it might say.

It's not very nice to dump someone by post, is it?

Just because they had a bit of a twist with Dave the Whatsit.

Two minutes later
Ripped it open.

Three minutes later
Well, the nub and the gist is...

I think...

That Masimo says he thinks that he was a bit out of order. And that Dave had been to see him and said that we were just mates having a laugh.

But (and this is the worrying bit) Masimo said he thought that maybe I wanted just to have fun with my mates. And that maybe I am too young for a relationship with him.

He doesn't know.

He is thinking.

He wants me to think too.

And that we can meet at the Stiff Dylans gig on Saturday, and then we will talk.

He just signed it "Masimo".

No kisses.

Not a "I am missing you and want to snog you within an inch of your life."

Hmmm. So am I semi-dumped?

Fifteen minutes later

The one person I would like to talk to about this is the Hornmeister.

But I can't.

I had to make do with Jazzy Spazzy.

Phoned Jas

I told her about the note.

"I think what the note means is that I have got another chance. To show that I want to be with him. And that I am not a twisting fool. I am, in fact, a sophisticate wise beyond my years. And so on."

She just went, "Hmmmm."

"He is, in fact, asking me to reveal my inner maturiosity, of which I have got bloody bucketfuls as it happens. And he is requesting me to put away my inner fool. That is what I think."

"Hmmmmmmmmmmm."

What does she mean, "Hmmmmmmmmmmm"?

Midnight

"Hmmmmmmmmmmm" does not mean "Yes yes, I agree with you."

It means "Hmmmmmmmmmm".

Anyway she can "hmmm" away. I am going to start my campaign of maturiosity tomorrow.

FIRE!!! I'm gonna teach you to burn!

Tuesday September 20th
Stalag 14
Break

It's bloody nippy noodles outside.

Mabs said, "Shall we work out a new disco inferno dance for Saturday's gig? To warm us up?"

I said, "Er, well, it's a bit soon after our last triumph, don't you think?"

Rosie said, "No. A triumph is not a triumph until you have gone too far."

Jas said, "I'm freezing."

 353

To change the subject away from mad dancing, that I am now eschewing with a firm hand, I said, "Well, Jas, we are all freezing. Why don't you use some of your very well-known forest skills and start a lovely campfire? I bet you've got your special fire-making stick in your rucky, haven't you?"

Jas said, "Don't be silly."

I said, "I'm not being silly. I'm being frozen to within an inch of my life. Anyway, you can't do it without Hunky, can you? You're frightened of fire."

"I am not frightened of fire."

"Yes you are."

"No I'm not."

"Look at me, Jas. I'm a flame and I'm coming near your fringe."

And I started doing an ad-hoc flame improv, wiggling my body and making my arms all snakey, touching Jas's fringe and making a *whooshing* noise.

Jas was getting quite red and there was deffo a touch of tomato about her ears.

Rosie, Jools and the rest of the gang started snaking and shaking about, going "*Whoosh whoosh*".

Jas finally lost her rag and said, "I can make a fire! Go and get some twigs and I'll show you."

Excellent!

Ten minutes later
Brillopads.

Jas actually did it. She rubbed her special little fire-making stick in a wedge thing. She did happen to have her special "rubbing sticks" with her in her haversack. I don't know why, but I knew she would have. She is very secretive about her rucky. I bet she has several changes of different type weight pants in there. And possibly a collection of molluscs. We may never know. At least, I may never know because I will never be putting my hand in there. My hand will never be upon her lock and that is a fact!!!

Anyway, it was really jolly sitting round our little campfire. It was made mostly out of crisp packets. To be fair, there was more smoke than flame, but we pretended we were really really warmey warm. I said, "Shall we sing the old traditional campfire song, little Ace Gang pallies?"

And they all went, "Yeah!!!"

And I said, "What is it?"

Then I remembered some old crap recording of *Top of the Pops* in the 70s that my dad had. I'd shown it to the gang. I said, "Let's sing 'Fire' by that bloke who wore a helmet that was actually on fire. And when he sang on *Top of the Pops*, his helmet set fire to the ceiling. By the way, Ro Ro, do NOT mention that to Sven. He's bound to want to do it and then it's goodbye to any club that we go to."

Anyway, where was I? Oh yes, we were just sitting round our campfire singing, "FIRE!!! I'm going to teach you to burn. FIRE! I'm gonna teach you to learn!!!" when out of nowhere came Wet Lindsay. The octopus in the ointment. With her assistant fascist, ADM. She saw us round our innocent "campfire" and went absolutely ballisticisimus.

She was yelling, "You absolute twits!!!!! Step away, step away!!! Monica, get Mr Attwood and tell him there is a fire in the fives court..."

Twenty minutes later
What a fuss and a kerfuffle.

Mr Attwood practically pooed himself with delight. He's been standing by with flame retardant since *MacUseless* when somebody accidentally set fire to Nauseating P. Green. The fact that the "inferno" had gone out by the time he got there didn't stop him. He came leaping up and made us stand and watch from "a safe distance" (the edge of the fives court) while he donned his special breathing apparatus. He was shouting through the mask, "There may be toxic fumes."

I was yelling, "It's out, Mr Attwood!"

But he couldn't hear me.

He squirted his extinguisher thing until there was foam up to the top of his welligogs. Quite, quite extraordinarily bonkers.

Three minutes later

He took off his mask and looked at the huge pile of foam.

He said, "I've made the area safe – I'll just radio in to Headquarters to say I've achieved a result safety-wise and no casualties."

From his "fire sack" he fished out an enormous walkie-talkie thing.

Wet Lindsay said, "Right, you lot, the headmistress's office. NOW!"

Oh no, not Slim.

She frogmarched us off, chuntering on to ADM and giving me the evils every now and again. She just absolutely loves it times a million.

If she can upset me, she's made up.

Jas said, "Oh, now I'll never get to be a prefect. This is all your fault, Georgia. Again."

I said, "Er, I think you are the firestarter, crazy firestarter Jas."

Rosie said, "Do you think Slim will beat us to death with her chins?"

As we sloped along at one mile an hour, we could hear Mr Attwood shouted into his walkie-talkie. "Z Victor 1 to B.D. Are you receiving me? Over."

Astonishingly barmy.

Jools said, "Who is he talking to?"

And I said, "He's talking to Headquarters. And you know who that is, don't you?"

Ellen said, "No, I... er... is it... erm, is it, like... Headquarters or something?"

We just looked at her.

I said, "He is talking to the radio in his shed. And do you know who is listening? No one."

Outside Slim's office

I asked "permission" to go to the piddly-diddly department and Wet Lindsay came with me. Like I was going to escape through the loo window! Actually, I did do that once, but that is not the point. As I was in the cubicle, trying not to make any piddly-diddly noises because I didn't want her to hear me, she said, "You really are the most appalling little tart, Georgia Nicolson. Robbie did the right thing dumping you and Masimo must be dying to get rid of you."

I started to say, "Actually, I think boys like girls with foreheads..."

But she said, "Nicolson, if you don't want to spend the rest of the term recovering from a very bad hockey injury, I advise you to SHUT UP right now."

As I walked back under armed guard, I thought, how could Robbie kiss her?

Erlack.

I think he must have clinical depression after I stopped going out with him. When she had been yelling at me, I could see right up her nostrils. Also she didn't have mascara on and her eyelashes were like albino mouse eyelashes. No, they weren't as nice as that; they were like duck eyelashes. And ducks don't have eyelashes.

I hate her times a million. When I get over enticing Masimo back into my web of luuurve, I will concentrate on ruining her life and saving Robbie.

Outside Slim's office
Three minutes later
The Little Titches, also known as the Dave the Laugh fanclub, were in the outer torture chamber with the Ace Gang when I got there. Wet Lindsay went off to get Elvis.

I said, "Hello, Titches, what are you up for? GBH? Titchiness?"

Ginger Titch said, "We were making up a tribute to Dave the Laugh in the loos."

And I said, "Where is the crime in that?"

And the littlest one said, "We broke the loo seat with our stamping."

"There is no justice in this place. It squashes any sign of creativitosity."

The Little Titches nodded. Ginger said, "Miss, do you like Dave the Laugh the bestiest? We do."

All of the gang looked at me and I went a bit red.

Jas said, "Yes, do you "accidentally" like Dave the Laugh, Georgia?"

Ellen was looking and blinking and started saying, "Why would... I mean, what... Dave and... well, what is that..."

Rosie started shouting "FIRE!! I'm gonna teach you to burn, FIRE!!" and doing *whooshing* and flame dancing when Slim opened her door suddenly and said, "I'm glad that you are all in such a jolly mood. Let's see if we can change that. You two first-formers in my room, now."

The two Little Titches started to follow her. After her gigantic bottom had waddled off, they got to her door and looked round. I saluted them by putting my finger on my nose and making it stick up like a piggie.

They saluted back and even did a little grunt.

They are top girls for Little Titches.

Five minutes later

We could hear muffled shouting and then a bit of crying.

Rosie said, "She is beating them with her chins."

God, if Slim was going to go ballistic over a loo seat, we were deffo going to get a severe mental thrashing.

Then Wet Lindsay arrived, accompanied by Mr Attwood. In a wheelchair. What????

Was he too lazy even to walk across the playground?

A man in his physical condition should not be in charge of the safety of high-spirited youth.

Or any people.

Or anything.

Wet Lindsay looked at me like I was snot in a skirt. It turned out that Elvis had slipped in his own foam and done his back in. I bet he hasn't.

He was moaning on for England, as usual.

"How am I supposed to do my job now?"

I was going to say, "Oh, you know, the usual way, sitting perving in your hut."

But I didn't.

He was rambling on.

"You have no thought for others. When I was a boy, we had respect for our elders."

Moan moan. Here we go. It will be, "In my day we used to enjoy ourselves just by picking our own noses."

I said, "Well, as it happens, Elvis, er, I mean Mr Attwood, I agree with you. You are clearly too old to be working. It's cruel. In fact, I am going to have a word with our headmistress and suggest she gives you the big goodbye you so richly deserve."

Wet Lindsay had her usual spazerama attack.

She said, "Shut up and grow up!"

Charming.

Slim's office

Oh, I am soooo bored with being told off. It is giving me the megadroop. I should be at home glamming myself up for the Luuurve God and practising my new sophisticosity. Just in case he forgives me. Instead of which I am in an office counting chins.

Slim was completely jelloid. In fact, her whole body was having a chin-a-thon. Of course, it was me who got it in the neck. As if I started the bloody fire. I just did a bit of *whooshing*.

Slim said, "It's always you, isn't it, Georgia? What happened this time? Is it another miscarriage of justice?"

Well, at least she was being reasonable for once.

I said, "Well actually, Miss, yes it is. You see it was minus 50 outside and we were terribly cold, so J... I mean we, decided to use our woodland skills that we learned on our magnificent camping trip with Herr Kamyer and..."

Slim looked at me.

"You mean you set fire to some rubbish in the fives court."

I said, "Well, that's one way of putting it."

Mr Attwood lurched to life.

"I'm in agony, Headmistress, because of an act of senseless arson. By arsonists."

I don't know what it is about the word arse-onists, but it does give me the inward hysteria. Mr Attwood had more or less said "arse" in front of Slim. I daren't look at Rosie.

Slim looked at me.

"It's always you, Georgia. Why can't you grow up?"

I nearly said, "I'm growing as fast as I can. Look at the size of my nungas!"

Wet Lindsay had to put her oar in.

"The trouble is, of course, that she does lead the others into it."

Oh yeah, that'll be the day.

I started to say, "Well actually, funnily enough, this time it was..."

And Jas looked at me like an annoying fringey puppy. Dear God, she actually did want to be a prefect. It is vair nice of me to even be mates with her under the circs.

It's an act of charity really. And when I had mentioned my plan for sophisticosity she had said, "Hmmmmmmmm mmmm."

But then she looked at me again. A bit tearful. Oh, bloody hell.

It had to be done.

I said, "Oh, OK, yes, it was my idea..."

Rosie and Jools said, "Well, not really. We all..."

But I ploughed on.

"Whatever they say, they are my mates and they are covering for me. It was my idea, but it was only a tiddly tiny firey thing."

Mr Attwood said, "I bet that's what the baker said about the fire he started that turned into the Great Fire of London."

What is he rambling on about? We're not even in London.

Anyway, the long and the long of it is that the others have got a ticking-off and reprimands and I have got detention...

and worst of all... have to "help" Mr Attwood this term. Again.

Oh, what larks we'll have.

Not.

Detention
4:00 p.m.

Jas squeezed my arm as she left for home and pressed a secret stash of Midget Gems into my hand. She said, "You are truly my bezzie mate of all time, Georgia."

And she is not wrong. I am without doubtosity top mate of all time.

4:05 p.m.

Luckily, I have got Miss Wilson as my prison guard so I will be able to make best possible use of my time.

First of all, I am going to plan my Luuurve God re-entrancing plan.

Fifteen minutes later

The Luuurve God re-entrancing plan.

1. "You are never alone with your lippy and mascara."
I am going to make a sort of pouch that fits under my
bra and pants so that I have a secret supply at all times.
Even if the Luuurve God pops up unexpectedly (oo-er)
I can refresh by reaching for my pouch.

NB. Make my pouch out of nice softy soft
material so that I can wear it in bed. In case the
Luuurve God pops up unexpectedly in the night.
(Oo-er.)

2. I will exude sophisticosity with just a hint of glaciosity. I
think the European Luuurve God likes this sort of
thing. He is not, after all, a crude Viking like Sven who
quite frankly wouldn't recognise glaciosity if it hit him
in the face. On the contrary, Sven would think you
were playing hard to get because you were a lezzie and
that would give him the Horn.

Four minutes later
3. Be nice. This means regrettably I will not be disco
dancing like a tit any more. When the Stiff Dylans play,
I will waft around like a... wafting thing on waft

♡ 367

tablets. I will laugh lightly, but at no time don a false beard.

False beards are over. I will never wear the beard again.

Ditto horns.

And finally...

4. I will not do arm-wrestling or any kind of wrestling with Dave the Laugh.

Dave the Laugh is no longer a laugh to me. He is Emma's boyfriend and my mate.

Actually, I wonder where he is? I haven't seen him for yonks. Ah, well. Stop thinking about Dave the Laugh. He is not in this re-entrancing document.

Five minutes later

Blimey, I have finished my manifesto and it is still not time to go home. Miss Wilson is humming and reading something. It had better not be some humming idea she has for the school play. I am not doing a humming version of *Rom and Jule* and that is a fact. I am not humming in tights.

Four minutes later

I know what I will do next. I will make another scale for the Ace Gang. On how they too can become great mates like what I am.

Ten minutes later

Great mates scale.

1. Offer a mate a Midget Gem without being asked.
2. Share your last Jammy Dodger even though you really want it and your mate may be flicking her fringe about.
3. Listen to your mate rambling on about themselves when you have got vair important things to do yourself (e.g. nails, plucking etc.).
4. Be with your mate through thick and thin. Or even if they are both thick and thin. Tee-hee. I made a great mate-type joke there. Did you see??? Which leads me to Number 5.
5. Always be game for a laugh even though you may be blubbing on the inside.

Crikey, I am coming out of this scale VAIR well indeed. But as everyone knows, I do not blow my own trumpet. I just blow my own HOOOOORN.

No, I don't. And that brings me to my tip-toppy of the toppimost great mate scale.

6. Even when they have all the reason in the universe to be top dog (i.e. when they are the girlfriend of a Luuurve God, even if it is slightly on a sale-or-return basis) a top mate does not blow their own trumpet. Or snitch on her less fortunate mates.

6:00 p.m.
On my way home at last. Miss Wilson said, "Well, now that's over, I expect you are excited about our workshop for *Romeo and Juliet.*"

Oh no, the humming in tights.

Miss Wilson was rambling on.

"I've been busy coming up with some original ideas. I think it's important to keep up with you modern girls. I hope we can make this a... erm... groovy production."

Oh dear God.

I was walking along as fast as I could out of the school gates. She is wearing a knitted hat. It has a bobble on it.

That is all I am saying. I am not being bobble-ist.

She turned left out of the gate with me. Please, please let her not be going my way. I had done my detention!!!

She was still going on.

What if she linked arms with me?????

"I know you girls might think that us teachers are not very, you know... hip."

What? She was trying to be my mate! Please don't let her tell me about her growing feelings for Herr Kamyer. Maybe she'll call him by his first name. I don't even know what that is. I don't want to know. I bet it's Rudi!!!! Stop being my friend!! I've got enough on my plate without having to be friends with knitted people.

She didn't hear my inner screaming though. She said, "Yes, I think you will see that I do listen to your ideas and so on. For instance, when Jas suggested that perhaps Juliet could have a little companion – a sort of puppet dog – I thought 'Bingo'!!"

I couldn't stop myself, even though I had taken a vow of silence until she shut up or I died. I said, "Er, Miss Wilson, do you remember your last 'Bingo' idea? Do you remember, you said that juggling would be 'happening', but what actually 'happened' was that Melanie toppled over with the weight of her own basoomas and the oranges bounced into the audience."

Miss Wilson said, "Well, that's the excitement of theatre, isn't it? The danger, the risk!"

"Yes, my grandvati said an orange nearly took his eye out, so..."

Miss Wilson fortunately saw a bus coming and scampered off to get it. Thank the Lord.

It really is tragic how keen she is to get on with us. Touching really, if you like that sort of thing. Which I don't.

Thank goodness no one I knew saw me walking along talking to a teacher. I may just as well have gone to a leper colony if they had. Or become a policewoman.

Twenty minutes later

My road at last. Angus was round in Naomi's garden. He likes to go over to Mr and Mrs Across the Road for his evening poo.

Mr and Mrs Across the Road are vair unreasonable about

it. They say he always chooses to poo in their rare heathers windowbox. I explained to them, that is because the soil is nice and softy and he doesn't have to do any digging. But you can't tell people.

When he last came over to complain, Mr Across the Road said, "How long does his breed of cat live? Is it nearly over?"

I said with great dignitosity (I like to think), "Angus is half Scottish wildcat and sometimes he hears the call of the wild and longs to poo somewhere that reminds him of home. Hence the heather."

Mr Across the Road stomped off though. Some people don't understand the poetry of life. Or even the poo-etry of life. Hahahaha. I have just made an inward joke.

one minute later

When Angus saw me, he did his weird croaky miaow thing. And waved his tail about. His tail is still a bit crooked from his car accident. (The accident being that the car wasn't the huge mouse on wheels that Angus thought it was.) Otherwise, he is top dog catwise.

He came bounding over, purring around my legs. Which is nice, but it makes it really difficult to walk without falling over and breaking your neck. Now he has started his pouncey game. He pretends my ankles are his prey and hides behind something until my ankles loom in view. Then he tries to kill them.

I managed to beat him off with my rucky.

Then I noticed that Oscar, Junior Blunder Boy and all-round idiot, was lurking around on his wall, pretending to talk on his phone to all his mates. A.k.a. the Blunder Boys. He was going, "Yeah, check it... for real... awwwrite."

Absolute bloody wubbish of the first water.

I'd be amazed if he can work his phone and keep his trousers up at the same time. I used to prefer him when he just played keepie-uppie for ages. Now he's taking an interest in me, if you know what I mean, and I think you do.

When he stopped pretending to talk on his phone, he shouted over to me. "Ay, girl! Do you believe in love at first sight... or am I going to have to walk by again?"

Then he flicked his fingers and said, "For real."

Good Lord.

I didn't say anything.

What is there to say?

Besides "Go away" a LOT.

As I walked in my gate, Naomi came slinking along, waggling her bottom about. She displays no glaciosity or sophisticosity. Things are very different in the cat world. If I was a pussycat, entrancing a Luuurve God, I would merely have to lie on my back and display my girlie parts to him. Or maybe lick my bum-oley area, and not only him, but every boy in the area would be following me around like fools.

Angus and Naomi slunk off together under Dad's useless clown car. Vati has got a fur driving-wheel cover now. There is absolutely no need for it. Mind you, there is no need for Dad either.

Front room
One minute later
Vati was in his recreational area, a.k.a. lying on the couch getting fatter.

He lurched into life when I tried to slope up the stairs.

He said, "Where have you been until now?"

I said, "Why? Have you been waiting to tell me how much you appreciate me as a daughter and that although you will never be seeing me again once I am twenty-one, you have liked me entertaining you through your twilight years?"

"No, I bloody well didn't want to say that and stop being so bloody cheeky. Where have you been?"

"Erm, I was doing extra hockey."

"What, without your boots or kit which is thrown on the floor of your bedroom or 'rubbish tip', as I call it?"

I said, "Father, why have you been in my room? You know it is *verboten*. I may write to my MP and..."

He is sooooo violent. His slipper just missed my ponytail.

I wandered into the kitchen. Mum, Libby and Gordy were making some cakey thing. Which I will not be eating under any circumstances, including famine. Libby was covered in dough stuff. It was clinging to her raincoat and wellingtons. She came running over to me yelling, "It's bad boy, it's Gingeeeee! Kissy kiss, Ginger."

Oh gadzooks. She started climbing up my legs like a mad monkey in boots.

Oh good, now I am covered in cake mix, hurrah. Things are really looking up.

Mum said, "What did you get detention for this time?"

Why is everyone sooooo suspicious? I am not surprised I get detention all the time because no one will give me a chance. I could show her my "how to be a great mate" scale, but I won't.

I grabbed a sausagey thing from the cooker. It may have some nutritional value, you never know.

I was just going up to my room when Mum said, "Dave popped round earlier. He's a cool-looking boy, isn't he? If I was a few years younger, I wouldn't mind tangling tonsils with him."

Oh, how very disgusting.

I took the sausage/spam thing out of my mouth. I felt besmirched.

I said, "Mum, what were you wearing when he came round?"

She looked at me.

"Why? This."

I said, "What – that tiny skirt and even tinier top? I'm surprised he didn't call the prostitute police."

She snapped then.

"Don't be so bloody cheeky."

Libby joined in then. She stood with her hands on her hips and yelled, "Yes, bloddy chinky."

9:00 p.m.
I wonder what Dave was going to say?

I wish I'd been in, instead of being a great mate. I would have really liked to see him.

And he's not bad on the great mates scale himself. He talked to the Luuurve God for me.

Maybe I should phone him. And thank him.

One minute later

No, I can't because of my new re-entrancing a Luuurve God plan.

I am going to distract myself by making my little pouch.

9:15 p.m.

I am wearing my pouch. I am going to sleep in it tonight to make sure it is softy soft enough and so on. If I wake up in the night, I might feel for it (oo-er) and do a practice application.

9:20 p.m.

Libby is practising her snogging skills on Mr Potato Head. Surely this can't be right at her age? Shouldn't she mostly be pretending to be a fairy and playing with elves?

This is disgusting. Libby is going "mmmmmmmmm naiiice" and making lip-smacking noises.

I shouted downstairs.

"Hello, my sister Libby, also your daughter, is snogging a potato in my bed. What are you going to do about it?"

Dad started yelling uncontrollably. I wonder if he is having the male menopause? If he starts growing breasts, I will definitely be running away with the circus. Although to be fair, he would have a better chance of getting a job with them.

I could hear him going on.

"Connie, have you been using my bloody razors again? I've nearly cut my chin off."

Ah well, time for bobos.

I went back into my room and shut the door.

Libby is now doing a sort of smoochy dance with Mr Potato Head. It involves a lot of botty-wiggling.

What do they teach her at playschool? When I was little, we used to do face-painting and so on. Our tiny faces covered with little flowers and hearts. Libby wrote BUM on Josh's face in indelible marker.

I said to Bibbs, "Don't you want to take Mr Potato Head into your nice bed? In your own room. In your own lovely, snugly..."

She put her face really near mine and said, "Shhhhhhhhh."

Midnight

I had to read *Heidi* to Libby and Mr Potato Head. She never tires of tales of cheese. I do.

The bit that makes her laugh the most is when the little crippled girl falls out of her wheelchair.

It's not right.

Suddenly he got his maracas out

Wednesday September 21st
Assembly
9:00 a.m.

Oh, hurrah! We are having an "ad-hoc" assembly. No proper hymns that we can improvise hilarious lyrics to. No "Breathe on me BREAST of God" or "There are some green PANTS far away without a city wall..."

Hang on a minute though, things are looking up. On to the stage came Herr Kamyer in a check shirt and a cowboy hat. With a guitar. And he is accompanied by Miss Wilson on ukulele.

I said to Rosie, "I didn't even know she could play the ukulele."

Two minutes later
She can't.

This is torture. I don't know if you have ever heard the Country and Western version of "All things bright and beautiful", but I thoroughly don't recommend it.

I said to Rosie, "Quickly leap on stage and grab Herr Kamyer's guitar and kill him with it."

She said, "Righty-o," and started moving along the line. When she got to ADM on guard duty, she said to her, "Women's trouble" and skipped off to the loos.

Damn.

Fifty-five million years later we were set free. Well, free if you think double maths is freedom. Which it isn't.

Maths
Oh, shut up about numbers, why don't you?

Lunch
Behind the fives court. Right, this was my chance to

introduce the question of sophisticosity into the whole boynosity area.

I began, "I'd like to open this meeting of the Ace Gang…"

They were all looking at me attentively. Well, if you call people chewing and fiddling with their fringes and being fools attentive.

I went on, "I have called this meeting of the Ace Gang…"

Jools said, "One for all and all for one and one in all for one of us and so on?"

I said, "Yes, well, shall we get on?"

Ellen said, "Shall we do the group hug?"

I said, "I think we can take the group hug as done."

Mabs said, "I really like the group hug."

Oh dear *Gott in Himmel*.

Four minutes later

The group hug practically turned into a love-in. Rosie would not let me go. She knows it annoys me so she keeps doing it.

Eventually though, I beat her off and started again.

"The thing, the serious thing I want to discuss is…"

Rosie said, "My Viking wedding?"

"Well, no I…"

But it was too late. She had her beard out.

Afternoon break

I will try again.

Mr Attwood wheeled past us, tutting. Tut away, lunatic man.

Two minutes later

We watched while he got stuck trying to get up the ramp into the science block. Unfortunately, the Titches were passing and he harassed them into pushing him. While they were huffing and puffing, he actually opened a sandwich and started eating it.

I said to the gang, "He luuurves ligging about in that wheelchair. I bet he hasn't even got a bad back."

Rosie said, "Have you thought about being a nurse? I think you've got the hands for it."

I didn't get the chance to mention the sophisticosity question because Jas started going on about Tom. Is he going to go to college in Hamburger-a-gogo land? Blah blah blah. He wants to go visit the maybe college after Chrimboli.

Should she go with him? Blah blah blah.

What she actually said was, "Should I go with him? It's an area very rich in wildlife."

I said, "Oh well, you must go then. You can set fire to most of Texas and gather crusted newts to your heart's content. I only wish I could come. However, I have a life and maybe a boyfriend..."

Jas got into her huffmobile. Typico. Anything to do with Hunky or her fringe and she gets the hump. She was doing fringe-fiddling to the max.

I said, "Look, Jas, all I am saying is that we decided that you should let Tom ping off elastic-bandwise and then he can come pinging back. Possibly with gifts. Maybe some new owls."

"But you don't know that for sure, do you? I mean in *Rom and Jule*, Jule wakes up after pretending to commit suicide and Rom actually has committed suicide."

I looked at her.

"Jas, what has some old play got to do with it? It's a made-up story."

"It might not be."

"Well it is."

"How do you know – were you there?"

I wanted to kill her. I hate her in this mood.

"No, Jas, I wasn't there. I am not four hundred and fifty-five."

"Well then."

"Well."

This could go on for years. I decided to call a truce with old arsey pants.

"Look, Jas, Tom is not going to commit suicide, is he? He's just going to go to Hamburger-a-gogo land for two weeks. That'll be enough for him. When he sees the size of their shorts, he'll come scampering back."

"Well, maybe."

"Of course he will, and also they say 'aluuuuuuuuminum' there, don't they? He won't put up with that. Will he?"

"Well..."

"And mostly of all, he doesn't wear tights like Rom, does he?"

She didn't say anything, just went a bit red.

"Jas, whatever Tom has under his trousers is between you and him."

That did it.

It doesn't take much for her to expose her violent side. She really hurt my ankle. I'm glad that she doesn't have a sword in *Rom and Jule*. But does she have a dagger at the end? It could be a bloodbath if her fringe doesn't go right.

In the gym
Rom and Jule workshop
2:00 p.m.

The "workshop" exceeded even my very high expectations. Miss Wilson was in a sort of all-in-one "playsuit". She was tremendously excited.

We were lolling around on the mats when she started clapping her hands and waving a clipboard around wildly.

"Now then, girls, attention, please, on this very exciting day. Now, here we are. We are all in Verona. Can you hear the swish of the light summer wind in the blossom trees? The gay calls of the streetsellers?"

(Rosie started honking with laughter.) But Miss Wilson was immersing herself in the gay calls and the breeze.

"We are all young, full of life and passion. Come on, girls, let's get up and show that passion. Feel the passion. Just go with the flow. Grab a tambourine or a drum if you like!!! Use the whole space!!!!"

Ten minutes later
I have rarely seen anything more alarming than Miss Wilson being free and passionate. And keep in mind, I have seen her in her nuddy-pants and with her soap on a rope.

She was careering around, banging her tambourine...

At one point, she got on the wall bars and threw bean bags around.

She was yelling, "Waaaaaaaaaa Waaaaaaaaa."

Quite sensationally mad.

I said to Jools mid-leap, "Poor Rudi Kamyer has no chance."

Twenty minutes later
As a climactic end to the workshop, Rosie showed her inner passion by pulling her nick-nacks down and mooning at us.

I am aching with laughter. My ribs hurt.

Hey and guess what? When I popped to the piddly-diddly department because I thought I might have an accident,

I saw Elvis Attwood having a sly fag. And he was walking about normally. He can walk!

Home time
Hurrah hurrah!!!

Just walking out of Stalag 14 main building, all sweaty and shiny with our berets pulled down to our eyes for comedy effect, when we noticed that Tom and Robbie were waiting at the gates.

Hell's teeth.

Jas said, "How's my head?"

I said, "Alarmingly red. How's mine?"

She looked at me and went, "Blimey."

We had to think quickly. The boys hadn't seen us because they were chatting with a few passing girls that they knew. So we dashed off to the science block loos to do emergency repair work.

I put my head upside down under the hairdryer. My hope was that Robbie secretly liked the Coco the Clown look. Jas opted for the hair pulled back in a tight little ponytail, which frankly I think is a bit of a mistake, as it exposed her very, very red ears.

I didn't say though, because I didn't want her to have a complete tiz and to-do.

As we were doing lippy and mascara (thank goodness for my pouch), Jas said, "Anyway, why are you bothering about Robbie? Masimo is your one and only, isn't he?"

"I know, but once you have been out with someone you have to keep up appearances so that every time they see you, they think, 'Oooh, I wish I could snog her to within an inch of her life.' That is just the dating code."

"Apart from if it was Mark Big Gob."

"Please don't mention him."

"Or Whelk Boy."

"Jas, just shut up and turn your skirt up."

At the gate, I was casualosity personified until Robbie said, "Hello, Georgia."

He's a good-looking bloke. And nice with it. With very blue eyes, and a firm but tender mouth. Also he has charming snogging skills, his varying pressure technique for instance... hang on a minute, was that him or Dave the Laugh?

Robbie was looking at me. Had I said anything out loud?

I said, "Hi, Robbie, nice to see you."

My brain went on chatting to him, "Yeah, nice to see you, you hunky brute. Why are you with old Ms No Forehead when you could be in a triple-sided manwich with me and the Luuurve God?"

Shut up, brain. That is disgusting!!!!

Tom said, "Hi, Lindsay, all right?"

And it was Ms No Forehead herself. The Bride of Dracula... I looked down at my watch (which I haven't got) and said loudly, "Oh, is that the time? I must dash."

And I hoiked up my rucky. I said to Jas, "Are you walking?"

And she looked a bit dithery.

Hang on a minute. She wasn't choosing between walking with me or walking with the Hunky Brothers and WET LINDSAY, was she?

Oh yes she was.

Lindsay ignored me as if I was invisible girlie and said, "Jas, are you going on Saturday? Maybe we could meet up before, that's if Robbie can do without me. Can you, babe?"

And she went and kissed him on the cheek. Then she pointed to her own cheek. And sort of pouted. And he had to kiss her cheek.

Dear God.

It got worse. I was sort of mesmerised by horror.

She put on an ickle girlie voice and said, "Can ickle Lindsay go to de big club all by her lickle self?"

Christ on a bike.

It was horrific. It was like when Mr Next Door came to tell me off and he was wearing his shortie dressing gown and I could see his legs.

As I walked off – walking home without my so-called bestie – Tom called after me, "See you later, Gee."

And Robbie said, "Yeah, see you Saturday."

I noticed that Jas didn't dare say anything. I don't know why I bother being a really great mate to her. Boys are nicer than girls.

I'm going to show her my Great Mates Scale and suggest she tries being one. (A great mate, not a scale.)

Home

Bum-ty has got a ladder. He's crouching at the top of it. I don't think he likes his ladder. I think he is up there because it makes him slightly further away from the staring cats.

He hasn't said a word and his feathers are starting to fall out. Libby has been showing him pictures of cheese.

7:00 p.m.
I've got German homework. I have to write about the Kochs. Hurrah!!!

When he set the homework, I said to Herr Kamyer, "Can it be about the Kochs going out? Because the little Kochs like to go out, don't they? Although the bigger Kochs prefer to stay in."

The Ace Gang had a mini larf-fest but Rudi didn't get how full of hilariosity I truly am. He just looked at me with his blinky eyes and said (seriously), "*Ja*, Georgia, zat is a *gut* idea, vy not haf ze Kochs havink a wild party???"

Which made us laugh even more.

I have said it once and I will say it again, I luuurve the Kochs and the comedy magic that is the German language.

Also, Herr Kamyer's idea of a wild party is probably a game of Scrabble with Miss Wilson where they don't keep the score.

7:30 p.m.
I am looking through my German slang book for inspirationosity for the Koch party.

Two minutes later

Bottom is *arsch*. To fall arse over tit is *auf die Schnauze fallen*.

Two minutes later

This cannot be true. With knobs on is *mit schnickschnack*.

I think, in all honesty, the first person to make up der German language was a clown. Or alternatively, a *blodman* (berk).

8:00 p.m.

Looking through my window.

Aaah, there is Cross-eyed Gordy stretching out on the wall.

Now he is half sitting up, swatting at something. What is he doing?

Oh, it's a bee. He's up on his hind legs swatting at the bee. He's sort of hopping along on his hind legs swatting the bee.

One minute later

Angus has joined him on the wall.

He's watching Gordy hopping along swatting the bee and

he is moving his head about. Following the bee.

It's the bee dance. Hop hop, swatty swat, movey head, movey head. Super cats do the bee dance.

One minute later
Not any more.

Angus has eaten the bee. He just leaped up and ate it.

He didn't even chew it.

Two minutes later
Lying down on my bed, recovering from the excitement of bee dancing.

I wonder who is going to be Rom? Everyone who has tried out so far has been an utter fiasco. Miss Wilson said she might have to look outside our year. Crikey, what if she asks Rudi Kamyer to do it?

Phone rang
Aha! This will be my so-called bestie ringing up to apologise.

Mum yelled up, "Georgia, it's for you."

I lolloped downstairs, taking my time, building up my

dignitosity. I said formally into the phone, "Yes. What is it you want to say?"

"Usually, I like you to say, 'What is it you want to say, Hornmeister' but I'll let you off because I am in a casual Devil take the hindmost mood."

Dave the Laugh! My heart skipped a little beat. I said, "Guess what? Wet Lindsay talked like an ickle girl to Robbie. It was horrific. Do boys like that sort of thing in girls?"

Dave said, "It depends on what the girls are wearing."

"What?"

"Boys are very visual."

"Er, Dave, I think you mean very stupid. Anyway, it doesn't matter what Wet Lindsay wears. It can't disguise her Octopussyness."

"Listen, Chaos Queen, how's every little thing? Is your girlfriend still stropping around, rifling through his handbag, or is it all tickety-boo?"

"Well, he wrote me a note, but I haven't seen him yet. It'll be the first time on Sat. He says we should take it easy and that maybe he overreacted a bit."

Dave said, "A bit? That's like Hitler saying 'Oooh, I just meant to go for a little walk, but then I accidentally invaded Poland.'"

"No, Dave, it isn't anything like that."

"You didn't know that Hitler invaded Poland, did you?"

"Of course I did."

"You don't know where Poland is, do you?"

"Dave, I am not a complete fool."

"Where is it then?"

"It's clearly, you know, near..."

"Yes?"

"The top bit."

Dave laughed. "You are good value, Kittykat."

I was a bit red, but at least I had avoided saying that I was sort of "on trial" maturiosity-wise with the Luuurve God...

Dave said, "So you'll be at the gig on Saturday?"

"Yes, will you be there?"

"Probs."

"Dave?"

"Yep..."

"Well, Dave, will you, can you, will you not be too funny and not talk to me and so on?"

"You want me to not talk to you and not be funny and so on?"

He sounded a bit weird.

I said, "Only until, you know, the whole thing, the whole pants and comedy twisting thing dies down."

He said, "You must really like him..."

I didn't say anything.

He said, "Listen, I have to dasharoo. S'laters." And he hung up.

I think he's miffed.

Dear God, you just get one boy off the numpty seat and another one goes and sits on it.

10:00 p.m.

Why do cats do this? They loll about snoozing in weird places for hours.

It's never their cat basket.

Why would anything want to have a snooze on the top of the kitchen rubbish bin?

Or the loo seat?

Or the fruit bowl?

Then, after all that snoozing all day, at 10:00 p.m. they wake up and go utterly bananas. Tearing up and down the stairs. Leaping from the sofa to the television, missing and falling down the back of it. Diving into plastic bags. Wrestling with their own feet. Then shooting up the curtains and doing ad-hoc sailors' hornpipe stuff coming down...

Why?

Where does leaping up curtains and doing the hornpipe occur in primitive cat life?

In bed
10:30 p.m.

Time for snoozy snooze and Luuurve Goddy dreams.

I've almost forgotten what the Luuurve God looks like.

Thirty seconds later

Yummy scrumboes though, I know that much.

And also, Grrrrrrrrrr.

Oh dear God, I actually said that out loud. I am growling at myself.

I have got snogging withdrawal baaaaad.

In fact, maybe I have forgotten how to snog.

Oh no. I may have lost my skills puckerwise.

I need to practise.

10:35 p.m.

I have done something so disgusting and weird that even I am ashamed of myself.

One minute later

This may be another thing I will not be mentioning this side of the grave.

One minute later

I hope that God and Baby Jesus were momentarily looking aside. Like I am sure they do when you are having a poo.

Or when Uncle Eddie does his baldy-o-gram.

One minute later

I can't get the thing that I will never talk about ever again out of my brain.

One minute later

I can't stand this. OK, I admit it!!!!

I looked at Mr Potato Head and considered practising puckering up on him.

There you are – it's out now.

one minute later

Yes, I momentarily thought about snogging my little sister's cast-off.

one minute later

I wonder where snogging a root vegetable would come on the Snogging Scale?

Minus 50 I should think.

I bet Jas snogs her owls.

11:00 p.m.

I hope Dave is just having a minor hump. We are, after all, mates.

Yeah, that will be it. He will just be having a No. 7 (walking on ahead, metaphorically).

It won't be the full Humpty Dumpty.

So that's all right.

2:00 a.m.

Woke up from a dream that I was at a fancy-dress party. I was painted purple and in the nuddy-pants because I had gone as a jelly baby. Then Dave the Laugh came by really slowly with a girl on his back. I said, "What have you come as?"

And he said, "A tortoise."

I said, "Who's the girl on your back?"

And he said, "That's Michelle... Do you get it – me-chelle?"

And he was laughing and laughing. But not in a nice way.

Friday September 23rd
8:15 a.m.

I really need some new shoes for Saturday night. Maybe my vati is in a sunny, Devil take the hindmost sort of mood about money this morning.

I said, "Dad... I couldn't help noticing how... er... shiny, your car is. You do keep it lovely."

"No."

"Dad, I..."

"Goodbye."

I can't believe it.

Mum came mumming in, in her knickers. Well, if you can call them that.

Hang on a minute.

402

I said, "Mum, are you wearing a thong?"

She is. She is wearing a thong!

I said to her, "If you have a road accident, I will not be coming to explain your underwear to the emergency services."

She just looked at me and went off into the bathroom... Well. Then I remembered my new shoes.

I shouted to her, "Mum, could I just borrow..."

Before I could finish, she shouted back. "No."

What is the point of parents? They wonder why the youth of today goes wrong. If they would merely give us what we wanted and keep away from us, all would be well...

Instead of Mum just lending me her black Chanel stilettos and everything being nice and easy, I am now going to have to sneak into her wardrobe, smuggle them out in my bag, wear them, sneak back into her room and replace them.

They force us into a life of crime.

8:30 a.m.
On the way to school
Jas needn't think I have forgotten about her blatant lack of best mateyness. And her creepy-crawly pants behaviour around Wet Lindsay.

I am going to have the hump with her for once and see how she likes that. I am going to avoid her house and go a different way. That will teach her that you can't... she is sitting on my gate.

Damn. I hadn't even had a chance to get in my huffmobile.

She hopped off the gate and said, "Gee, I'm really sorry about last night. I couldn't sort of get out of it because of Tom and Robbie. It's not Lindsay, but the boys are brothers and... well, you know... blood is thicker than not having a forehead."

I went, "Hmmph."

She got her Midget Gems out and offered me one.

I was a bit suspicious.

"Where have you been keeping these? It's not your special pantie hoard, is it?"

She said, "I just bought them new. You can open the packet and have any colour you like, even if it's not the top one."

Blimey, she is really pulling out all the stops.

On the way to Stalag 14

It's more fun being chummly wummlies with Jazzy Spazzy

than riding alone in the huffmobile.

I said, "Did you hear Wet Lindsay doing that ickle girl thing?"

Jas nodded like Noddy the well-known nodding dog from Nodland. And then she said, "I've decided I'm not going to go for being a prefect any more. I don't want to hang out with Wet Lindsay and ADM."

I said, "Who does? They don't even want to hang out with themselves."

But I was really pleased. I gave her a spontaneous outdoor hug. Even though we might have been seen by the Blunder Boys and created an outburst of "Get 'em off, you lezzies."

Five minutes later

We were in such a good matey mood that we did the top part of the snot dance along the High Street... I am soooo happy I've got my luuuverly bestie mate and gang and on Saturday I will be in the arms of a Luuurve God. Probably.

Break

We were in a spontaneous dance mood all day. But not in a getting-a-detention way. When Mr Attwood appeared around our camp (the fives court) in his wheelchair, we did a quick rendition of the snot dance. Just to cheer him up. In case he was feeling peaky at having to pretend to be crippled. But did he appreciate it? No, he did not.

In fact, as usual, he was shouting.

"You young buggers, I'll tell the headmistress about this!!"

I said, "Mr Attwood, we are merely trying to cheer you up with our girlish high spirits. Anyway, I am here to help. I am going to push you to the science block..."

He said, "I'm not going to the science block."

I said, "Are you sure?"

He didn't seem keen, but I started pushing his chair down the incline towards the lower part of the science block.

I said, "Oooh, we're really moving along now, aren't we, Mr Attwood? Are you enjoying yourself? I am."

He was yelling, "Oy oy, watch it, watch it!!!"

Then we started going faster and faster and I was singing, "He taught me to yodel... yodo-le-ee-heee. Do you know *Heidi*, Mr Attwood?"

He was shouting, "Never mind about bloody *Heidi*!"

I said, "Never mind about *Heidi*? It's a classic, Mr Attwood... Oh dear, oh dear... Oh NO! I've lost control of the chair. I can't stop it... We're going to crash into the science block! Save yourself, save yourself!!!"

At which point, Mr Attwood leaped out of his chair like a very old startled earwig. He was trotting along, pulling up his trousers and grumbling on, "Bloody fool, I could have been killed!"

But I fell to my knees and started yelling, "It's a miracle. It's a miracle. Look, everyone. He can walk. He walks!!!!"

And loads of people saw him, so everyone knew he was pretending, so he didn't dare do anything to me. Resultio! He was bang to rights, as our proud bobbies in blue might say (if they were in the mood).

Afternoon break
I explained my re-entrancing a Luuurve God plan.

Rosie said, "So your nub and gist is nicey-nice, glaciosity and pouch work?"

"*Mais oui.*"

Friday evening
8:00 p.m.
In bed with a face mask on. I've made it myself with mashed

♡ 407

up banana and cream. It feels disgustingly slimy. Like having Wet Lindsay on your face. OH MY GOD!!!

I want to scrub my brain out.

I hope the Luuurve God appreciates this. Although, of course, I don't necessarily want him to know about me being slathered in banana.

8:10 p.m.

I am going to lie here in my mask and imagine what I want to happen tomorrow night. I've barricaded my door with some drawers, so it should be cat and loon proof.

Not that anybody cares what I'm up to, as it's party headquarters downstairs. Mum has got some of her mad aquarobics friends round and Dad and Uncle Eddie and their new bestie Mr Across the Road are all making complete arses of themselves.

They are all wearing tight, light blue jeans for a start. What is that all about? Where have all the proper dads gone? Like in Dickens and so on. Dads in "Crap Expectations" and "David Copperpants" were either dead or had a proper job that kept them out of the house all day and most of the night.

My only idea of what a real dad could be like comes from Jas's dad. He wears Marks and Spencers casual slacks and a cardigan with a pocket for his pipe and bifocals. Like in the *Good Dad Guide Book*, which I haven't read and Dad certainly hasn't. And if I had read it, I know for a fact there would not be a chapter on "How to be a male stripper".

Anyway, where was I?

Aaaah, yes, relaxey vousey and Ohhhhmmmmmm...

Here we go and relaxxxxxxxxxxxxxxxxxxx...

So, here I am in my fantasy. I have arrived at the Sugar Club. Hmmmmm, I looked naaaice in my mum's fabby stilettos and my denim skirt and little cheeky waistcoat which emphasises my shape, but doesn't thrust my basoomas into the face of others.

My hair displayed *magnifique* bounceability and my skin glowed with the look that only four bananas mashed to a pulp can achieve.

Confident of my charms, I blinked my eyes slowly (forty-five layers of mascara are heavy). My nose, which once flung itself with gay abandon across my face, seemed a normal size. I have quite literally grown into my nose. Although this is not to suggest that I have an enormous head.

And when I say I have grown into my nose, I also don't mean that I am actually living in my nose, so stop it. And get out of my fantasy, whoever you are.

My Ace Gang and I entered the club and everyone looked round. Who is that, they asked themselves. She looks like someone who should go out with a lead singer or something... The band came on and started to play.

I was dancing by myself. I don't need a partner tonight because... there he was.

Up on the stage.

In the spotlight of life.

A Luuurve God.

And everyone knows that a Luuurve God on the stage is worth two on a bus.

He looked at me. I looked at him.

Time stood still.

Suddenly, he got his maracas out (leave it) and started playing. It was a tune called "Georgia, *mia bellissima*, Georgia".

It was about me.

He beckoned me on to the stage.

I looked shyly away, but the crowd started chanting, "We want Georgia, we want Georgia!!"

Smiling sweetly, I got up on to the stage. But I couldn't sing – why was I up there?

The Stiff Dylans started to really rock out. Robbie gave me a nice smile and nodded his head to me.

Suddenly, I knew what I was born to do.

I started to move to the beat.

I raised my arms and *WHOOOOSH*!

Flame dance to the right, flame dance to the left.

Whoosh whoosh.

The Ace Gang looked at each other and, smiling shyly, they too mounted the stage (I said leave it).

They acknowledged the crowd with a quick huddly duddly and then they joined in with the dancing...

We did a compilation of our greatest hits, flame to the right, flame to the left.

Whoosh whoosh.

Bogey dangle, bogey dangle.

Eyes shut for night-time Viking paddling,

Paddle, paddle to the right and to the left,

Then interweaving paddling.

And then, in a grand finale, we fell to our knees with a shout of HOOOORRRRN!!!!

As the crowd went wild, Wet Lindsay got her coat. A beam of light from the stage illuminated her lack of forehead. She beckoned to Robbie and he shook his head. She stormed off.

The Luuurve God helped me to my feet and stared in admiration. I knew what he was thinking (telepathically). "Aaaaah, beauty-io and talent-io all in one package-io."

He kissed my hand and then all up my arm. And then he started on my neck.

Thank goodness he didn't start at my ankles otherwise we would have been there all night.

As he got to my ears, I saw Dave the Laugh in quite a cool suit. He was just looking at me sadly, then he said to Emma, "Get your face on, love, we're leaving."

He looked angry and upset.

Hang on a minute, how did Dave the Laugh get in this? And also why is he such a downer??

I sat up in bed. He's spoiled my fantasy now, stropping around in the Humpty Dumpty.

For no reason at all. Ish.

Boo.

Two minutes later

I should have told him about the Titches' tribute to him when they broke the loo seat. That would have cheered him up. It's not like him to be moody. He's not an Italian Stallion.

In fact, that's one of the best things about him, that he is Dave the Laugh.

The key word being "Laugh".

One minute later

I wonder who Jas likes best out of Dave the Laugh and Masimo?

She's never said.

I might phone her and ask her.

Not that I am bothered.

In the hall
9:00 p.m.

I can hear the "grown-ups" giggling like fools. I glanced into the front room to see Dad crawling through Mum's friend, Big Beryl's, legs. He had a balloon in his mouth. It is very disturbing.

I went to use the phone and Mum came mumming out.

I said to her, "Mum, this is not some sort of wife-swapping party, is it? Because if it is, can I not have Big Beryl as my new mum?"

Mum said, "Don't call her Big Beryl."

I said, "You do."

And she said, "Yeah, but not in front of her."

That is sooo typical of the lax morals she has.

Thirty seconds later

Rang Jas.

Jas's mum, who is practically a saint in human form in my opinion, answered the phone. She even sounded glad to hear my voice – that is how nice she is. When I asked for Jas, she said, "I'll get her. She is just making an aquarium with Tom."

For politenessnosity I said, "Are you doing anything nice this evening?"

And she said, "Well, yes, Dad and I are jam-making actually."

I said, "I hope you've got your aprons on."

And she said, "Oh yes, dear."

And I know she does not lie.

As Mum passed again, staggering under the weight of

wine and lager, I said, "Jas's mum and dad are making jam."

She said, "Why is your face all slimy?"

Jas came on the phone all breathless and excited.

"Hi, hi, we've just put the gravel in and the miniature Ferris wheel. There's going to be a grotto area and…"

"Jas, fish don't go on Ferris wheels."

"Oh, I know that. It's for the crabs."

I didn't know what to say.

She went rambling on because she has little real idea of how mad she is.

"Anyway, what do you want? Have you decided what to wear? I've started learning my Juliet part. It's terribly sad."

You're not kidding, matey.

For friendlies sake, I pretended to be interested.

"Have you got to 'hark what pants through yonder windows break'? I like that bit – it's my fave."

She was, as usual, being Mrs Fussy Knickers.

"It's Romeo who says that and it isn't 'pants' it's 'light'…"

"Light, pants, owls… what difference does it make? I can't stand here discussing pants with you all night. I want to ask you a vair important question."

"What?"

"Who would you go out with? The Luuurve God or Dave the Laugh?"

"Oh noooooooooooooo, no, no, no and no. I am not answering that. You'll blame me for choosing the wrong one whichever one I pick, and anyway, it's nothing to do with me."

"Come on, Jazzy, I just want to know. I won't blame you or anything. I love you."

"Don't start that again."

"Come on, Jas."

"You promise you don't mind and you just want me to be honest? From my point of view?"

"Yep, as simple as that."

"Hmmmm."

There was a silence.

Apart from what sounded like chewing.

What was she chewing?

I bet it was her fringe.

I said, "Hello, what are you doing? Look, just be spontaneous!!! It's a simple, harmless question. Who would you choose? There's no pressure, JUST CHOOSE!!!!

She said, "Well... Dave the Laugh of course."

"What? What did you say?"

"Dave the Laugh."

"But I'm going out with the Luuurve God. You know, the grooviest, most good-looking Pizza-a-gogo dreamboat."

"I know, but I personally and hypothetically would choose Dave the Laugh."

"Why?"

"He's a laugh."

"Masimo's a laugh."

"When?"

"Jas, me and him have LOADS of laughs when we are alone. We are practically laughing the whole time."

"Well, that's good. I'm just saying that I have seen you have a laugh with Dave the Laugh, but I haven't seen you have a laugh with Masimo. He's not called Masimo the Laugh, is he?"

I said, "Well, I have to go now, Jas. Goodbye."

"You've not got the hump, have you?"

"Of course I have not got the hump, I assure you."

Why did she say Dave the Laugh?

10:30 p.m.

I can't get to sleep now.

I know why Jas chose Dave the Laugh. It's because she's frightened of doing anything unconventional. She probably thinks that Masimo is not really English.

He isn't.

11:00 p.m.
If she had parents like mine, she'd probably choose someone a bit different.

11:10 p.m.
Anyway, Dave is the "different" one. You wouldn't get Masimo doing run run leap.

11:15 p.m.
Or swearing in German.

11:16 p.m.
Or doing mad twisting.

11:24 p.m.
Or nip libbling.

Right, that's it. I am going to sleep. I am giving my brain

an official warning.

I know what, I will distract myself by reading through my part in *Rom and Jule*. I suppose I will have to learn it sometime.

I may as well get into the mood to be Mercutio.

I will climb into the tights of life.

Right, here we go...

Ten minutes later

Crikey. Miss Wilson said that Mercutio was the comedy part. He is supposed to be a laugh, but frankly, he's what I would call an "unlaugh". I may have to improvise some comedy moments with fake blood...

When I say "Ay ay a scratch, marry; tis enough. Where is my page? Go villain, fetch a surgeon," after I am stabbed to death, I could make fake blood spurt all over the page and they would be bound to have the ditherspaz and possibly fall off the stage.

Yes, I am beginning to see the possibilities of Billy Shakespeare's renowned comedy... Zzzzzzzzzzzzzzzzzzzzzzz zzzzzzzzzzzzzzzzzzzzz.

My tights runneth over

Saturday September 24th

I feel much better and excited about seeing the Luuurve God again and impressing him with my sophisticosity.

I feel cool as a cucumber that has been lying around in a fridge, reading books on coolness.

Phone rang

It was Jas.

"Where shall we meet? Hey, guess what? There's going to be an international band management type person coming tonight. If the Stiffs go on world tour, would you give up your education to go with them?"

"No, of course not. What is pleasure and travel and luuurve, compared to knowing how to say 'I have broken my glasses' in French?"

In my bedroom
The only blot on the landscape of luuurvenosity is sneaking Mum's shoes out of her wardrobe without being thrashed to within an inch of my life.

I must not arouse her temperosity in any way. Especially since she has been in such a bad mood since the balloon party thing. I don't know what Dad has done, but she doesn't like it. I don't like it and I don't even know what it is.

Anyway, I must be like the wily fox.

Foxy and wily.

Here I go as a foxy-wily thing.

In the kitchen
I said, "Do you want a cup of tea, Mum?"

Foxy wily, foxy wily.

She looked at me.

"Have you got my perfume on?"

I resisted the temptation to strop off and said, "No, it's just that well... I'm really excited about tonight, you know, making it up with Masimo and..."

She smiled at me.

"It's lovely being so into someone, isn't it? I remember when your dad used to..."

Oh no, she is going to talk about her feelings for Dad. I must stop her, and also get her to go out so I can get her shoes.

Two minutes later

In a fit of hysterical madness, I have found myself agreeing to go to the Wild Park with her tomorrow.

How did that happen?

I just said, "You need to go out more." Now I'm going out with her.

I meant to get her shoes.

In my bedroom

I have given myself a French manicure because that is vair vair European. And also because I don't know what an Italian manicure is.

Phone rang

Dad yelled up, "Georgia, it's another of your mates again. I am trying to work out a new dance routine with the magnificent baldy-o-gram and am constantly interrupted."

I didn't bother to reply.

He is wearing shorts around the house.

What if a normal person unexpectedly pops round?

He has leg hair that stops at his knees.

How grotesque.

I am beginning to feel a bit sorry for Mum.

It was Rosie.

"Sven has just cooked me a Viking snack."

"What is it?"

"Deep-fried Mars bar. I could paddle for miles now and still do a spot of pillaging and extreme violence at the end of it."

Just to check that my lecture on sophisticosity had got through to the Ace Gang I said, "What are you wearing tonight? There is no beard involved, is there?"

Rosie laughed, but not in a reassuring way.

"Toodle pip, see you at 7:30 p.m."

6:00 p.m.

Mum and Dad and Bibbs and Uncle Eddie have popped out to get a pizza in the loonmobile. I've just heard the roar of its massive quarter-horsepower engine *phut phut* off into the distance.

Before they went, I could hear Mum having a go at Dad in the driveway just under my window. She is deffo at No. 8, the quarter humpty (evils), on the Having the Hump Scale. Bordering on No. 9, the half humpty (evils and withdrawal of all snacks). This started because he didn't open the car door for her. She said, "Jim across the road has lovely manners – he opens doors for me."

Dad said, "Come on, love, you're a big woman, a very big woman. You can manage a little door. You could open it easily with one of your nungas."

I didn't hear the rest of it, but it was mostly Mum shouting and Libby yelling, "Bum bum, arsey ARSEEEEEEEY!"

Lovely.

7:15 p.m.

Got Mum's shoes, although they are not what you would call comfortable. They are what you would call agonising.

I'll wear my ballet pumps till I get there.

Oh, I am so nervy. I nearly stuck the mascara brush up my nose. Oh God, I may be turning into Ellen. She's only phoned me eight times to tell me that she is soooo excited about seeing Declan. I think that is what she said. Or something. What do you think? Or something? Shut up!!!!!!

Met the Ace Gang at Hennes

My worst fears are realised. Rosie is wearing a lurex catsuit...

She saw me looking and said, "Yes, it's groovy, isn't it?"

As we walked along, I said, "Please tell me that Sven has not got a matching catsuit."

She just winked at me.

Oh no, I bet he has.

And I bet it is snug.

Round the trouser snake area.

Oh noooooooo.

As we walked, I gave the gang the pep talk.

"Don't forget the plan. The key note here, is nicenosity and glaciosity. You have to be around me at all times, making

♥ 425

me look vair popular... Smiling is good, but no ad-hoc, full-on snorting and capering sort of laughing."

Sugar Club
9:00 p.m.
We're going in.

It's an amazing place. It's got a sort of "chill out" room. I know that because it says so on a notice. Ellen was going, "Is it like... if when... you know, you're hot or something and..."

Ellen should really live in that room. She is so dithery at seeing her "boyfriend" that she can hardly keep her head on.

In the tarts' wardrobe
I said, "I've got this new stay-on lipstick so even if someone had a wire brush, they couldn't get it off."

Rosie said, "Oh yeah, you say that but you should get Sven to test it. If anyone is a human wire brush, it's him. The gorgeous big brute."

I said, "Where is the gorgeous big brute?"

Rosie said, "With the lads. They are having a pre-club

game of footie in the park."

It's dark.

Why?

OK, big breaths (yeth, I thertainly have got big breaths. Shut up brain).

I've got my stilettos on. I am full to the tippy topmost of sophisticosity and *je ne sais quoi*.

Except in the knicker department, which has a touch of the jelloid about it.

What if Masimo has had second thoughts and he just comes over and says, "Face it, love, you're dumped"?

Although he of course would say "dump-io-ed".

10:00 p.m.
The Blunder Boys came lurgying in. Mark Big Gob had his hands in the back pockets of his jeans and some tiny fool hanging off his arm. His mouth is practically bigger than she is. As he passed by us, he said, "There's a party in my trousers and you're all invited."

And the Blunderers were going, "Oh yeah. Cool."

And laughing like constipated hyenas.

Prats.

10:30 p.m.

Oooh, this is agony, this hanging around pretending not to be hanging around. Where is he?

Then I saw him. He came out of the backstage area and he was wearing an electric blue suit with a blue shirt. Blimey, he looked so cool. And he's so sort of blokey. He's got a bit of designer stubble and his hair is a bit longer.

Every bit of me is separately jelloid. Now I know how Slim feels when all her chins are moving in a different rhythm.

He was talking to a group of St Pat's boys and then two tarts I vaguely knew from St Mary's came up, thrusting themselves at him. And giggling, like hens that had eaten too many worms and were having a worm rush. If you know what I mean and I think you do.

Mabs said, "You'd better move about a bit, Gee, otherwise he won't know you're here."

Jools said, "Look, there's a spare table. Let's go and sit down at it and then he will see us walking across."

Good point well made.

We started to walk over to the table.

Bloody hell, Mum's shoes were high. I'd better walk slowly. Oh, and do the flicky hair, hip to the right, hip to the left thing that boys are supposed to like. I don't know why they like girls who look like they have got false hips, but there you are. The whole bloody thing is a mystery.

Two minutes later

It is amazing though, boys really do like it. At last I reached the table and put my hand on it to steady myself. I'm exhausted. I may have to have a little lie-down under the table and...

"*Ciao*, Georgia."

I looked up and there he was. Looking at me with those dreamy eyes. They looked amazingly yellow. It must be the blue suit, but they were sort of like Angus's eyes. Not insane, clearly, but the colour was the same. And his skin is sort of olive, and his mouth, well, blimey is all I can say.

Thirty seconds later

So much for our plan of light sophisticated talk... the Ace

Gang were WUBBISH. They were just giggling and twittering on.

"Oooohhh, look at your nice shirt..."

"Ooooh, hahahha."

"Oooohh, I like your hair long it's... Ooooohhh."

Etc. like a bunch of mad doves.

Masimo said to me, "Miss Georgia, maybe at the end of the gig, I could walk you home."

Oh, thank God. He still liked me, at least a little bit.

I smiled at him (a contained smile, making sure that my nose didn't spread all over my face). I just smiled enigmatically and kept tight control over my nostrils. I wanted to say something, but I had lost all control of my bits and pieces.

My brain felt quite literally like a bag of wet mice.

He came and stood close to me and touched my face. He said, "Tonight there is, how you say, the men for management... they are wanting to speak with me in the break. So, *mi dispiace*, I will not be having you for myself until later... Sorry, *cara*..."

Then he kissed me softly on the hand and then behind the ear, and then two little kisses on my neck and then he looked me in the eyes – I was melting, I was melting – and put his mouth on mine. When he stopped, I came back to earth and saw the Ace Gang just looking at us. Masimo didn't seem to notice them. He stroked my hair and said, "*Cara*," and squeezed my bottom slightly as he left.

The gang were just silent after he had gone.

Then Rosie said, "Phwaooooor."

Jools, Mabs and Hons went, "Whooooooooaaaaaaah."

Jas said, "Cor."

And Ellen said, "He... that was... your ear... and er... so on."

I had to sit down quickly as the bottom part of me had turned into a jellyfish.

Ten minutes later

Jas tried to pretend that she had only said "Cor" because she was finding her inner passion as Juliet. Oh yeah.

As Billy Shakespeare would have said, "Prithee, lackaday and also WHATEVERS!!!!!"

I couldn't help saying to her, "Don't forget, you chose Dave the Laugh not the Luuurve God that you have just said 'Cor' to."

Jas went sensationally red.

"I knew this would happen. You said you hadn't got the hump, but you had. And I knew you would get it. I do not have the big red bottom for either of them. Hunky is my one and only."

I said, "Calm down, Jas. It's only the hypothetical red botty that you have got."

"I have not got the hypothetical red bottom. I haven't got the red bottom at all."

She has though.

As the band were tuning up and messing about with their equipment... oo-er (leave it), I tried to keep the conversation light and frothy so that I could tinkle with laughter and Masimo could see me out of the corner of his eye.

I said to Jas, "Speaking of *Rom and Jule*, has Miss Wilson found a Rom yet? Why can't we just have a bloke?"

Jas was glad to get back into boring rambling on about being a thespian. She said, "Miss Wilson says that in Shakespearian times there would be no women in the plays and so Juliet would have been played by a boy. And in our production, all the parts will be played by girls. She thinks it's an interesting reversal."

"Yes. But she is wrong. Anything she says is interesting is not. Think of the 'making our own musical instruments' fiasco. I had runner beans down my nick-nacks for weeks."

Rosie said, "Nauseating P. Green would make a cracking Romeo. She's got the glasses for it."

Jas went very red (tee-hee) and said, "Nauseating P. Green is one of the townspeople."

I said, "She could be all of the townspeople for all I care. The question is, who is going to be your boyfriend?"

Jas went even redder. She can never lie.

I said, "You KNOW, don't you, Jazzy? You know who your boyfriend is going to be!!!! Come on, tell."

She was getting redder and redder.

At that moment, Wet Lindsay and her silly "mates" came in. She went scampering over to the side of the stage and called Robbie to her. I don't think he really wanted to go. He is, of course, only human. I feel really sorry for him.

Astonishingly Dim Monica is not well-known for her fashion sense (the puffball skirt) but tonight she had outdone herself. Culottes are a bit of a risk anyway, but especially if your legs are only half a metre long. And your botty is a bit loomy. In fact, ADM looked like my vati in his shorts.

Jas was looking at them and manically fiddling with her fringe and suddenly it dawned on me.

I said, "It's not Astonishingly Dim Monica, is it? Oh, top!! Thank you, Baby Jesus!!!!!"

Jas was really red. She said, "No, don't be stupid. Of course it's not her!"

Then her eyes sort of swivelled to the stage.

Ohmygiddygodspyjamas.

No.

We all said, "No!"

But yes. Wet Lindsay.

Jas said, "It was Miss Wilson's idea."

I said, "Well, that's as maybe, but you must tell her that you cannot do it. It is against the European Code of Human Rights."

Jas said, "I did! I tried! I said, I said, I didn't want to be Juliet in that case, but then she was going to tell Slim and..."

As she was dithering and rambling on, Wet Lindsay came over to our table and said, "Hi Jas, great news about the play. I can only manage a few of the general rehearsals, but we ought to get together at mine for extras."

Then, only pausing to give me the look of death, she Octopussed off.

Jas was as red as I have ever seen her. And that is saying something.

Rosie said, "She wants you to go round to hers for 'extras', if you know what I mean. And I think we all know what she means."

Actually, it was quite funny in a way.

I said, "Oy, Jas, in the big snogging scene between Rom and Jule... what number do you think you will get up to with Wet Lindsay? Open mouth kissing with tongues?"

Jas was getting the defensive hump.

"Look, stop being so stupid. It's called acting – it's not snogging. It's only pretend snogging."

I said, "That's what you will say to Lindsay, but she won't take no for an answer. If she wants to do *Abscheidskuss* with you, she will."

Rosie leaped to her feet. "She might want to do *AUF GANZE GEHEN*!!"

And she started doing the flame dance around Jas. It was making me laugh a lot and not in a girlish, tinkling way. I was trying to pull myself together when Sven and the rest of the lads came in from their blind football.

Ten minutes later
The Stiffs are playing a new one: "Tell me about yourself sometime". Robbie and Masimo are doing lead vocals. Wow, they both look cool. And one of them is my ex and one of them is mine mine miney mine mine. I am indeed the SEX KITTY of all England!!!!!

Two minutes later
I'll tell you for free who does not think I am a Sex Kitty. Dave the Laugh. I saw him at the bar laughing with some of his mates and he caught me looking at him. And he stopped laughing and just nodded his head. Like I was just someone he knew, but didn't like that much. Then he turned his back on me and started talking and laughing again.

Fifteen minutes later
I am sitting by myself because it's a slow number and the gang are all smooching with their boyfriends. Dave is dancing with Emma. He does smoochy smooch for a bit and

then every now and again does fast twisting to the floor and sort of Cossack dancing. He used to do that with me. Emma is really laughing, but she is not joining in. I would have joined in. Like in the old days.

I think I might go to the tarts' wardrobe until the song's over.

Five minutes later

When I came back in, the band were playing the last number of the set. It's called "Hold me back" and it's really wild. One of the St Pat's boys I see quite a bit of at the footie and at gigs and so on, came over. I think he's called Chunky, but I can't be sure. He is a bit chunky, but in a nice way. Anyway, he asked me to dance. I was going to say no, but then I thought, I'm not the Virgin of Rheims. It's only Dave I have to be cool about, so I said yes.

Three minutes later

Oh no. Sven has started doing the conga.

I'm deffo not going to join in...

Oh, I've joined in.

I am doing the conga.

My shoes are killing me and also I am about two metres high. Please don't let me fall over and display my nick-nacks to a Luuurve God and also a Sex God.

Also, Masimo is bound to notice that Sven and Rosie are wearing matching lurex catsuits. And that they are my mates.

I must escape to recapture my sophisticosity. I do not want to do a second round of conga where I end up in front of the stage next to Rosie and Sven in matching lurex catsuits.

At a convenient moment, as we passed the door to the loos, I slipped off. I said a quick "*adios*" to Chunky and flung myself into the tarts' wardrobe...

I stumbled in and took off my shoes. Ow ouchy ow ouch. Why can't Mum buy sensible shoes? She'll ruin my feet at this rate. I took my tights off and stuck one of my poor feet into the sink.

That's when I saw four eyes looking at me...

"What in the name of arse?"

It was the Little Titches.

From their hidey-hole beneath the sink they said, "Hello, Miss."

I said, "Will you stop calling me Miss. And what are you doing under the sink?"

They got up. Well, I think they did. They are so titchy, it's hard to tell.

The Ginger Titch said, "We shouldn't really be under this sink."

I said, "You can say that again."

And the other one said a bit more loudly, "We shouldn't really be under this sink."

Dear *Gott in Himmel.*

I said, "Well, why are you then?"

"We snuck in the back way because we wanted to see the band. We're not allowed to do anything at home. It's like prison. Our parents just watch what they want on television and we have to eat what they have and so on."

Yeah, it's tough out there.

Ginger went on, "Do you think we could sneak into the club behind you and just go and say hello to Dave the Laugh?"

The other one said, "We've got something we want to give him."

Aaaahhh. That is so sweet.

I said, "Have you made him a card or something?"

Ginger said, "No, we just want to do No. a quarter on the Snogging Scale with him."

What what????

I said, "What in the name of arse is No. a quarter on the Snogging Scale, and by the way, how do you know about the Snogging Scale?"

The littlest one went a bit red.

"Because we heard you in the loos. We were hiding in there one break and we heard you and made our own one up."

You see. And Slim says I do nothing to set an example to the youth of today!

I said, "Go on then, what is it?"

They both said together, "It's kissing hands."

Oooooooh. This I have to see.

Three minutes later

Came out of the tarts' wardrobe. Ouch, bloody ouchy ouch. I'm sure my feet have swollen up. I am without doubt the patron saint of Titches.

I saw Masimo and the Dylans talking to some big blokes in suits. They started going up the stairs to the mezzanine floor of the club. I suppose for a bit of privacy for their meeting. Masimo saw me and blew me a kiss. Robbie was behind him and he smiled at me too. Double resultio!! But then Wet Lindsay arrived on the scene and slimed up the stairs behind Robbie and put her hands over his eyes like a blindfold.

She said, "Guess who, babe?"

Ooohhhh, it was so full of embarrassmentosity. Robbie looked really uncomfortable because she was just hanging around his neck and the others were waiting to get on with the meeting. If she starts doing all that "Wickle Lindsay can't climb up the BIG stairs", we'll all have a communal throw-up.

In the end, he disentangled himself and Wet Lindsay went to the far end of the club.

Erlack.

How can Robbie stand it?

Two minutes later

Jas was sitting on Tom's knee, and as I came up to her, I heard her say, "I think the crabs are moving their little wheel."

I said, "Jas, go and distract your new boyfriend, Wet Lindsay, while I sneak the two Titches in to see Dave the Laugh."

She said, "Why would I do that?"

I said, "Because you are an all-round tip-top egg. Isn't she, Tom?"

Tom kissed her cheek and said, "Yes, she is. But I'm very jealous of her new boyfriend."

Jas went all girlie and red. "Stop it, you two, it's just a play!"

I raised my eyebrows.

Jas quickly said, "Why do the Titches want to see Dave?"

"They want to do No. a quarter on the Snogging Scale with him."

Jas said, "There isn't a quarter."

I said, "There will be in a minute if you get your skates on. Please, Jazzy Spazzy, let the Little Titches get to No. a quarter with Dave. They are unhappy at home – they are not even allowed Jammy Dodgers."

In the end, Jas sloped off to do distracting-the-octopus work.

It'll cost me twenty-two million years of talking to her about Hunky going off to Hamburger-a-gogo land, but as I have said, I should really be knighted for my services to small humankind.

442

Four minutes later

The Titches are marching smartly behind me, being inconspicuous. If you think that hunching your shoulders and looking furtively around like mad hamsters is inconspicuous.

Dave was still at the bar, joshing with his mates.

No sign of Emma. She was probably off somewhere practising her smiling.

I was quite nervy now that we were actually behind him. I hadn't really thought about how it might go. What if he was genuinely horrible to me, in front of everyone?

Girdey loins, girdey loins.

The Little Titches were practically vibrating with excitement.

I tapped Dave on the shoulder.

"Dave, could I just have a word?"

He turned round and looked at me.

Now I deffo had the droop. He wasn't smiling – or talking. He didn't even have the good manners to say hello.

I said, "Well, erm, I've got the Titches with me."

They bobbed out from behind me and Dave smiled at them.

"Hello, little Sex Kittys."

They bobbed back behind me, but said together, "Hello, Dave the Laugh."

He was being nice to them, but not to me. I ploughed on. "They wanted to ask if they can do something for you."

Dave raised his eyebrows and then he looked at me and went, "Gnot nis nit?"

I said, "I beg your pardon?"

He looked at me again and went, "GNOT nis nit?"

It was like really crap ventriloquism, you know, when someone tries to say "bottle of beer" as a ventriloquist, without moving their lips, and it comes out "gottle og geer"?

Well, like that.

I said, "Dave, why are you keeping your mouth shut?"

Dave looked at me with his eyes very wide.

"Necoz nime nog sunosed nu sneek nu uuu."

What is he doing?

The Titches said, "He says he is not supposed to speak to you."

Oh, I see.

I said, "I never said don't speak to me."

"Nu nid."

"Dave, if you keep this up, we'll be here all night."

"Nay norry."

"Nay norry?"

Ginger said, "He says you have to say sorry."

Oh, *sacré bleu*. Oh, all right then.

I said, "I'm sorry."

Dave shook his head.

"Nay norry narti."

Nay norry narti? Were we doing some sort of crap Olde English songe? Were we going to start morris dancing and hitting each other with tambourines now?

Little Titch said, "He wants you to say sorry, Vati."

This was ridiculous.

Dave was just looking at me, sipping his drink. Leaning on the bar.

I said, "Oh, gadzooks, OK. I'm sorry – Vati."

Dave said, "Oh, hello, Georgia. I didn't see you hiding behind the Titches."

He is sooooo annoying. But anyway, at least he was talking to me again.

I smiled at him and he smiled back. He's got a lovely smile.

Shut up, brain.

Anyway, I had a mission.

"The Titches wanted to see you and do their tribute to you."

One of the Titches said, "We got a reprimand each for it."

Dave said, "Good girls."

In a lunatic way, it was quite touching to see the Titches do their little tribute.

They stood in front of him and did actions as they sang (badly):

"We love you, Dave the Laugh, we do" (nodding and touching hearts and pointing at Dave)

"When we're not near to you, we're blue" (pretend crying)

"We love you, Dave the Laugh, we do" (more nodding)

"Oh, Dave the Laugh, we love you!!!" (manic stamping and snogging of their hands).

They really snogged their hands, a bit like Libby with Mr Potato Head.

And also the stamping was truly manic. I'm not surprised they broke the toilet seat.

Dave is not often lost for words, but he acted as if he had never had small girls snogging their own hands in front of him before.

He was laughing and he said, "That was, and I am proud to say it... sensationally mad."

Then they went all red.

Ginger said, "Faaanks, Dave, you are the bestiest. Bye, Miss. Huddly duddly."

And off they scampered.

I felt rather proud.

I am like the Godmutti.

It was just me and Dave, as the rest of his mates had backed off when the Titches had started their tribute to him. They had sloped off to "impress" some girls that were being harassed by the Blunder Boys.

I said to Dave, "Fanks for that, Dave."

He said, "Forgive me if I'm right, but aren't we not talking to each other?"

"That's not what I said."

"It is."

"Well, I know, but I only meant until Masimo cooled down and got off the numpty seat."

"And has he? Or will he be attacking me with his hair gel when I go to the wazzarium?"

I didn't want to have to talk about the Luuurve God to

Dave. It made me feel funny, so I said, "I'm looking forward A LOT to *Rom and Jule*; comedywise I think it will outdo *MacUseless*. There might be clowns and for the *pièce* of resistance, Jas is going to snog Wet Lindsay."

That got his attention.

He said, "Now you're talking my language. I've always loved the Bird of Avon, as you know. I thought Melanie's basooma juggling was a triumph, but now, girl snogging? As Billy himself would have said, 'My tights runneth over'."

I started laughing.

Then Dave looked at me. Quite intensely. Whenever I get near him, I feel sort of hypnotised. Well, my lips do... They were puckering up without my permission... Nooooo. He looked down and away, and then he said, "It's not a topless production, is it?"

Just at that point Emma came back. All Emma-ish. Why is she so keen on everything? She gave me a hug and linked up with Dave. She said, "Hi, Gee. Is it all cool with Masimo? If I didn't have the best boy, I would say that he was deffo the fittest."

Then she turned and kissed Dave on the cheek. "But no one compares to the Hornmeister."

Dave smiled and I smiled. But I didn't really want to smile. And I don't think he felt on Cloud 9 actually.

I didn't want to hang around with the two of them. It felt a bit odd.

So I did S'laters.

And went into the tarts' wardrobe for a bit of a sit-down on the loo, feet up in the air sort of thing.

Is Dave happy with Emma?

She's so nice. ALL THE TIME.

Why is that?

Is she really nice, or is she just pretending to be nice so that everyone thinks she is nice?

As I was sitting there in the cubicle, Jas came in. I knew it was her because no one else could have such an irritating way of blowing her nose. On and on. Not just one little blow and have done with it. Sort of little ones and then a big trumpeting one.

I hobbled out of my cubicle and there she was, sitting on the sink. Looking all miz.

Oh no. Now we would have to talk about Hunky for the next millennium. Still, she had helped me with the Titches.

She said, "I can't do it. I can't snog her..."

I tried to cheer her up. I owed her really.

"But, Jas, look on the bright side. Think how great it will be when she commits suicide. It'll bring the house down. We could buy those football clacker things. Or come on doing some ad-hoc celebratory Scottish dancing."

Jas said, "You'll have been dead for fourteen scenes by then, it's OK for you."

I could see she was upset.

"Look, we just need to think of some sensible way of dealing with her. Perhaps a chemistry experiment that goes tragically wrong as she happens to be passing?"

Jas just looked at me.

Then I said, "I've got it, by George, I've got it!!! We extend the puppetry motif that Miss Wilson is so vair vair keen on and we suggest that Romeo and Juliet have massive papier mâché heads. So you never actually see your real head and the snogging is just a question of aiming your massive heads at each other."

Jas said, "I don't want a big papier mâché head."

I said, "I am only trying to help, Jas. If you don't want to be helped...

End of the gig

Lurking around like Lurkio at the stage door. It's a bit nippy noodles. I am nervy, but sort of happy. Also, and I have to admit this, I am really, really happy that Dave is being OK with me. I hate it when he gets the monk on.

As I was just thinking that, he loomed up with Emma and a crowd of his mates.

One of the lads said, "Are you up for a late snooker needle match, Dave? Haven't seen much of you lately, mate."

Dave said, "Maybe actually."

Then Emma pulled on his hand. "Oy, Hornmeister, don't forget we've got an early start for the sculpture park tomorrow. Mum and Dad planned to set off at 9:00 a.m."

Sculpture park?

Mum and Dad?

I looked at Dave and raised my eyebrows. He looked back and as Emma pulled him away, he pretended to do crying.

He didn't seem a sculpture park sort of guy to me.

What did I know, though? I have just remembered I have accidentally agreed to go to the Wild Park tomorrow with my mum and look at horned budgies or whatever.

Rosie and the rest of the gang trolled off as soon as the Dylans came out. There was a bit of banter between the lads and it seems that the management stuff has gone well.

Masimo still hadn't appeared. I had Dave's voice in my head going "Emergency hair gel application". Shut up, Dave.

The Ace Gang were all linked up, singing, "Give me an H, give me an O, give me an R, give me an N, what are you giving me? The HOOOOOORRRRNNNN!"

Just then, I felt two arms around me.

"Aah, Miss Georgia, you are noodly nips as you say. Come here inside my coat."

And he opened his coat and snuggled me in. I could feel his heart beating. The other Dylans were leaving and shouting, "Nice one, talk on the blower tomorrow about the London gig."

What London gig?

Also where was I?

It was snugly in the coat and everything, but I couldn't tell what was going on. I popped my head up through the collar to breathe a bit, just in time to see Wet Lindsay tucking Robbie's scarf into his parka. Oh, leave him alone, Slimy

Head. I don't know if she thought-read, but she turned round and gave me the worst look.

Poor Robbie.

Poor Jas. Who would want a boyfriend like Wet Lindsay?

I must help both of them.

We scootered home through the twinkly night. The streets were quite busy and in fact we passed the Ace Gang still all linked up. Seeing them trying to get past a bloke walking his dog was hilarious. As we passed by them, Masimo sounded his horn and they all yelled back, "Hooorn!"

Masimo laughed and pulled my arms around him tighter. Blimey, this was a bit like having a real relationship, like you read about. I hope I know how to do it. If my mutti and vati were anything to go by, Masimo would be wearing enormous pants by the end of the week. I couldn't imagine Masimo in enormous pants. I bet he's got those really groovy Pizza-a-gogo ones... Stop thinking about his pants!!!

When we got back to my place, it was a beautiful clear night and the moon was beaming down at us. Like a big smiling custard pie in the sky. If you have seen one of those.

Masimo stopped his scooter at the bottom of our road so

that there could be no spying or "joining in" from my parents. Also I took Mum's shoes off and put on my flats when I got on the scooter. (I suggested that I had brought my "scootering shoes" with me to Masimo. Which I think is rather sophisticated.)

12:30 a.m.
We're sort of snuggled behind a hedge. Or Snog Emporium, as I call it.

Blimey, snogging Masimo is like going to Heaven in a bread basket and back.

And I don't even know how I would get into a bread basket. But that is luuurve for you.

Masimo whispered a lot of Italian stuff to me. It sounds so romantica and groovio gravio.

Of course, he might have been saying, "I can see a bogey up your nose."

I must learn some more Pizza-a-gogo-ese because conversation is a bit tricky in between the snogging.

Ten minutes later
The snogging is deffo top drawer though.

I wonder how far he got on the Snogging Scale with his ex?

Shut up, brain, just snog.

Five minutes later

I like it that he kisses so softly and gently uses his tongue. Not like Whelk Boy, when it was like being attacked by whelks.

Two minutes later

We even touched tongues and sort of kissed with them. Blimey. It's fabaroonie to learn new stuff about the game of luuurve.

Also I do like his hand technique... He put one hand on the back of my neck and one on the base of my spine. It made all of my body feel sort of linked up to him. Yum.

Two minutes later

Something horrific happened. We were doing No. 5 when I heard the unmistakable sound of a lunatic shouting in the dark.

I looked carefully round the hedge and up our street. It

was Mr Next Door, in his shortie nightgown. He was shouting and the Prat brothers were yapping.

There is something a bit funny about the Prat brothers (besides the obvious fact that they are poodles)... In the moonlight, they look sort of dark blue with white things stuck on them.

Masimo said, "*Come?* What is that?"

I whispered, "That is Mr Next Door going barmy."

Masimo pulled me back into the Snog Emporium. And he kissed me so hard that all the blood drained from my head and went into my ballet pumps. Through the love daze, I could vaguely hear things kicking off.

Mr Next Door was raving on.

"He's a bloody disgrace. They've got a show tomorrow, I've been dyeing them all day. Now they're covered in feathers."

What was he on about?

I had to have a look.

We crept up along the hedge a bit so we could see.

Mr Next Door had a broom and a shovel. And he was standing at our gate. I heard a door being opened and then more shouting.

"What the bloody hell is going on?"

Oh no. I recognised those mad tones. It was my vati.

Then another voice joined in.

"Don't worry, Bob, I'm right behind you... oo-er."

Oh dear God. Uncle Eddie.

I said to Masimo, "Erm, I'd leave now if I were you. This is going to get ugly."

And that's when my vati and Uncle Eddie hove into view. Both wearing undercrackers.

The Luuurve God whispered, "Is that, er, your father, and is that, how you say, his boyfriend?"

I nearly shouted out, "NOOOOOOO, that's not his boyfriend!"

Four minutes later

I eventually persuaded the Luuurve God to leave. It took a bit of kissing and pleading. I don't think he really understood what was going on. Who could?

I've said it once and I will say it again, why can't everyone just speak English? The Americans give it a bit of a go – why can't other nations?

In the end, after kissing all of my fingertips, he crept off.

By this time, lights were coming on in the street. I took a deep breath as soon as I heard Masimo scooter off and came out from the bushes.

As I passed Mr Next Door's gate, Angus and Gordy dropped on to my head from the wall. They didn't hurt themselves though, because they gripped on to my shoulders with their horrible sharp claws.

I couldn't help it. I yelled out, "Oh, buggering buggeration."

Dad heard me and yelled, "Stop that bloody foul language, young lady. You'll wake up the sodding neighbourhood."

Oh, the irony.

Uncle Eddie said, "Evening, Georgia," as if it was teatime.

I said, "Look, we all want to go to bed. Is there something we can do to clear this up? What have your poodles done to frighten Angus and Gordy? Cats are very sensitive, you know."

Mr Next Door practically had a fit. He couldn't speak.

Dad could, sadly.

"Don't you start, young lady. Get yourself in the house!"

I didn't mind going in actually. Angus and Gordy had both

fallen asleep on my shoulders and they are not anorexic. It was like having a huge snoring fur coat on.

The front door was open. And my mum was hiding behind it.

She said quietly, "What the hell is going on?"

I said, "It's unbelievable! Vati and Uncle Eddie are both in their undercrackers."

She came out from behind the door.

And she was wearing a shortie black negligee.

What is this? Desperate Husbands?

I looked at her and said, "To be frank, I feel let down by all of you. I'll just say goodnight, Mother."

As I went up the stairs, she said, "Hang on a minute – those are my bloody Chanel shoes in your bag!!!"

Damnity damn damn.

How much shouting can one family do???

And what a bloody fuss about nothing. Angus had, from the kindness of his own heart, taken a gift into the Prat Poodles' kennel. All right, it was a half-alive pigeon that was probably flapping about a bit. And yes, the Prat brothers had fallen into the pond as they tried to escape. But what normal person dyes their poodles blue?

And then complains if they fall into a pond that THEY built?

That is the question.

1:30 a.m.

It's all gone quiet now, thank the Lord.

What a fiasco of a sham. At one stage, there was shouting inside and outside my house.

Even Libby woke up and shouted through the open window and threw Mr Cheese at Mr Next Door before she snuggled back into bed... My bed.

I tried to get in as well, but Libby, Gordy, Angus and Mr Potato Head were all sleeping horizontally. In the end, I went into Libby's bed.

I had to feel my way in the dark.

I didn't turn the light on because I really didn't want to see her sheets. I'll just say this: they crackled when I got in. And my feet touched something soft at the bottom. Pray God it was playdough...

How to Make Any Twit Fall in Love With You

Sunday September 25th

Morning

Mutti and Vati are not speaking to each other...

It was all, "Would you ask your mother to pass me the butter?" etc.

So childish.

Still, I had a Luuurve God, so what did I care? I was just about to go up to my room for a bit of a daydream about our poptastic lives together when Dad said, "Will you explain to your mother why Uncle Eddie and I were in the garden in our underpants?"

I said, "Certainly, Father. Mum, Dad is going out with Uncle Eddie. Face it. Move on."

Dad hit me over the head with his newspaper.

"Tell her we were practising a new routine for the baldy-o-gram when the fool next door started..."

Mum interrupted. "Tell your father I am sick of his japes with his pals."

I said, "She says you should go and live in a house with men like yourself and leave us alone. We'll write."

That did it.

Dad has "roared" off in his "car".

In my room

Where every clud has a silver lining. Dad "roaring" off having the numpty means that we won't be able to go to the Wild Park to look at more horned budgies etc.

I'm distracting Libby from poking Bum-ty with a fork with cheese on it, by reading her *Heidi* in a Chinese accent. She is hysterical with laughter. It's making me laugh actually. I do love my sister. There is something so gorgey about her little dimply face. She's got amazingly long eyelashes.

When we got to the famous wheelchair falling off the mountain top bit she looked up from laughing and then said, "I lobe my funny Gingky." And gave me a really big cuddle.

Blimey, it brought tears to my eyes.

Especially as Libby accidentally stabbed me with her fork.

Ten minutes later

I could hear Mum on the phone, and then she called up the stairs.

"Georgia, get dressed. We're off on our lovely trip to the Wild Park."

Oh God.

Twenty minutes later

We are off to the Wild Park with two of Mutti's mates, Pippy and Scottish Jo. They picked us up in their car. Wow, I am actually riding in a proper car that people don't point to and laugh at. Also it's quite peaceful because Mum, Pippy and Jo just talk all the time. Libby is combing what is left of Panda. She tried to warm him up by putting him in the oven. Most of his bottom is burnt to a crisp. She is happy though.

Gor blimey, Mum and her mates talk WUBBISH. I am glad that me and my mates are not so superficial. They are just talking about men and clothes and men.

I can just dollydaydream about my boyfriend and what I will wear when I next see him.

I must say, I can't really believe that he likes me.

And really fancies me.

Wow.

I'm a bit tired from last night and my lips ache a bit.

In a nice way.

I wonder if you can strain lips by too much snogging?

Jas said she did once. She got a sort of pucker spazerama.

Didn't she do puckering exercises for it?

Pucker relax.

Pucker relax.

Two minutes later

Erlack, she will soon be kissing Wet Lindsay unless something good happens.

Maybe I could suggest to Miss Wilson that we do mime kissing?

I am a genius!! Miss Wilson loves mime.

I wonder if Rudi and Miss Wilson have snogged yet?

Fifteen minutes later

Even though I am trying not to listen, Mum and her mates are going to join this women's group that teaches you how to become a goddess and make men do anything for you. Crikey.

It sounds a bit like *How to Make Any Twit Fall in Love With You*.

Apparently, the nub and the thrust is that men *like* to do stuff for women. So, you ask them to do something and then you say thank you. And that is how you train them.

I said, "Are there any dog biscuits involved?"

But they were too full of themselves to reply.

Wild Park

Wow and wowzee wow. We had the tippytop of times. Honestly. When we got there, I said I was very happy to stay in the car.

I said, "I've seen a bison on *Look North* or something and also some monkeys that Lady Dave Attenborough was lolling about with and that will do me, thank you."

But I was glad as a glad thing on glad tablets that Mum made me get out.

Because we found Angus's wild family.

Honestly.

His Scottish wildcat cousins.

They were sooooo cool. The kittens looked just like Angus when I first found him in the garden in Och Aye land. Doing flying face-pouncing. One kitten would unexpectedly and for no reason hurl itself through the air and pounce directly on another kitten's face. Then it would grab on with its front paws and do bunny kicks with its back legs.

Libby kept yelling, "Me want naaaice pussycats" and trying to climb into their cage with them.

One of the keepers said, "They are not pets. They are wild animals."

I said, "You don't need to tell me that. I used to keep Angus on a lead, but he ate it. Let us in, mister."

Libby even said, "Please, Mr arsey man."

Ten minutes later
We're in!!!

Oh, what a hoot. Libby and I had a bucket each of dead chicks and some rabbit legs.

We tugged on one end of a rabbit leg and the kittykats pulled on the other end. In between spitting at us.

I love them I love them.

We took some pictures to take home with us to show Angus what his family look like and also a little tartan mousey.

Mum and her mates were ridiculously embarrassing around the keepers who were quite fit, in an overall and welligoggy way...

On the way home

Libby is "feeding" tartan mousey with bits of chicken feather she has stuffed in her welligogs. I hope that is all she has down there. She was very interested in what the wild kittens' poo looked like.

5:30 p.m.

When we got home, Dad wasn't in so Mum went off to have a bath.

She is sensationally cheered up and all full of herself now.

I said, "What's for supper?"

And she said to me, "Find something in the fridge. And give some to Bibbs. She's allowed to watch children's TV for half an hour. I'm having a long aromatherapy bath. I will use ylang ylang, I think, for its sensual overtones."

I said, "Mum, you don't need sensual overtones, you need sensual undertones."

She didn't get it though, she just went rambling on.

"This is 'me' time."

And she went off into the bathroom.

Ten minutes later

I made Bibbs and me cheese on toast, but remembered that we must eat a balanced diet, so put some tomato sauce on for the vit. C content. If my legs start getting all bendy like Grandvati's because of rickets, I hope Mum will find her ylang-ylang-smelling skin a comfort.

Libby is sharing her cheese on toast with tartan mousey. They are watching "Pudsey and Sudsey go on holiday" or something. Anyway, weird creatures with no necks in bathing suits.

As I left, she went to get her swimming costume and rubber ring. She lobes Pudsey and Sudsey's holiday.

In my bedroom
Ten minutes later
Mum's not the only one who can have "me" time. I can have "me" time for me to have some "me" time.

Aaaah... soooo, the Luuurve God.

I'll start with the tongue-kissing episode and...

"GET OUT! Oooooh, how disgusting. Don't stand on there, you'll..." *SPLASH!!!!!*

Then more yelling and splashing and Mum saying, "Don't let it touch my... Ohmygod, it's touched me... Put that snorkel, owwww..."

MIAOOOOWWWWWW...

"Lalalalalala...... Heggyheggyho..."

What the hell was going on?

Four minutes later
Mum's "me" time turned into "us" time.

I went down to see what had happened and there was water everywhere in the bathroom. Mum was standing in a bath towel, shouting. Libby was in her swimming costume with a snorkel, sitting in the bath singing "Bum bum pooey pooey bum bum" in two centimetres of water. And Angus and Gordy were sneezing and soaking and trying to scrabble up the sides of the bath.

Mum stormed off into her bedroom and I said to Libby, who was now putting her rubber ring on, "What happened, Bibbsy?"

She looked at me cross-eyed, like I was a fool, and said very deliberately, "Me came on my HOLIDAYS wif my fwends. Get in, Gingie."

Back in my bedroom
All is calm again.

I will get into my bed to look at my part (oo-er) in *Rom and Jule*.

Lovely and snugly, I may just have a little zizz before I settle down to...

Not.

Have you any idea what it is like to have two wet cats, a soaking tartan mouse and a toddler covered in soap in your bed?

Fifteen minutes later

Libby has dried off a bit now and the cats have bogged off to murder stuff. They only stayed in my bed long enough to get warm and dampen the sheets.

Libby still has her rubber ring on, but it could be worse, she could have Mr Fish in here with us.

Three minutes later

It IS worse.

She has got Mr Fish in here with us.

Five minutes later

If I hear "Maybe it's beCOD I'm a Londoner" one more time, I may have a nervy spaz.

Three minutes later

Mr Fish's batteries went. I will never be mean about Baby Jesus again.

Also I was just saying to Libby that she should lie down and have a little snooze when she dropped off to sleep, sitting up.

Amazing.

I carried her to her own room, which wasn't very easy actually with the rubber ring, but it does mean I have the whole of my bed to myself!!!!

Ten minutes later
Now then, back to Billy Shakespeare land. Otherwise known as "Twits in Tights".

Ten minutes later
Mercutio just lurks around Rom, more or less telling him off and then dies. I am going to call him Merc-lurk-io.

Twelve minutes later
I wish I could be bothered to get up and phone Jas. In Act 11 she has a whole night of snogging with her boyfriend, Wet Lindsay. She will have got further on the Snogging Scale than she has with Hunky. I bet she wishes she hadn't been so mean about my brilliant papier mâché head idea now.

She is vair stubborn.

Right, I am going to get some shut-eye.

10:32 p.m.

Oh, how vair vair inconsiderate some people are. I can hear Mum's voice booming all over the house. She is on the blower to one of her mad aquarobic mates.

Mum said, "Well, I'm deffo going to do it. At the very least it will shake Bob up, and stop him being so bloody lazy. Madame Betty said be there at 7:00. The workshop actually starts at 7:30 p.m... What? Oh, yes, OK, look, I'll just get the list, hang on."

I heard the phone being put down and Mum going off somewhere.

Oh, really, some people are trying to sleep.

I could hear her scuffling around.

I shouted down, "Mum, it is a school night you know. Some of us are trying to sleep."

Libby shouted from her bedroom, "Shut up, Ginger."

One minute later

Mum was just going on and on.

"Right, you've to bring a towel, a sarong to wear... it says you can keep your pants on if you wish. Erm... some coloured scarves and a boiled egg. Yep, yep. Oh and some oil. OK, see you there... S'laters."

God. Her workshop thing sounds horrific. What do a boiled egg and coloured scarves have to do with being a goddess? It sounds more like one of Miss Wilson's improvised drama workshops. Although, thank the Lord, Miss Wilson has never said, "You can keep your pants on if you wish."

How utterly horrific.

Ten minutes later
Oh, that reminds me, I mustn't forget to ask Miss Wilson about fake blood for my dying scene.

We've got another read-through on Thursday. I wonder if Jas's new boyfriend will be there. She might be. Maybe I could accidentally chop her head off with my sword.

Two minutes later
Ouch. I just leant on my pouch by mistake. I must remember to replenish my supplies. You must never be caught with an empty pouch.

Phone rang
Oh, this is so selfish!!!!

I yelled down, "Mum, will you please not discuss your lady parts on the phone with your friends. I have an artistic temperament."

Mum yelled up, "Georgia, it's Masimo, or are you asleep for school tomorrow?"

Ohmygod.

I tore out of bed and quickly applied a bit of lippy from my pouch. I did a bit of puckering up on the way down the stairs so that he could sense my Sex Kittykatnosity down the phone.

(Oo-er!)

Picked up the phone and...

"Hello."

"*Ciao, cara*, I just have phoned to say..."

Then he started singing a song down the phone. Something in Italian. Also he was playing the guitar as an accompaniment. How was he holding the phone? Perhaps he had an assistant?

It's nice and everything, but what do you do? Nod along to it? Join in? I was just holding the phone away from my earlug, because it was a bit loud, when the key turned in the lock and Vati came in. And he looked at me with the phone and a song coming out of the end of it.

He said, "Don't tell me there's a bloody singing clock now."

And stumbled off into the bedroom.

Monday September 26th
In the kitchen
I noticed an egg boiling away. I can't even begin to think what Mum and her mad mates are going to be doing with that.

On the way to Stalag 14
How many times do we all have to do this? Get up, go to school, again? Before everyone admits it's a crap idea?

Break
Thank the Lord.

Fives court
Brrr! Blimey O'Reilly's trousers, it's nippy noodles.

We've buttoned our coats together like in the old days. We are quite literally a tent with six heads and sleeves.

Three minutes later

Snuggly buggly. We have to sort of thread the snacks up to our mouths through the collar bits.

Rosie and Jools made me laugh a lot by doing duo Twix eating. One started at one end and the other at the other end. Vair amusant. And as Rosie said, "Strangely erotic."

Wet Lindsay came by, but apart from tutting at us, what is she going to punish us for? Coat abuse?

She said, "The rest of them I am not surprised at, but I am sorry you have chosen to join in, Jas."

Jas didn't say anything, but after Ms Slime had gone off we all went, "Oooooooohhhhh" like in "Oooooooohhh, get you!"

Geoggers

We are doing about deserts.

What would you do to survive if you got stranded in one?

I said, "Phone a friend?"

But, as usual, I got *nuls points* for my hilarious sense of fun and adventure.

It's all so tremendously dull. You have to put your car mirrors out to catch the sun and blind any passing plane etc.

Dig a ditch and lie in it. Dear God, just kill me, that's what I say.

Jas, of course, is in Seventh Heaven.

Her hand was shooting up all the time.

Saying stuff like, "You could catch water at night because of the diurnal change in temperature."

Oh, SHUT UP!!!!

Just as I thought I might have to pull my own head off to stop the boredom, Rosie passed me a questionnaire that she had made up.

Dear All,

Suppose you were stranded on a desert island with your family and with no food. Not even Jammy Dodgers. Who in your family would you eat first? Here are a few ideas.

Who does least work?

Who eats most?

Who would make the most nutritious meal?

Who would be the easiest to track down and catch?

And my answer to all of the questions was: Dad.

PE

As a "treat" and because the weather is so bad, Miss Stamp has allowed us to stay indoors. It's a miracle really because she is such a sadist. Once she made us play hockey in the fog. You couldn't see your hand in front of you. You'd hit the ball off in the general direction of where you thought someone was and then go after it, if you heard someone go "Owwwww".

When I reached the goal, the goalie had wandered off into the fog somewhere. By the time she got back I had scored 19 goals, but Miss Stamp disallowed them.

Which is typical.

When I protested she said, "Georgia, no one else was playing, you were just running about by yourself and shooting goals into an empty net. That is not hockey."

I said, "Well it's my kind of hockey!!!"

479

She said I had taken stupidity to new heights, which is a bit rude.

Anyway, happy days. Today, as our special "treat", we are playing shipwreck in the gym. While everyone else dashed about, the Ace Gang all climbed to the top of the wall bars. You're supposed to leap about from a piece of equipment to a mat to a whatever, but unless Miss Stamp actually came up the bars and removed us, we were technically safe.

Anyway, she didn't notice at first because Nauseating P. Green created an accidental diversion by destroying the mini trampoline.

While we were hanging about, we had a discussion about the fact that we all now had boyfriends.

Jas said, "I feel like I've known Tom all my life. I feel we have always been together."

I said, "So do I."

Rosie said, "It's just a complete laugh with Sven."

I said, "Yes, but do you feel natural?"

Rosie said, "You'll have to ask Sven that, love!"

And laughed like a drain.

I said to the others, "But what I mean is, besides the

snogging... what do you actually do with boys when you've got them?"

Ellen said, "I well... how do you really know if you've got them or something... you know... what if you haven't got them or something..."

I said, "Thank you for that, Ellen. It's cleared it up for me."

Changing rooms

Getting changed. My brain is still burbling on.

Should I see my "boyfriend" every day? Or every two days?

Is the Luuurve God going to sing to me every night?

Am I supposed to phone him and sing to him when it's my turn?

Could I do an improvised dance instead?

How do you know these things?

Why am I expected to do lessons as well as boy stuff?

4:00 p.m.

Bell went.

Thank the Lord. Freedom.

Cloakroom

I was just getting my coat on when Jools came in. I thought she'd gone home. She was a bit breathless.

"Gee, I've just run all the way back. Masimo is at the gate on his scooter."

Ay caramba!!

Look at my head!

Eight minutes later

Emergency make-up routine and upside-downy blowdrying hair. I have made the gang surround me so that I can get to the gate without my beret. It may look a bit odd, us all walking like a big crab, but that is the penalty of luuurve.

And it does mean that I can emerge with hair bounceability in front of my boyfriend (oo-er).

Masimo was sitting on the seat of his scooter with his legs crossed. He had jeans and Chelsea boots on and a long cardigan.

He said to the gang, "*Ciao.*"

And they all said "*Ciao*" back.

Then we stood around a bit.

Erm.

Masimo came and stood in front of me. He put his hands on my face and kissed me on the mouth. Then he said, "Hello, gorgeous."

And he snogged me properly. I had my eyes open because I felt a bit, erm, unrelaxed with 500 girls passing by.

The gang were shuffling about behind me, I could sense it and then Jas said loudly, "Well, I'm off... er, are you off, Rosie?"

And Rosie said, "Er, yes, I'm off, off as, erm, anything."

And they were all saying even more stupid things than normal.

"*Hasta la vista.*"

And "Toodle pip."

After they had all gone, Masimo was still just casually stroking my hair and kissing me softly on the lips.

I didn't want to push Masimo away, but... it was all a bit weird. I just wanted to get away from Stalag 14.

At last I said, "Erm, shall we go?"

And he smiled and gave me a last big smacking kiss.

Just then, I caught sight of an elephant in a coat out of the corner of my eye.

Oh dear God, Slim.

I looked away.

Masimo gave me another smackeroonie and then put a helmet on my head.

And we roared away.

Perhaps it had really been an elephant in a coat. Perhaps it was a special surprise for the production of *Rom and Jule*.

You never know.

Ish.

Café Noir

Actually, it was quite cool being the "girlfriend" when Masimo's mates and so on came into the café.

It is mostly band talk though.

In fact, Masimo had to drop me off home and go talk to the band round at Robbie's about their London gig.

Which is this coming weekend.

Am I a pop widow already?

10:00 p.m.

Learning my part for the school fiasco. AGAIN. I thought Merc-lurk-io was supposed to be the "larf" factor. All I can say, once more, is that Billy Shakespeare had a very odd idea of fun.

Oh dear God.

This is wubbish jokes.

Mostly I describe the Queen of the Fairies for about a million years. Apparently, all she does is drive along in a tiny wagon "over men's noses as they lie asleep".

They wouldn't be asleep for long if someone drove a wagon over their nose. I tell you that for a fact.

Because, as it happens, I have had a wagon driven over my nose. When I was asleep. Libby put Gordy in her Thomas the Tank Engine when he was a kitten and made him drive up the "big big hill" (my nose).

Twenty minutes later

Oh, this is just wubbishnosity of the highest order. I can't go on in tights and say this:

"Her waggoner, a small grey-coated gnat."

Three minutes later

Oh, tee-hee-hee, I've got to a great bit. Jas's big snogging scene with her "boyfriend".

I'm going to phone Jazzy Spazzy.

Jas answered the phone.

"Jas."

"What?"

"Why are you saying what like that?"

"Like what?"

"Anyway, have you got to your brilliant bit in *Rom and Jule* when your boyfriend climbs into your bedchamber for the night?"

She put the phone down, which is a bit rude.

Ten minutes later

OK, this is the summary of *Rom and Jule*.

It starts with a bit of fighting between two families. When I say families, I mean boys stropping around and so on. Jule is not allowed to do what she wants by her vati because she is only a girl and he will not let her have any fun. (Typico.)

However, her family throws a party and Rom gatecrashes it with his mates. I am in this bit and I go along with Rom to party and dancey aroundy like ye fool.

Which actually might be a bit of a larf.

I will note down some suggestions for Miss Wilson for my interpretation of my part (oo-er).

My dance note is: Perhaps Scottish dancing here.

After the party there is a bit more fighting.

Note for Miss Wilson: Plenty of tomato ketchup here.

Then I have my big death scene and I die telling that hilarious world-renowned joke, "Ask for me tomorrow and you shall find me a grave man."

Do you get it? Do you see?

Die... grave... ?

Oh, it's a side-splitter.

And thankfully, that is it for me. I can scamper off backstage.

To play around with the backstage lads (oo-er).

If the play gets that far that is.

Because I tell you this for free, if Dave the Laugh and his mates have anything to do with building the scenery, the balcony scene is bound to quite literally bring the house down.

Five minutes later

Anyway, what happens next after I die? Not that I care because I won't be watching.

Hmmm.

Rom and Jule spend the night together getting up to hanky panky and possibly rudey-dudeys. We will never know because it's all in some sort of verse about the moon and so on.

Then they get married secretly.

Note for Miss Wilson: Papier mâché heads can be "happening" and "now". They have the "Bingo!" factor.

As a v. good plan, Jule goes to the vicar to ask for help and advice. (The vicar is not "Call me Arnold" but for all the use he is, he should be called "Call me Arnold".)

Back on stage, Jule pretends to take poison and die, Rom finds her, thinks she's dead so he commits suicide. She wakes up and stabs herself.

Note: Plenty of blood capsules and liver here.

The end.

It's a lovely, cheery little tale.

For the sake of the audience, I must make my comedy fight scenes last as long as possible.

Maybe I could accidentally kill Jule's comedy puppet dog.

Note here for Miss Wilson: Comedy dog gets it.

11:00 p.m.

I heard Mum come in from her workshop. Uh-oh.

Dad called out, "Hello, Connie."

But she is not talking to him so... there was a bit of silence and then she said, "Bob, would you run me a bath with some rose oil in it and get me a cold glass of wine, please?"

What? Yes, in your dreams, Madame Zara.

Ten minutes later

He's doing it. How amazing.

Surely just doing something with a boiled egg and a coloured scarf doesn't make Dad turn into, erm... unDad.

Slim's snogging lecture

Thursday September 29th
French
As they probably say in *la belle France*, *qu'est-ce que c'est le point of France?*

3:00 p.m.
Read-through
Had our first proper read-through of *Rom and Jule*.

Our star-studded cast features:

Me as Merc-lurk-io

Miss Prissy Knickers (Jas) as Jule

Ellen as Tybalt (or something, what do you think... oh, am I the page as well or something?)

Rosie in a *tour de force* and also possibly a beard, as the Nurse.

The octopus in the ointment is, of course, waiting for Ms No Forehead to come and be Rom.

Then Miss Wilson said, "I'm afraid Lindsay cannot be at the read-through today. She has to go for an interview for college."

We all pretended to cry and shouted out, "Ah prithee, lackaday."

"Have you seen my tights?"

"Gadzooks!"

And so on for a while.

As Nauseating P. Green was only "townspeople", she read the Rom part.

She was so excited her glasses steamed up.

I said to Jas, "You lucky, lucky tart."

But Jas shoved me away.

She always takes these things soooo seriously. And I think she really does believe that it is the story of her and Hunky.

Halfway through it was complete chaos with Rosie shouting, "Am I on? Shall I wear my Nurse's beard?"

And Jas was saying stuff like, "But what is my motivation here? Why would I suddenly go across to the balcony window? Perhaps I heard a night owl?"

Absolute wubbish stuff. Jas insists on getting owls in everything. I just wanted to get to the fighting bit. I said to Miss Wilson, "Have you got the swords yet?"

And she dithered about, saying ridiculous stuff like, "Perhaps for now you could use a pointed finger."

Is she mad?

Yes is the answer you are searching (not very far) for.

I said to Miss Wilson, "May I just illustrate my point vis-à-vis the ultimate crapnosity of trying to have a sword fight with a pointed finger?"

I did the bit where we have the fisticuffs and Tybalt stabs me (Merc-lurk-io) to death.

I put my finger up and said, "Tybalt, you rat catcher! Will you walk?"

Which is my fave bit actually.

Then Ellen (as Tybaltio) says, "I am for you", or in Ellen's case, "Er, is it this bit or something, do I, is it for..."

I said, "Ellen, just say 'I am for you' and then fight me to the death."

Bloody hopeless.

Ellen came shuffling over, pointing her finger at me. Ooooh, scary. I jabbed my finger at her and she stuck her finger in my waist. Which I didn't notice actually, until I said, "Come on, get on with it. Stab me to death with your index finger."

And she said, "I, er, I just did."

I looked at Miss Wilson and said, "Do you see? We need swords and plenty of them, and blood. And maybe a bit of old liver. Have you got blood bags?"

Rosie said, "I can make severed fingers out of sausages."

At which point a strange woman came in. In really bright clothes.

Miss Wilson was all over her like a rash. Bobbing like a bobbing thing.

"Oh, girls, girls, this is Miriam. She has come to improvise with us this morning. She has trained with *Le Coq*."

Ten minutes later

We just about managed to get ourselves under control. I thought Rosie might have to go to the school nurse she was laughing so much.

Nauseating P. Green was the only one who looked a bit puzzled. She was blinking and saying, "What is so funny?"

Rosie said, "I don't think P. Green understands how vair *amusant* a grown-up saying she has trained with *Le Coq* is. I don't think she gets it."

I said, "She wouldn't get it if it came in a big bag labelled 'IT'."

And I am not wrong.

Twenty minutes later

If we thought Miss Wilson was odd, Miriam took the biscuit odd-wise. She was mega odd. And a half.

She was dressed mostly in coloured scarves, with two or three round her head and she wore big shoes and kept falling over things.

Rosie said, "Is Miriam breaking those shoes in for a clown?"

Sadly, Miriam WAS a clown.

We weren't allowed to just say our boring old lines. We had to do mime and clown gestures.

We had to find our inner clown.

4:00 p.m.

Still, it passes the time.

Thank God, the final bell.

As we slouched off to the cloakroom, I said to the gang, "I'm bloody exhausted, and I will tell you this for free, I am not wearing tights and a big red nose."

Jools said, "She won't really make us wear the noses, will she? I thought we were just wearing them to please Mad Miriam."

Jas said, "Actually, I found it quite liberating doing the clowning. I found a different part of Juliet, sort of more playful. She is just a teenager after all. Like us."

We all looked at her.

I said, "She is five hundred and fifty years old."

Jas was ready to do storming off in the huffmobile when I said, "Actually, you might be right, Jas. If you and your boyfriend, Wet Lindsay, wear clown noses, that would put proper snogging out of the question. *Voilà*! Bob *est l'oncle*!!"

4:05 p.m.

Things are hotting up in the Miss Wilson and Rudi Kamyer department. They walked out of the school gates together tonight. Miss Wilson looked like she was showing him her inner clown. Bobbing her head around like a demented pigeon. Rudi took off his glasses and cleaned them with his scarf. That is how vair vair excited he was.

Luckily, it's German tomorrow.

Three minutes later

Crikey, Masimo is at the gates again! Back to the bloody loo for me for glamour work.

6:00 p.m.

They are awfully demonstrative, the Pizza-a-gogo types.

And also not inhibited.

When he saw me, the Luuurve God actually came through the school gates into the playground. And then he snogged me among the milling girls. Who were all squeaking and shrieking like wild geese.

It seems a bit sort of pervy snogging someone in the school playground.

I don't know why.

I don't associate Sex Gods with school.

Or anything to do with rudey-dudey or snoggy-poos.

In fact, when we had so-called "Sex Education" with someone called Mrs Tampax (probably), I had my fingers in my ears and was humming.

It's just not right...

The Ace Gang sloped off and Masimo took me home on his scooter.

7:00 p.m.
In my private boudoir of luuurve
He has given me a little locket.

Crikey.

It's a heart with a photo of him inside.

He's on a beach in his jeans and he doesn't have a top on.

I must never ever ever mention this to Dave the Laugh.

I can imagine what he will say.

Anyway, shut up. I am not imagining what he will say.

10:00 p.m.
The Luuurve God says he will miss me when he goes to

Lunnern town this weekend. But a little break doesn't hurt anyone I say.

Two minutes later
I seem to be the only one who does say it though. The rest of the gang are practically glued to their boyfriends. What happened to the one for all and one for one and all in all fandango?

Four minutes later
I heard Mum call out to Dad, "Bob, would you put a hot-water bottle in bed for me? And a cup of hot chocolate would be lovely. Thank you."

I don't know what is going on with Mum and Dad, but it's weird.

Mum keeps asking Dad to do things, and he keeps doing them.

Two minutes later
Unfortunately, she hasn't said, "Hand over your money and make your way to Europe."

I have pinned a photo of the wildcats on the shed door

so that Angus can look at them.

He likes it a lot. He stares and stares and then does that silent miaowing thing.

Then he starts shaking.

I can see him through my bedroom window.

I thought it would be a relief for Bum-ty but unfortunately Angus divides his time equally between staring at his photo and budgie staring.

Friday September 30th

Hurrah. Nearly freedom. Thank you, Baby Jesus, for leading us through another week of pain and tribulation (triple maths and "David Copperpants").

Lurching out of assembly. Which was only bearable because Slim nearly fell up the stairs when she went on to the stage. She so clearly can't see where her feet are.

Wet Lindsay came up to me after assembly and said, "Nicolson, the headmistress wants to see you in her office, now."

What had I done?

What?

I knocked on Slim's door and she said, "Come."

499

Oh God.

Ten minutes later
One of the most embarrassing things in the history of embarrassmentosity has happened.

It was so horrific. I may have to go lie down in the loos.

Two minutes later
Hawkeye was taking Geoggers and when I walked in late, she said, "So pleased you managed to fit us into your busy schedule, Georgia. Sit down and treat us to your description of the formation of an oxbow lake."

Oh God.

Break
The Ace Gang all crowded round me at break going, "What happened?"

"Did the clown lady complain?"

Rosie said, "Yes, did she tell that we laughed at *Le Coq*?"

I looked at her.

I said, "She talked about snogging."

Rosie opened her eyes wide.

"Oh my God."

I said, "Slim has given me a sex lecture."

The Ace Gang went, "Nooooo."

"Oh yes. An onion bhaji has talked to me about snogging."

All the Ace Gang went, "Erlack, that is soooo disgusting."

Rosie said, "Phone the police now."

Oh, I feel dirty.

Rosie said, "Did she actually say, 'What number have you got up to on the Snogging Scale?' "

"No, thank God. It was mostly 'inappropriate behaviour in front of the younger girls... Running before I could walk... Saving yourself for the right young man... All in good time'. In fact, a quick summary would be, 'Blah blah blah rave on rave on. Tremble tremble... Have some pride and dignity'."

Rosie said, "What she means really is, don't tart around so much."

"Thank you for that, Rosie."

Lunchtime
I feel besmirched.

♡ 501

I asked Miss Stamp if I could have a shower even though we haven't had games today. She said, "Go on then, but I'm coming to keep an eye on you."

Bloody hell, this place is quite literally like *Prisoner Cell Block H*.

Two hours later

How dare Slim talk about my private parts.

I don't talk about hers.

I don't even think about hers.

Oh God!!!!

I just have done!!!

Last lesson of the week and fortunately it's German

I may even get a light snooze in before home time.

I said that to the gang.

"I am *absolutement* full of exhaustosity. I feel like I have been through the mangle of luuurve."

Which I have.

Rosie has been reading her *German for Fools* book again.

She said to me, "Prat is *Volltrotte*!"

It's a *sehr* musical language.

Basoomas in German is *mopse*.

As the bell rang, Rosie leaped up and did comedy beard work.

She had her beard underneath her desk and she was pretending to beat it off her face and yelling, "Herr Kamyer, Herr Kamyer, *ich glaub mich knutscht ein* Hamster!!!"

Herr Kamyer blinked through his glasses and then said very quickly, "*Guten Abend.*"

And walked out quickly.

I said, "What did you say?"

And Rosie said, "I think a hamster is snogging me."

4:10 p.m.
I was quite relieved when I got to the school gates and there was no sign of the Luuurve God. Slim is sure to be on snogging alert somewhere, probably with binoculars. She could quite easily hide them about her person and you would never know.

4:20 p.m.
As we walked along as a gang, it was nice and jolly.

And a relief to be away from Stalag 14.

♥ 503

And just to have the weekend stretching before me.

No one has got a proper plan for the weekend as there is no gig or anything, but we are going to have a ringaround. I feel really happy and free. I don't know why.

Rosie said, "*Rom and Jule* could do with a bit of livening up, couldn't it? Music wise? Couldn't we ask Miss Wilson if we could have a song or two? Cheer things up a bit in among the suicide and fighting?"

Hmmmm.

Four minutes later

We are all skipping along (yes, I do mean skipping along) singing songs from *The Sound of Music*. It was that ye olde Shakespearean classic, "The hills are alive with the sound of tights, with tights I have worn for a thousand years"!!!!!

We were just all singing, "I go to the hills when my tights are loneleee..." when Dave and the lads leaped out from behind a tree.

I was so flustered I nearly fell over.

When I got my breath back, I said, "Have you been following us?"

Dave said, "Yes."

I said, "Well that's not nice, is it?"

Dave said, "Yes. It is."

"No, it's not."

"It is. I particularly noticed your basoomas wiggling about when you were skipping."

"That's disgusting."

"I liked it."

"Don't you feel ashamed, sneaking about and so on?"

"*Nein, ich* feel *gut!*"

I said, "I think you will find you are a bit of a *Volltrotte*."

He said, "*Ach, Scheissenhausen!*"

He does make me laugh.

Five minutes later

We all lolloped along together. The lads were in top moods because of a *coup d'état* they had done at school. They had drawn a massive boy's trouser snake on the playing field with weedkiller.

They'd done it under cover of playing footie and then just waited for it to emerge.

Dave said, "Top-class group work."

I very nearly told them about my "snogging lecture" from

Slim, but I didn't want to talk about the Luuurve God in front of Dave the Laugh.

I did tell him about Mad Miriam and how we had had to find our inner clown.

Dave said, "Has your inner clown got a Horn?"

At the bottom of the hill everyone else peeled off to go home. The casual plan is to go to the cinema tomorrow eves. Dave walked along with me. He pushed me in the arm and loosened his tie and smiled at me.

"Long time since we did this, isn't it, Kittykat? You're too frightened of the call of my Magnetic Horn to be alone with me, aren't you?"

I said, "Er, Dave, I am not frightened of your Magnetic Horn and that is *le* fact."

He said, "You are."

"I'm not."

"You are."

"I'm not and just repeating something doesn't make it an argument."

"It does."

"It does not... hang on a minute, we're doing it again. Stop it..."

506

There was a silence then he said, "No, you stop it."

He is soooo annoying. Funny though.

We didn't talk about the Luuurve God or Emma, although I half expected her to come running up behind us with some warm milk for Dave or something. Is that what happens to girls around boys – they just turn into zombie girls?

Somebody should try telling my mum that she is supposed to be a man-pleaser. She asked Dad to polish her shoes last night. And he did! What is all that about?

When we reached my turn-off, Dave said, "So what are you up to tomorrow night?"

I said, "Well, I... erm, the rest of them want to go to the cinema, but you know... it'll be like Snog Central and... I..."

He looked at me with his crinkly eyes.

"And your girlfriend is not around."

I said, "Oy... but, well, yes, I guess."

There was a moment's pause and then Dave said, "Well, I'll be on my jacksie as well, so maybe see you there. S'laters."

Blimey.

When I got to my house, Masimo was sitting outside on his scooter chatting to Mum and Libby! Libby had got his

♡

spare helmet on, so was essentially a helmet on a pair of legs. I could hear her laughing inside the helmet.

Five minutes later

Why doesn't Mum go in with Libby? I keep raising my eyebrows and looking at her in a meaningful way, but she doesn't know what I mean.

Masimo has put his arms around me, and I am half sitting on his knee. I feel weird in front of my mum.

Oh joy unbounded, Oscar is lurking about. Does he really think that wearing a baseball cap backwards is going to get him a girlfriend? Also, when he jumped over his gate, he caught his shoe in his falling-down jeans fiasco and head-dived into his dad's perennials (quite literally oo-er).

Sad really.

Also, I can't help noticing, I am in my school uniform. This is not the air of sophisticosity I am aiming for.

Also, even though nothing was going on with Dave the Laugh, except just matewise, I couldn't help thinking what would have happened if the Luuurve God had seen us skipping along together. Talking about Dave's Magnetic Horn.

Dave seemed more like Dave the Laugh again. He hadn't

shown any sign of numptiness, which is good.

Not that I care really, but well, you know.

Don't you? I hope you do because I certainly don't.

As my brain burbled merrily on by itself, Masimo said, "*Cara*, I must go. We are driving, now, for London. I am missing you. *Bellissima* Georgia." And he kissed me on the lips. In front of my mother. Dear God.

Mum said, "How beautiful. See you when you get back and good luck with everything."

Then Masimo went and gave her two kisses on either cheek. He said, "*Bella mama.*"

My mother practically collapsed on the spot. Then she laughed like a fool and said, "Ooohhh."

The romantic mood was spoiled a bit by the complete fandango of getting the spare helmet off Libby. First of all she said, "No, I laaaaaike it. It's mine."

And ran off to hide.

Of course, being a helmet on legs doesn't make it easy to hide. Nor does the fact that she thinks just standing very still behind a small tree makes her invisible. When I went and got her, she kicked my leg and said, "Shhhh, Gingey, I am hiding, you bad boy."

I lured her out of it by the Jammy Dodger bribe. She couldn't eat them with the helmet on, but I also had to promise to read her *Heidi*. AGAIN!!!

Mum tried to help by suggesting I read something called *The Magic Faraway Tree* by Enid Blyton.

At least it's trees instead of cheese.

Reading The Magic Faraway Tree
Twenty minutes later

Why do they let impressionable children read this sort of thing? It has even freaked Libby out because it is so insane. There is some bloke called Moonface in it. And he has got a moonface. Literally. Isn't that a bit moon-ist?

In my bedroom

It's odd having someone really like you. Am I that brilliant? Maybe all Pizza-a-gogo boys are like Masimo.

Hang on a minute, Rom is a Pizza-a-gogo type. It's all fitting together now. Rom only snogged Jule once before he shinned up her drainpipe (oo-er) and then he married her and committed suicide.

Perhaps all Pizza-a-gogo boys are the same.

Two minutes later

If I hear a scrabbling noise outside my bedroom window one night, it might not be Angus dragging some half-eaten cockroach for me to look at. It might be Masimo wanting a midnight wedding.

Crikey. I've already got a locket.

8:30 p.m.

Masimo phoned just before he set off.

He said, "Miss Georgia, will you wait for me?"

I was thinking, blimey, mate, it's only a day and a half. But I said yes.

I hadn't really thought about it before, but I suppose if he did go on tour, we might not see each other all the time.

And there would be loads of girls around him.

But he is not a red-bottomed Hornmeister, is he?

The question is... am I?

Two minutes later

No, I am most certainly not. I am the girlfriend of a Luuurve God and that is the end of the story.

Oh yes, I have dabbled in the cakeshop of life, but those days are well and truly over now.

I have settled for an Italian fancy. And I am not a jam tart.

Three minutes later

What did Dave the Laugh mean when he said he would be on his jacksie?

Four minutes later

I phoned Jas.

"Jas?"

"Hmmm."

"Are you going to deffo go to the cinema?"

"Yes, I think so. The only thing is, if Tom has got some special stones he was talking about, then we would put them in the aquarium."

"Right, so it's either the cinema or putting stones in a tank. I see. Erm, Jas, is, erm, are, Dave the Laugh and Emma going?"

"Why?"

"It's just a question, Jas."

"I know, but it's nothing to do with you pretending I fancy Dave the Laugh, is it?"

"You have a vair suspicious nature; it's sad."

"Well, why are you asking me? Anyway, Emma has gone on a sketching weekend with her art teacher, so she won't be there."

In my room
The vair weird thing was that I was sort of looking forward to going to the cinema now.

What was all that about?

Half an hour later
Just for the crack of being with your mates.

That's all.

You know, relaxing and watching a film with your mates.

Simple, uncomplicated stuff.

Sven finds his inner woman (unfortunately)

Saturday October 1st

9:00 a.m.

Something's vair vair wrong. It's so quiet.

What is so weird?

9:10 a.m.

I know what it is. No one has come barging into my room making me do stuff.

Also, I am in my bed, by myself.

No cats chewing my hair.

No Libby dancing around in suspiciously bulging pongie pants.

one minute later

No, I tell a lie, I am not alone. I have got Mr Potato Head with me. I didn't realise at first because he has got his sock "nightdress" on...

Urgh, Mr Potato Head is going a bit green.

I can't believe I nearly snogged him when I had snogging withdrawal.

I don't fancy him half so much now he is losing his looks!!!!

Hahahahahahaha.

Shut up.

Why is it so quiet though?

Oh, I thought it was too good to be true. I can hear the distinct approach of some portly bloke lumbering up the stairs to my b.o.l. (boudoir of luuurve). It will be Vati larging in with some ludicrous scheme to go and look around some pie factory somewhere. For hints on how to get even larger in the botty department.

The steps stopped outside my door and there was a knock.

What?

Then Vati said from outside the door, "Georgia, I have

brought you a cup of tea. Your mum said you would like one. May I bring it in for you?"

What was this? It must be some plan of his to get me to do something horrific, like come and watch him play "football" with his mates. Twenty-two out-of-condition men lumbering around a pitch for twenty minutes before most of them are sent off for fighting. (Or, as happened when I last went, Uncle Eddie got sent off for having a fag and a beer with the goalkeeper. During the game.)

Two minutes later
I said, "You can come in with the tea as long as you just leave it and don't say anything."

Three minutes later
Am I suddenly living in *Wind in the Willows* and Dad is kindly old Badger? He didn't say anything to me, just put the tea down and smiled at me and went away.

It must be some sort of trick to lull me into a false sense of security.

He was even almost normally dressed. In a proper jumper and trousers.

Not leatherette or anything.

Crikey.

Fifteen minutes later

This is the life, just lying here letting my pores breathe.

I wonder if I should start to cleanse and tone?

Also I must remember to replenish my pouch. I've gone through all my lip gloss in the last few days because of all the unexpected popping up that has been going on. Vis-à-vis the Luuurve God.

He'll be in Lunnern now hanging around with the Chelsea set.

Do I want it to go well or not?

What do management people do anyway?

Five minutes later

At least I have got my locket.

My precious locket of my beloved Luuurve God.

Where is my locket by the way?

Fourteen minutes later

I forgot I had put it in my pouch, in case I was body-searched on the way out of Stalag 14 for smiling or something.

I am going to phone Jas and see if she is coming tonight. And make her come anyway.

Downstairs

There is quiet music playing from the bathroom. As I picked up the phone, Dad came by with another cup of tea. He'll probably throw it over me and start yelling about the phone bill.

But he just smiled and said, "Good morning; sleep well?" and knocked on the bathroom door.

Mum said, "Come."

And Dad shuffled in with the tea.

Something really weird was going on. Mum was hardly ever out of the bath and Dad hadn't gone ballistic in hours.

Has he turned into a Stepford Dad?

One minute later

Jas answered the phone.

Before I could say anything she started going, "Guess what, guess what's the bestiest thing ever!!"

Oh, what did that mean? The best thing on Planet Jas could be anything.

I said, "Something to do with a new strain of vole poo? You've got a stuffed barn owl? No, no, don't tell me. Your pants have a new all-weather stretch gusset?"

She was going, "Nope, nope, you will never guess, it's so soooooo bestie!"

I said, "Jas, if it's anything to do with the newts getting a helter skelter I don't think I can bear the excitement."

She was too excited to notice my amusingnosity. She just burbled on. "The *Rom and Jule* thing, it's all, well... it's all fabby and marv. In fact, it's a miracle."

"I think you will find it's a tragedy, unless Miss Wilson has rewritten the ending so that Jule wakes up in time and finds her inner clown, with hilarious consequences."

Jas was talking over the top of me.

"Tom just told me, she's got to take a uni bursary exam. She can't be in it!!"

"Who?"

"Wet Lindsay!!!!"

Oh, joy unbounded.

Ten minutes later

Mind you, it would have been vair amusing to see Jas snogging Wet Lindsay. In an horrific, road crash sort of way.

Also Radio Jas tells me that there has been a change of plan cinema experience wise. I can't decide if it is good or bad.

Or a combo of good and bad. Goba. Or maybe even bago. Depending on how you look at it. Shut up, brain.

Rosie's parents have gone away for the night and she is planning on having the cinema experience at her place.

Hmmmmm.

I phoned her and said, "When you say 'cinema experience', what exactly do you mean by that?"

She said, "You know what I mean, my little pally. All of us in the dark, snogging and eating popcorn."

I said, "Yes, but the added mystery ingredient in the usual 'cinema experience' is that there is a film on."

Rosie assures me that there will be a film on, a "special" film. But she won't tell me what it is as she wants it to be a "lovely surprise".

Now I am frightened.

And I can't quite be sure that Dave the Laugh will be

there. And I can't ask anyone to check. If I ask Radio Jas and say, "Please will you not tell anyone I am asking, just use subtlenosity," Dave would be on the blower within five minutes saying, "Why do you want me to come to the cinema experience? Can't you resist my Magnetic Horn?"

What shall I do if he isn't there? I will be the goosegog fool of all time. But I can't just leave if he's not there because otherwise that looks like I really meant to see him.

And then the cat would be out of the bag.

Racing down the hill with the bag over its head.

Why is it in the bag anyway?

Speaking of cats, when I went down to the kitchen for a soothing plate of cheesy wotsits to calm my nerves, Angus was playing with his tartan toy mousey.

He was biffing toy mousey with one paw and then biffing him back with the other. Then picking him up by his neck and shaking him. Then he biffed toy mousey really hard and it went under the fridge.

Angus started trying to reach under with his paw. But he couldn't reach. Then he started his croaky miaowing and the looking at me pathetically fiasco.

Three minutes later

I was chomping away on the cheesies. I must keep my strength up for my maybe goosegogging experience tonight.

One minute later

Angus was still trying to reach toy mousey and still looking pathetically at me.

Two minutes later

Oh, I can't stand this.

I lay down on the floor and put my arm under the fridge to try to reach toy mousey. Angus was pressing my bottom with his paw as I was doing it. Sort of encouraging me, I suppose.

Two minutes later

It's right at the back. I can sort of touch it with my fingers, but I can't reach it to pull it out.

Two minutes later

I got the washing-up brush and nearly got it.

Oh, bloody hell, it's gone a bit further back.

Three minutes later
Just about got it.
  Just a centimetre or two more.

One minute later
Got it!!!
  Stood up. Blimey, I'm a bit dizzy.
  I said to Angus, "There you are, now don't..."
  He's just biffed it straight back under the fridge.
  And started his croaky miaowing and looking thing.

6:30 p.m.
When I went back in the kitchen for more cheesy wotsits,
Mum was down on the floor scrabbling under the fridge for
toy mousey.
  I didn't say anything.

6:45 p.m.
She's got it out.

6:46 p.m.
He's biffed it back under the fridge again.

7:00 p.m.

Libby is being taken over to Grandvati's because Mum and Dad are going out on a "date". Which is sad. They even said "date". Erlack.

As I was setting off to Rosie's "cinema experience", Vati was faffing around adjusting his fur steering wheel. I tried to just sneak off past him but he spotted me and said, "Have a nice time, but you won't be having as nice a time as us because your mother and I are off to paint the town red."

I said, "Don't you mean beige?"

And just for a moment I caught sight of my dear old dad, the dad I know and... well, the dad I knew. He went all red and ballistic-looking and started shouting, "You're not bloody funny, and what time will you be in? Because I am telling you this for free..."

Then he sort of stopped himself as Mum came out all tarted up and forced this very scary smile on his face. I watched while he opened the mirthmobile door for her and put Libby in the back.

Then I watched as Libby did a bit of kicking of the car seats and shouting. "Me want Bum-ty, me want Bum-ty!!! Go get her, Big Uggy!!!!"

And Dad went back into the house and came out with Bum-ty in her cage. Bum-ty seems to have less and less feathers. And she has gone off her Trill.

I'm not surprised with the twenty-four-hour cat staring that goes on.

Tonight Angus even managed to get on top of Bum-ty's cage. Even though Dad has fixed it to the light fitting and it's suspended from the ceiling.

Angus must have used the sofa as a launch pad, leaped up the curtains and hurled himself on to the cage from there. In a Devil take the hindmost kat-i-kaze diving episode. It's only because his paws are so huge that he couldn't get them through the bars.

7:15 p.m.
Anyway, at last the Swiss Family Mad streaked off at one mile an hour.

Some people live life in the fast lane. My dad lives life in the bus lane.

As I strolled along, I nearly caught up with them. I had to take really tiny steps to avoid walking alongside.

At Rosie's

Sven answered the door in an usherette's uniform. If you can imagine that. It's not easy, I know. He had a sort of mini-skirt on with platform boots. And a lot of eyeshadow and lippy.

Not expertly applied I have to say.

Sofas and chairs were arranged in front of their big-screen TV and Rosie was in charge of popcorn. I say in charge. What I mean is she was stoking up the popcorn maker, a duck that made popcorn that came shooting out of its beak.

The Ace Gang were all there by the time I arrived. Hons, Jools, Ellen, Mabs and Sophie, all snuggling up to their "boyfriends" already.

It was so crowded, I even wondered if the Little Titches might pop up from behind something. I'm not kidding. I wouldn't be surprised. If they have even a whiff (half a whiff) that Dave the Laugh might be in the area, they would be scampering around trying to get near to him.

Is he in the area though?

Fourteen minutes later

No sign of Dave the Laugh.

Goosegog land was approaching.

Oh God, this was going to be horrific.

Even now it was horrific and the film hadn't even started. The one hilarious moment was when Ellen did the classic bobbing around like a pigeon wondering which side to put her head for the snog.

Maybe I could pretend I had a sudden pressing piddly-diddly scenario and sneak out through the bathroom window.

Just then the doorbell rang. Sven the usherette went to answer it and carried in Dave the Laugh.

Dave said, "I like a big girl."

I didn't say anything. I felt a bit shy actually. And sort of nervy.

Dave got his popcorn and then came and sat down next to me.

I have to say, even though I am not interested in this sort of thing, that he looked, well, quite fit. For a matey-type mate.

The film was the sing-along version of *The Sound of Music*.

No, I am not kidding.

Sven (the usherette) introduced it by saying, "This is a film about the *unter*garments. We are haffing the singing about pants and the lederhosen. Let's groove!"

And then he switched the lights out.

We were plunged into complete darkness. Everyone was going, "Oo-er" and "Phwoooaar" etc. for a bit.

Then, in the darkness, Dave the Laugh said loudly, "Oy, Georgia, is that your hand on my knee, you cheeky, cheeky minx?"

What what???

It turned out to be Sven's hand. Sven was crawling around trying to find the control for the screen.

We sang, we ate popcorn. The film even had the bouncing ball lyrics because it was the sing-alonga one.

It should have been crapnosity personified, but it was not.

And the best thing was that the goosegog factor was vair low because no one really had any time for snogging.

My ribs really, really did hurt from laughing so much.

Sometimes we had reversed the film so that we could get the song again. We sang them all:

"The hills are alive with the sound of pants."

"Idlepants", as I have said many, many times, is one of my all-time hits.

Rosie said, "I am deffo going to have songs from *The Sound of Music* at my Viking wedding. The Vikings love a bit of yodelling."

It was after midnight before we came out. When we got to the end of Rosie's road, the rest of them walked off because they all lived in the same direction. They were yelling, "Pants for the memory!"

"*Guten Nacht, Volltrotte!*"

"*Abscheidskuss* all round!"

Till there was only Dave and me left.

It was a lovely soft night and as we walked along, I felt all warm and yummy inside.

Dave said, "I'll walk back along your way in case you are attacked by voles."

I said, "Fanks."

We didn't link up or anything and walked a bit apart. You know, in a sort of matey way. I think.

Then Dave said, "Well, I don't know what you think, missus, but I thought that was quite literally a hoot and a half. I thought your yodelling in 'The lonely goatherd' was, well, good is not the word."

I said, "Oy, mate, I have practised yodelling for weeks. Libby makes me read *Heidi* at least four times a day."

As we got near my house, Dave said, "Ah well, better say *Auf Wiedersehen*, pet."

And we both stood looking at each other in the half light.

He has got the most dreamy eyes. I don't know what it is, but I always feel like I could look at him for ages and ages. (Not in an Angus and Gordy looking at Bum-ty way.)

I don't know how much time went by because for once my brain froze.

I sort of felt like Baby Jesus, all full of love.

Dave put his hand on my face and just gently stroked it. Then he traced his finger around my mouth.

Oh no, stop puckering!!!

He looked down at me still with his finger on my lips and said, "I don't know what it is about you, Kittykat, but for me you are the most beautiful girl in the world."

Then he kissed me, just a little kiss.

I sort of reached up to kiss him back, but he stepped back then and pulled his coat collar up.

He breathed in really deeply and then cleared his throat and said, "Hmmm, that was a bit unexpected... but anyway, dig you later."

I didn't know what to say. Or do.

I just stood there.

I wanted to do all sorts of things. Grab him, run away, laugh uncontrollably. Snog, go to the loo, do a bit of the flame dance. I don't know!!!! Who is in control here?

As I dithered around, he walked off home.

When I got in, Mum and Dad were still up. And they weren't alone. Uncle Eddie was there. He's just "popped" by after a baldy-o-gram night. He hasn't been round much since the undercrackers at midnight scenario. Dad said they were "letting things cool down" neighbourwise.

I said, "Why, are you pretending that you and Uncle Eddie are not gay?"

Anyway, sadly, they seem to be together again.

As I tried to scamper upstairs, Uncle Eddie said, "This is one for you, Georgia. A man goes to the doctor and says, 'I keep thinking I'm a cartoon character. One day I'm Mickey Mouse, this morning I was convinced I was Bambi.' And the doctor says, 'It sounds to me like you're having Disney spells.'"

I looked at him as he rocked and hooted with laughter, going, "Do you see??? Do you see... Disney spells!!!"

What is the point of Uncle Eddie?

In bed

1:00 a.m.

Blimey.

Well, the cinema experience turned out to be a hoot and a half. The laughter, the pants, the yodelling.

One minute later

The nearly accidentally snogging Dave the Laugh AGAIN!!!

What in the name of arse is going on?

Two minutes later

What about Masimo?

I think I may have a touch of guiltosity.

Two minutes later

Although I don't know why I should have guiltosity – I haven't really done anything wrong as such. Involuntary puckering is not a capital offence.

One minute later

In fact, I will probably mention it in a light-hearted way to the Luuurve God.

You know, tell him what larks we had at the "cinema experience".

Two minutes later

Although explaining the "Idlepants" thing might take the rest of my life, given that I can't even say "What time is it?" in Italian.

Oh, I am just a crazy, mixed-up kid!!! It's not fair. If you look at the relativitosity of time and pretend that my life is a big clock... and I'm at three o'clock, it's only about five minutes since I first learned to do my shoes up at kindergarten. And so how come I am supposed to be an expert at relationships???

I only started snogging last year. (Half past two.)

Shut up about the clock fiasco!!!!

I didn't even have any basoomas eighteen months ago... (i.e. quarter to one... shut up, shut up, brain!!!).

I was practically just a nose on legs.

Two minutes later

OOOhhh. I'm never going to be able to go to sleep now.

I wonder if Dave is feeling the same.

I hope he is because it's his fault. He snogged me. I only did accidental puckering up.

It was him who said I was beautiful.

Am I?

Had a look in the mirror.

Erm, well, as I said, I have sort of grown into my nose, but I don't exactly as such look like a supermodel.

Perhaps boys like all sorts of girls not just supermodelly types.

Dad likes Mum, for instance, and does not think she looks like a mad prostitute.

In fact, he is very bloody keen on her these days.

I wonder if she is putting something in his food?

Five minutes later

I'm going to count sheep to get to sleep.

Three minutes later

Oh buggeration, the sheep keep changing into Masimo, and

then Dave, and then Robbie, and then Masimo and then two Daves. And then Dave with a clown nose on, leaping over the fence. And then Masimo with a handbag. Then Dave and Masimo fighting and leaping over the fence.

I will never ever sleep again. I zzzzzzzzzzzzzzzzzzzzzzz.

I may have a slight fence burn

Sunday October 2nd

Yipppeee we are going to take Angus to the kittykat park!

Mum has gone ballistic because Angus was going on and on, miaowing and rubbing round her legs. Tripping her up when she tried to walk anywhere. He's had his food so she put some water down for him in his bowl. He looked at it and then instead of lapping it up, he leaped in it and splashed it all over the floor and her.

She tried to chuck him out, but he ran off into the front room and he's managed to get himself into the back of the armchair.

She said, "He's not coming with us."

I said, "Mum, he's excited. He is hearing the call of the wild."

She said, "Go and get his lead. I'm putting my gardening gloves on."

We eventually got Angus out of the armchair and on his lead. It was all going quite well until he had a spontaneous spaz attack and wound himself round and round my legs...

When Pippy turned up in her car, Mum said to Dad, "You don't mind not coming, do you, Bob? Perhaps you could fix the shed roof this afternoon. I would be so thrilled if you did."

I looked at her in an "are you mad" way.

As if Dad will agree to that. The last time he fixed a ceiling, he went into the attic to have a look, walked in between the rafters and now his big fat footprints are there for ever.

To my absolute amazement, he gave her a big kiss on the mouth (oh, dear God) and said, "All right, my queen. Missing you already."

As we got in the car, I said to Mum, "Is Dad on drugs?"

And Mum said, "No, but the whole thing I have learned from Madame Betty is..."

I said, "Mum, can I just stop you there. If this is anything to do with boiled eggs and so on, I would rather not know."

She didn't take any notice of me, but just went on chatting to Pippy about stuff they had learned in their stupid workshop thingy.

I was trying not to listen because it was making me feel a bit queasy. Stuff about thinking you are the sexiest woman alive etc. Telling yourself how gorgeous you are.

On and bloody on.

When Mum said, "Next week we are doing how to release your inner lushiousness," I had to stuff two bits of scrumpled-up paper handkerchief in my ears.

Wild Park!!!

Angus luuurved his wild cousins. The wildcat ladeeez luuurved Angus too, the little furry minxes, laying on their tum tums with their girlie parts flying free.

He really howled when we finally managed to get him away.

To cheer him up because he was still yowling and bonking about in the car, I sang "Wild Thing" to him.

I even improvised a little kittykat disco inferno dance.

And I did the paw actions for him.

He let me work his paws for a bit before he started spitting.

Home

Dad had hit himself with the hammer, and also the door of the shed had fallen off. So an excellent result DIY-wise.

He was in a foul mood when we got in.

I thought it was too good to last.

It was a bit of a relief to see the Portly One back to normal. He was vati-ing around, moaning and limping. Which is ironic, seeing as he had hit his thumb with the hammer.

Bobo time

Libbs is still at Grandvati's so I am going to enjoy my bed. Just the luxury of lying on it, without something hideous sticking in my back. Or Libby farting loudly all night.

Anyway, I've got to get myself in the right frame of mind to welcome back my Luuurve God.

I wonder what time he will be back?

He'll probably call me tomorrow.

I'd better check on my loveliness.

Maybe I should have an overnight egg-yolk face pack?

Two minutes later

No, maybe not. The last time I did I thought that my face had gone paralysed in the night.

Anyway, according to Dave the Laugh, I am beauty personified just as I am.

Which is handy.

I wonder why he said that to me?

The most beautiful girl thing.

Was it a joke?

Why weren't we laughing?

Anyway, shut up, brain.

Going upstairs

I said, "Goodnight, Mater and Pater. Please keep the noise down."

Dad said, "Oh, by the way, that Italian boy phoned. Masimo, is it? He says to tell you that he is back and he will see you tomorrow. And to think of him and put your hand on your locket. I told him that was going too far."

I said, "Dad, I hate you."

Masimo is back.

That's fab, isn't it?

I thought Dave might have rung. You know, just for a matey chat. But he didn't. I expect Emma is back and he'll be, you know, seeing her. Or something. Which is fine by me.

Monday October 3rd

Miss Wilson brought in the puppet dog for Jas. It is hilariously crap. And it is a glove puppet. It doesn't even look like a dog. I think it is a bear. Jas was supposed to work her own dog. She got into a terrible state in the balcony scene.

Miss Wilson suggested that the puppet dog "senses" that Rom is down below in the garden. She said to Jas, "When you, Juliet, say, 'Romeo, Romeo, whyfore art thou, Romeo,' the little faithful dog could bark..."

I said, "Erm, just as a matter of interest, Miss Wilson... wherefore art Romeo?"

Miss Wilson said, "Yes, well..."

I said, "Couldn't the dog double up as Romeo? I think that would be great. Try it, Jas. Get the doggie to say some of Rom's bits."

Jas was getting vair vair red indeedy. She was revving up the huffmobile, big time.

She said to me, "Georgia, shut up about Romeo being the doggy."

I said to her, "I am only trying to help things go with a swing, aren't I?"

Two minutes later

Miss Wilson announced the new Rom.

And the surprise news is that it's going to be... Melanie Griffiths.

She's a nice girl, Melanie, but she really has got ginormous basoomas.

I said to Rosie, "I don't fancy her chances of climbing up the balcony and not toppling over."

Possibly taking out several villagers on her way down.

But it's not really my prob, as I am dead by about page six.

Frankly, it's not really worth putting the tights on for.

Ten minutes later

Jas was on the edge of a nervy b. trying to do the barking and tail-waggling thing for the doggy and being Juliet as well.

In the end, she threw the glove puppet to the floor and burst into tears.

Ten minutes later

It's a dream come true for Nauseating P. Green because she is doubling up as townspeople and doggie. As I say, it's a dream come true for her, but not for anyone else. It's very hard to concentrate on her dog work, as immediately behind the dog is her not unlarge loomy face with huge glasses on it.

Miss Wilson looked a bit worried when Nauseating P. Green suggested an improvised "fetch the stick" moment.

I said to the gang, "Pamela will be doing method acting. She will almost certainly be sleeping in a dog basket tonight."

Jas is not amused of course.

Rom and Jule, otherwise known as Mrs Grumpy Knickers and Melanie, didn't do the kissy kissy bit. Actually, costumewise, there really is going to have to be quite a bit of strapping down. Otherwise Rom won't be able to get near enough to Jule to snog her.

Twelve minutes later
At last we got to the good bit. My fighting bit.

Miss Wilson said, "I was chatting with, erm, Herr Kamyer..."

We all went, "Oh, yes..." And winking and so on. Miss Wilson bobbed madly about.

"Yes, and by a stroke of good fortune, Herr Kamyer did *épée* as a young man. Competitively."

Rosie said, "Miss Wilson, why are you telling us about Herr Kamyer going to the piddly-diddly department?"

Miss Wilson looked completely baffled (no change there then). She said, "I don't understand..."

Rosie said, "You said Herr Kamyer did a pee as a young man. Competitively."

Miss Wilson started giggling like a goose.

"Oh, oh, I see... no, no, I said EPEE... it's a form of swordfighting."

Good Lord.

So Herr Kamyer is going to teach us to swordfight.

We may as well book the hospital now.

Ten minutes later

Hurrrahhhhhhh! God Bless King Harry and gadzooks etc.

Jas has perked up again now she doesn't have to do any barking.

Or have Wet Lindsay as her boyfriend.

Maybe everything is going to be OK.

We've got the lads coming in for the first tech run-through this week. Wait till Dave the Laugh hears that Melanie Griffiths is going to be Rom.

Lunchtime

Lolling about in the fives court.

Wet Lindsay and ADM came lurking over just looking at us. What are they looking at?

Octopussy called over to Jas, "Sorry about the play, Jas, but I've just got so much to do, the university thing and now the band going off to live in London."

What? What did she know about the band?

♥ 545

Then she went on talking to ADM. But loud enough for us to hear every word.

She said, "Robbie was so pleased to see me when I popped round last night. It's like he'd been away for months. And he is so cool at snogging. I had a boyfriend before him who was so inexperienced he didn't even know where to put his hands."

I said to Rosie, "I could have told him where to put his hands – round her throat until her goggly eyes popped out. Hell's teeth, she is such a smug bucket."

Jools said, "Did you know they were moving to London?"

No I didn't is the answer.

Wet Lindsay was still going on. I'm sure for my benefit.

"Yeah I could go to uni in London of course. I haven't applied anywhere there but, you know, I could. I think it would break Robbie's heart if I didn't go. I can tell he daren't ask me to go with him, just in case I say no."

Oh whatever!!

As a bit of light relief the two Little Titches came skipping up. All titchy and excited. Ginger Titch said, "Miss, Miss, we've got something to tell you. It's a secret."

I said, "Your library book's not a day overdue, is it?"

They shook their little heads. Then they did sort of "looking" at Wet Lindsay.

Then they did sort of "looking" to the science block. Ginger Titch said really quietly, "Follow us in a minute."

Then they did ludicrous waving and saying goodbye to me.

I wondered if they had been having Mad Miriam for theatre studies.

One minute later

I scooted over to the science block. Wet Lindsay had seen me go, but she was too busy talking about her own no forehead or something to ADM.

The Titches nearly gave me a heart attack by leaping out from a rhododendron bush.

"Miss, quick, he's here. He wants you to go and see him. He's down at the back of school, by the lower playing-field fence."

My heart skipped. Blimey, this was a bit thrilling. I could tell him about Melanie Griffiths and...

That's when I realised I'd been thinking the Titches meant Dave the Laugh, but they meant the Luuurve God.

I did quick pouch work and hair bounceability and sloped off down the fields.

The afternoon sun glanced off the trees and their autumny leaves and then I saw him.

He smiled that wonderful smile of his. God, he's good-looking. He actually looks like a pop star.

He shouted, "*Cara*, I came round 'ere to the back, for not getting trouble. I had to see you. I rang you."

Have you ever kissed someone through a fence? I don't as such recommend it.

In fact, I think I may have slight fence burn on my mouth.

Which is unusual.

When I got back, the gang was agog (two gogs).

Rosie said, "So, what did he say?"

Ellen dithered into life. "Is he, will he, is he, are they???"

Jools said, "Go on, tell us everything."

I said, "Well, I dunno really. The Stiff Dylans have got a major management company now, but they have to be, you know, where it's all happening."

Ellen said, "Where, I mean is it... is it happening... here?"

I said, "Not as such."

Jas said, "So is it true, they are moving to London?"

I said, "That is the nub and gist."

Jas came and put her arm around me in a sudden lezzie attack. She said, "I know just how you are feeling. The Tom thing has made me know the meaning of heartbreak."

"Er, Jas, Tom's only going to pop over to Hamburger-a-gogo land for a week and a half. Masimo is moving to the throbbing metropolis."

Rosie said, "Oo-er."

The bell went for double physics. At least I can take my mind off things by amusing myself with Herr Kamyer.

Masimo wants to take me out to talk everything over tonight.

What is there to talk over though?

He has been asked to go to London for his career.

He's not going to not go, is he?

I am on the rack of luuurve again.

Marvellous.

Double Physics
Two hours of unadulterated boredom and *merde*. If we

weigh atoms or whatever, I may eat my own head. Just to stop me being so bored.

Oh good, we are doing about "light". The only "light" in all of this is Herr Kamyer.

There is something so keen about him. Why? Has he just got the keenness gene? Mostly I think teachers come and teach because they hate us and want to make us suffer. But Herr Kamyer likes us. He does. If I had a conscience... well, I'd... well, I don't know what I would do. But thankfully I haven't.

To illustrate the difference between light and dark, Herr Kamyer had drawn the curtains and switched the lights off. Which was crap because it was still light outside and the curtains were see-through.

I said, "Herr Kamyer, we don't really experience dark any more, do we?"

He looked at me through his roundey glasses.

"*Ach zo*, Georgia, how do you mean zis?"

"Well... because of the lights in cities and you know global thingy and everything."

He said, "Global thingy?"

I said, "*Ja, ja*, zat is what I mean. We don't know what it is like to be in the dark."

He looked at me. "*Ja*, that is a *gut* point. No-vhere is completely dark."

I said, "Except for the photography dark room. Let's go in there and see what it is like to be completely in the dark."

Herr Kamyer said, "Vell, I don't know if..."

I got to my feet.

"*Ja, ja*, to the dark room."

The Ace Gang surged out, followed by the rest of the class.

The dark room is quite small and you could probably get about five people in comfortably. When we opened the door, it was quite literally pitch-black in there. Herr Kamyer stepped in and said, "*Ja*, now zen, girls if we go in maybe five at a time, we..."

At which point, all twenty-five of us crammed into the room and I slammed the door.

It was hysterical. I could hear Herr Kamyer, but I couldn't see a thing. It was just jampacked in.

And we were all shrieking and yelling, "Where am I?"

Herr Kamyer was shouting, "Now, ver is *der* door, girls? Calm down."

Then there would be the crash of some glass thing.

And the shrieking started again.

Rosie was shouting, "We're doomed, we're doomed!!!!!"

"Is that the door knob... oo-er."

Etc. etc.

After a few minutes of this, someone found the door handle and we piled out. Herr Kamyer came out last. His hair was all mussed up and his glasses were on sideways.

I couldn't stop laughing.

I said to him, "Now that is what I call dark."

5:00 p.m.

As I walked up our driveway, the mirthmobile was parked by the garage. Looking out of the back window was Bum-ty in his cage.

He is still up his ladder even though the cats are not around him. Mum must have left him in the car to give him a staring-free holiday.

In my room

Masimo is coming at 7:00 p.m. I said I would meet him in town, but he insisted on picking me up. I am going to make sure I am waiting by the gate to avoid any chance of Dad "talking" to him.

I'm a nervy wreck.

I've already changed my clothes four times. I have to get out of my bedroom before I go mad.

In the kitchen

Mum was doing her nails.

I could see Libby through the back window. She has got the washing-up bowl on the grass and is surrounded by Pantalitzer doll, Mr Fish and all her toys. She must be giving them a bath. She's obsessed with baths.

I said to Mum, "If someone really liked someone and had the chance to go off with them to somewhere really exciting, should they go?"

She looked at me.

"Someone really likes someone and wants to go off with them to somewhere really exciting."

Yes, yes, what is this? Simpletons' hour?

She was still rambling on though.

"And does this someone have any money to go off somewhere really exciting?"

"Not as such."

"Well, you can't go then, can you?"

Oh, she is so annoying. And unreasonable.

Half an hour later

I didn't mean to, but I have accidentally told Mum the whole story.

She was sort of not too bad about it.

In a bad way.

She said that she thought fifteen was too young to make a big commitment, away from home and away from your family and mates.

I said, "Well, I agree with the mates thing, but the family..."

She said, "And also, what will you be living on? Will your Luuurve God pay all the bills while you... erm... what is it you do exactly?"

I hate her and wish I hadn't told her anything.

I could just go.

She can't stop me.

What do the girlfriends of pop stars do actually?

I would miss the gang. Leaving all my pally wallys...

Phoned Jas

"Jazzy, I'm sorry that I ever dissed your owls. And also your fire-making stick thing. It is well good."

Jas said, "What is this all about? I'm not going to get into any trouble, am I? You haven't got some new mad idea about papier mâché heads, have you?"

Oh, she is so full of suspicionosity.

I said, "No, it's just that I am on the horns of a dilemma vis-à-vis Masimo and I know I wasn't vair nice to you about Hunky going to Hamburger-a-gogo land."

Jas said, "Well, I know you didn't mean to be nice, but in fact you have been accidentally nice on purpose. I have told Tom that I want him to be happy and if he wants to go to college there, he should fly free and then we'll see what happens next. And he's going to go."

"Jas, did you really set him free like a rubber band? Wow. And also wowzee wow wow."

Jas said, "I'm a bit freaky-deaky about it, but you can't stop people doing what they want. And anyway, I might go to York and see what it's like there. Apparently, they have a very active wildlife centre."

I said, "Steady on, Jas, are you hearing the call of the owl?"

Crikey. I think committing suicide on stage is bringing out the best in Jazzy.

I may spontaneously buy her Midget Gems tomorrow.

7:00 p.m.
Sitting on the gate waiting for the Luuurve God.

Oscar just came blundering up and said to me, and I quote, "Your legs must be tired because you've been running through my mind all night. Check it."

Dear *Gott in Himmel*.

I didn't say anything.

There is nothing to say.

It was getting a bit dark and nippy noodles. I'd compromised bikewear-wise by wearing a short skirt, but with thick tights and long boots. So hopefully, there would be no "gusset incident".

Masimo zoomed round the corner into my street. He had a leather flying jacket on. Which was vair cool.

He killed the engine on his bike and slowly took off his helmet. Then just sat on his seat looking at me. Sort of in an admiring way. Looking me up and down. Oh, good, my legs had gone all jelloid. I was going to fall off the wall and reveal my gusset before I even got on the bike.

I heard Oscar say, "Tosser".

And not in an ironic way seeing as it was coming from an absolute spoon.

Masimo just half turned in his seat and looked at Oscar. He said, "Ay you, monkey boy, vamoose."

And Oscar spat on the floor. (Why? Did he think Masimo was frightened of spit?) And then shuffled off, like he had meant to go anyway.

By the time Masimo got off his bike and came over to me, I had managed to gain some control of my legs.

Also I had remembered to wear my locket round my neck. Which was a lucky break because it was the first thing he kissed.

Er... was that odd?

Shut up, brain. Dave the Laugh has deffo started camping in my brain, twittering on about stuff. That is the problem with seeing too much of him. He gets in there with his annoying jokes. Although the boy's penid on the school playing field is, it has to be said, comedy gold.

I only wish I could tell the Luuurve God about it... but I can't.

Five minutes later

We zoomed off and went to Ciao Bella's. Which is a quite groovy pasta place. In the centre of town. I've never actually been in it because it's quite new. And when we had passed it, I was with Dad, Libby and Grandad, and Dad said there was too much glassware around. And the waiters looked a bit too namby pamby to deal with Libby and Grandvati.

One hour later

I suppose this is what my new Lunnern life will be like. Stopping off at bijou restaurants for a quick supper before... well, before what? Extended snogging?

The Luuurve God told me that the management people want them to move to London quite soon. Then he just looked at me and smiled. He touched my cheek.

"What do you think, Miss Georgia?"

Everyone is so bloody keen on me thinking all of a sudden. It's not what I do.

Masimo had tiny molluscs in spaghetti. Like little clammy things.

I'm bloody glad I had a pizza because if I had had molluscs

and spaghetti, I might have managed to choke and strangle myself at the same time. I feel like I am on the verge of an enormous visit to Strop Central, stopping only at nervy tiz headquarters.

Masimo said, "If you don't want me to go, I will not go. I can always do my music. Maybe I could write some songs for the band."

But it didn't seem right somehow.

He got hold of my hand.

"You are young – this is big decision for you. But, if you like, I will find for us a place to live. I have friends there, and you could go for your college there."

Go for college to do what?

9:30 p.m.
When I came in, Mum was mumming around.

She said, "Are you OK?"

I said, "What do you think?"

She said, "Would you like a hot choccy?"

"As if that will help."

"You do want one though, don't you?"

In the Kitchen

She went, "Sooo?"

I didn't mean to tell her, but I didn't have enough room left in my brain to think about it any more.

I said, "He said if I didn't want him to go, he wouldn't go."

She said, "Hmmm."

I said, "Mum, if you are going to annoy me by hhhhhmmmming I may as well go and tell some bees about it."

She put her arm around me.

"Look, I'm wanting to try and find out how you feel, that's all."

Well, she is not on her own there.

Mum says this is good practice for me, trying to figure out about love and how I feel.

She says I shouldn't be afraid to lose someone by saying the wrong thing.

She also said that girls make the mistake of thinking they should do what they think boys want.

After a while I said, "In a nutshell, Mum, are you saying that I should strop around doing what I want?"

560

She said, "Yep, boys like that. And also you will find that if you try to be good and nice and girlie and make sacrifices, you will get madder and madder at the boy. And he won't even know why."

In my bedroom
What in the name of Beelzebub's Y-fronts is that supposed to mean?

In bed
Why do I have to keep doing stuff?

Making decisions and so on.

It's bad enough knowing what shoes to wear but now, suddenly, it's all: What do you want to do as a job?

I don't know!! is the answer. I've only just really learned how to get up and go to school EVERY BLOODY DAY!!!

And now it's: Do you want to go to London and be a pop star's girlfriend?

I don't know!!! is the answer. It's only a minute and a half since I got a pop star. I don't know what you bloody do with them day after day.

I feel like stabbing something with my pretend sword.

Midnight

I can't wait for the swordfighting thing.

Maybe bludgeoning Ellen to death (metaphorically) will give me a bit of light relief.

Whey-heyyyy!!

Tuesday October 4th

Bum-ty has made a desperate bid for freedom! He is up the big tree next door.

Apparently Libby thought he needed a bit of a wash and blowdry, and got him out of the Robinmobile and into the washing-up bowl. When she went to get the hairdryer he must have staggered off.

He is free, free, free!!!!

Free from the cat staring.

He can fly free and wild with his sparrow friends.

As I walked to school, I could see lots of his sparrow friends all gathering on the branch near him.

Staring at him.

He is shuffling up the branches.

They are just staring.

Stalag 14
Ace Gang meeting

The gang are taking a vote on what I should do vis-à-vis the Luuurve God situation.

The options are:

a) Tell the Luuurve God not to go

b) Bravely tell him to go with a quivering lip (not him having the quivering lip, me having it... keep up)

c) Bog off to London with him and Devil take the hindmost. Our Lord Sandra will take care of me

d) The mysterious option d

It's a secret ballot paper, where you put a cross next to the option you choose.

However, I know which is Ellen's because she has ticked everything and then crossed it out and then ticked everything again.

OK, the result is: one vote for **c**. (That will be Rosie. In fact, I know it is because she put a cross with a little beard on it.) The rest are **b**s.

Sad really.

I sort of knew that would happen.

I said, "How come no one voted for the mysterious option **d**?"

Mabs said, "What is it?"

And I said, "I don't know. That is why it is so mysterious."

Lunchtime

Jas had a secret rendezvous with Tom in the alleyway by the science block. I had to be the guardey dog type person.

That is the kind of top pal I am.

Actually, since she has decided to let Tom *boing* off on his elastic band she is getting quite un-Jasish. Less Miss Hufty Knickers and more Ms Loosey Goosey Knickers... With just a hint of Devil take the hindmost about the gusset area. She even applied a bit of lip gloss. In school hours!!! The little rebel. And she turned her skirt over. As she went off to meet Hunky, I said to her, "Jas, you're not wearing a thong, are you?"

And she didn't say no.

Or hit me.

Or fiddle with her fringe.

Hmmmmmm.

As I was lolling about, minding my own business, Elvis Attwood came shambling and perving along. With a hosepipe. He's probably pretending to clean the windows.

I said, "Your hosepipe is very big, Mr Attwood."

He, as usual, went sensationally ballistic for no reason.

He said, "Don't think I don't know what you're up to."

I said, "What am I up to?"

He said, "No good, that's what."

What kind of sense does that make? When he filled out his form to be a caretaker, they should have given him the lowdown about being a caretaker.

Stuff like, "If you take this job as caretaker at a girls' school, there will be quite a lot of girls there. At school. Do you see?"

It would have saved an awful lot of trouble.

I watched him turn the nozzle on the hose to start the water coming out. But nothing happened.

He really has got vair colourful language for a man who fought in the Boer War.

I watched him as he grumbled back along the hosepipe. He had got it wrapped round a bollard by mistake. He untangled it but then, with a huge *whoosh*, the trapped water came shooting out. The hosepipe snaked around like a bonkers python. A bonkers python that was chasing Mr Attwood. He was soaking wet before he managed to get to the tap.

Python hose even shot his hat off.

Quite, quite top entertainment.

The bell rang and Jas came scampering back going, "Oh, Hunky is sooo umm, I think I'll love him for ever no matter what happens..."

Yes, anyway, as we went back into the Temple of Doom, we saw Wet Lindsay slamming into the sixth-form common room. Phew, she was red and scary-looking.

I said to Jas, "What's the matter with her? Perhaps she tried to wear a hat today and it fell down over her eyes and she realised she has no forehead."

Jas looked a bit owly.

And tapped her nose.

What is that all about?

Afternoon break

We've just heard on the Bush Telegraph, i.e. Jas, that Robbie has dumped Wet Lindsay. Tom told Jas that Robbie is deffo skipping off to London town with the band, but he is not taking the Wet Wipe with him. He has escaped from the slimy, slimy girl!!!!

Yessssss!!!!! And thrice Yesssssss!!!

At the fives court

I said, "I think you will all agree that this is a victory in the fight against slimenosity. Robbie's bid for freedom calls for a celebration Viking bison disco inferno dance. But with a little added *je ne sais quoi*. In honour of the occasion."

So we did the Viking inferno dance, but at the end, instead of falling to our knees and yelling "Hoooorn", we yelled, "Duuuuuummmmmmped!!!!!"

Which was slightly unfortunate timing, as Octopussy Girl herself and ADM came round the corner.

We sat down quickly and passed around refreshing Midget Gems. I looked at Lindsay and let a little smile play around my lips.

If looks could kill, I would have been deader than a dead

person on dead tablets. In dead land.

Wet Lindsay had tiny little mousey eyes from crying. I would feel a bit sorry for her, but she is such a mega cow and a half, and horrible to the Titches. And anyway, I've got used to hating her. It's a bit of light relief.

ADM was saying to her, "How do you feel?"

Wet Lindsay said, really loudly so that she was sure we would hear, "Well, to be honest, I let it happen. You know, I've sort of encouraged him to think he left me, but it's only to save his pride really. I mean when I went up to uni for my interview, there were loads of really fit boys there. Robbie is quite nice-looking, but there are better, much hotter boys."

What an enormously ludicrous Octopussy slime pot she was.

As we got up to go in, I looked at her and opened my eyes in a really ironic way.

She shouted at me, "And you can shut up, Georgia, you tart."

How can I shut up when I haven't said anything?

What is she going to do now – give me a reprimand for telepathic talking?

6:00 p.m.

Masimo called when I got home.

"*Cara*, I am off for meeting with the band. We are having talking about our plans, you know. How are you feeling?"

I said, "You know, a bit freaky-deaky."

"*Che...*"

"I mean I... oh, I don't know how to say it in Italian... but, well, I think it should be option **b**. On the whole."

In the end, the Luuurve God said he will pop round before his meeting to talk to me for a little while. Even if he can't understand what I am saying, it's still nice of him to come and see me.

7:30 p.m.

Sitting outside at the bottom of our garden in the dark. Masimo has put his coat around me and him, and we were looking up at the stars. Winking and a-blinking. But not giving any advice as such.

I even rescued Our Lord Sandra from Libby's teapot tonight. I've been looking for him/her for ages. I thought if I made a shrine for him, like I used to, it might help me know what to do. He had a BluTack foot before, but since I last saw him he seems to have lost a whole leg. I propped him up with Mr Potato Head. Libby doesn't lobe Mr Potato Head since he started going green, but I know Lord Sandra loves him... It doesn't say that he loved vegetables as such in the Bible. It doesn't say that he said "blessed are the leek", but he had whatsit, unconditional love, for all kind.

It was nice having him there. Still heavily rouged, it has to be said. But it doesn't alter his innernosity of goodness.

I suppose I didn't exactly have a conversation with him, but I did get the feeling that option ♭ would be the right thing to do.

Anyway, where was I? Oh yes. Masimo was being so sweet to me. When I look at him, I can't believe that he really likes me; he could have anyone he wanted. And actually, if he goes to London, he probably will.

Masimo said, "Georgia, Georgia."

And he kissed me softly on the mouth, and on the nose. (He's brave, I thought! Shut up, brain.) He was looking down at me.

"This for you is hard, but let me 'elp you."

I was glad to hear that because frankly I needed some 'elp.

He said, "This is how it is, for me. I have more years than you. I think, yes, it is *bene, molto bene*, that we have good offer for the band... but, I am man, I am good singer, another band will come."

I started to say, "But I..."

He put his finger on my mouth.

"For you, it is big thing because you have not so many years. For you, you are afear that I will be sad not for to go to London. But no, for me is cool."

God, he was nice.

I started again, "But I..."

He said, "Let me finish, then you think more."

I nodded, but really I was thinking, Oh, good grief, please no more with the thinking. Cut my head off, please.

Masimo said, "I think if I go to London without you and say we will still be going out, you will be unhappy. You will not know where I am. You like big attention. You are big attention girl. You are like 'Me, me, me!!!'"

I thought er, no, I am not. I was only chatting with Lord Sandra earlier about the bestnosity of choosing option ♭.
But he didn't seem to think being a "Me, me, me" girl was a bad thing. He was smiling at me.

"Georgia, that is good. That is why I like you. But you would be not good if I am busy always away from you. For me, I can say, 'I am your man, I will be thinking of you and no one else,' but you will not like. You will say, 'What about me, me, me!'"

Blimey.

When he said "Me, me, me", it really sounded like Libby. That's a bit alarming. I might be a me, me, me girl, but I'm not like Libby. I'm grown up. I haven't ever written BUM on a boy's forehead in indelible ink. (Although, to be honest, I am quite tempted to do it to Junior Blunder Boy.)

Shut up, brain. Concentrate.

Masimo had to go.

He said, "I think maybe I will be saying that, for me this time, I will not be going with the band. And that is for me good also. I will have you, and we will know each other, and then something else will happen. Later maybe we go to London together. *Ciao, bella.*"

I wanted to weep and weep. It was so sort of overwhelming.

And sort of grown up.

And sort of crap.

In bed

Looking through my window into the night sky.

And at the tree next door.

I can't see Bum-ty anywhere.

One minute later

The sparrows look a bit fatter to me.

Is this what happens when you do something wild?

You pay the price.

Is that what would happen to me if I went to London?

I would be eaten by cockney sparrows?

Ten minutes later

Is Masimo actually going to give up his chance with the Stiffs for me?

Ooooooh I need someone to talk to about it.

If the Hornmeister could be bothered to keep in touch like a mate, I could ask him.

I think.

Actually, I'll be seeing him the day after tomorrow deffo because the "lads" are coming in after Stalag 14 for a tech read-through. Or "two hours of mayhem" as some people might call it.

I've learned my Merc-lurk-io part, which is a minor miracle given that he rambles on about the Queen of the Fairies for about a million years.

On the plus side, we are doing the swordfighting thing with Herr Kamyer tomorrow.

I may be able to work out my inner turmoil by whacking a big sword around. Oo-er.

Wednesday October 5th
In the gym
Sword workshop

Herr Kamyer changed into his "sportswear" for the swordfighting. Although he kept his socks and sock suspenders on. We knew this because his trackie bums were ankle-length.

Miss Wilson practically bobbed her way to the loony bin she was so excited to have "Rudi" near her. She was saying, "Now pay careful attention to Herr Kamyer. He is the expert, and this needs to be very precise because it could be dangerous. Over to you, Herr Kamyer."

Rosie said, "She is deffo wearing Mivvy today."

Herr Kamyer took off his glasses.

We all went, "Ooooohhh, sir... why, you're beautiful," and so on.

"Now zen, girls, vat ve are doing *ist* choreographing ze fighting. Ve are not wildly waving our weapons around."

We all went, "Whey-heyyyyy!"

Fifteen minutes later

Good Lord this is a larf. Nauseating P. Green has been stabbed twice and she isn't even in the fight scene. It's her arse; it just seems to attract the sword like a magnet.

Ellen (Tybalt... or something, er, what do you think) and me (Merc-lurk-io) have this fab fight backwards and forwards across the stage. Thrust, thrust, parry, thrust, thrust... "Oooh, sorry about that, Pamela"...thrust, thrust.

The only pity is that we are not allowed fake blood capsules. Miss Wilson said that, not only would it be slippery and dangerous, but that she thought it would be "more creative" for us to come up with our own artistic interpretation of blood being spilled.

Oh no.

Oh yes.

Fourteen minutes later

Of course it involves balloons and scarves. I knew it would. And free-form dance.

Dear God.

The village people come on when I am stabbed, with red balloons and scarves. Miss Wilson said, "Now then, you village people, you have become blood, you are blood. Blood corpuscles. Spilling out of the wound. Pumping and pumping! Wave those scarves and balloons. Interweave in a dance of blood and death."

Good Lord.

Nauseating P. Green said, "Should I still be the dog and blood at the same time?"

Miss Wilson said, "No, no, Pamela, put your dog on the side of the stage. You can leave it with one of the technicians."

I said to Rosie, "If it's Dave the Laugh she hands it to, she'll either never see it again or the next time she does see it, it will be wearing comedy glasses. Probably hers."

Oh, I am exhausted. The whole afternoon has been absolute top entertainment.

And I never thought I would say that about Stalag 14.

I'm full of exhaustosity, and even saying that is making me vair tired.

Gordy got stuck in a beer mug. Honestly. I don't know what to say.

Masimo called.

He sounded a bit down.

"*Ciao, cara*. Did you have good day?"

I said, "Yeah, we did swordfighting and it was tremendously crap. For the school play. *Rom and Jule*."

He laughed. "Yes, I am glad you are more happy. I look forward to seeing you in it."

Oh no. No, no, no, no, no. Not in my tights. No.

Before I could say the no, no, no business he went on.

"The management, they call today, and they are upset. They say it might not be so good for the band. If I am not with them. I don't know. I say, Robbie he is good and they say yes, but it is more good with two."

Oh, bloody hell, now I was ruining six people's lives. Oh good.

Masimo is going off for another meeting with the band. Also he knows that Robbie has dumped Wet Lindsay.

I said, "Yes, well, every clud has a silver lining."
He didn't get it though.

What should I do?

What if the management say that they won't take the Stiff Dylans without the Luuurve God? I would be the most hated girl in town since Big Fat Mary the Hateful. Whoever she was.

I wish I could talk to Dave the Laugh. It seems ages since I saw him.

I hope he hasn't got the hump with me again.

It wasn't my fault he said I was beautiful.

I hadn't meant to be.

I'm not.

Looking in my mirror

Especially as there is the suspicion of a lurker on my chin.

Oh no.

In bed
8:15 p.m.

Some absolute fool (Vati) has replaced Mr Fish's batteries.

8:30 p.m.

Mr Fish is still singing "Maybe it's beCOD I'm a Londoner" and wriggling about. I said to Libby, "Turn him off now, he's tired."

Libby gave her mad heggy heggy ho laugh and said, "He's singing!!!"

I said, "I know he's singing, but it's time for bobos now. Let's tuck Mr Fish under the blankets so that he doesn't... erm... get..."

Libby said, "Fwightened."

"Yes, let's tuck Mr Fish up so he doesn't get frightened."

"Fwightened."

"Fwightened."

My life is a mockery of a sham of a fiasco.

Dreamt that I was fighting off lurkers.

It was disgusting actually.

I was in *Rom and Jule*, giving it my all in my tights, and the lurkers came lumbering and lurking up to me. Surrounding me. And when I hit them with a sword, they exploded like custard bombs. But they didn't give up; they just kept coming up to me all wriggling and exploding and singing... "Maybe it's because I'm a LURKERER!!!"

Just call me Pongo

Thursday October 6th
French

Madame Slack had *le* nervy spaz today. She is vair highly strung. (Or should be.) We only laughed when we read in our *Français* textbook that the slang for a lady lavatory attendant was *une dame pipi*. And she started tutting and muttering in French.

She said we were childish.

Caca is to poo. Hahahahahaha.

To get her own back, she told us that the slang insult for English people is *Les Rosbifs* (the roast beefs) or *Les Biftecks* (the steaks).

581

Then she laughed like *le* drain.

I said to Rosie, "*Oooh là là*, she has really hurt my feelings now by saying I am a roast beef. I may never play the violin again."

What is the matter with the Froggy-a-gogo people?

First technical run-through with the lads

I feel a bit nervy. I don't know why. The lads are due in a min. We are all huddled in the loos doing lippy work. Miss Wilson wanted us to wear our costumes. But in a fit of geniosity Jools said, "Miss Wilson, I think we should try and keep the, erm... mystery, and, er..."

I said, "Sheer bloody excitementosity."

Jools said, "Yes, keep the excitementosity down to a manageable level, by wearing casual clothes in rehearsal."

Essentially, what she is saying is that we will not be donning our tights in front of the lads until we absolutely have to.

Miss Wilson said, "Yes, yes, I see what you mean. Let the, the, mystery and excitement gather. Yes."

Of course, Jas was a bit miffed. She is keen as *la moutarde* to get into her Jule gear:

a) because she is a girlie swot and b) because she has a quite flattering dress to wear and a blonde wig. Which personally I like a LOT, due to its lack of fringeyness. I wonder what Jas will do with her hands when she hasn't got her fringe to fiddle with?

Try to fight off Melanie's basoomas, I should think. I don't think the binding is very secure on Rom's costume. When they last tried to strap her into her tunic, two buttons popped off and nearly blinded one of the villagers.

She must be a 34H if she is a day.

We are rehearsing with a ladder and a bit of scaffolding for the balcony scene... Mr Attwood is standing by with his first-aid kit. I bet he is hoping that Melanie strains a basooma and he has to put it in a splint.

Ten minutes later

Nauseating P. Green has brought some proper dog biscuits in for her puppet dog. Which she told everyone is called Pongo.

Jas said to P. Green, "I can't just call you Pongo you know. It's not in the script."

P. Green said, "No, but you will know that it's my name, and I will know it's my name."

♡ 583

I said, "Er, Pamela, how will we know it's your name if no one says your name?"

And Nauseating P. Green said, "I've got it on my dog collar."

And she has.

4:30 p.m.

The lads arrived.

We were all on the stage when they came in.

They sounded like they kicked the door open and all surged in at once. We sort of huddled at the back of the stage while they whooped and yelled.

I said to Rosie, "Can you see Dave the Laugh anywhere?"

And she said, "Are you having the General Horn?"

I said, "Nooo. I just can't see him and..."

At which point he walked in and waved at us all on the stage. He said, "Settle down, girls. I am here."

He went over to Miss Wilson and said, "May I say how thrilled I am that once more we can help you as you fill your Shakespearean tights."

Miss Wilson had a bit of a ditherspaz. Dave can look smiley and sincere while he says the rudest things.

She said, "Well, thank you, I, well, I am not, erm, filling, well I mean, I won't be, I'm not in the play of course. Would you boys start by looking at our lighting plan and the scenery that needs, erm, painting?"

Dave said, "Of course, sir. I have only the finest handpicked lads with me."

Fifteen minutes later
On the side of the stage, while Miss Wilson chalks stuff on the stage and so on.

Dave came up behind me. I had sort of felt too shy to go up to him and although he had caught my eye and winked, he was busy chatting to all the other girls.

He is an appalling flirt.

The girls were all giggling and being girlie.

Pathetico. I wonder if Emma would be so smiley if she could see him now.

He looked at me for what seemed like ages. Then he came really close to me. Oh my God. He said, "Hello, Miss. Show us your sword."

My head nearly fell off. Why does he come and stand so close to me?

♡ 585

I was so happy to see him though.

So I showed him my sword.

He said, "Ummm, groovy."

I said, "How did you manage to get handpicked?"

And he said, "Kittykat, as you know I am the vati. The vati is always handpicked, and the vati's mates are also handpicked."

I said, "Yes, yes, but who does the handpicking?"

And he said, "Hello."

5:30 p.m.

For a while, I forgot that I was on the horns of a whatsit. And also prob up shi cree without a padd.

As I predicted, when P. Green handed over Pongo to become a blood corpuscle, it was the last she saw of him. Until he appeared on the balcony with a false beard and a pair of comedy glasses at the suicide scene.

Actually, the lads were relatively well behaved. Probably because they were so mesmerised by Melanie's basoomas, especially when she tried to get up the ladder. They all offered to give her a hand up.

The *pièce de résistance* was, of course, the snogging scene.

You have never seen anything like it. Twenty lads at the side of the stage. All like seeing-eye dogs. I wouldn't mind, but it isn't even proper snogging. It's bloody mime snogging and they still were drooling like drooling droolers.

There is some crap music and then Jule and Rom start going into slow motion. Their eyes meet at the dance and then they walk over to each other. Then they pucker up really slowly: puckering and moving their heads from side to side, with their arms flailing about. And then there is the sound of waves crashing and they pretend to fall back and be swamped by the waves.

Then they do the slow-motion puckering and arms flailing thing again, and then the waves crash again and they fall back again.

It's WUBBISH snogging.

It's like in *Thunderbirds*, that crap puppet show, where you can see the strings, and the puppets' feet are about a metre off the ground.

However, in Melanie's case, it is not only the arms that are slow-motion flailing around. It is her nunga-nungas as well.

At the end of the big snogging fiasco all the lads went, "Phwoooaar."

As I have said, often, boys are sensationally weird.

Twenty minutes later

Rosie got a bit of a telling-off for ad-hoc beard work during her Nursie scene.

As I have often said, she has two styles of acting: with or without the beard.

Ten minutes later

My fight scene with Ellen was a triumph, dahling, a triumph.

At the end of it Dave the Laugh said to me, "I don't care what anyone says, I think you were marvellous."

6:30 p.m.

As we were all piling out of "rehearsal", Tom turned up in the hall. Jas went all pink, but amazed me by not dashing over to him like a simpleton. He came over to her and said, "I came to take you for a romantic walk in the woods."

And got hold of her hand and they walked off.

Ooohh. Quite touching really. If you like that sort of

thing. And also, it has to be said, Jas'n'Tom's idea of a "romantic walk in the woods" is almost bound to involve cuckoo spit.

As we were all going along the corridor to get out of Stalag 14, I was next to Dave the Laugh. All his mates were round so I didn't feel like I could say anything to him about the Luuurve God situation. But the lads were preoccupied with flirting and farting and so on, and it was Dave who said, "Gee, about the other night."

I said quickly, "I know, I know, you just said something nice to me, to make me feel nice... it's OK, I didn't really believe it. You were just like being nice or something."

Dave said, "Well... not exactly..."

I was thinking, oh no, he didn't mean it at all. He's embarrassed now.

I didn't know what to say.

He said, "I'm a bit confused."

I said, "You don't need to talk to me about confused, I am Lady Confused of... well, I don't know where..."

He said, "Look, I just wanted to say..."

I said, "No, I just wanted to say..."

By this time, we were outside going towards the gates.

Dave said, "Look, you've chosen Masimo and..."

I said, "Yeah, I know, but well..."

Dave said, "But well what..."

I didn't know what to say.

I said, "Just, yeah, I know, but well..."

Dave looked at me. He sighed. "God, Georgia..."

I said, "I know."

But I don't.

And that's when I saw Masimo waiting for me on his scooter.

Dave said, "You'd better go, Kittykat. I'm off to see Emma."

But he didn't sound pleased. He sounded sort of sad.

Oh double *merde*.

Saturday October 8th

Jas phoned up.

"Gee, guess what? Dave the Laugh has finished with Emma."

What?

I said, "Really, how do you know?"

And she said, "Well, I've had Emma on the phone. She's

really upset. She couldn't speak at first. She just sort of hiccupped."

"Why did he say that he finished with her?"

"She said that he said that she was too good for him."

I said, "Well, to be frank, she is."

Jas said, "Yeah, but people always say that, don't they, when they dump people?"

Oh, here we go. Jas has gone back to her Wise Woman of the Forest ways.

I said, "Jas, forgive me if I'm right, but you have never been either the dumper or the dumpee, so how do you know so much?"

Jas was getting a bit numpty and I wanted to know all the juicy details so when she said, "I am a great observer of people," I didn't laugh or anything.

She was in full wisdomosity mood.

"Yes, it's like when you get dumped and people say, 'It's not you, it's me. I just need space.' And the space they need is exactly the height and width of the space that you are."

What is she on about?

I said, "What else did she say?"

Jas said, "Well, this is the weird bit, she said that he said there was someone else."

Ohmygod.

Someone else?

Dave had someone else?

And he said I was the most beautiful girl for him.

Whilst he had someone else?

Two someone elses.

Twits in Tights fiasco

Thursday October 13th
Dress rehearsal

Dave wasn't at the dress rehearsal.

Jas said that Emma has been off school.

I didn't ask for any details, because I feel so weird about the whole Dave the Laugh multi-girlfriend scenario, but Radio Jas cannot help herself.

She said, "I went round to see her and she was in her dressing gown watching daytime TV and eating Pringles."

I said, "Well, that's all right, isn't it. My dad does that."

Jas said, "Yes, but does your dad have a picture of Dave

the Laugh pinned on to a teddy?"

Oh, bloody hell.

I said to Nursie, "Erm, aren't we supposed to be teenagers with not a care in the world etc.?"

Rosie said, "I haven't got a care in the world apart from an itchy beard."

I wonder if Dave the Laugh is off with his new mystery girlfriend?

He's a bit of a swine if he is.

Just dumping poor Emma and going off with someone else.

Without a care in the world.

Dumping Emma and telling me I am the most beautiful girl in the world.

Still, he is not my problem.

He has proved himself to be a hard-hearted Hornmeister and gad-abouty boy.

At Home
6:00 p.m.
Masimo is coming to the Twits in Tights fiasco.

Ooohh noooo.

I tried to persuade him not to, but he says he wants to see me.

In fact, even though I have once again tried to pretend to my family that the show is next week, they don't believe me.

Which is a savage indictment of our relationship in my opinion.

I said that to Mum. I said, "I am very upset that you don't trust me. If I tell you that the production is next week, why oh why do you not believe me?"

And she said, "Because I was talking to Jas's mum and she said she would see me there tomorrow night."

Oh, typical.

Jas has told her parents the proper night of the show. That is so typical.

She wants everyone to see her pretend snogging and being thrown around by pretend waves.

6:30 p.m.
Oh, fabulous... EVERYONE is coming.

Grandvati phoned up to tell me the wonderful news.

I answered the phone and he said, "Hello, hello, anybody there?"

And I said, "It's me, Georgia."

And he said, "Well, what do you want?"

Oh God's pyjamas and matching slipperettes.

I said, "Grandad, you phoned me."

He said, "Did I? What did I want?"

It turns out that he and Maisie (his knitted girlfriend) are coming along to see *Rom and Jule* as a special celebration.

I said, "You won't like it, Grandad, it's all mime and slow motion."

And Grandvati said, "Is that big girl in it again?"

6:45 p.m.

No amount of pleading will make my mutti and vati not come along. And they are bringing Libby. I said, "No, there is no need for that. She doesn't want to come."

I said that to her, "You don't want to come along to the silly old *Rom and Jule* thing, do you?"

She said, "I laiike it. I laiike Mr Cheese best."

I said, "Ah well, Mr Cheese is not in it."

She kicked me very hard on the ankle.

When I bent down to rub it, she put her little face in mine.

And went cross-eyed.

"Mr Cheese IS COMING!!! BAD GINGER!!!"

One minute later

Oh, good, she is bringing Mr Cheese.

And Mr Fish, probably.

Five minutes later

Oh, well, maybe it will be all right. I'm only on for about a minute anyway and then I can just lurk around annoying Mr Attwood, or trying to put Jule off with my amusing backstage pranks (which she will then kill me for).

8:00 p.m.

Masimo phoned again.

He sounds vair miz.

He said, "I 'ave been with the band all day. It is sad. They are my, how do you say it, mates now. I will be not having them for my mates when they go to London."

I said, "Oh, Masimo. Look, why, well, why... don't you, why don't you go with them? For a bit? To London."

There was a silence.

He said, "You want me to go?"

"No, no, it's just that you seem so unhappy, and..."

"But you will not come with me."

"I think, I am too... I don't think I have enough..."

"Money? I can get the money."

"No, I don't think I have enough... maturiosity."

"Mat... nosity? What is this?"

Then I sort of had a brainwave (ish) well, a brainripple anyway.

"It's just I don't want to leave my mates either. I have special mates and I don't want to leave them."

He said, "I understand, Georgia. I so like you, *cara*."

Oh, bloody blimey and also poooooooooooooooo.

Why can't everything be simple???

In the front room

The Blunder Boys are having a "gathering". Just outside our front-room window.

Mark Big Gob is clearly the lovechild of Mick Jagger and a cod. His gob is huge.

I can't hear what they are saying, thank God. It's just odd words like "wicked" and "yeh mon" and I did hear Oscar say,

"She wan' me baaaaaad."

As if.

Also they were doing that really crap boy smoking. You know, holding the fag upside down and taking really big drags on it.

Angus hopped up on to the windowsill and was looking at them.

Doing his staring thing.

When they noticed him, I could hear them going on.

"Look at the stupid cat. He is rank."

"Hey, stupid cat, want to kiss my arse?"

On and on.

Angus was just looking and looking at them.

Ten minutes later

He is still looking at them.

But they are not saying anything.

In fact, they are looking a bit shifty.

Two minutes later

They have all shuffled off somewhere else.

Yes!!!!!

Super cat scores again!

He has quite literally outstared them.

In bed

Dear Lord Sandra, please give me some advice.

What shall I do about Masimo?

Three minutes later

I have decided that I am going to remove Mr Potato Head and if Lord Sandra falls over, that is a sign that I should tell Masimo that he should go to London.

If Lord Sandra stays upright, then I should have a full-on relationship with the Luuurve God.

Five minutes later

What does it mean if Lord Sandra just leans slightly to the left?

Rom and Jule: the tragedy (you're not kidding, mate)

Friday October 14th
Final run-through

We're giddy with excitement (ish).

Jas was asking me about her puckering technique.

She said, "Does this look like real snogging?"

And made a little face like a fish.

I said, "Jas, if that is how you snog Tom, I am not surprised he is high-tailing it to Hamburger-a-gogo land."

She stropped off because she seems to forget that we are bestie mates of all time, weathering the storms of luuurve together. She seems to have forgotten that.

That and her emergency supply of Midget Gems, which I am looking after for her.

I have to give her one when she comes off stage in between scenes, so that she has the courage to face her audience.

Good Lord.

I wonder if Dave the Laugh will turn up tonight.

I bet he feels horrible about Emma.

Maybe he is consoling himself with his mysterious girlfriend.

Not that it is any of my business.

11:00 a.m.

I cannot believe this place. Us artistes are being made to do ordinary lessons. How can that be right? We need to be limbering up. Stretching our vocal cords and our tights etc.

Maths

Miss Stamp does not seem to understand that my answers are meant ironically.

Lunchtime

Lolling around trying to conserve our strength.

Wet Lindsay came sliming by. Hasn't she died yet?

She said, "What a bloody bunch of losers and liggers you are."

Charming.

I said, "Actually, we are trying to relax before this evening's gala performance."

She didn't even bother to reply.

Rosie said, "Better to have loafed and lost than never to have loafed at all."

Lindsay turned round then.

She said, "What is that supposed to mean, Mees?"

Blimey, was there going to be a fight?

By the way, although people suggest the youth of today do not pay attention to boring stuff, I will just say this. The French for a fight between two girls is *un crêpage de chignons* (a fight between hairstyles).

I said to Rosie, "Are you going to be having *un crêpage de chignons* as a warm-up for tonight's fiasco? Don't ruin your beard."

But then Wet Lindsay just turned away and said, "You're not worth it."

And stormed off.

But fortunately for us, she stumbled on the top step of the science block.

I said, "If you fall down those stairs and break your legs, don't come running to me!"

Oh, we laughed. But quietly.

Sort of quietly but hysterically at the same time.

Jas said, "Emma said that she might turn up tonight."

Oh dear God.

What if she flung herself on stage and grabbed my sword?

7:30 p.m.
Showtime!!!
The roar of the greasepaint, the smell of the crowd.

Backstage
Jas was pacing backwards and forwards. And even though she has no fringe on her wig, she is still managing to fiddle about with her forehead. It is vair annoying.

She said, "Do you think everyone will know it's a tragedy?"

I said, "I guarantee tonight that after our moving interpretation of *Rom and Jule*, there will not be a dry seat in the house."

Especially as my grandvati and Libby are coming and they have trouble in the piddly-diddly department. But I didn't say that bit to Jas.

No sign of Dave the Laugh. He must really be having a bad time.

I hope he is all right, even if I am eschewing him with a firm hand because of his new secret girlfriend that I don't even care about.

7:31 p.m.
Dave the Laugh turned up.

He looked a bit dark around the eyes, like he hadn't slept much. But he greeted all his mates with the usual slapping and "You idiot" sort of carry on.

He saw me and said, "Nice tights, Kittykat... and enormous beard."

I didn't mean to talk to him. I was going to give him my cold-shoulderosity work for being a cad and a bounder but unfortunately I couldn't help smiling at him.

605

Actually, even though he looked tired, he did look really lovely.

7:41 p.m.
After he had been joshing around with the others he came over to me and said, "All right, Kittykat?"

And suddenly, I felt like crying. I wanted him to just get hold of me.

I said, "Well, not really. It's all been a bit..."

He said, "I know, it really has been all a bit... but come on, gird your gusset and cheer up. It will be all right. The Hornmeister is here."

By the side of the stage
Melanie has done her best as Rom, but she is struggling against enormous odds (oo-er).

As soon as she came on, I could hear my grandad say, "Bloody hell, she's a mature lass."

She did her best, but she is not really an actress as such.

In fact, as Dave the Laugh said, "The only thing moving about her performance is her wig."

Every time Nauseating P. Green came on as the puppet dog,

I could hear Libby howling with laughter. And unfortunately, I could see her howling with laughter. This was because she had three seats to herself on the front row. One for her, Pantalitzer doll, Scuba-diving Barbie and burnt-bottom Panda, one for Mr Fish and one for Mr Cheese. Mr Cheese was not naked as he is at home – he had on his lovely macintosh.

Ramble ramble *Rom and Jule.*

At last it was my big fight scene. I took a deep breath and adjusted my beard.

Before I went on, Dave gave me the thumbs up and said, "Give it your all tightswise! I'm right behind you, oo-er."

Onstage

My dying was another triumph darling, a triumph! I even improvised recovering a bit, just when everyone thought I was a goner.

I could see Dave the Laugh by the lighting console, rubbing his hands like he was a masterchef or something. The lights dimmed to atmospheric red and through my half-closed eyes I could see the "blood corpuscles" dancing up to me like twits and waving their red scarves about.

Then, as last year, once again the stage was plunged into complete darkness.

I couldn't see a bloody thing. I heard someone whisper (loudly), "Which way is off?" then there was a bit of a bang and someone in the dark said, "Bloody hell, what's that?" and then Mr Attwood's voice saying very loudly, "You've just put your foot in my first-aid kit."

It was an absolute shambles.

I stood up and started sort of shuffling along sideways in the dark when the lights suddenly came up again.

I could see the audience quite clearly.

Looking at me.

I thought about doing some Irish dancing but it didn't seem right somehow. I kept on shuffling because I couldn't just lie down again. Then someone shouted out, and I am pretty sure it was my dad, "It's a bloody miracle. He's alive!!!" And the audience applauded, so me and the blood corpuscles had to bow.

Backstage

I looked at Dave the Laugh and he shrugged and said, "Technical hitch but the show must go on, Kittykat."

He has no shame.

Also he said it was an accident waiting to happen.

I said, "What was?"

And he said, "Putting me in charge of lights."

Miss Wilson went bobbing out on to the stage and said, "Erm, despite the erm, technical hitch, erm we will carry on... please ignore the erm, Mercutio walking off. He is in fact dead."

I could hear Dad and Uncle Eddie booing.

The next scene was Melanie's big climbing on to the balcony scene. All of the lads crowded round the sides of the stage. The atmosphere was so stiff with hormones I could have cut it with my sword. But sadly, I had broken it trying to open a bottle of lemonade backstage.

Melanie put her foot on the lower rung of the ladder and then reached out to haul herself up to the next rung. All of the lads and the audience went "Oooooooohhh" and then she went for the next rung and they all went "Oooooooohhh". It was riveting to watch.

Finally, she got to the balcony and hauled herself up on to it. As she stood up and opened her arms to speak, all the buttons on her tunic pinged off. And as she looked down in horror, Dave the Laugh said really loudly, "Are these my basoomas I see before me?"

After show

I like to think the play was a unique experience for everyone. Lots of people came backstage and said they had quite literally never seen anything like it.

We were all doing a mad conga backstage, wearing beards, when Masimo came in.

I had completely forgotten he was coming.

I felt so awful.

He looked at me in my beard with Dave the Laugh and the others.

Oh no.

He wasn't going to challenge Dave the Laugh to another fisticuffs at dawn, was he?

I wouldn't really blame him this time.

In fact, I would lend him my handbag.

Shut up, brain.

Then he smiled at me.

It was a really lovely smile.

I went over to him and he said to me, "*Cara*, can

we talk for a minute? Not too long away from your friends."

And he wasn't being mean or anything, just really lovely and soft.

We went off down the corridor and through the fire exit to the outside. Which was great as I thought my head was going to explode into flames.

He looked at me and stroked my face.

Thank God I had quickly removed my beard.

He said, "Georgia, I am going to say this, for you. I am going for London. I will go, now, tonight."

I went, "But, but..."

And he said, "I don't think I can speak long, for my heart. But I see how this is for you. I know you like me much, but you are, your heart is here. I will not make you choose. I am going. Be happy. I do not think I will ever meet anyone like you again... *Ciao*."

And he gave me the longest, softest kiss. I couldn't speak. My head had frozen over.

And he just went.

I should run after him. I should say something.

But.

I went back into the theatre. Like I was in a soup. I sat down by the loos.

How did I feel?

I don't know.

I must have been sitting there for about five minutes when Jas came out.

She saw me and came over to me.

First of all she was saying, "People cried when I died." Blah blah ramble ramble.

But then she stopped and said, "Gee, what is it?"

I said, "Masimo has gone off to be with the Stiff Dylans in London."

She put her arm about me.

"Oh, Gee. How do you feel?"

I said, "I dunno; funny."

She said, "Oh I'm sorry. You've liked him for ages, I know. And he is lovely. I know I said the Dave thing but I think you really were right to like him, but..."

I looked up at her and even though she was fiddling with her wig, I didn't mind.

I just said, "But what?"

She looked a bit thoughtful.

"Well he always made you nervous, and you know, we're only like, well we're not like Jule, are we? I mean, we aren't going to get married, are we? Just yet... or... well, I think we need our pals. And we need to grow up a bit together. Like a little family."

I looked at her.

"I would really miss you if you weren't here, Jas."

She said, "I know, and I would really miss you."

And she gave me a big hug.

Then she said, "We'll be all right, little pally. I bet you something really nice will happen now. It will all work out in the end."

I said, "How do you know that?"

And she said, "I don't know, it just does. Do you want a Midget Gem?"

I nodded. I did quite want one as it happened.

She went off and I just sat there again.

I was looking down at the floor when I heard her coming back again.

I said, "Can I have the black one?"

And Dave the Laugh said, "You cheeky minx."

I looked up at him.

He said, "Jas told me."

I looked at him.

He has the loveliest smile.

I said to him, "You said 'Are these my basoomas I see before me,' and everyone heard you."

He said, "I know, I am the vati."

I said, "Yeah, you are the double-timing vati."

He said, "What do you mean?"

"You know, your secret girlfriend that you dumped Emma for."

He looked at me.

"You may be the thickest chick alive. You're the secret girlfriend, you daft tart."

And he kissed me.

I said, "So, do you, want to be my girlfriend? I mean, do you want to..."

He put his arm around me.

"Go on then, Sex Kitty, I'll be your girlfriend. It'll probably all end in tears. Mine. But... I am Dave the Biscuit. I will survive. Give us a snog and possibly a *rummachen unterhalb der Taille*. Go on, you know you want to."

And I did want to.

The end

So as Billy Shakespeare said, "Forsooth and verily all endeth happily in the snogging department."

Probably.

Or something?

What do you think?

I'll be the last to know.

Georgia's Glossary

bhaji · A bhaji is an Indian food. An onion bhaji is brown and round and full of fat, hence my hilarious joke about Slim looking like one. I exhaust myself with my good humour, I really do.

Blimey O'Reilly · (as in "Blimey O'Reilly's trousers") This is an Irish expression of disbelief and shock. Maybe Blimey O'Reilly was a famous Irish bloke who had extravagantly big trousers. We may never know the truth. The fact is, whoever he is, what you need to know is that a) it's Irish and b) it is Irish. I rest my case.

BluTack · Blue plasticine stuff that you stick stuff to other stuff with. It is very useful for sticking stuff to other stuff. Tip-top sticking stuff actually. I don't know why it's called BluTack when it clearly should be called Blue Sticking Stuff. Also, blue is spelt wrong, but that's life for you.

bobos · As I have explained many, many times, English is a lovely and exciting language full of sophisticosity. To go to sleep is "to go to bobos", so if you go to bed you are going to Boboland. It is an Elizabethan expression... Oh, OK then, Libby made it up and she can be unreasonably violent if you don't join in with her.

brillopads · A brillopad is a sort of wire pad that you clean pans and stuff with (if you do housework, which I sincerely suggest you don't. I got ironer's elbow from being made to iron my vati's huge undercrackers). Where was I? Oh yes. When you say "It was brillopads" you don't mean "It was a sort of wire pad that you clean with," you mean "It was fab and groovy." Do you see? Goodnight.

Bugger(ation) · A swear word. It doesn't really mean anything but neither do a lot of swear words. Or parents.

bum-oley · Quite literally "bottom hole". I'm sorry but you did ask. Say it proudly (with a cheery smile and a Spanish accent).

catsuit · An all-in-one suit thing with trousers and a zipper up the front. Usually evening wear. It is supposed to be sexy, and perhaps it is, but try getting out of one quickly if you have to pay an emergency lavatory call. Like a grown-up version of a romper suit.

Chuntering · When people are moaning on, they are said to be "chuntering". An example of chuntering would be my dad saying, "Why can't you tidy your room like a normal person. I found two pizzas and a dog bone in there that must have been there for weeks. A decent person would tidy their room. An ordinary person... blah blahh chunter chunter."

clown car · Officially called a Reliant Robin three-wheeler, but clearly a car built for clowns by some absolute loser called Robin. The Reliant bit comes from being able to rely on Robin being a prat. I wouldn't be surprised if Robin also invented nostril-hair cutters.

clud · This is short for cloud. Lots of really long boring poems and so on can be made much snappier by abbreviating words. So Wordworth's poem called "Daffodils" (or "Daffs") has the immortal line "I wandered lonely as a clud". Ditto *Rom and Jule*. Or *Ham*. Or *Merc of Ven*.

Dark room · Oh stop being so lazy – you know what a dark room is. It's a room. And it's dark. Leave it. Leave the dark room.

div · Short for "dithering prat", i.e., Jas.

DIY · Quite literally "Do It Yourself"! Rude when you think about it. Instead of getting someone competent to do things around the house (you know, like a trained electrician or a builder or a plumber), some vatis choose to do DIY. Always with disastrous results. For example, my bedroom ceiling has footprints in it because my vati decided he would go up on the roof and replace a few tiles. Hopeless.

Epée · A form of swordfighting. All swordfighting is hilarious, but *épée* takes the biscuit comedywise because: a) there is a comedy opportunity for misunderstanding that someone is not actually saying... a pee, and b) when you fight with an *épée* it is a sword with a bit on the end so that you cannot hurt anyone. Which has to be one of the most pointless things around. (Do you see? Do you see what I did there? "Pointless." Do you see? Oh, I am so vair vair tired.)

fives court · This is a typical Stalag 14 idea. It's minus forty-five degrees outside so what should we do to entertain the schoolgirls? Let them stay inside in the cosy warmth and read? No, let's build a concrete wall outside with a red line at waist height and let's make them go and hit a hard ball at the red line with their little freezing hands. What larks!

fringe · Goofy short bit of hair that comes down to your eyebrows. Someone told me that American-type people call them "bangs", but this is so ridiculously strange that it's not worth thinking about. Some people can look very stylish with a fringe (i.e. me) while others look goofy (Jas). The Beatles started it (apparently). One of them had a German girlfriend and she cut their hair with a pudding bowl, and the rest is history.

f.t. · I refer you to the famous "losing it" scale:
1. minor tizz
2. complete tizz and to-do
3. strop
4. a visit to Stop Central
5. f.t. (funny turn)

6. spaz attack
7. complete ditherspaz
8. nervy b. (nervous breakdown)
9. complete nervy b.
10. ballisticisimus

gadzooks · An expression of surprise. Like for instance, "Cor, love a duck!" Which doesn't mean you love ducks or want to marry one. For the swotty knickers among you, "gad" probably meant "God" in olde English and "zooks" of course means... Oh, look, just leave me alone, OK?

geoggers · Geoggers is short for geography. Ditto blodge (biology) and lunck (lunch).

gob · Gob is an attractive term for someone's mouth. For example, if you saw Mark (from up the road who has the biggest mouth known to womankind) you could yell politely, "Good Lord, Mark, don't open your gob, otherwise people may think you are a basking whale in trousers and throw a mackerel at you!" Or something else full of hilariosity.

goosegog · Gooseberry. I know you are looking all quizzical now. OK. If there are two people and they want to snog and you keep hanging about saying, "Do you fancy some chewing gum?" or "Have you seen my interesting new socks?" you are a gooseberry. Or for short, a goosegog, i.e. someone who nobody wants around.

gusset · Do you really not know what a gusset is? I do.

Hoooorn · When you "have the Horn" it's the same as "having the big red bottom".

On my jacksie · It means on my own. All aloney. On my owney. It is of course Olde Englishe and was formed because "jacksie" rhymes with... erm... alonesie.

Jammy Dodger · Biscuit with jam in it. Very nutritious(ish).

jimjams · Pyjamas. Also pygmies or jammies.

knickers · Americans (wrongly) call them panties. Knickers are a particular type of "panty" – huge and all encompassing. In the olden days (i.e., when Dad was born) all the ladies wore massive knickers that came to their knees. Many, many amusing songs were made up about knicker elastic breaking. This is because, as Slim, our headmistress, points out to anybody interested (i.e. no one), "In the old days people knew how to enjoy themselves with simple pleasures." Well, I have news for her. We modern people enjoy ourselves with knicker stories too. We often laugh as we imagine how many homeless people she could house in hers.

Le Coq · Hahahahahahahaha. Do you see why this is so funny??? For the same reason that the Koch family are so funny. *Le Coq* is alarmingly, the name of a mime school in *le* gay Paree. People go there to learn how to look as though they are trapped behind a glass wall etc. No one knows why.

Leper of Rheims · Oh come on, you must know who the Leper of Rheims is. Oh blimey. Well. He was living in Rheims – erm – in ancienty times and he had dodgy skin. And as we all know the Rheims-type people (the Rheimsonians) can't abide a poor complexion so they ignored him. The end.

loo · Lavatory. In America (land of the free and criminally insane) they say "rest room", which is funny, as I never feel like having a rest when I go to the lavatory.

Merc-lurk-io · a.k.a. Mercutio. He is Rom's friend in *Rom and Jule* and supposed to be the "comedy" element in the tragedy. But as far as I can see, he just hangs around in a lurking way. Hence my vair vair amusant nickname. Occasionally, he stops lurking to fight and complain. Much like my vati.

Midget Gem · Little sweets made out of hard jelly stuff in different flavours. Jas loves them A LOT. She secretes them about her person, I suspect, often in her panties, so I never like to accept one from her on hygiene and lesbian grounds.

nippy noodles · Instead of saying "Good heavens, it's quite cold this morning," you say "Cor, nippy noodles!!" English is an exciting and growing language. It is. Believe me. Just leave it at that. Accept it.

nub · The heart of the matter. You can also say gist and thrust.

This is from the name for the centre of a wheel where the spokes come out. Or do I mean hub? Who cares. I feel a dance coming on.

nuddy-pants · Quite literally nude-coloured pants, and you know what nude-coloured pants are? They are no pants. So if you are in your nuddy-pants you are in your no pants, i.e. you are naked.

nunga-nungas · Basoomas. Girls breasty business. Ellen's brother calls them nunga-nungas because he says that if you get hold of a girl's breast and pull it out and then let it go, it goes nunga-nunga-nunga. As I have said many, many times with great wisdomosity, there is something really wrong with boys.

Och Aye land · Scotland. Land of the Braves. Or is that Indiana? I don't know, and I know I should because we are, after all, all human beings under our skins. But I still don't care.

Pantalitzer doll · A terrifying Czech-made doll that sadistic parents (my vati) buy for their children, presumably to teach them early on about the horror of life.

Pizza-a-gogo land · Masimoland. Land of wine, sun, olives and vair vair groovy Luuurve Gods. Italy. The only bad point about Pizza-a-gogo land is their football players are so vain that if it rains, they all run off the pitch so that their hair doesn't get ruined.

red-bottomosity · Having the big red bottom. This is vair vair interesting *vis-à-vis* nature. When a lady baboon is "in the mood" for luuurve, she displays her big red bottom to the male baboon. (Apparently he wouldn't have a clue otherwise, but that is boys for you!!) Anyway, if you hear the call of the Horn, you are said to be displaying red-bottomosity.

rucky · A rucksack. Like a little kangaroo pouch you wear on your back to put things in. Backpack.

sailor's hornpipe · As I have pointed out many, many times, England is a proud seafaring nation and our sailors on the whole are jolly good chaps etc. However, when they were first invented in the olden days, they had a few too many rums and made up this odd dance called a "hornpipe", which largely consists of hopping from foot to foot with your arms crossed. Well, you did ask.

Scheissenhausen · Quite literally (if you happen to be a Lederhosen-type person) a house that you poo in (*scheiss* is poo and *haus* is house). Poo house. Lavatory. Or rest room as Hamburger-a-gogo types say. No one knows why they say that. Oh no, hang on, I think I do know. When they all lived in the Wild West in wooden shacks, one room was both their bedroom and their lavatory. Cowboys didn't mind that sort of thing. In fact they loved it. But I don't.

Silly beggars · Playing "silly beggars" is an old-fashioned term used by the elderly insane, when they are suggesting that the youth of today are acting stupidly. Which of course, as we all know, they never do.

Sing-alonga · This is when you have the lyrics to songs printed along the bottom of a film. So that the audience can sing along. (Not the lyrics to any songs... just the lyrics to the songs in the film. Otherwise you would be there all day and night.)

spoon · A spoon is a person who is so dim and sad that they cannot be allowed to use anything sharp. That means they can only use a spoon. The Blunder Boys are without exception all spoons.

Strawberry Mivvy · Is an ice lolly. It has red-coloured ice on the outside but inside (when you have sucked like a mad sucking thing) you find the ice cream centre. Hurrah!! People who eat them usually end up with red lips and chin. Often with a slight red moustache effect. Miss Wilson of course took it the whole hog and managed to get red nostrils. Either that or she had applied lippy in the dark with a spoon.

The Sound of Music · Oh, are we never to be free? *The Sound of Music* was a film about some bint, Julie Andrews, skipping around the Alps and singing about goats. Many, many famous and annoying songs come from this film, including, "The Hills Are Alive With the Sound of PANTS", "You Are Sixteen Going on PANTS" and, of course, the one about the national flower of Austria, "IdlePANTS".

Titches · A Titch is a small person. Titches is the plural of titch.

vino tinto · Now this is your actual Pizza-a-gogo talk. It quite literally means "tinted wine". In this case the wine is tinted red.

waz · Another expression for piddly-diddly department. Possibly named after the sound the piddly diddly makes as it comes out of the trouser area. I don't know, to be frank. Only boys say it. And who knows why boys say anything? The whole thing is a mystery.

wazzarium · A place where you go to have a waz.
p.s. You will not be finding me in there.

welligogs · Wellington boots. Because it more or less rains all the time in England, we have special rubber boots that we wear to keep us above the mud. This is true.

whelks · A horrible shellfish thing that only the truly mad (like my grandad, for instance) eat. They are unbelievably slimy and mucuslike.

Wild Thing · This is a 60s song sung by a band called The Troggs. It is about a wild thing. That is how simple life was in the 60s. If you had a Wild Thing now (which believe me, I do) people would not say it was groovy, they would put a restraining order on it.

Great Mates Scale

1. Offer a mate a Midget Gem without being asked.

2. Share your last Jammy Dodger even though you really want it and your mate may be flicking her fringe about.

3. Listen to your mate rambling on about themselves when you have got vair important things to do yourself (e.g. nails, plucking etc.).

4. Be with your mate through thick and thin. Or even if they are both thick and thin.

5. Always be game for a laugh even though you may be blubbing on the inside.

6. Even when they have all the reason in the universe to be Top Dog (i.e. when they are the girlfriend of a Luuurve God, even if it is slightly on a sale-or-return basis) a top mate does not blow their own trumpet. Or snitch on her less fortunate mates.

Meet Georgia's crazy cousin
Tallulah Casey in

Out Now!
Read on for a sneak preview . . .

CHAPTER 1

On the showbiz express

I've come to Yorkshire by mistake
Chugging towards Dother Hall

Wow. This is it. This is me growing up. On my own, going to Performing Arts College. This is goodbye Tallulah, you long, gangly thing and helloooooo Lullah, star of stage and... owwwwooo. Ow and ow.

The train lurched and I've nearly knocked myself out on the side of the door. I'm bound to get a massive lump. Oh good, I can start college with two heads...

In my brochure it has a picture of a big manor house and on the front it says:

Dother Hall, world-renowned for its excellence in the Arts. This magnificent centre of artistry is set amongst the beautiful Yorkshire Dales. With its friendly northern folk offering a warm welcome to visitors, think Wuthering Heights *but with less moaning!*

I've been looking over the top of my brochure at the bloke opposite. He is the grumpiest man in the universe probably.

He's got no hair on his head, but he has loads of red hair shooting out of his ears. Like there are a couple of red squirrels nesting in there. Which would be quite good actually, as they are an endangered species.

His wife said to him, "Oooh look, Fred, the sun's coming out."

And he said, "It can please its bloody self."

Is this what Yorkshire folk are like?

I wonder if anyone is missing me at home?

I wonder if they are saying, "Where is Tallulah?"

I think I know the answer to that question, and it is, "Who?"

Connor will just move into my bedroom and make it smelly and then leave.

It will be next week before my grandma notices that my egg-cup hasn't been used. When I tried to explain to her that I was going to performing arts college in Yorkshire for the summer, she said, "Will you bring a trifle back?"

Maybe she thought I said I was going to Marks and Spencers for the summer.

Mum didn't comment because as usual she wasn't there. She's gone to Norway to paint.

Not people's houses. She's doing her art.

When I stayed over with cousin Georgia, I asked her what sort of painting the Norwegians did and she said, "It's mostly sledges."

I thought she meant they painted sledges a lot, but she said, "No, my not-so-little cousy, they paint WITH sledges."

She said the official term for that kind of work was 'Sled-werk', and that it was one of the reasons why Norwegians had such big arms and had therefore become Vikings (for the rowing). And that if I dropped 'Sled-werk' into a conversation at art college, people would be impressed and not notice my knees...

Georgia knows a lot of stuff. Not just about painting, but about life. And boys. She wears a bra. It's a big one. She showed me her special disco inferno dancing and her lady bumps were jiggling quite a lot.

I wish I wore a bra. And jiggled.

It's so boring being fourteen and a half.

She's nice to me, but I know she thinks I'm just a kid.

When I left she gave me her 'special' comedy moustache. She's grown out of it and thought it would suit me. She said, "Always remember, Lullah, if in doubt, get your moustache out."

I do love Georgia and wish I lived near her. I haven't got a sister and it's not the same having a brother. Connor mostly likes to talk about what he's going to kick next.

And that I am like a daddy long-legs in a skirt.

And how he could win a kicking contest with a daddy long-legs.

Is that normal in a boy?

Well, all will be revealed when I start my new life at Dother Hall.

Georgia's also given me a secret note to read on my first day at college. She says she will write to me. But will she?

I will look at the college brochure again to get me in the creative zone.

Let me see.

Aaaaaah, yes, yes. These are my kind of people.

This is more like it.

Here is a photo of a girl leaping around in the dance studio. The caption says:

Eliza loses herself in the beauty of modern dance.

As far as dancewear is concerned Eliza has gone for big tights.

As indeed she needs to.

Oh and here's a photo of a boy.

What on earth is he holding?

Let's see.

The caption says:

Martin has made an instrument. Here he is holding his own small lute.

Crumbs.

Martin has got very bright lips.

Perhaps he is a mouth-breather, that makes your lips go very red.

Or perhaps it is lipstick.

I suppose anything goes in the crazy world of dance and theatre! Hey nonny no, this is my new world, the world of showbiz!

But what if the course is full of people who can sing and dance and everything, and are really confident?

And hate me because of my nobbly kneecaps?

Uh-oh, we are arriving at my station. I must get my bag down. I'll get up on the seat and try and reach it... Oh great balls of fire, I've just accidentally kicked Mr Squirrel as he was getting up.

What does, "You great big dunderwhelp, use your bloody gogglers!" mean in English?

I bet it's not nice.

His wife said, "Take no notice, love, if there was a moaning medal, he'd win it hands down."

I let them get off first.

How come everyone else in my family is the right height and I have knees that are four feet above the ground?

I swung the train door open and saw the sign:

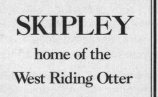

SKIPLEY
home of the
West Riding Otter

To be continued . . .